"Is this StarClan?" Yellowfang called. "Is there anyone there?"

A moment later a small dark-pelted cat padded out of the shadows. He gave Yellowfang a long look, and solemnly shook his head. "There is a cat coming," he meowed, "a cat who should never be born, whose life will bring fire and blood to the forest, yet StarClan is powerless to stop him!"

Yellowfang stared at him in horror. "Is there nothing we can do?"

The dark cat dipped his head. "Only one thing can stop the tide of hatred this birth-cursed cat will bring: the courage of a mother to know her destiny."

Yellowfang gasped. "What do you mean? Is this a prophecy?"

"It is a *warning*," the dark cat whispered.

Book One: Into the Wild

Book Two: Fire and Ice

Book Three: Forest of Secrets

Book Four: Rising Storm

Book Five: A Dangerous Path

Book Six: The Darkest Hour

THE NEW PROPHECY

Book One: Midnight

Book Two: Moonrise

Book Three: Dawn

Book Four: Starlight

Book Five: Twilight

Book Six: Sunset

POWER OF THREE

Book One: The Sight

Book Two: Dark River

Book Three: Outcast

Book Four: Eclipse

Book Five: Long Shadows

Book Six: Sunrise

OMEN OF THE STARS

Book One: The Fourth Apprentice

Book Two: Fading Echoes

Book Three: Night Whispers

Book Four: Sign of the Moon

Book Five: The Forgotten Warrior

Book Six: The Last Hope

DAWN OF THE CLANS

Book One: The Sun Trail

Book Two: Thunder Rising

Book Three: The First Battle

EXPLORE THE WARRIORS WORLD

Warriors Super Edition: Firestar's Quest

Warriors Super Edition: Bluestar's Prophecy

Warriors Super Edition: SkyClan's Destiny

Warriors Super Edition: Crookedstar's Promise

Warriors Super Edition: Yellowfang's Secret

Warriors Super Edition: Tallstar's Revenge

Warriors Field Guide: Secrets of the Clans

Warriors: Cats of the Clans

Warriors: Code of the Clans

Warriors: Battles of the Clans

Warriors: Enter the Clans

Warriors: The Untold Stories

Warriors: The Ultimate Guide

MANGA

The Lost Warrior

Warrior's Refuge

Warrior's Return

The Rise of Scourge

Tigerstar and Sasha #1: Into the Woods

Tigerstar and Sasha #2: Escape from the Forest

Tigerstar and Sasha #3: Return to the Clans

Ravenpaw's Path #1: Shattered Peace

Ravenpaw's Path #2: A Clan in Need

Ravenpaw's Path #3: The Heart of a Warrior

SkyClan and the Stranger #1: The Rescue

SkyClan and the Stranger #2: Beyond the Code

SkyClan and the Stranger #3: After the Flood

NOVELLAS

Hollyleaf's Story

Mistystar's Omen

Cloudstar's Journey

Tigerclaw's Fury

Also by Erin Hunter

SEEKERS

Book One: The Quest Begins

Book Two: Great Bear Lake

Book Three: Smoke Mountain

Book Four: The Last Wilderness

Book Five: Fire in the Sky

Book Six: Spirits in the Stars

RETURN TO THE WILD

Book One: Island of Shadows

Book Two: The Melting Sea

Book Three: River of Lost Bears

Book Four: Forest of Wolves

MANGA

Toklo's Story

Kallik's Adventure

Book One: The Empty City

Book Two: A Hidden Enemy

Book Three: Darkness Falls

Book Four: The Broken Path

ERIN
HUNTER

An Imprint of HarperCollins*Publishers*

www.harpercollinschildrens.com

Library of Congress Cataloging-in-Publication Data
Hunter, Erin.
Yellowfang's secret / Erin Hunter. — 1st ed.
p. cm. — (Warriors, super edition ; bk. 5)
Summary: Yellowfang is a loyal ShadowClan cat through and through—but she is haunted by a dark secret from her past that could threaten the future of the warrior Clans
ISBN 978-0-06-208216-9 (pbk.)
[1. Cats—Fiction. 2. Prophecies—Fiction. 3. Adventure and adventurers—Fiction. 4. Fantasy.] I. Title.
PZ7.H916625Yel 2012 2012019087
[Fic]—dc23 CIP
AC

Typography by Hilary Zarycky
20 21 CG/BRR 20 19 18 17
❖
First paperback edition, 2014

Special thanks to Cherith Baldry

ALLEGIANCES

SHADOWCLAN

LEADER

CEDARSTAR—very dark gray tom with a white belly

DEPUTY

STONETOOTH—gray tabby tom with long teeth

MEDICINE CAT

SAGEWHISKER—white she-cat with long whiskers

WARRIORS

(toms and she-cats without kits)

CROWTAIL—black tabby she-cat

BRACKENFOOT—pale ginger tom with dark ginger legs (Yellowkit's father)

ARCHEYE—gray tabby tom with black stripes and thick stripe over eye

HOLLYFLOWER—dark-gray-and-white she-cat
APPRENTICE, NEWTPAW

MUDCLAW—gray tom with brown legs

TOADSKIP—dark brown tabby tom with white splashes and white legs
APPRENTICE, ASHPAW

NETTLESPOT—white she-cat with ginger flecks

MOUSEWING—thick-furred black tom

DEERLEAP—gray tabby she-cat with white legs

AMBERLEAF—dark orange she-cat with brown legs and ears

FINCHFLIGHT—black-and-white tom

BLIZZARDWING—mottled white tom

LIZARDSTRIPE—pale brown tabby she-cat with white belly

APPRENTICES (more than six moons old, in training to become warriors)

FROGPAW—dark gray tom

NEWTPAW—black-and-ginger she-cat

ASHPAW—pale gray she-cat

QUEENS (she-cats expecting or nursing kits)

FEATHERSTORM—dark brown tabby (mother to Raggedkit and Scorchkit)

BRIGHTFLOWER—orange tabby (mother to Yellowkit, Nutkit, and Rowankit)

POOLCLOUD—gray-and-white she-cat

ELDERS (former warriors and queens, now retired)

LITTLEBIRD—small ginger tabby she-cat

LIZARDFANG—light brown tabby tom with one hooked tooth

SILVERFLAME—orange-and-gray she-cat (Brightflower's mother)

THUNDERCLAN

LEADER **PINESTAR**—red-brown tom with green eyes

DEPUTY **SUNFALL**—bright ginger tom with yellow eyes

MEDICINE CAT **GOOSEFEATHER**—speckled gray tom with pale blue eyes

APPRENTICE, FEATHERPAW

WARRIORS	(toms and she-cats without kits)
	DAPPLETAIL—tortoiseshell she-cat
	ADDERFANG—mottled brown tabby tom
	TAWNYSPOTS—light gray tabby tom
	HALFTAIL—big dark brown tabby tom
	SMALLEAR—gray tom with very small ears
	ROBINWING—small brown she-cat **APPRENTICE, LEOPARDPAW**
	FUZZYPELT—black tom **APPRENTICE, PATCHPAW**
	WINDFLIGHT—gray tabby tom
QUEENS	(she-cats expecting or nursing kits)
	MOONFLOWER—silver-gray she-cat
	POPPYDAWN—long-haired dark brown she-cat
ELDERS	(former warriors and queens, now retired)
	WEEDWHISKER—pale orange tom with yellow eyes
	MUMBLEFOOT—brown tom, slightly clumsy with amber eyes
	LARKSONG—tortoiseshell she-cat with pale green eyes

WINDCLAN

LEADER	**HEATHERSTAR**—pinkish-gray she-cat with blue eyes
DEPUTY	**REEDFEATHER**—light brown tabby tom

MEDICINE CAT — **HAWKHEART**—stone-gray tom with flecks of darker brown fur

WARRIORS — (toms and she-cats without kits)

DAWNSTRIPE—pale gold tabby with creamy stripes
APPRENTICE, TALLPAW

REDCLAW—dark ginger tom
APPRENTICE, SHREWPAW

ELDERS — (former warriors and queens, now retired)

WHITEBERRY—small pure-white tom

RIVERCLAN

LEADER — **HAILSTAR**—thick-pelted gray tom

DEPUTY — **SHELLHEART**—dappled gray tom

MEDICINE CAT — **MILKFUR**—gray-and-white tabby
APPRENTICE, BRAMBLEPAW

WARRIORS — (toms, and she-cats without kits)

RIPPLECLAW—black-and-silver tabby tom

TIMBERFUR—brown tom

OWLFUR—brown-and-white tom

OTTERSPLASH—white-and-pale-ginger she-cat

QUEENS — (she-cats expecting or nursing kits)

LILYSTEM—pale gray queen

FALLOWTAIL—light brown she-cat with ginger patches around her muzzle, flecked with gray

ELDERS (former warriors and queens, now retired)

TROUTCLAW—gray tabby tom

CATS OUTSIDE THE CLANS

MARMALADE—large ginger tom

PIXIE—fluffy white she-cat

RED—orange she-cat

BOULDER—gray tom

JAY—elderly black-and-white she-cat

HAL—dark brown tabby tom

Prologue

❧

Starlight shone down into a large cavern through a ragged hole in the roof. The faint silver sheen was just enough to show a tall rock jutting from the floor in the center of the cave, flanked by soaring rock walls, and at one side, the dark, gaping hole of a tunnel entrance. The shadows in the mouth of the tunnel thickened, and six cats emerged into the cavern. Their leader, a speckled gray tom with clumped, untidy fur, padded up to the rock and turned to face the others.

"Sagewhisker, Hawkheart, Milkfur," he began, nodding to each cat as he named them, "we, the medicine cats of the four Clans, are here to carry out one of our most important ceremonies: the creation of a new medicine cat apprentice."

Two more cats lingered by the tunnel entrance, their eyes huge in the half-light. One of them shuffled his paws as if they had frozen to the cold stone.

"For StarClan's sake, Goosefeather, get on with it," Hawkheart muttered with an impatient twitch of his tail.

Goosefeather glared at him, then turned to the two young cats by the tunnel. "Featherpaw, are you ready?" he asked.

The bigger of the two, a silver-pelted tom, gave a nervous

nod. "I guess so," he mewed.

"Then come here and stand before the Moonstone," Goosefeather directed. "Soon it will be time to share tongues with StarClan."

Featherpaw hesitated. "But I . . . I don't know what to say when I meet our ancestors."

"You'll know," the other young cat told him. Her white pelt glimmered as she touched his shoulder with her muzzle. "It'll be awesome, you'll see. Just as it was when I became Milkfur's apprentice!"

"Thanks, Bramblepaw," Featherpaw murmured.

He padded up to Goosefeather, while Sagewhisker, Milkfur, and Hawkheart sat a couple of tail-lengths away. Bramblepaw took her place at her mentor's side.

Suddenly the moon appeared through the hole in the roof, shedding a dazzling white light into the cave. Featherpaw halted and blinked in astonishment as the Moonstone woke into glittering life, blazing with silver.

Goosefeather stepped forward to stand over him. "Featherpaw," he meowed, "is it your wish to share the deepest knowledge of StarClan as a ThunderClan medicine cat?"

Featherpaw nodded. "Yes," he replied, his voice coming out as a breathless croak. He cleared his throat and tried again. "It is."

"Then follow me."

Goosefeather turned, beckoning with his tail, and took the few paces that brought him close to the Moonstone. His pale blue eyes shone like twin moons as he spoke. "Warriors of

StarClan, I present to you this apprentice. He has chosen the path of a medicine cat. Grant him your wisdom and insight so that he may understand your ways and heal his Clan in accordance with your will." Flicking his tail at Featherpaw, he whispered, "Lie down here, and press your nose against the stone."

Quickly Featherpaw obeyed, settling himself close to the stone and reaching out to touch its glimmering surface with his nose. The other medicine cats moved up beside him, taking similar positions all around the stone. In the silence and the brilliant light, the new medicine cat apprentice closed his eyes.

Featherpaw's eyes blinked open and he sprang to his paws. He was standing chest-deep in lush grass, in a clearing of a sunlit forest. Above his head, the trees rustled in the warm breeze. The air was laden with the scent of prey and damp fern.

"Hi, Featherpaw!"

The young tom spun around. Approaching him through the grass was a tabby-and-white she-cat with blue eyes; she gave him a friendly flick with her tail as she drew closer.

Featherpaw stared at her. "M-Mallowfur!" he gasped. "I've missed you so much!"

"I may be a warrior of StarClan now, but I am always with you, my dear," Mallowfur purred. "It's good to see you here, Featherpaw. I hope it's the first time of many."

"I hope so, too," Featherpaw responded.

Mallowfur kept walking, brushing through the grass until she joined a ginger tom at the edge of the trees; together the two StarClan cats vanished into the undergrowth. Close to the spot where they had disappeared, another StarClan warrior crouched beside a small pool, lapping at the water. Heartbeats later, a squirrel dashed across the clearing and swarmed up the trunk of an oak tree, with two more of Featherpaw's starry ancestors hard on its tail.

Featherpaw heard his name being called again. "Hey, Featherpaw! Over here!"

Featherpaw glanced around the clearing. His gaze fell on a black tom, almost hidden in the shadows under a holly bush. He was small and skinny, his muzzle gray with age.

The dark-furred cat beckoned with his tail. "Over here!" he repeated, his voice low and urgent. "Are your paws stuck to the ground?"

Featherpaw shouldered his way through the long grasses until he stood in front of the tom. "Who are you? What do you want?"

"My name is Molepelt," the cat replied. "I have a message for you."

Featherpaw's eyes stretched wide. "A message from StarClan, my first time here?" he breathed. "Wow, that's so great."

Molepelt let out an irritable grunt. "You might not think so, when you've heard what it is."

"Go on."

Molepelt fixed him with an icy green gaze. "A dark force is

on its way," he rasped, "with the power to pierce deep into the heart of ThunderClan. And it will be brought by a Shadow-Clan medicine cat."

"What?" Featherpaw's voice rose to a high-pitched squeak. "That can't be right. Medicine cats have no enemies, and they don't cause trouble for other Clans."

Molepelt ignored his protest. "A long time ago, I was the ShadowClan medicine cat," he went on. "My Clanmates and I did a great wrong to another Clan—a Clan that belonged in the forest as much as any of us, but was driven out through our selfishness and hard-heartedness. I knew then that what we did was wrong, and I have waited, my heart filled with dread, for the Clans to be punished."

"Punished? How?" Featherpaw asked hoarsely.

"The time has come!" Molepelt's green eyes were wide, and he seemed to be gazing into the far distance. "A poison will spring from the heart of ShadowClan, and spread to all the other Clans." His voice became a soft, eerie wailing. "A storm of blood and fire will sweep the forest!"

Featherpaw gazed at the old cat in horror. Before he could speak, a powerful black-and-white tom pushed his way through a clump of ferns and padded up to the holly bush.

"Molepelt, what are you doing?" he demanded. "Why are you spilling all this to a ThunderClan apprentice? You don't know that this is the time!"

Molepelt snorted. "You were once my apprentice, Hollow-belly, and don't you forget it! I *know* I'm right."

Hollowbelly glanced at Featherpaw, then back at Molepelt.

"Things are different now," he meowed.

"What do you mean? What's going to happen?" Featherpaw asked, his voice shaking.

Hollowbelly ignored him. "There's no reason to punish ShadowClan," he continued. "What happened was too long ago. The medicine cat code will keep the Clans safe."

"You're a fool, Hollowbelly," Molepelt growled. "The medicine cat code can do *nothing* to save the Clans."

"You don't know that for sure!" When Molepelt did not respond, Hollowbelly turned to Featherpaw. "Please, say nothing about this," he meowed. "There is no need to spread alarm, not when the future is lost in mist even to StarClan. Promise me that you won't tell any of your Clanmates. Promise on the lives of your ancestors!"

Featherpaw blinked. "I promise," he whispered.

Hollowbelly nodded. "Thank you, Featherpaw. Go well." Nudging Molepelt to his paws, he led the old medicine cat away into the trees.

Featherpaw gazed after them. After a few heartbeats he scrambled out from underneath the holly bush and staggered into the sunlit clearing. "Even if Molepelt was telling the truth, it makes no sense!" he meowed out loud. "How can ThunderClan be threatened by a ShadowClan medicine cat?"

CHAPTER 1

"ShadowClan warriors, attack!"

Yellowkit burst out of the nursery and hurtled across the ShadowClan camp. Her littermates, Nutkit and Rowankit, scurried after her.

Nutkit pounced on a pinecone that lay at the foot of one of the pine trees overhanging the clearing. "It's a WindClan warrior!" he squealed, batting at it with tiny brown paws. "Get out of our territory!"

"Rabbit-chasers!" Rowankit flexed her claws, growling. "Prey-stealers!"

Yellowkit leaped at a straying tendril from the brambles that encircled the camp; her paws got tangled in it and she lost her balance, rolling over in a flurry of legs and tail. Scrambling to her feet, she crouched in front of the bramble, her teeth bared in a growl. "Trip me up, would you?" she squeaked, raking her claws across its leaves. "Take that!"

Nutkit began to scan the clearing, peering around with narrowed amber eyes. "Can you see any more WindClan warriors on our territory?" he asked.

Yellowkit spotted a group of elders sharing tongues in a

shaft of sunlight. "Yes! Over there!" she yowled.

Nutkit and Rowankit followed her as she raced across the hard brown earth and skidded to a halt in front of the elders.

"WindClan warriors!" Yellowkit began, trying to sound as dignified as her Clan leader, Cedarstar. "Do you agree that ShadowClan is the best of all the Clans? Or do you need to feel our claws in your fur to persuade you?"

Littlebird, her ginger pelt glowing in the warm light, sat up, giving the other elders an amused glance. "No, you're far too fierce for us," she meowed. "We don't want to fight."

"Do you promise to let our warriors cross your territory whenever they want?" Rowankit growled.

"We promise." Silverflame, the mother of Yellowkit's mother, Brightflower, flattened herself to the ground and blinked fearfully up at the kits.

Lizardfang cringed away from the three kits, shuffling his skinny brown limbs. "ShadowClan is much stronger than us."

"Yes!" Yellowkit bounced up in the air. "ShadowClan is the best!" In her excitement she leaped on top of Nutkit, rolling over and over with him in a knot of gray and brown fur.

I'm going to be the best warrior in the best Clan in the forest! she thought with glee.

She broke away from Nutkit and scrambled to her paws. "You be a WindClan warrior now," she urged. "I know some awesome battle moves!"

"Battle moves?" a scornful voice broke in. "You? You're only a kit!"

Yellowkit spun around to see Raggedkit and his littermate,

Scorchkit, standing a couple of tail-lengths away.

"And what are you?" she demanded, facing up to the big dark tabby tom. "You and Scorchkit were still kits, last time I looked."

"But we'll be apprentices soon," Raggedkit retorted. "It'll be moons and moons before you start training."

"Yeah." Scorchkit licked one ginger paw and drew it over his ear. "We'll be *warriors* by then."

"In your dreams!" Rowankit bounded up to stand next to Yellowkit, while Nutkit flanked her on her other side. "There are *rabbits* who'd make better warriors than you two."

Scorchkit crouched down, his muscles tensed to leap at them, but Raggedkit blocked him with his tail. "They're not worth it," he mewed loftily. "Come on, runts, watch us and we'll show you some *real* battle moves."

"You're not our mentors!" Nutkit snapped. "All you know how to do is mess up our game."

"Your game!" Raggedkit rolled his eyes. "Like you wouldn't go squealing into the nursery if WindClan really attacked our camp."

"Would not!" Rowankit exclaimed.

Raggedkit and Scorchkit ignored her, turning their backs on the younger kits. "You attack me first," Scorchkit ordered. Raggedkit dashed past his littermate, aiming a blow at Scorchkit's ear. Scorchkit swung away and pounced on Raggedkit's tail. Raggedkit rolled over onto his back, all four paws ready to defend himself.

Annoyed as she was, Yellowkit couldn't help admiring the

older toms. Her paws itched to practice their battle moves, but she knew that she and her littermates would only get sneered at if they tried.

"Come on!" Nutkit nudged her. "Let's go and see if there are any mice in the brambles."

"You won't catch any, even if there are," Raggedkit meowed, rising to his paws and shaking debris from his fur.

"I wasn't talking to you." Nutkit's fur bristled and he bared tiny, needle-sharp teeth. "Kittypet!"

For a moment all five kittens froze. Yellowkit could feel her heart pounding. Like her littermates, she had heard the elders gossiping, wondering who had fathered Raggedkit and Scorchkit, asking one another if it could be true that Featherstorm's mate had been a kittypet. The young she-cat had often strayed into Twolegplace, and she'd never been obviously close to any of the toms in the Clan. But Yellowkit knew that it was something you should never, never say out loud.

Raggedkit took a pace closer to Nutkit, stiff-legged with fury. "*What* did you call me?" he snarled, his voice dangerously quiet.

Nutkit's eyes were wide and scared, but he didn't back down. "Kittypet!" he repeated.

A low growl came from Raggedkit's throat. Scorchkit's gaze darkened and he flexed his claws. Neither of them looked one bit like a soft, fluffy kittypet. Yellowkit braced herself to defend her littermate.

"Nutkit!"

Yellowkit turned at the sound of her mother's voice.

Brightflower was standing beside the thornbush that shielded the nursery hollow. Her orange tabby tail was twitching in annoyance.

"Nutkit, if you can't play sensibly, then you'd better come back here. You too, Yellowkit and Rowankit. I won't have you fighting."

"Not fair," Nutkit muttered as all three littermates began trailing toward the nursery. He scuffed his paws through the pine needles on the ground. "They started it."

"They're just stupid kittypets," Rowankit whispered.

Yellowkit couldn't resist glancing over her shoulder as she reached the thornbush. Raggedkit and Scorchkit stood in the middle of the clearing, glaring after them. The force of Raggedkit's anger scared her and fascinated her at the same time. Behind it she could sense something else: a black space that echoed with fearful questioning. She thought of her own father, Brackenfoot, who told stories of patrols and hunting and Gatherings at Fourtrees, who let his kits scramble all over him and pretended to be a fox so they could attack him. Yellowkit loved him and wanted to be like him.

What must it be like, not to know who your father is? Especially if every cat thinks he was a kittypet?

Then Yellowkit realized that Raggedkit's gaze had locked with hers. With a squeak of alarm she ducked underneath the branches and tumbled down into the nursery after her littermates.

CHAPTER 2

"I'm bored," Nutkit complained. "Let's go play in the warriors' den."

Yellowkit blinked at him. "Are you mouse-brained? The warriors will rip our pelts off."

Three sunrises had passed since the quarrel with Raggedkit and Scorchkit. Yellowkit still felt uneasy around them, and tried to avoid them around the camp.

"You're a scaredy-mouse!" Nutkit taunted her. "Go on—peek under the bush. I dare you!"

I can't back down now, Yellowkit thought, bracing herself as she gazed across the clearing to the thick bramble bush where the warriors slept. Like all the ShadowClan dens, theirs was a shallow dip in the ground, sheltered by tightly woven thorns and enclosed by the circle of brambles. The dens surrounded a clearing beneath pine trees, with the entrance to the camp at one end and a large lichen-covered rock, known as the Clanrock, at the other.

Rowankit nudged Yellowkit. "Don't do it! Brightflower's got her eye on us. Look over there." She angled her ears to where Brightflower and Brackenfoot were sharing a vole beside the fresh-kill pile. In between mouthfuls, Brightflower was turning her head to check up on her kits.

A wave of affection for her mother washed over Yellowkit. *I'm glad I look like her,* she thought. She had seen her own reflection in a puddle once, and almost thought she was gazing at a tiny copy of Brightflower. Though her pelt was gray, not orange tabby like her mother's, she had the same broad, flat face, snub nose, and wide-set amber eyes.

I want to be just like her, and *just like my father,* Yellowkit thought. *A warrior and a queen. I'll have lots of kits, and I'll bring them up to be great warriors for our Clan.*

"I know a game!" she announced. "You be my kits, and I'll teach you how to catch frogs."

"Okay!" Rowankit sat in front of Yellowkit, and wrapped her tail neatly around her paws.

Nutkit rolled his eyes, but said nothing as he came to sit beside Rowankit.

Yellowkit let out a hiss. "I never saw such untidy kits," she scolded. "Nutkit, have you been rolling around in the brambles? And Rowankit, just *look* at your chest fur. Give it a good lick *right now*!"

Rowankit let out a tiny *mrrow* of amusement as she started to lick her chest fur. Nutkit wriggled as Yellowkit used her claws to pick imaginary thorns out of his pelt.

"This is a dumb game," he muttered. "And *your* pelt's not so great, either."

Yellowkit gave him a light swat around the ear. "Don't you dare speak to your mother like that!"

She stood back, checking her littermates' fur carefully, then nodded. "Much better. Now, kits, listen up. We're going to learn how to catch a frog. Nutkit, pay attention!" She flicked her tail over her brother's ear as he watched the jerky flight of a white butterfly. "The most important thing to remember about frogs is that they jump."

"Can I be the frog? Can I?" Rowankit asked, bouncing up and down in excitement. "I can jump really high!"

Yellowkit let out a sigh of exasperation. "No! You've got to *listen*."

Brightflower was padding across the clearing toward them. Her eyes were warm and amused. "That looks like a good game," she meowed. "Yellowkit, you'll make a great queen one day."

"And a warrior!" Yellowkit insisted.

"Of course," Brightflower purred. "If that's what you want."

"It is! I'll be the best—" Yellowkit broke off as she spotted Cedarstar emerging from his den beneath the oak tree.

The Clan leader bounded across the clearing and leaped up onto the Clanrock. "Let all cats old enough to catch their own prey join here beneath the Clanrock for a meeting!" he yowled.

Yellowkit turned to her mother. "What's happening?"

"Wait and see," Brightflower replied. "Come sit with me and your father."

Sweeping her tail around all three kits, Brightflower led them across the clearing to where Brackenfoot sat beside the fresh-kill pile. Meanwhile, more of the Clan cats were gathering. Sagewhisker, the medicine cat, slid out from her den in the shadow of the Clanrock and sat down facing her leader. Poolcloud, her belly heavy with kits, hauled herself out of the nursery and padded slowly over to the entrance of the warriors' den, where her mate, Toadskip, had just appeared. Toadskip's apprentice, Ashpaw, bounded up to join them. The other two apprentices, Frogpaw and Newtpaw, broke off their play fight, shook their pelts, and sat down to listen. Crowtail, Archeye, and Hollyflower pushed their way out of the warriors' den.

Finally Raggedkit and Scorchkit appeared from the nursery, followed by their mother, Featherstorm. Their fur was gleaming and they paced proudly across the camp to stand at the front of the crowd of cats.

Yellowkit suddenly realized what was going on. "They're being made apprentices!"

"Shh!" Brightflower responded. "Nutkit, stop scratching your ear."

"I wish it was *our* turn," Nutkit whispered to Yellowkit. "We've got to wait *forever*."

Yellowkit nodded. "Four whole moons." *Raggedkit and Scorchkit look so grown-up,* she thought. *I can't believe I'll ever be an apprentice.*

Cedarstar looked down at the two older kits. "Cats of ShadowClan," he began. "Today we are gathered for—"

Yellowkit squirmed, trying to get comfortable. Her hind paw was tingling as if she'd stepped on a thorn. She twisted around, lifting her pad in an attempt to see it.

Cedarstar broke off, looking down at her.

"Yellowkit!" Brightflower hissed. "Stop wriggling!"

"I've got a thorn in my paw!" Yellowkit wailed.

"Keep still, then. Let me look." Brightflower peered at Yellowkit's paw, then gave it a brief sniff. "There's nothing there," she snapped. "Stop fussing and listen to Cedarstar."

Yellowkit realized that all of her Clanmates were staring at her. She wished that she could sink into the earth floor of the camp and disappear. "Sorry," she muttered, hanging her head. Her paw was still painful, but she gritted her teeth and tried to ignore it.

"Cats of ShadowClan," Cedarstar began again, "we are here for one of the most important ceremonies in the life of any Clan, the making of new apprentices. Raggedkit and Scorchkit have reached their sixth moon, and it is time for them to begin their training."

A murmur of appreciation came from the surrounding cats, though Yellowkit heard a quiet comment from Toadskip, who was sitting nearby. "Training half kittypets!" he murmured into Archeye's ear. "We'll be making hedgehogs into apprentices next."

Yellowkit started to bristle, but Raggedkit and Scorchkit hadn't overheard their Clanmate's unkind words. The two kits stood with their heads and tails erect and their whiskers quivering; Yellowkit thought they looked as if they would burst with pride.

"Raggedkit, come forward." Cedarstar beckoned to the dark tabby tom with his tail. "Brackenfoot," he went on, "you are ready for another apprentice, and you will be mentor to Raggedpaw. I trust you will pass on to him your warrior skills and your loyalty to your Clan."

My father is going to be Raggedpaw's mentor! A tingle of jealousy shot through Yellowkit. *Now Brackenfoot will spend more time with Raggedpaw than he does with us.*

Brackenfoot dipped his head. "You can trust me, Cedarstar," he meowed.

Raggedpaw trotted toward him, and Brackenfoot stepped forward to touch noses with his new apprentice.

As they withdrew into the circle of watching cats, Cedarstar called Scorchkit forward. "Crowtail, Scorchpaw will be your first apprentice," the Clan leader meowed. "You have proven yourself as a warrior and I know you will pass on all that you have learned to him."

Her eyes shining, the small black she-cat padded to the Clanrock and gazed up at her leader. "I'll do my best, Cedarstar," she responded.

Scorchpaw bounded over to her, and the two cats touched noses.

"Raggedpaw! Scorchpaw!" Every cat in the Clan yowled the new names and pressed forward to congratulate the two new apprentices. But Yellowkit and her littermates hung back.

"They're not so great," Nutkit muttered. "Wait till we're apprentices. We'll show them!"

Now that the meeting was over, Yellowkit flopped down on one side and brought her hind leg forward so that she could take a good look at her paw. Pain was still throbbing through it. But however much she probed between her pads, she couldn't find the thorn. Sitting up, she saw that Brackenfoot and Crowtail were leading their new apprentices through the gap in the brambles that circled the camp.

They're going to see the territory, Yellowkit thought enviously. *I wish I could go with them.* But right now she could hardly put her hind paw to the ground. *Maybe I should go see Sagewhisker.*

But as Yellowkit made her way toward the medicine cat's den, hopping awkwardly on three legs, she saw a patrol emerging from the tunnel into the camp. Mudclaw was in the lead with Mousewing; both were carrying mice. Nettlespot followed, dragging along a squirrel nearly as big as she was. Deerleap, one of the most senior warriors, had caught a blackbird. Last of all came the young pale brown warrior Lizardstripe, limping as if her hind paw was hurting her too.

"Better see Sagewhisker about that thorn," Mudclaw mumbled around his mouthful of prey. "Your paw might get infected if it's not seen to."

"I'm on my way." Lizardstripe sounded irritated. "This is the last time I go chasing mice underneath a thornbush." She limped past Yellowkit and vanished between the rocks into the medicine cat's den.

Yellowkit waited patiently until Lizardstripe emerged again, this time walking almost normally. "Thanks, Sagewhisker," the warrior called over her shoulder.

Sagewhisker poked her head out from her den. "Give it a good lick," she instructed. "And see me again tomorrow so I can make sure it hasn't gotten infected."

Yellowkit stumbled forward, ready to tell Sagewhisker about the thorn in her own foot, but when she put her hind paw on the ground, she realized the pain had gone. The thorn must have fallen out. She looked around her, trying to see it on the grass, but there was nothing that looked sharp enough. *Oh well, as long as it doesn't hurt anymore.* She pressed her paw harder on the ground, making sure it was truly better.

"Hey, Yellowkit!" Rowankit's voice interrupted her.

Yellowkit looked up to see both her littermates standing beside a broken tree stump not far from the elders' den. New branches had started to sprout from the remains of the trunk, making a shady cave.

"Come over here!" Nutkit squealed. "We've found a fox and her cubs. We've got to drive them out of our camp!"

For a heartbeat Yellowkit believed him, and her neck fur bristled. Then she realized this was just another game. *Oh, yes, the elders will make really scary foxes!*

Silverflame was peering out of the elders' den as Yellowkit bounded over to join her littermates. Her fur stood on end and her teeth were bared. "This is our den!" Silverflame hissed. "Stay away, or I'll strip your fur off and feed you to my cubs!"

"Go on, attack them!" Littlebird peered over Silverflame's shoulder. With her ginger pelt she looked a lot like a fox cub. "I just fancy a nice fat kit!"

"No!" Yellowkit yowled. "This is ShadowClan's camp! No foxes allowed!"

She hurled herself at Silverflame, trying to grab ahold of the old she-cat's fur. Silverflame batted at her with soft paws, her claws sheathed. Rowankit and Nutkit raced past them into the den.

"Out! Out!" Nutkit squeaked.

Yellowkit and Silverflame rolled into the open; Yellowkit ended up on top, clinging to Silverflame's belly fur. "Do you give in?" she demanded. "No more eating cats?"

"No more, I promise," Silverflame responded. Then she let out a gusty sigh. "Go on, my old bones won't stand much more of this." As Yellowkit bounced off her, Silverflame sat up and shook her gray-and-orange pelt, panting a little as she caught her breath. She blinked affectionately at Yellowkit and a purr rose in her throat. "Well fought, little one," she mewed. "I can see you're going to be one of the best warriors in Shadow-Clan."

You're right about that, thought Yellowkit, her chest swelling with pride. *Watch out, foxes!*

Chapter 3

Yellowkit found it hard to get to sleep that night. She had often complained about the nursery seeming too crowded, but now that Raggedpaw and Scorchpaw had left for the apprentices' den, it felt oddly empty. Featherstorm had returned to the warriors' den, so the only cats in the nursery besides Yellowkit and her littermates were Brightflower and Poolcloud, whose kits were close to being born.

I'll never get to sleep if Poolcloud keeps snoring, Yellowkit thought crossly, wriggling around in the moss and pine needles that lined the floor of the nursery.

"Keep still," Brightflower mewed drowsily. "How is a cat supposed to get any rest?"

With a snort of annoyance Yellowkit curled up and wrapped her tail over her nose. Peering over the top of it, she could just make out Rowankit tucked close into their mother's side, and Nutkit sprawled on the moss, his legs and tail twitching as if he was dreaming about racing through the forest.

I wish StarClan would send me *a good dream,* Yellowkit thought.

She slept at last, only to wake again with a start. A faint dawn light was filtering through the brambles. Poolcloud was still snoring softly; Brightflower and Rowankit were curled up together. Nutkit was squirming about in the bedding, letting out soft moans of pain.

Yellowkit realized what had woken her; her belly felt heavy, and every couple of heartbeats pain shot through it. *I guess Nutkit's belly is hurting, too.* She prodded her brother gently with one paw. "Do you have cramps in your belly?" she whispered.

Nutkit's eyes blinked open and he peered blearily at his sister. "How do you know?"

"My belly is aching too," Yellowkit retorted, wincing as another deep cramp coursed through her. She pressed her belly hard against the moss as if she could squash the pain out of it. "We've got to tell Brightflower," she grunted. "She'll get Sagewhisker."

"No!" Nutkit's eyes stretched wide with alarm. "Yellowkit, don't, please."

"Why not?" Yellowkit asked. She narrowed her eyes at her brother. "What have you been up to?"

Before Nutkit could reply, Brightflower raised her head, twitching her whiskers in annoyance. "Will you kits settle down?" she began. "This isn't the time for playing. You—" She broke off and her gaze grew more intent, swiveling from Nutkit to Yellowkit and back again. "What's the matter?"

"Our bellies are hurting," Yellowkit replied, her words ending with a low wail as another wave of pain surged over her. "Please get Sagewhisker."

Before she had finished speaking, Brightflower had risen to her paws, careful not to disturb the sleeping Rowankit, and padded across the moss to give each of her kits a careful sniff. "Have you been eating something you shouldn't?" she asked. "Tell me quickly, now. Sagewhisker will need to know."

"No, I—" Another gasp of pain interrupted Nutkit. "All right," he went on when he could speak again. "I found a dead sparrow among the brambles yesterday. I only tasted it to see what it was like . . ."

"Nutkit!" Brightflower let out a sigh of exasperation. "You *know* what I've told you about eating crow-food. You too, Yellowkit. How could you be so stupid?"

"But I didn't!" Yellowkit protested.

Her mother gazed at her sternly. "Eating crow-food is bad, and lying about it is even worse," she meowed.

Hot indignation surged through Yellowkit, almost driving out the pain in her belly. "I'm not lying!" she insisted. "I never even saw the stupid sparrow! Tell her, Nutkit."

"I didn't see Yellowkit there, but . . ." Nutkit's words ended in a groan.

"And how do you suppose you got a bellyache if you didn't eat it?" Brightflower twitched her tail-tip angrily. "I'm very disappointed in both of you, especially you, Yellowkit. Now come outside so you don't disturb Rowankit and Poolcloud. I'll go get Sagewhisker."

Yellowkit didn't argue any more as she scrambled out of the moss and pine needles. Still simmering with indignation, she clambered up the side of the hollow and wriggled under the branches of the thornbush. The sky above the pine trees was pale with the approach of dawn. Just inside the entrance to the camp, Mousewing was on guard, his black pelt barely visible against the brambles. He yawned and stretched, not noticing Brightflower as she bounded across the clearing to the medicine cat's den.

Wincing from the pain in her belly, Yellowkit flopped down beside her brother and waited for her mother to reemerge from the den with Sagewhisker.

"You'd better tell Brightflower the truth about eating that sparrow," Nutkit murmured. "You're only making it worse for yourself."

"For the last time, I did *not* eat any dodgy sparrow," Yellowkit snapped. "I've got more sense!"

Nutkit gave her a disbelieving look, but said nothing more. A moment later Sagewhisker emerged from her den and trotted across to the nursery, followed closely by Brightflower.

"Kits!" the medicine cat exclaimed, dropping a bundle of leaves as she halted in front of Yellowkit and Nutkit. "If it's not one thing, it's another. Have you *no* sense?"

"What are you going to give us?" Yellowkit whimpered, sniffing at the leaves as another spasm cramped her belly. "Are you going to make us sick to get the bad stuff out of us?"

Sagewhisker gazed at her intently. "That's exactly what I'm going to do," the medicine cat meowed. "And this is the herb we need for it: yarrow." Bending her head, she gave Nutkit and then Yellowkit a long sniff. "Brightflower tells me you've been eating crow-food," she continued.

Nutkit let out a moan of pain. "It was only a mouthful . . . two, maybe."

Sagewhisker sighed. "Or three, or four. Now you know why we teach kits not to do that."

"Will they be okay?" Brightflower fretted, giving Nutkit's ears a comforting lick.

"They'll be fine," Sagewhisker assured her. "Right, kits, I want you to eat this yarrow. It will make you sick and then your belly will feel a whole lot better."

Nutkit gave the herbs a suspicious glare. "Are they yucky?"

The medicine cat nodded. "They are pretty yucky," she admitted. "But would you rather have a yucky taste, or the bellyache?"

"I'll eat them . . . I guess," Nutkit responded.

"Not here, please," Brightflower mewed. "We don't want a mess right outside the nursery."

In spite of Nutkit's feeble protests, she picked him up by the scruff and carried him toward the edge of the camp. Sagewhisker padded alongside, carrying the yarrow, while Yellowkit followed, staggering a little as pain roiled through her insides.

By now, the dawn light had strengthened; several warriors had emerged from their den, and Stonetooth, the Clan deputy, was organizing the dawn patrols. Yellowkit felt a pang of envy as she spotted Raggedpaw and Scorchpaw with their mentors. She quickened her pace, stumbling a little, hoping the apprentices wouldn't spot her and ask what was happening.

In the shelter of the thorns at the edge of the clearing, Sagewhisker laid a few yarrow leaves in front of Nutkit, and the rest of the bundle in front of Yellowkit. While Nutkit was still hesitating, Yellowkit lapped up the leaves, wincing as the bitter juices filled her mouth.

"Yuck!" she gasped, gagging as she tried to swallow.

After a few heartbeats she managed to force the vile stuff down. Almost at once she felt her belly give an enormous heave, and she vomited up several mouthfuls of slime. She passed her tongue over her lips, trying to get rid of the taste.

"That's good," Sagewhisker murmured approvingly, as Nutkit too brought up the contents of his belly. "Brightflower, take them back to the nursery. They should sleep now. When they wake they can have some milk, but no food today. I'll check on them later."

"Thank you, Sagewhisker." Brightflower dipped her head to the medicine cat. "And let that be a lesson to you," she added to her kits. "No more crow-food."

"But I didn't eat crow-food!" Yellowkit's indignation surged up again now that her belly didn't hurt anymore. *It's not fair! Why won't any cat believe me?*

Brightflower let out a hiss. "No more!" she mewed. "I won't punish you for lying this time, because you've suffered enough, but don't let it happen again."

Without waiting for Yellowkit to respond, she grabbed Nutkit by the scruff and headed for the nursery. Yellowkit padded after them, her head down and her tail drooping. Her belly was sore from vomiting, and she could still taste the bitter yarrow, but what made her really miserable was the thought that her mother believed she was a liar.

* * *

Yellowkit pushed her way into the open, yawning and arching her back in a long stretch. She was bored. Behind her in the nursery, Nutkit was still asleep, half-buried in the moss as if he was exhausted from his disturbed night and his upset belly.

But I feel fine, Yellowkit thought. *Except my belly's growling.* Brightflower had just reminded her that Sagewhisker had said she and Nutkit couldn't have anything to eat until tomorrow. *I'll never last that long!* Yellowkit wailed inwardly. *I'll be as weak as a mouse.*

Blinking, she gazed around the camp. Hollyflower and Crowtail were sharing tongues outside the warriors' den, while the elders were gossiping in a patch of warm sun beside the tree stump. Yellowkit caught a scrap of their conversation.

". . . sent that WindClan warrior squealing all the way back to his camp," Lizardfang meowed. "We didn't put up with any nonsense from WindClan in *my* day, let me tell you."

"No, and not from ThunderClan either," Silverflame purred.

Yellowkit's heart swelled with love for the old she-cat. *Maybe if I go over there she'd tell me a story.* Then she shook her head. *No, more likely I'd have to listen to Lizardfang yakking on about all the WindClan warriors he chased off.*

In the middle of the clearing, Rowankit was playing by herself, tossing a ball of moss into the air and catching it on her tiny extended claws. Yellowkit didn't feel like joining in.

I wish I could go out and explore the territory like Raggedpaw and Scorchpaw.

Flicking her tail and trying not to look as if she was going anywhere special, Yellowkit padded across the camp toward the fresh-kill pile. The sun was shining, and the patches of sky visible through the trees were a clear blue. But there was a chill in the air, and the leaves on the huge oak tree where Cedarstar made his den were beginning to turn yellow. Greenleaf was coming to an end.

Yellowkit felt hungrier than ever when she approached the fresh-kill pile and the enticing scents of vole and squirrel flooded her jaws. She absolutely had to have something to eat if she was going to sneak out of the camp.

One little mouse couldn't hurt. . . .

"Hey, Yellowkit!"

Yellowkit jumped guiltily. Turning to see who was calling her, she spotted Sagewhisker sunning herself at the entrance to her den.

Uh-oh!

"Nothing until tomorrow," the medicine cat warned her. "I'm surprised you can even think about eating yet."

"I'm *starving*!"

Sagewhisker stifled a purr of amusement. "Would you rather have a bellyache, little kit?"

Yellowkit scuffled her forepaws in the earth of the camp floor. "I guess not."

"Why don't you come and help me with a few things?" the medicine cat suggested. "All the apprentices are out, and I need someone to give me a paw sorting my herbs. It might take your mind off your empty belly."

"Okay." Yellowkit perked up. She liked the sharp scents of herbs in the medicine cat's den, and she needed something to stop herself from thinking about food. She followed Sagewhisker back into the den. Beyond the narrow entrance that lay between two boulders, a tiny clearing opened out, edged by thick clumps of fern. At the far side a pool of clear water reflected the pine trees above.

"The herbs are over here." Sagewhisker padded to one side of the clearing. "I dig holes in the ground to keep them fresh, and cover them up with fern fronds."

She picked up one of the fronds and laid it aside. Yellowkit peered into the hole beneath; a few withered leaves lay at the bottom.

"That's marigold," Sagewhisker meowed. "It's good for infected wounds, but as you can see, those scraps aren't much good. Lift them out and pile them up by the entrance. Later on I'll carry all the rubbish out of the camp."

While Yellowkit obeyed, Sagewhisker uncovered the next hole; it held only two or three shriveled berries.

"Should I add those to the pile?" Yellowkit asked, dipping her paw into the hole, ready to scoop out the berries.

Sagewhisker shook her head, flicking her tail across to block Yellowkit's paw. "No, those are juniper berries. I know they're past their best, but they're so useful for bellyache and shortness of breath, I won't dare throw them away until the fresh ones are ready. It won't be long, thank StarClan."

Yellowkit nodded, giving the berries an interested sniff. "Silverflame wheezes sometimes," she remarked. "Do you give her juniper berries?"

"I do." Sagewhisker dipped her head. "You're learning fast, Yellowkit."

Yellowkit felt proud of herself. *This is so useful! I'll know about herbs and everything when I'm a warrior!* "What's in the next hole?" she asked.

"These are daisy leaves," Sagewhisker replied, uncovering a pile of fresh leaves. "Good for Lizardfang's aching joints. I only collected them yesterday, so we don't have to throw them out."

Yellowkit followed her along the row of holes, while Sagewhisker told her about each different herb and what they were used for, sorting out the withered ones so that Yellowkit could pile them up at the entrance.

"There, finished!" Sagewhisker mewed at last, dusting off her paws. "Well done, Yellowkit. You've been a big help."

"It was fun," Yellowkit replied, realizing with a start that it was true. *I had no idea how much you have to learn to be a medicine cat!*

"And your belly feels fine now?"

Yellowkit nodded. "Still empty, though," she mewed.

Sagewhisker touched Yellowkit's ear with her nose. "Then you'll remember to stay away from crow-food in future."

Yellowkit heaved a deep sigh. "Yes, okay," she muttered.

There wasn't any point in arguing. She knew that no cat was going to believe her. *But if it wasn't the crow-food,* she asked herself as she padded back to the nursery, *what* did *make my belly ache like Nutkit's?*

CHAPTER 4

Yellowkit's paw landed squarely on top of the quivering mouse, and it went limp. Her jaws watered as she bent her head to take the first succulent bite, when something slammed into her back. Her eyes flew open, her dream fled away, and she found herself in the nursery. Poolcloud's kits, Foxkit and Wolfkit, were wrestling together in the moss, rolling over so they were half on top of Yellowkit.

"Get off!" she muttered, giving the nearest kit a shove. *I could almost taste that mouse!*

Yawning, Yellowkit sat up. Brightflower and Poolcloud were still asleep, but beside her in the mossy nest Nutkit and Rowankit were beginning to stir. *There's something odd about the nursery this morning,* Yellowkit thought. The light was different, and there was a clean, cold scent in the air that she had never smelled before.

Curious, Yellowkit scrambled over the moss and stuck her head through the branches. Her jaws gaped and she let out a gasp of astonishment. The camp lay under a thick white covering, and more of the white stuff weighed down the branches of the encircling pine trees.

"Wow!" Yellowkit squeaked. "What happened?"

Nutkit and Rowankit appeared beside her, their eyes round as they gazed out.

"Did WindClan do this to us?" Nutkit growled. "I'll shred their fur!"

"No." Brightflower pushed her way out of the nursery, her paws sinking into the white stuff, and turned to look back at her kits. Her eyes were warm with amusement. "This is snow. We get it sometimes in leaf-bare."

"Where did it come from?" Rowankit asked.

"It falls out of the sky," Brightflower explained. "Like rain, but snow looks like falling feathers."

Extending one paw, Yellowkit dabbed at the white stuff. "It's *cold*!"

Nutkit let out a yowl of excitement and launched himself into the snow, his weight hardly denting the surface.

"Wait for me!" Yellowkit charged after him, with Rowankit a tail-length behind. She could hear more squealing from the nursery, telling her that Foxkit and Wolfkit were following. "This is fun!"

But as Yellowkit raced across the camp after her littermate, she felt as if something was holding her back. Rowankit overtook her with an excited squeak. Trying to force her legs to run faster, Yellowkit realized that the snow was clogging up her thick fur, dragging at her and slowing her down. *That's not fair!* she thought indignantly.

A moment later her paws skidded out from under her as Foxkit crashed into her. "Got you!" the younger kit squealed.

"You're as slow as a hedgehog, Yellowkit!"

Struggling out from underneath her denmate, Yellowkit looked at the other kit's smooth ginger pelt. No wonder it was easier for her to run fast in the snow. Taking a breath as she tried to shake the clots of snow from her pelt, she felt her mouth burning in the crisp, dry air. "I'm thirsty," she announced. "I'm going to get a drink."

"You just want an excuse to stop running," Foxkit taunted.

Yellowkit opened her jaws to respond, then decided that arguing with Foxkit wasn't worth it. *Four moons old, and she thinks she knows everything.* Glancing around the camp, she spotted the early morning light gleaming on a pool of melted snow just outside the warriors' den. Silverflame was crouched beside it, lapping steadily. Yellowkit went to join her, but Silverflame didn't look up. The old cat must have been superthirsty. She always seemed to be drinking these days.

A sharp pain stabbed at Yellowkit's belly as she started to drink the icy water, and her fur prickled as though a storm was brewing. Yellowkit tilted her head on one side. There had been storms in the heavy days of greenleaf, when gray clouds would cover the sky and the air felt hot and damp, but today the sky was clear and pale, and the rising sun cast blue shadows across the snow-covered camp. A cold, dry breeze ruffled the white surface. *No storms today,* Yellowkit told herself.

"Hi, Yellowkit." Silverflame paused in her lapping at last. "Enjoying your first snow?"

Yellowkit turned to reply, and winced at the look of exhaustion and pain in the old she-cat's eyes. "It's okay, I guess," she replied. "Silverflame, are you all right?"

Silverflame shrugged. "It's just the moons catching up with me," she mewed. "Don't worry, Yellowkit."

"This cold weather does nothing for old bones," Littlebird agreed as she emerged from the elders' den and headed for the fresh-kill pile. Glancing back, she added, "Are you coming, Silverflame?"

The she-cat shook her head. "I'm not hungry. The young ones need to eat more than I do."

Yellowkit frowned. *What does Silverflame mean? All cats need to eat!* "Come on," she urged, giving Silverflame a gentle push. "Let's go together and find something tasty."

"Okay." With a huge sigh Silverflame rose to her paws.

Yellowkit thought that the elder's paw steps looked a bit shaky as she padded over to the fresh-kill pile. Littlebird was already clawing the snow away from it, revealing the heap of frozen prey.

"Here, try this frog." Yellowkit dragged it out of the pile and set it down in front of Silverflame.

The elder blinked at the frog for a couple of heartbeats as if she had never seen one before, then lowered her head and took a small bite. Yellowkit chose a mouse for herself, but kept an eye on Silverflame as she was eating. The old cat was barely picking at her prey. In the sharp, slanting sunlight, Yellowkit could see Silverflame's bones showing beneath her fur, as if the elder hadn't been eating properly for days.

After two or three more bites of the frog, Silverflame pushed it toward Yellowkit with one paw. "I've had enough. You finish it."

She turned and tottered away, vanishing into the elders' den. Yellowkit stared anxiously after her. She didn't want to finish the frog; the mouse she had eaten was weighing heavy in her belly, and she wondered if there might have been something wrong with it. Her fur was still prickling, too.

There was a rustle of frozen brambles and Sagewhisker emerged into the camp. She carried a few frostbitten twigs in her jaws, and as Yellowkit bounded over to her she recognized shriveled juniper berries clinging to them. "Sagewhisker!" she called, catching up with the medicine cat just outside her den.

Sagewhisker carefully laid the twigs down. "What is it, Yellowkit?"

"It's Silverflame," Yellowkit explained, struggling to stop her voice from shaking. "I think she's sick. She doesn't want to eat anything."

Sagewhisker blinked at her. "Silverflame is old," she mewed. "And leaf-bare is hard for the newest and the oldest members of the Clan."

"But she . . ." Yellowkit's voice died away. *There aren't any herbs to stop a cat from getting old,* she thought miserably.

"I'll look in on her," Sagewhisker promised.

Yellowkit nodded, knowing she had to accept what the medicine cat said. *I wish I could do something to help.* Then she remembered how thirsty Silverflame always seemed. *She must get so cold, coming out to drink at the pool. If I found some moss, I could bring her a drink into her den.*

Feeling better now that she had a plan, Yellowkit plunged through the snow to where a fallen tree lay among the thornbushes that surrounded the camp. As she pushed her way beneath the spiky branches she dislodged clumps of snow that showered down over her head and shoulders. Yellowkit let out a snarl as she shook the icy flakes from her pelt.

The moss-covered tree was just ahead of her. But as she reached out to strip off a pawful of moss, Yellowkit heard voices on the other side of the brambles. Curious, she scrambled over the tree trunk and wriggled farther through the thorns, her paws tingling with excitement as she realized she was almost outside the camp. Peering cautiously through the branches, Yellowkit saw a flat stretch of ground enclosed by the dark trunks of pine trees. The surface of the snow was churned up, and Brackenfoot was standing with Raggedpaw in the middle of the rough patch.

"You've learned that move really well," Brackenfoot was meowing. "Now you need to work on getting more power into your swipe. Let's try it again."

Yellowkit watched, fascinated, as Brackenfoot crouched down in the snow and Raggedpaw charged at him, darting in to rake his paw over his mentor's ear, and leaping back before Brackenfoot could retaliate.

"Better," Brackenfoot praised him. "Try again. Harder!"

This time Brackenfoot rose to his paws and waited with muscles tensed for Raggedpaw's attack. As Raggedpaw struck out, Brackenfoot ducked so that the blow only ruffled his fur. Raggedpaw leaped at him again and suddenly the two cats were locked together, swiping at each other with all four paws as they struggled to pin the other to the ground.

Yellowkit drew in a breath of mingled excitement and

horror, terrified that her Clanmates would injure each other, until she noticed that they were fighting with sheathed claws.

I can't believe how good Raggedpaw is, she thought with a twinge of envy. *He's still only an apprentice!*

A moment later, Raggedpaw let out a yowl of triumph. He was standing on top of Brackenfoot, his forepaws pinning down his mentor's shoulders, while one hind paw was fixed firmly on his tail. Brackenfoot was panting, his eyes half-closed and his muscles limp. Yellowkit's eyes widened in dismay and she flexed her claws, ready to dash out and defend her father.

"I won!" Raggedpaw meowed. His eyes blazed as he looked down at his mentor. "I'm the best fighter in the Clan!"

Before the last words were out of his jaws, Brackenfoot surged upward, flinging Raggedpaw off him and rolling him over in the snow. "What was that again?" he asked mildly as Raggedpaw scrambled up with snow clumped all over his pelt.

Yellowkit let out a gleeful *mrrow* to see that her father hadn't lost the battle after all. *Raggedpaw thinks he's so great . . .*

Raggedpaw glared at his mentor. "You cheated! You pretended to be beaten!"

"And you think that an enemy won't do that when you fight in a real battle? You're doing well, Raggedpaw, and you'll be a great fighter one day, but you still have a lot to learn."

Raggedpaw shook himself, spraying snow everywhere. His shoulders sagged. "You're right," he admitted. "I'm sorry. Will you teach me that move?"

"Another time," Brackenfoot promised. "We've done enough for today. Let's get back to camp, and you can take something from the fresh-kill pile."

"Thanks!" Raggedpaw's eyes glowed. "I'm *starving*!"

Brackenfoot turned toward the camp entrance and Raggedpaw was about to follow. Suddenly he froze and Yellowkit shrank back as she realized the apprentice was staring straight at her.

"What do you think you're doing?" Raggedpaw demanded. "Hey, Brackenfoot, Yellowkit's spying on us!"

Brackenfoot glanced back, spotting his daughter among the thorns. "Don't be such a mouse-brain," he told Raggedpaw. "Yellowkit can watch if she wants. She might learn something."

Raggedpaw let out a snort of disgust, but said nothing more. Her fur hot with embarrassment, Yellowkit scrambled backward until she reached the fallen tree again. Tearing off a pawful of thick moss, she scampered across the camp to soak it in the puddle before carrying it to the elders' den.

"Here, Silverflame," she mumbled around her mouthful as she poked her head underneath the branches. "I brought you a drink."

All three elders were huddled together in the shelter of the stump. Littlebird narrowed her eyes at Yellowkit. "Keep that wet moss away from our bedding," she snapped.

"Yes," Lizardfang agreed. "You should know better than to bring it in here."

Yellowkit suppressed an angry hiss, remembering she

ought to be polite to the elders, even when they were being a pain in the tail.

"Leave her alone," Silverflame meowed. "That was a very kind thought, Yellowkit." Gesturing with her tail, she added, "Put the moss down there, well away from the bedding."

When Yellowkit had obeyed, Silverflame stretched out her neck and lapped at the dripping fronds. "Great StarClan, that's good," she murmured. "Thank you."

Shooting a smug glance at the two other elders, Yellowkit was about to reply when she heard Cedarstar's voice from outside in the camp.

"Let all cats old enough to catch their own prey join here beneath the Clanrock for a meeting!"

"For StarClan's sake, what now?" Lizardfang complained.

Dipping her head briefly to the elders, Yellowkit backed out of the den, almost colliding with her mother as she spun around to see what was going on.

"There you are!" Brightflower exclaimed. "I've been searching everywhere for you."

"Why? What's happening?" Yellowkit mewed.

Just behind her mother, she spotted Rowankit and Nutkit, looking unusually well groomed. Nutkit was bouncing up and down on his paws, while Rowankit's eyes were wide and shining.

"You're going to be made apprentices," Brightflower explained.

Yellowkit stared at her. "Now?"

"Yes, now, and just look at you!" Brightflower darted out

a paw and snagged a spiky twig that was stuck in Yellowkit's pelt. "Any cat would think you'd been wriggling through thorns all day."

Yellowkit stood still while Brightflower gave her a quick grooming, flicking bits of thorn and moss out of her fur, and smoothing it with strong strokes of her tongue.

Meanwhile the cats of ShadowClan were gathering around the Clanrock. All three elders poked their heads out from under the branches that shaded their den. Deerleap and Amberleaf appeared from the warriors' den, followed closely by Toadskip and Featherstorm. Brackenfoot and Raggedpaw, who were eating beside the fresh-kill pile, finished their prey quickly and turned to listen; Crowtail and Scorchpaw padded over to join them.

Yellowkit's belly began to churn. *Every cat will be looking at me! What if I get something wrong? Who will be my mentor?*

"This is going to be a hard leaf-bare," Cedarstar began. "With snow on the ground, we need all the hunters we can get, and border patrols to defend our territory when the other Clans get hungry. So this is a good time to strengthen Shadow-Clan by making new apprentices. Rowankit, come forward."

Rowankit swallowed nervously, then padded forward until she stood beneath the Clanrock.

Cedarstar's gaze swept over his Clan. "Finchflight," he meowed, "you have served your Clan well and you deserve to have another apprentice. I know you will pass on your skills to Rowanpaw."

Rowanpaw gave a little skip of delight at the sound of her

new name, then trotted over to Finchflight and touched noses with him. The black-and-white tom let out an approving purr.

Cedarstar beckoned Nutkit with his tail. "Nutkit, come forward," he meowed.

Nutkit paced proudly across the clearing.

"Amberleaf," Cedarstar continued, dipping his head to the dark orange she-cat, "you are a skilled warrior, and I know you will give Nutpaw the training he needs."

Nutpaw's got Amberleaf! Yellowkit barely stopped herself from exclaiming out loud. *She's so strict!* All the young cats were a bit afraid of Amberleaf, who had a scathing tongue when she was annoyed; Yellowkit remembered being scolded by her when she accidentally hit the warrior on the head with a ball of moss.

Nutpaw looked nervous as he padded across to Amberleaf to touch noses, but relaxed as the she-cat murmured, "I'll make you the best warrior you can be."

Yellowkit's heart began pounding harder. When Cedarstar beckoned to her, she padded across the clearing with as much dignity as she could muster.

StarClan, please don't let me trip over a twig!

"Deerleap, you are a wise and experienced cat," Cedarstar mewed. "I know that you will pass on your qualities to Yellowpaw."

Yellowpaw spun around to face Deerleap. The gray tabby she-cat had stepped into the clearing, waiting for her. As she approached her mentor, Yellowpaw saw the friendly gleam in Deerleap's eyes, and decided she was very satisfied with the choice that Cedarstar had made for her.

"I'll do the best I can, I promise!" she mewed fervently as they touched noses.

Any reply was drowned in the cheers of the Clan as they greeted the new apprentices by their names. "Nutpaw! Yellowpaw! Rowanpaw!"

Yellowpaw saw Brightflower and Brackenfoot standing side by side, identical expressions of pride on their faces and in their shining eyes. She felt happy enough to burst.

"Okay," Deerleap meowed to Yellowpaw when the noise had died down and the cats were beginning to drift away. "Why don't we go out for our tour of the territory before it gets dark?"

"Great!" Every hair on Yellowpaw's pelt bristled with excitement. "Let's go!"

But as she followed Deerleap across the camp toward the brambles where Nutpaw and Rowanpaw were already vanishing with their mentors, she staggered as a sharp pain shot through her belly. She couldn't suppress a yelp.

Deerleap turned around. "What's the matter?"

Yellowpaw could hardly stay on her paws. The pain filled her body, darkening her vision. She had never felt anything so bad.

"Pain . . . it hurts . . ." she managed to gasp.

"You'd better see Sagewhisker," Deerleap meowed.

"But . . . I want to see the . . . the territory," Yellowpaw protested.

"The territory won't go away." Deerleap's voice was determined. She laid her tail across her apprentice's shoulders. "Come along."

As she stumbled across the camp, Yellowpaw fought against her disappointment. *I want to start training* now. *I don't have time to be sick.*

But when she reached the medicine cat's den, there was no sign of her.

"You looking for Sagewhisker?" Toadskip was on his way to the fresh-kill pile. "I saw her go into the elders' den."

"Thanks, Toadskip." Deerleap led the way toward the tree stump.

When they approached the den, Yellowpaw heard drawn-out moans, as if a cat was in agony. Yellowpaw's pain had ebbed a little, but her fur felt strange and began prickling, harder and harder with every paw step she took. She was scared of what she might find in the elders' den, and could hardly force herself to go in.

When she ducked underneath the outer branches of the den, she saw Silverflame stretched in her nest, her body twisted and her eyes glazed with pain. Sagewhisker was crouching over her, while Lizardfang and Littlebird huddled together at the far side, their faces full of fear and pity. The floor was strewn with different herbs, their sharp scents mingling with another sweetish smell that made Yellowpaw gag.

Silverflame is really sick!

"Yes—what is it?" Sagewhisker snapped, not shifting her gaze from the old she-cat.

"I had a pain . . . but it's nothing," Yellowpaw stammered.

"Okay." Sagewhisker paused to chew up a mouthful of

leaves. "See me tomorrow if it doesn't clear up."

"I will. Thanks."

Unable to bear watching Silverflame any longer, Yellowpaw backed out of the den.

"Are you feeling okay now?" Deerleap asked, a tinge of impatience in her voice. "Because if you are, we can set off."

Yellowpaw nodded, trying to ignore the nagging pain in her stomach; when she breathed in the scent of the herbs it had faded to a tolerable ache. "I'm fine," she insisted.

Deerleap led the way through the brambles. Excitement surged over Yellowpaw as she followed, almost driving out her anxiety about Silverflame. Heartbeats later, she stood outside the camp for the first time. Pine trees stretched into the distance on every side.

"Wow!" she breathed. "The forest goes on forever!"

"Not quite," Deerleap responded, a glint of amusement in her eyes. "Come on. We'll go this way."

The ground between the trees was flat and almost clear of undergrowth. Yellowpaw spotted tracks crisscrossing it: the spiky claw marks of birds, cat paw prints from an earlier patrol, and larger prints, tipped with claws, that she had never seen before. She paused to sniff at them and picked up a trace of a rank smell that felt faintly threatening.

Deerleap had halted and was looking back. "Come on, Yellowpaw."

"What's this?" Yellowpaw mewed.

Deerleap gave the tracks a swift glance. "Fox," she stated.

Yellowpaw shivered and glanced around, half expecting

to spot a slim russet shape slinking among the trees. She had never seen a fox, but she had heard plenty of stories about them.

"It's okay," Deerleap told her. "That scent is stale. But we need to keep a lookout whenever we're outside the camp."

Yellowpaw flexed her claws, wondering what it would be like to fight a fox. Movement among the trees caught her eye, but no fox appeared. Instead, it was a ShadowClan hunting patrol. Cedarstar was leading the way back to camp, with Archeye and Featherstorm, all of them carrying prey. Deerleap called a greeting, and the Clan leader waved his tail in acknowledgment.

A short while later the pine trees thinned out, replaced by bushes mounded with snow and reeds whose feathery tops rattled together in the breeze. The flat ground became uneven, with hidden hollows filled with snow. Yellowpaw let out a squeak as she slid down a dip and sank deep into the powdery white stuff. *Deerleap is going to think I'm a stupid kit!*

But Deerleap just waited until Yellowpaw struggled out, and didn't make any comment. "When the weather is warmer, the ground here is marshy and wet," she meowed. "It's a good place for catching frogs."

Yellowpaw nodded. *Silverflame used to enjoy frogs,* she thought, remembering how the elder hadn't been eating properly for ages. She realized that Deerleap had asked her a question and had paused, waiting for an answer.

"Sorry," Yellowpaw muttered. "What was that?"

Deerleap sighed. "I asked what you thought would be

the best way to catch a frog."

"I . . . um . . ." Yellowpaw thought fast. "Hide in the reeds and jump out at it?" she suggested.

Her mentor twitched her whiskers. "That might work. But remember frogs can swim too. It's best to find one on land. Two cats can hunt better than one: one to cut the frog off from the pool it came out of, and one to catch it. We'll practice with the other apprentices when newleaf comes."

"Great!" Yellowpaw responded, though her thoughts of Silverflame moaning in agony dampened her enthusiasm.

They came to the edge of the marsh and padded through another belt of pine trees. The trees grew more sparsely here, and reddish, hard-edged shapes loomed beyond the last of them, as tall as the highest trunks.

"We're coming to the edge of ShadowClan territory," Deerleap mewed. "Can you smell our scent markers?"

Yellowpaw sniffed and nodded. She felt proud that the ShadowClan scent was so strong. *That warns other Clans not to mess with us!*

"Over in that direction," Deerleap went on, angling her ears toward the ominous shapes, "is Twolegplace. We don't go there. It's a place for dogs and kittypets, not warriors. Those are the dens where Twolegs live."

Yellowpaw gazed at the unnaturally straight walls with square holes dotted across their sides, some high up and some closer to the ground. Low wooden barriers surrounded each den, rather like the thorns that surrounded ShadowClan's camp. As Yellowpaw watched, a kittypet appeared, balancing carefully on the top of the wooden wall before jumping down to the other side.

"That cat was wearing something around its neck," she observed.

Deerleap nodded. "A collar. Most kittypets have them. It signifies that they belong to Twolegs, and can never be free. Just be thankful you'll never have to wear one."

Yellowpaw watched for a little longer, but the kittypet didn't reappear. She wondered what it would be like to live in the Twolegplace. It looked cold and hard and empty, and she was glad when Deerleap moved on again, through another belt of woodland where pines were mixed with other trees. The bare branches creaked over Yellowpaw's head.

Yellowpaw soon became aware of an acrid stench in the air, and a dull roaring that grew and died away again. "Is that *thunder*?" she mewed.

"You'll see what it is in a few heartbeats," Deerleap told her.

When Yellowpaw came to the edge of the trees she stumbled to a halt. In front of her lay a narrow stretch of ground that led away in both directions as far as she could see. The snow that lay upon it had been churned up in straight lines, leaving dirty brown ridges. Underneath, Yellowpaw could make out a hard, black surface. The acrid stench rose from it in waves, smothering all the other scents of the forest.

"What's *that*?" Yellowpaw gasped. She stretched out a paw to touch the surface.

Immediately Deerleap flicked her tail in front of Yellowpaw. "Keep back," she warned.

At the same moment the weird roaring sound began again. Yellowpaw tensed as a small creature appeared at the far end of the path; it grew bigger as the roaring grew louder. Soon she could make it out more clearly: It was an unnatural glittering scarlet, and it had round black paws that seemed to eat up the ground. Heartbeats later it swept past, spattering Yellowpaw with dirty, half-melted snow. For a moment its bellowing and vile reek filled the air; then it was gone, dwindling into the distance as the sound died away.

"It didn't spot us!" Yellowpaw mewed in relief.

"Mostly they don't," Deerleap responded. "They keep to the Thunderpath, and don't bother us provided we stay away from it. But cats have died trying to cross, so don't even think about it."

"*That's* the Thunderpath?" Yellowpaw asked. "Then that must have been a monster! Brackenfoot told us about them when we were in the nursery. He said the monsters have Twolegs in their bellies, but I thought that was just a tale for kits."

"No, it's true," Deerleap meowed.

"Those things *eat* Twolegs?"

"Not exactly." Deerleap sounded puzzled. "The Twolegs get out of them again, and they seem okay. I don't know what it's all about, but then, Twolegs are strange."

The stink of the monster was dying away, and as she tasted the air Yellowpaw could pick up another scent she didn't recognize. It was the scent of cats, but harsher than the warm, comforting ShadowClan scent she was used to.

"What's that yucky smell?"

"That's ThunderClan," Deerleap explained, waving her tail toward the trees on the other side of the Thunderpath. "Their territory is over there."

"Really?" The scent marks seemed so close; Yellowpaw imagined a patrol of hostile ThunderClan cats charging across the Thunderpath, invading her territory. Her neck fur started to bristle and she dug her claws into the ground.

They'd better not try it!

But there was no movement among the trees on the opposite side of the Thunderpath, nothing to suggest an enemy patrol was lurking there. Feeling slightly disappointed, Yellowpaw turned away.

"Where do we go next?"

"Follow me." Deerleap led the way alongside the Thunderpath and stopped at a point where the ground fell away into a deep cleft that became a tunnel leading into darkness. The sides were lined with squared-off stones.

"Did Twolegs make that?" Yellowpaw mewed.

"They did." Deerleap sounded pleased and a little surprised that Yellowpaw had guessed right. "Don't ask me why. It leads under the Thunderpath and up on the other side."

"Into ThunderClan territory? They could come right through it and attack us!"

"No, it's still our territory on the other side, all the way to the hollow at Fourtrees. It's the way we go for Gatherings."

Yellowpaw's paws tingled. *Now that I'm an apprentice, I'll get to go to Gatherings!* When she was three moons old, she had begged and begged to go to a Gathering. Silverflame had promised to tell her everything that happened, and the day after, she had kept her promise.

She made it sound so exciting . . . I hope she'll be better by the next full moon, so we can go together.

She was dragged abruptly out of her memories as Deerleap flicked her on the shoulder with her tail-tip. "Wake up!" her mentor chided. "We've still got a long way to go."

They walked on, sticking close to the Thunderpath with the Twoleg dens fading into the trees behind them. "Over there," Deerleap continued, "is another tunnel. That one leads straight into WindClan territory. What do you think that means?"

"Trouble!" Yellowpaw exclaimed.

"Right. So what should we do about it?"

"Patrol really carefully?" Yellowpaw suggested. "And . . . er . . . put really strong scent markers around our end?"

Deerleap nodded. "Exactly. Good thinking, Yellowpaw."

A few fox-lengths farther on, Yellowpaw spotted Rowanpaw trotting toward them with her mentor, Finchflight.

Rowanpaw waved her tail. "Isn't this great?" she called. "Our territory is awesome!"

Yellowpaw mewed agreement, but there wasn't time to stop and chat. Deerleap was forging ahead, and Yellowpaw had to scurry to keep up. By now the sun was starting to go down, staining the snow as red as blood. Shadows began to gather under the trees, and the monsters that swept past on the Thunderpath had glaring yellow eyes that cut through the darkness.

Eventually Deerleap veered away from the Thunderpath and headed back to the trees. Darker shadows loomed ahead, and Yellowpaw tried to hide her nervousness as Deerleap plunged into them. Finally her mentor stopped.

"What can you smell?" she asked.

Yellowpaw parted her jaws and tasted the air. "Very strong ShadowClan scent," she reported. "Are we near the border again?"

"We are. But is there anything else?"

Yellowpaw took in another breath, trying to distinguish other scents beneath the overpowering scent of ShadowClan.

"Oh!" she exclaimed. "Something really nasty! Is it another Clan?"

"No, that's the Carrionplace." Deerleap flicked her tail toward the shadows.

Peering more closely, Yellowpaw made out huge heaps of evil-smelling stuff. Weird shapes that gleamed in the half-light poked out of a mountain of sludge and debris. A shiny fence, like a thick, regular cobweb, surrounded them. "What's that stuff?" she mewed. "How did it get there?"

"Twolegs bring it in yellow monsters," Deerleap replied with a look of disgust. "It's Twoleg crow-food. And before you ask, I don't know why they dump it there."

"Yuck!" Yellowpaw passed her tongue around her jaws. "I can almost taste it from here."

"Stay away from it," Deerleap warned her. "More rats than you can imagine live in those heaps, and even experienced warriors think twice before messing with them."

"There's no *way* I'd want to go there," Yellowpaw assured her. She was happy to leave the Carrionplace behind and head back into the forest. Night had fallen, and the first warriors of StarClan were appearing in the sky. The snow gleamed eerily beneath the trees.

"What's over there?" Yellowpaw curled her tail to where the pine trees stretched on and on until they melted into shadow.

"More forest," Deerleap replied. "No cats go that way. We have enough territory without it."

Yellowpaw felt a stab of relief that they didn't have to go any farther. Her paws were frozen and starting to feel sore. *I've never walked so far,* she thought.

"We're almost back at the camp," Deerleap announced. "You can pick out a piece of fresh-kill and then find yourself a nest in the apprentices' den."

Yellowpaw blinked; she hadn't considered that she wouldn't be sleeping in the nursery anymore, and she wondered if Raggedpaw and Scorchpaw would welcome her and her littermates. But she pushed that thought to the back of her mind. There was something more important that she had to do first.

I need to know how Silverflame is.

She followed Deerleap through the thorn tunnel and into the clearing.

"Did you enjoy seeing the territory?" Deerleap prompted.

"Yes, it was great, thanks," Yellowpaw responded, her paws itching to carry her toward the elders' den.

"Off with you, then." Deerleap flicked her ears. "I'll see you at dawn tomorrow. We'll start your training with hunting practice."

Yellowpaw knew she should feel excited about that, but her anxiety about Silverflame was growing stronger with every heartbeat. She ducked her head to her mentor and bounded across the clearing to the elders' den. Just as she reached it, Brightflower emerged.

"How is Silverflame?" Yellowpaw demanded.

"Growing weaker," Brightflower replied. Her face was solemn. "Be brave, little one. We have to accept that it's time for her to walk with StarClan."

Chapter 5

"No!" Yellowpaw gasped. "She can't leave us!"

"I'm sorry, but she has to." Brightflower bent her head to touch Yellowpaw's ear with her nose.

Yellowpaw could see the desperate anxiety in Brightflower's eyes. *I know how I'd feel if Brightflower was dying. She must feel the same now that it's her mother who's going to join StarClan.*

"I want to see her!" she choked out.

Brightflower nodded. "You can, but you must be very quiet." She stepped back and allowed Yellowpaw to slide underneath the branches into the elders' den.

Silverflame was lying on her side, her legs splayed out as if she were running. Her eyes were half-closed and her chest heaved with rasping breaths. Sagewhisker crouched over her while Littlebird and Lizardfang watched from the corner, their eyes gleaming in the darkness.

Yellowpaw felt as though her pelt were on fire as she drew closer to the old, sick cat. She reeled back, blinking. "She's so thirsty!" she whispered to Sagewhisker. "Why don't you give her something to drink? Why aren't you treating her pain?"

Sagewhisker looked up, her eyes full of grief. "There's

nothing more I can do," she murmured.

"There must be!" Yellowpaw wailed.

"Yellowpaw." Littlebird rose to her paws and gave Yellowpaw a gentle nudge. "Come with me."

"No!" Yellowpaw felt as if her whole world was full of pain and her grief for Silverflame. "I want to stay with her."

"You can't help her now," Littlebird mewed softly. "Come away."

Yellowpaw let herself be urged toward the entrance. Before she ducked under the branches, she looked back. "Good-bye, Silverflame," she whispered.

There was no sign that Silverflame had heard her. She drew a breath that rattled in her throat. As Yellowpaw climbed out of the den, she strained her ears for the next breath. It didn't come.

"She's dead, isn't she?" Yellowpaw whispered.

Littlebird nodded. "She hunts with StarClan now."

Yellowpaw dug her claws into the ground. "She shouldn't be dead. Why didn't Sagewhisker save her?"

"It wasn't—"

Yellowpaw cut off Littlebird's words with a yowl of rage. "She *should* have saved her! What good is a medicine cat if she can't do that?"

"Come for a walk with me," Littlebird meowed gently.

"Yes, go with Littlebird." Brightflower, who had waited outside the den, touched her nose to Yellowpaw's ear.

Her eyes blurred by sadness, Yellowpaw followed the small ginger tabby out of the camp. She realized that Littlebird was heading for the marshes Deerleap had shown her earlier. It felt as though the tour of the territory had happened in another life.

"Medicine cats can only do their best with the knowledge that they have," Littlebird told her. "StarClan wanted Silverflame to walk with them. Look," she added, pausing beside a shrub with a few pale green leaves clinging to its spindly branches, "there's the juniper bush that Sagewhisker used to help Silverflame's pain. And in newleaf there's also coltsfoot for shortness of breath—"

"But none of it did any good," Yellowpaw snarled. "Sagewhisker should have found something better." She lashed her tail. "What's the use of being a medicine cat if you can't heal your Clanmates?"

"Death is part of life," Littlebird meowed, resting her tail on Yellowpaw's shoulder. "Every good warrior goes to StarClan, and that's a glorious place to end up." She raised one paw and pointed at a star that was shining above their heads. "Look, Silverflame is watching over us now."

"But I want her back in the Clan," Yellowpaw whispered. The star was too far away to mean anything, and how could any cat know that it was Silverflame?

"Every cat has to leave sometime," Littlebird murmured. "Until then, all we can do is try our hardest to be the best for our Clan."

As leaf-bare dragged on, the hard frost made the grass sharp enough to pierce a cat's pads like thorns, and prey stayed deep inside their holes. Yellowpaw felt as if her belly was flapping, it was so empty, but Deerleap kept her on a grueling training regime.

"I have to get up before any of you," Yellowpaw grumbled to Nutpaw as she licked a paw and tried to rub sleep out of her eyes. "Some mornings we're even out before the dawn patrol! And it's never enough if I catch one piece of prey. Oh, no—we can't come back to camp until I've caught two or three."

"You're doing great," Nutpaw muttered. He was still curled up in the moss of the apprentices' den, and he sounded half-asleep. "Deerleap is a fantastic mentor."

Yellowpaw snorted, though she was pleased that she had managed to impress her brother. *I'm trying really hard,* she thought. *Surely I'm going to be a good warrior with all this training?*

"Yellowpaw!"

"Uh-oh." Yellowpaw flinched at the sound of her mentor's voice. "Coming!" she called as she scrambled out of the den.

Deerleap was standing a fox-length away, impatiently flexing her claws. The first faint light of dawn was creeping into the sky; Yellowpaw could barely see the outlines of the trees. Stonetooth was emerging from the warriors' den. He arched his back in a long stretch and his jaws parted in a yawn.

Yellowpaw blinked and tried to look alert. "Where are we going today?"

"I thought we might try near the big ash tree," Deerleap replied. "No cat has hunted there for a day or two."

Yellowpaw's sleepiness vanished as she headed into the forest after her mentor. The air was crisp and cold; her paws pattered on the hard ground, and she made a conscious effort to walk softly. The dawn light was strengthening as the ash tree came into sight. Deerleap gestured with her tail for Yellowpaw to take cover behind some brambles.

"Keep perfectly still," she instructed. "Look, listen, and scent. What can you pick up?"

Yellowpaw drew herself up, her whiskers quivering with concentration, and tried to focus all her senses at once. At first she could hear nothing but the breeze in the bare branches of the ash, and the soft sound of her own breath. Then a familiar scent wafted into her jaws and she pricked her ears.

Blackbird!

She poked her head out from behind the brambles and spotted the bird pecking among the roots of the ash tree. Remembering to check the direction of the breeze, she worked her way around the outside of the thicket and dropped into her hunter's crouch to creep up on the bird from the other direction. Stealthily, paw step by paw step, Yellowpaw edged forward, her gaze fixed on her quarry. She was aware of Deerleap watching her, which made her even more determined. *I've got to make a good catch!*

But before Yellowpaw came within pouncing distance, she accidentally stepped on a dead leaf. It crackled under her paw, and the blackbird, alerted by the tiny sound, fluttered up onto a low branch.

"Mouse dung!" Yellowpaw hissed.

She padded back to Deerleap, who was still in cover behind the brambles.

"Okay," her mentor mewed. "What did you do wrong?"

"I stepped on a leaf." *Duh!*

"And why did you step on a leaf?"

"I wasn't aware of everything around me," Yellowpaw admitted. "I was so focused on the blackbird that I didn't think about where I was putting my paws."

Deerleap gave her an approving nod. "Good. You'll remember next time, won't you?" Glancing out from the thicket, she added, "And now you get another chance."

Yellowpaw poked her head out and saw that the bird was back among the tree roots, pecking away as if it had forgotten the threat.

I'll get you this time!

Checking the wind direction again, she crept forward; this time she looked down at the ground in front of her, assessing everything that lay between her and her prey. She avoided a fallen twig, and used a clump of frostbitten grass for extra cover. At last she was close enough to pounce; bunching her muscles, she shot forward in an enormous leap, and sank her claws into the bird before it realized she was there. Once the limp body was securely in her jaws, she trotted back to her mentor.

"Well done," Deerleap purred. "That was a perfect bit of stalking."

Yellowpaw felt warm all over; Deerleap's praise had to be earned. "It's a little scrawny," she confessed after she had dropped the bird on the ground.

"Never mind. Any piece of prey is welcome in weather like this."

The ground was too hard to dig a hole and bury the fresh-kill while they kept hunting, so Yellowpaw scraped leaves over it before starting to search the area for more prey, moving in widening circles around the ash tree. But it seemed as if nothing else was moving in all the frozen forest. Claws of frost dug deep into Yellowpaw's pelt, and she was almost ready to ask if they could go back to camp when she spotted a flicker of movement between two stones. Swiftly she flashed out a paw and was startled to find that she had hooked a lizard on her claws. It wriggled for a heartbeat and then was still.

"That was lucky," Deerleap commented. "You don't usually see those in weather as cold as this."

Yellowpaw swelled with pride as she carried her two pieces of prey into the camp. Nutpaw and Rowanpaw were standing by the fresh-kill pile with their mentors.

"We've been on a hunting patrol!" Nutpaw mewed, scampering up to Yellowpaw. "I caught a mouse!"

"And Rowanpaw caught a starling," Finchflight added. "They've both done very well."

"Well, there's no point in standing around watching our fur grow," Deerleap meowed. "What about giving the apprentices a joint training session? They could all do with practicing their battle moves."

"She never stops, does she?" Rowanpaw muttered into Yellowpaw's ear as the other two mentors murmured agreement and led the way to the thorn tunnel.

"At least fighting will keep us warm," Yellowpaw pointed out.

She and her littermates followed their mentors to the shallow training scoop not far from the camp. Raggedpaw and Scorchpaw were already there with Brackenfoot and Crowtail.

"Watch this," Crowtail mewed. "They're getting really good."

The two older apprentices were circling cautiously around each other. Raggedpaw flashed out a paw, but Scorchpaw leaped backward and the blow never connected. With a yowl Raggedpaw pushed off with his hind legs and thrust himself into the air. Yellowpaw winced, expecting him to land on Scorchpaw and knock him to the ground. But while Raggedpaw was still in the air, Scorchpaw twisted onto his back. He splayed out all four legs, claws extended. Raggedpaw landed on Scorchpaw's belly, and immediately Scorchpaw fastened his four sets of claws in Raggedpaw's shoulders and haunches. Then he rolled over, pinning Raggedpaw to the ground.

"Enough," Crowtail meowed, and the two apprentices broke apart. "Now try it again, and Scorchpaw, you leap this time."

"That's a brilliant move!" Rowanpaw exclaimed.

"It's a good one to remember if a cat leaps on you in battle," Brackenfoot explained as the older apprentices circled each other again. "Often the cat who's underneath has the worst of the fight, but this way you can get back in control."

"Can we try?" Yellowpaw asked when she had seen the move demonstrated for the second time.

"Of course," Deerleap meowed. "That's what we're here for. Yellowpaw, you can work with Nutpaw. Scorchpaw, you practice with Rowanpaw."

Rowanpaw looked slightly disconcerted at the thought of working with an apprentice who already knew the move, and Scorchpaw was obviously not too happy about being paired with a younger cat. But they knew better than to argue.

"Keep your claws sheathed," Brackenfoot instructed. "We don't want any shredded fur."

Each pair of cats began circling. Yellowpaw was leaping down onto Nutpaw, who had his paws extended ready for her, when she heard a startled yowl from Rowanpaw. At the same time a sharp pain sliced through her shoulder. She let out a screech and crumpled to the ground at Nutpaw's paws.

"For StarClan's sake, what's happening?" Finchflight exclaimed, bounding over to his apprentice. "Rowanpaw, are you okay?"

As Yellowpaw rolled over, gasping with pain, she saw her sister sprawled on the ground on the far side of the training area. Blood was welling slowly from punctures in Rowanpaw's shoulder.

"Scorchpaw, we said sheathed claws!" Crowtail snapped.

"Sorry," Scorchpaw muttered. "I forgot."

"I don't understand how two apprentices could be injured at the same time," Amberleaf meowed, padding up to Nutpaw. "What did you do?"

"Nothing!" Nutpaw's eyes were wide with dismay. "I never touched Yellowpaw, honestly!"

"Whatever. It still hurts," Yellowpaw snapped, scrambling awkwardly to her paws.

"I'm okay." Rowanpaw sat up, turning her head to swipe her tongue over the spots of blood on her shoulder. "I want to try again."

"Okay," Finchflight meowed. "But let's *all* be more careful this time."

The pain in Yellowpaw's shoulder was fading, but she was wary of being hurt for a second time. When they practiced the move again, she knew she wasn't giving it her best effort.

"Grab your opponent harder," Deerleap advised. "Don't think about what his paws are doing. Just concentrate on hanging on to him and pinning him down."

"I think that's enough for today," Finchflight decided, when the apprentices had practiced the move once more. "Rowanpaw, you'd better see Sagewhisker about those scratches."

Rowanpaw nodded, though Yellowpaw noticed that the claw marks weren't bleeding anymore, and her sister hardly limped at all as they headed back toward camp. While Rowanpaw padded off to the medicine cat's den, the rest of the apprentices and their mentors gathered around the fresh-kill pile.

"Yellowpaw, do you think you should see Sagewhisker too?" Deerleap prompted.

"No, I'm fine," Yellowpaw mumbled through a mouthful of the squirrel she was sharing with Nutpaw.

Deerleap looked doubtful. "You'd better take the rest of the day off," she mewed, giving Yellowpaw's shoulder a sniff.

"I can't see any injury, but you never know. Get some rest, and see Sagewhisker if the pain doesn't clear up." She turned away to choose some prey for herself.

Yellowpaw didn't want to rest. *I feel okay now,* she thought. *Maybe I just landed badly.*

When she had finished her share of the squirrel, she decided she would go off by herself to practice the new move. She still wasn't used to being able to leave the camp on her own and she felt a thrill of confidence as she strode out through the thorns. When she had found a secluded spot in a hollow screened by holly bushes, she tried the move again: first the leap, and then rolling over to splay out her paws, ready to grab her opponent.

It doesn't work so well with only one, she thought, disappointed.

"Do you want any help?"

The voice startled Yellowpaw; she looked up to see Raggedpaw standing at the top of the hollow. "No, I'm fine," she mewed, scuffling her forepaws in the earth.

Ignoring her refusal, Raggedpaw padded down to join her. "You really need a partner to do that move," he meowed.

Yellowpaw gave her fur a shake. *I'd be mouse-brained not to let him help me.* "Okay," she agreed. *Won't Deerleap be surprised when she sees I can do the move perfectly!*

Raggedpaw gave her a brisk nod. "I'll leap and you grab," he told her. "That way, you get to practice the difficult part."

At first, Yellowpaw was afraid that she was going to be squashed into the forest floor by the heavier apprentice. "I can't get my paws in place fast enough," she complained, sitting up and shaking scraps of dead leaf off her fur.

"You have to watch me more closely," Raggedpaw replied. "You should know when the leap is coming, and be ready. Try again."

This time, Yellowpaw spotted the tensing of Raggedpaw's muscles before he leaped. She rolled onto her back and spread her paws wide. "Got you!" she yowled as she wrapped her paws around him and flipped him over.

Raggedpaw scrambled to his paws and gave her a cool nod. "Better."

Better? Yellowpaw thought indignantly. *It was brilliant!*

"You'll be able to do it next time you're in a training session," Raggedpaw went on. "Now I've got to go. I want to hunt before it gets dark."

"Thank you!" Yellowpaw called after him as he climbed back out of the hollow. "You really helped!"

Raggedpaw didn't respond. Yellowpaw stood blinking after him, surprised by her feelings of gratitude. *Maybe he's not so bad after all.*

Chapter 6

The early morning sunlight sparkled on the dewy grass and on the cobwebs draped across bushes and clumps of bracken. Yellowpaw paused to taste the air. The scent of damp earth flooded her jaws, with a trace of fresh green growth.

Newleaf will be here soon.

Yellowpaw and her littermates were following Deerleap, on their way out of camp for a training session. As she leaped over a broken branch, she spotted a hint of green. She turned back, pushing the branch aside, and discovered a few delicate shoots poking up through the covering of rotting leaves. Very gently Yellowpaw scraped away the debris, giving the shoots a chance to reach the sun. Bending down to give them a good sniff, she thought, *I'm sure I've smelled this in Sagewhisker's den before. It must be an herb.*

As she straightened up, she heard yowls of excitement, and the two newest apprentices, Foxpaw and Wolfpaw, hurled themselves over the branch. Yellowpaw leaped backward to avoid being knocked over. Two sets of flying paws stomped down hard on the tiny shoots, crushing them into the earth.

"Mouse-brains!" Yellowpaw called after them, her fur

bristling in fury. "Watch where you're going!"

Brightflower, Foxpaw's mentor, and Blizzardwing, who was mentoring Wolfpaw, followed their apprentices more slowly. Brightflower gave Yellowpaw an inquiring look as she passed, but Yellowpaw just shrugged and brought up the rear.

The rest of the apprentices and their mentors had gathered in a clearing not far from the marshes. Wolfpaw and Foxpaw were charging around the edge, shouldering aside Nutpaw and Rowanpaw if they happened to get in the way.

Rowanpaw padded over to Yellowpaw. "They're even more annoying than Raggedpaw and Scorchpaw."

Still angry over the damaged shoots, Yellowpaw nodded. "They're acting like kits."

Deerleap called the cats together. "Today we're going to do a hunting exercise," she announced.

"Aww, do we have to?" Wolfpaw interrupted. "That's so boring! I want to fight!"

Deerleap gave him a freezing glare. "If you like, Wolfpaw, you can go back to camp and search the elders for ticks."

"Uh . . . no." Wolfpaw's tail drooped. "I guess hunting is okay."

"Thank you so much," Deerleap went on, an edge of sarcasm in her tone. "This morning you're going to work in pairs. Nutpaw and Rowanpaw, you can work together. Yellowpaw, you go with Foxpaw." Her tail-tip twitched. "Wolfpaw, seeing as there isn't another apprentice to partner with, you'll have to work with me."

Yellowpaw was torn between enjoying Wolfpaw's appalled

expression, and dismay that she had to work with Foxpaw. She glanced at the younger apprentice, and saw that Foxpaw was giving her a dubious glance in reply.

Okay, you don't like this any more than I do, Yellowpaw thought. *But we have to put up with it for the sake of the Clan.*

Deerleap directed Yellowpaw and Foxpaw to head through the marshes and toward the Thunderpath. "Come back here when you've each caught one piece of prey," she directed. "And remember, you're working *together.*"

Yellowpaw padded carefully across the swampy ground, practicing her mentor's instructions to *look, listen, and scent.* Meanwhile Foxpaw leaped from grassy clump to grassy clump, often landing instead in the shallow pools and splashing muddy water over her bright ginger pelt.

Yellowpaw rolled her eyes. *I suppose it's one way of disguising your scent from the prey.* She could hear the distant roar of the Thunderpath when Foxpaw gave an excited little bounce. "I can smell a pigeon! This way!" She dashed off.

"She won't catch a pigeon or anything else racing about like that," Yellowpaw muttered. She had picked up the pigeon scent at the same moment, but she had also scented something else.

"Cats—and not ShadowClan cats," she mewed softly as she followed Foxpaw. "This could mean trouble."

She caught up to Foxpaw within sight of the Thunderpath. The young ginger she-cat was standing in the middle of a puddle of feathers, gazing down at them with a look of dismay.

"Some other cat got here before us," she told Yellowpaw.

"I can see that." The scent of strange cats was stronger than ever. "And not a ShadowClan patrol."

"How do you know?" Foxpaw asked.

Yellowpaw ignored the question. *If she can't smell that* . . . She cast around the pool of feathers, her nose to the ground, until she spotted cat paw prints leading away in the direction of the Thunderpath.

"Look at this," she meowed, beckoning Foxpaw with her tail. "See how small and light those paw prints are?" she pointed out when Foxpaw reached her side. "I'll bet a moon of dawn patrols that they were made by WindClan cats."

"WindClan!" Foxpaw exclaimed. "Stealing our prey! They can't do that. Let's get them!"

She was ready to charge off, but Yellowpaw stood in front of her. "Wait!" she snapped. "Are you mouse-brained?"

"Are you scared?" Foxpaw retorted.

"Never!" Yellowpaw's voice was low and furious. "I just have some sense, that's all. What do you suppose two apprentices are going to do, alone on WindClan territory? What we have to do is go and find our mentors."

She raced back across the marsh. Foxpaw pelted alongside her, looking mutinous. When they reached the training area, only Brightflower and Blizzardwing were there.

"WindClan!" Yellowpaw gasped.

"Stealing our prey!" Foxpaw added, bouncing on her paws. "Are we going to attack?"

"Hold on!" Brightflower raised her tail. "Settle down and tell us what happened."

Yellowpaw began to explain what they had seen, trying to ignore Foxpaw's attempts to interrupt. While she was speaking, Deerleap and Wolfpaw returned, closely followed by Nutpaw and Rowanpaw.

"We can't let this pass," Brightflower meowed when Yellowpaw had finished. "We need to take a look. Yellowpaw, lead the way."

Yellowpaw was proud to pad at the head of the patrol as she took them through the marshes to where the pigeon feathers lay. Brightflower dipped her head to sniff at the cat paw prints.

"Fresh," she murmured. "And definitely WindClan. Two of them, I'd guess. Well scented, Yellowpaw."

"You have the best sense of smell," Deerleap meowed to Brightflower. "Why don't you follow these tracks and see where they lead? Take Blizzardwing with you in case the WindClan cats are still lurking around. We'll wait for you here."

Brightflower nodded and headed toward the Thunderpath, with Blizzardwing hard on her paws. Yellowpaw waited impatiently until she saw both warriors racing back.

"The paw prints lead to that new tunnel the Twolegs made under the Thunderpath," Blizzardwing reported. "And we know where that leads: WindClan territory!"

"What are we going to do?" Rowanpaw demanded.

Brightflower and Blizzardwing both looked at Deerleap, as senior warrior. She thought for a moment. "Blizzardwing, you should go back to camp and fetch reinforcements," she replied at last. "Foxpaw and Wolfpaw, go with him, and stay in the camp."

"What?" Wolfpaw exclaimed, dismayed. "We want to fight!"

"Yeah, we know some awesome moves," Foxpaw added.

"Certainly not," Deerleap meowed. "You're both too young for battle." Turning to Yellowpaw and her littermates, she added, "Do you feel ready for your first attack on an enemy?"

Yellowpaw's belly flipped over. "Yes!" she choked out.

Her littermates' eyes were wide with shock; they glanced at each other, then nodded.

"Not fair," Wolfpaw muttered. "We can fight as well as them."

Deerleap ignored his comment. "We'll wait for you near the tunnel entrance," she told Blizzardwing.

The white tom rounded up the younger apprentices and set off back to camp. When they had gone, Deerleap led the way along the line of the tracks until they came in sight of the narrow tunnel that led to WindClan. Yellowpaw could smell the WindClan scent even more strongly here.

"We'll stop here," Deerleap announced, halting beside a clump of long, marshy grass. "Settle down so you can't be seen. And if any WindClan cats come out of the tunnel, don't even twitch a whisker until I give the word."

Yellowpaw obeyed, crouching down in the grass between Rowanpaw and Nutpaw. Her claws were extended and her muscles tensed to leap on any trespassers, but no cats had appeared by the time that Yellowpaw picked up a stronger

ShadowClan scent and heard an approaching patrol brushing through the grass.

Deerleap rose to meet them, signaling to the apprentices to do the same. Stonetooth, the Clan deputy, was in the lead, with Brackenfoot and Crowtail close behind. Yellowpaw was surprised and a bit disappointed to see that Raggedpaw and Scorchpaw were with their mentors. She'd wanted herself and her littermates to be the only apprentices to face down WindClan this time.

"Where's Blizzardwing?" Deerleap asked.

"He stayed to help guard the camp," Stonetooth meowed. "Just in case WindClan thinks it can bring the battle to us."

Deerleap sniffed. "I'd like to see them try."

Excitement bubbled up inside Yellowpaw as the patrol prepared to leave. "We'll make WindClan sorry they ever touched our prey."

"Calm down," Raggedpaw mewed. "This is what warriors do."

"Yeah," Scorchpaw added. "It's just part of living in a Clan."

"It's your first time in battle too," Nutpaw snorted, "so don't pretend you're not excited."

Yellowpaw could see that her littermate was right. Scorchpaw was working his claws in the grass, and Raggedpaw's amber eyes gleamed.

Stonetooth gathered the patrol with a wave of his tail. "I'll lead," he announced. "Brackenfoot, you bring up the rear, and keep an eye out for trouble behind." The pale ginger tom nodded. Turning to the apprentices, Stonetooth went on. "Listen to everything I say. We won't attack right away. We'll give WindClan a chance to explain themselves first."

"Like they'll be able to explain WindClan scent and pigeon feathers inside our borders," Deerleap snarled.

The patrol set off in single file. Yellowpaw was close to the rear, just ahead of Raggedpaw and her father. The tunnel under the Thunderpath was narrower than she had realized—much smaller than the one Deerleap had shown her on their first tour of the territory—and dark. Yellowpaw jumped, her heart beginning to pound, at a roaring noise that seemed to fill the whole of it.

"It's okay," Brackenfoot meowed from behind her. "It's only monsters going past on the Thunderpath."

Forcing herself to relax, Yellowpaw followed the scent of Crowtail, who was walking in front of her. *I wonder what would happen if we met WindClan cats coming the other way.* She tried to work out how she could use her battle moves in such a tight space. Soon she could scent fresh air coming from somewhere ahead. A few heartbeats later Crowtail scrambled upward, showering scraps of earth and debris down on Yellowpaw. Blinking, Yellowpaw followed, and broke out into the open. As Raggedpaw and Brackenfoot emerged after her, she took a huge breath and looked around.

I'm on WindClan territory now!

Yellowpaw felt as if every hair on her pelt was standing on end with the thrill of being across enemy borders. Behind her, monsters roared up and down the Thunderpath. In front, a wide stretch of grass swelled to the horizon in an unbroken sweep. Wind blew from the hilltop toward the ShadowClan cats, ruffling their fur and bringing with it the scents of cats and rabbits.

Stonetooth waved his tail. "This way. Stay together."

"I'm surprised the WindClan cats can catch anything in these open spaces," Yellowpaw mewed to Nutpaw as they followed the Clan deputy toward the top of the moor.

"I know," Nutpaw agreed. "I can hardly hear myself speak, with the wind in my ear fur."

"Look!" Rowanpaw flicked her tail over Yellowpaw's shoulder.

Gazing upward, Yellowpaw spotted a scrawny WindClan warrior outlined against the sky. The cat stood motionless for a heartbeat, then turned tail and vanished down the other side of the hill.

"Gone to warn his Clanmates," Nutpaw muttered.

"I still can't believe how skinny they are!" Yellowpaw mewed. "And their smell is weird, like rabbits and windblown grass."

She remembered the first time she had seen WindClan cats, at her first Gathering almost a moon ago, but the memory was blurred. *There were so many cats . . . so much noise . . .* She had looked forward to her first Gathering for as long as she could remember, but it had been overwhelming, busy and full of chatter and conflicting scents. Yellowpaw had felt too timid to go and talk to any cats from the rival Clans, instead staying among the ShadowClan apprentices. Afterward she had felt stupid and embarrassed for being so shy, but Deerleap told her lots of apprentices felt that way, and sometimes even senior warriors. The next Gathering would be easier, she promised.

Now Yellowpaw felt strong and confident as she strode out across the moor. *I'm part of a ShadowClan patrol. I'm going to fight for my Clan!*

When the ShadowClan cats reached the brow of the hill, they spotted a patrol of WindClan cats heading across the moor toward them. Stonetooth halted, signaling with his tail for the rest to do the same. "We'll let them come to us," he meowed.

Leading the WindClan patrol was a light brown tabby tom. Yellowpaw remembered Deerleap pointing him out to her at the Gathering; he was Reedfeather, the WindClan deputy. Stonetooth stepped forward to face Reedfeather as the WindClan cats approached.

"What are you doing on our territory?" Reedfeather demanded.

"Don't you know?" Stonetooth challenged. "We found pigeon feathers on our side of the Thunderpath, with WindClan scent and paw marks. You've been stealing our prey!"

"We've done nothing of the sort," Reedfeather retorted. "We chased that pigeon from our own territory, and that makes it WindClan prey."

"That's not true, and you know it," Stonetooth growled, sliding out his claws.

Reedfeather tensed his muscles, his neck fur bristling. Yellowpaw could smell his fear. The WindClan patrol was smaller, and the cats looked too weak and skinny to fight well.

For a moment Yellowpaw felt a pang of sympathy. *These cats look as if they haven't had a good meal in moons. Maybe they deserved that pigeon.* Then she gave herself a shake. *That's mouse-brained! I'm a ShadowClan warrior—or I will be soon—and these are my enemies!*

"You need to leave," Reedfeather hissed. "You're not welcome on our territory."

"We're not going anywhere until you've been taught a lesson," Stonetooth responded.

Yellowpaw saw Reedfeather's gaze flicker. "All right," he mewed wearily. "You've made your point. We'll stay on our own side of the border from now on."

Stonetooth didn't reply with words. Instead, he leaped onto the WindClan deputy, bearing him to the ground. A heartbeat later, fighting exploded all around Yellowpaw. For a moment she stood frozen; the whole world seemed to be filled with screeching, clawing cats, and she didn't know which paw to use first.

Then she pulled herself together and lunged at a WindClan cat who was on top of Nutpaw, pummeling him with strong paws. The WindClan cat lashed out at her with a wild blow that only riffled her whiskers, then scrambled away.

"Thanks!" Nutpaw gasped.

Yellowpaw whirled around as she felt a burning scratch all down one side, but she couldn't spot the cat who had dealt the blow. Instead, a huge dark tabby tom bore down on her, his amber eyes blazing. Yellowpaw gulped. She had thought of these cats as small and skinny, but they were full-grown, and this one was much bigger than she was. Frantically she tried to remember her battle moves. She darted at the WindClan tom, intending to strike a blow and spring back out of range, but the tom was ready for her. He ducked away from her claws and swiped her so hard over the ear with one forepaw that she staggered and for a heartbeat the sky went dark. She lashed out again, remembering the move that Raggedpaw had helped her practice, but as she tried to twist in the air the tom batted her down so that she landed all wrong.

He's too strong, Yellowpaw thought despairingly as she struggled to her paws again.

"Out of the way!" A voice sounded in Yellowpaw's ear and a paw scooped her to one side. With a gasp of shock she saw Raggedpaw flash past her and hurl himself onto the big tom. Raggedpaw's claws dug into the WindClan warrior's shoulders and blood started to well up. With a yowl of pain the tom flung Raggedpaw off and fled. Raggedpaw sprang to his paws, ignoring Yellowpaw, then dashed into a fight between Scorchpaw and Reedfeather.

Yellowpaw stayed where she was, panting. *Raggedpaw thought he had to rescue me!* she thought indignantly, but she couldn't help admiring his courage and his fighting skill. As she rose to her paws again she winced with pain; it felt as if every scrap of her pelt had been ripped off. But when she checked her fur and flexed each paw in turn, she couldn't find any wounds except for the scratch along her side.

Glancing around to find another opponent, Yellowpaw realized that the fight was all but over. Most of the WindClan cats were pelting across the moor. Reedfeather was the last to break away and race after his Clanmates, with Rowanpaw hard on his paws.

"No!" Stonetooth commanded. "Rowanpaw, come back!" As Yellowpaw's sister returned, growling angrily, the Clan deputy continued, "There is no need to pursue a defeated enemy."

Yellowpaw thought she could discern sympathy in the deputy's voice and his eyes as he gazed after the vanishing WindClan patrol. But he did not admit as much out loud. Instead he raised his tail. "Back to our territory," he ordered. "There's nothing more to do here."

As they headed back down the hill toward the tunnel, the apprentices bunched together.

"Did you see me scratch that black she-cat's nose?" Nutpaw puffed. "She ran like a rabbit!"

"I did the latest move Finchflight taught me," Rowanpaw put in. "The WindClan cat looked so surprised!"

Yellowpaw couldn't join in their chattering. With every heartbeat, she was growing more annoyed that Raggedpaw had flung her aside in the battle. *None of the other apprentices had to be rescued. Does he think I can't fight?*

The rest of ShadowClan greeted the returning patrol with yowls of welcome.

"Thank you all," Cedarstar meowed, meeting them in the center of the camp. "You have shown our enemies that we in ShadowClan have teeth and claws to defend what is ours. Tonight we will hold a feast in your honor."

Extra hunting patrols went out, and as the sun set the whole

Clan gathered in the clearing to eat. Yellowpaw felt proud and a bit embarrassed when she and the rest of the patrol were allowed to choose the best pieces of fresh-kill before any of the other warriors.

"I can't believe we got to go on a real mission!" she whispered to Nutpaw as she settled down with a plump starling.

"I wish I'd been there," Toadskip meowed, digging his claws into the floor of the camp. "But I was out on a hunting patrol. I have the worst luck."

"There'll be other chances," Hollyflower told him with a twitch of her whiskers. "WindClan isn't going to go away."

"And ShadowClan will be ready for them," Archeye added.

A shiver of delight went through Yellowpaw as she listened to the senior warriors. *I'm glad I belong to such a strong Clan!*

When the Clan was full-fed and lay drowsily sharing tongues, Stonetooth rose to his paws and told the story of the battle against WindClan so that every cat could hear.

"WindClan won't bother us again for a very long time," he finished, "and part of that is thanks to the five apprentices who were with us. Our Clan should be proud of them."

"Those are wise words," Cedarstar responded, rising to stand beside his deputy. "And from what you tell me, there is already a new warrior among us. Raggedpaw, come here."

The dark tabby tom sprang up from his place beside Scorchpaw. For a moment he hesitated, glancing around wildly; then he padded forward to stand in front of his leader. Murmurs of surprise rose from the rest of the Clan.

The Clan was silent again as Cedarstar raised his tail and

began to address them. "I, Cedarstar, leader of ShadowClan, call upon my warrior ancestors to look down on this apprentice," he meowed. "He has trained hard to understand the ways of your noble code, and he has proven in battle that he is worthy to become a warrior. Raggedpaw, do you promise to uphold the warrior code and to protect and defend your Clan, even at the cost of your life?"

Raggedpaw's voice rang out clear and confident. "I do."

"Then by the power of StarClan I give you your warrior name," Cedarstar went on. "Raggedpaw, from this time on, you shall be known as Raggedpelt. StarClan honors your courage and your skill in battle." He bent his head to rest his muzzle on Raggedpelt's head, and Raggedpelt licked his shoulder in response.

"Raggedpelt! Raggedpelt! Raggedpelt!" the Clan yowled, their eyes gleaming in the gathering darkness.

Yellowpaw joined in somewhat reluctantly. *I still feel bruised all over from being thrown out of the way as if I was a troublesome kit.* She noticed Scorchpaw looking furious that he hadn't been made a warrior along with his brother, and felt a stab of sympathy. *It must be tough, falling behind your littermate.*

As the yowls died away, Yellowpaw was surprised to see Raggedpelt padding across the clearing toward her. He halted in front of her and dipped his head. "Yellowpaw, I'm sorry I pushed you aside in the battle," he mewed. "It's not that I think you can't fight, but that WindClan cat was too strong for you."

Yellowpaw opened her jaws for a stinging retort, then

stopped herself. Remembering the huge WindClan tom, she had to admit he was right. *I'd be licking my wounds in Sagewhisker's den right now, if it wasn't for Raggedpelt.* "It's okay," she muttered.

Raggedpelt let out a brief purr. "I'm looking forward to joining you on patrols when you're a warrior," he told her, then dipped his head again and padded off to join the other warriors.

Rowanpaw leaned closer to Yellowpaw, a glint of amusement in her eyes. "Raggedpelt likes you," she teased.

"Don't talk nonsense," Yellowpaw retorted. "He's just a Clanmate, that's all."

But as she watched Raggedpelt join Brackenfoot and Featherstorm outside the warriors' den, Yellowpaw felt a warm glow spreading through her from ears to tail-tip.

Raggedpelt came looking for me. Maybe he doesn't think I'm a troublesome kit anymore!

CHAPTER 7

A full moon floated in the sky, shedding silver light over the four great oaks of Fourtrees. With her Clanmates all around her, Yellowpaw followed Cedarstar as he wound around clumps of fern toward the bottom of the hollow. The ShadowClan cats were the last to arrive, and the slopes were already crowded with the cats of the other three Clans.

It was only Yellowpaw's second Gathering, and she was still daunted by the number of eyes gleaming from the shadows, and the unfamiliar scents. The yowls of the assembled warriors echoed around the hollow, with the four trees looming above them all.

"You'll be fine," Brightflower murmured, slipping to her side as they reached the base of the slope.

"Of course you will," Brackenfoot agreed. "I used to get nervous when I first went to Gatherings. Look, sit here." He waved his tail to a spot sheltered by overarching fronds of bracken. "You'll get a good view, but you won't be seen easily, and the ferns will keep other cats from crowding you too much."

Yellowpaw touched her father's shoulder with her nose,

grateful for his understanding, then settled down in the spot he had pointed out. She watched as Archeye, Featherstorm, and Toadskip padded past her, and the rest of her Clan found spaces for themselves.

"Who are those cats?" she asked Brackenfoot, angling her ears toward two sleek, well-fed warriors. "I don't remember seeing them last time. They look . . . different somehow."

"That's Oakheart and Timberfur from RiverClan," her father replied. "We don't see much of them because we don't have a border with them."

"The reason they look plump and shiny is because they eat fish from the river," Brightflower added. "But they're just warriors like the rest of us."

Yellowpaw wrinkled her nose. She had caught a minnow once, in one of the streams that ran through ShadowClan territory, and she hadn't much liked it. *I'm glad I'm not a River-Clan cat.*

She couldn't ask any more questions because Cedarstar leaped onto the Great Rock to join the other three leaders. Yellowpaw's nervousness ebbed, and she felt a prickle of curiosity. *What news will the other leaders tell us tonight?*

Then she suppressed a sigh as Foxpaw bounced into sight, pushing her way through the undergrowth to Raggedpelt's side.

"Raggedpelt!" she panted. "There are some RiverClan apprentices over here, and I've been telling them how you fought off the WindClan warriors. Come and meet them."

Raggedpelt shook his head.

"Come on!" Foxpaw nudged him impatiently. "They want to see your fighting moves."

Yellowpaw spotted a glint of anger in Raggedpelt's eyes. "No," he meowed. "The Gathering is a time of peace. There's no fighting allowed—and you shouldn't be stirring up trouble by talking about battles between the Clans."

Foxpaw glared at him. "You think you know everything, just because you're a warrior now!" Spinning around, she stormed off.

Raggedpelt shrugged and started looking for a place to sit. Still feeling slightly in awe of his new warrior status, Yellowpaw stood up and went over to him.

"Foxpaw is a stupid furball," she muttered. "You were right not to—"

She broke off as WindClan scent wafted over her and she realized that several young warriors had surrounded her and Raggedpelt, pacing around them so they couldn't keep an eye on all of them at once. Yellowpaw recognized at least one of them who had been in the battle on WindClan territory. He was the first to speak.

"Not so brave now, are you?" he sneered. "Not without your mentor and your Clanmates."

Yellowpaw felt Raggedpelt tense beneath his fur. "This isn't the time to talk about fighting," he replied.

One of the other WindClan cats gave a snort of disgust. "That's a good excuse!"

"Go away, flea-pelts!" Yellowpaw snapped. "You wouldn't dare say that to Raggedpelt if he was allowed to fight you."

"Oh, so you're Ragged*pelt* now," a third WindClan cat put in. "ShadowClan must be really short of warriors."

"Yeah, he needs an apprentice to defend him," the third cat mewed contemptuously. "Just what you'd expect from a kittypet."

Yellowpaw saw Raggedpelt freeze. *That's the worst thing any cat could say to him!*

Raggedpelt's claws slid out. He spun around to face the cat who was taunting him. "What did you just call me?" he snarled, his voice low and dangerous. "Say it again, and I'll slice your ears off!"

No! Yellowpaw thought, fighting back panic. *Raggedpelt will get into all kinds of trouble if he fights at a Gathering.* Swiftly she jumped between the two cats. "Where did you hear that?" she challenged the WindClan warrior.

"Every cat knows it," he retorted. "Still, I admit that Raggedpelt fights well . . . for a soft kitty."

Raggedpelt was shouldering Yellowpaw aside when a new voice broke in. "What's all this?"

Yellowpaw looked up to see Reedfeather, the WindClan deputy, striding toward them through the bracken. His eyes were narrowed and his neck fur bristling.

"Uh . . . we were just . . ." one of the young WindClan cats began.

"Get back to your own Clanmates," Reedfeather meowed sternly. "The Gathering is about to start."

For a heartbeat Yellowpaw thought that the cat who had started all the trouble was about to protest. Then he clearly thought better of it, and slunk past his deputy to the place farther around the hollow where most of WindClan was assembled. His friends followed him, their heads down and their tails drooping. Reedfeather's glance swept across Yellowpaw and Raggedpelt, and he gave them a tiny nod before he padded after his Clanmates.

Raggedpelt's claws were still digging into the soft earth of the hollow. His fur bristled and his eyes blazed as he watched the WindClan cats depart.

"Calm down!" Yellowpaw whispered. "Cedarstar can see you from up there."

The anger died from Raggedpelt's eyes, to be replaced by something dark and shadowed. "I hate it when they gossip about me."

Sympathy surged up inside Yellowpaw. *It must be terrible, not knowing who your father is,* she thought, remembering how much she owed to Brackenfoot. "Have you asked Featherstorm about your father?" she mewed hesitantly.

"Over and over." Raggedpelt sighed. "But she won't tell me. She says it doesn't matter, as long as I'm only loyal to ShadowClan."

But Yellowpaw could tell that it did matter to Raggedpelt. "What about Scorchpaw? Does he know anything?"

Raggedpelt shrugged. "Scorchpaw doesn't care. But I . . ." He let his voice trail off.

Yellowpaw was stretching out her tail to touch his shoulder when a yowl rang out across the clearing.

"Cats of all Clans!"

Looking up at the Great Rock, Yellowpaw saw Pinestar, leader of ThunderClan, standing in front of the other leaders, ready to start the Gathering. Raggedpelt settled down beside her, and there was no more time to talk.

All the same, Yellowpaw thought, *I won't forget this. I have to help Raggedpelt somehow. This isn't over.*

Curled in her nest later that night, Yellowpaw found it hard to settle down. Though she was tired from the Gathering, she couldn't get Raggedpelt out of her mind. *I've always known who my mother and father are,* she thought. *Even if Brackenfoot had died, I'd remember him. And I love that I look like Brightflower,* she added to herself, giving her thick tail a lick. *It means I feel safe in my Clan. Raggedpelt ought to be able to feel that, too.* She heaved a deep sigh as she remembered how bravely Raggedpelt had attacked the WindClan tom. *He's such a brilliant warrior! There's no way that he's half kittypet . . . is he?*

Suddenly Yellowpaw sat up, disturbing Rowanpaw, who muttered something crossly and wrapped her tail over her ears.

"Raggedpelt deserves to know the truth," Yellowpaw whispered out loud. "Whatever happens, nothing is more important than that, surely? I have to find out who his father is!"

She woke as dawn light began to seep into the apprentices' den. Careful not to disturb her denmates, she slid into the open. Everything was quiet in the camp. Hollyflower, who was on guard duty beside the gap in the brambles, was yawning, but no other cat was stirring.

I have to get this done before Deerleap comes looking for me.

Yellowpaw padded across the camp to the elders' den and poked her head inside. She still felt a pang of grief to see only two cats curled up in the thick moss. *Silverflame should be here too.*

Scrambling inside, Yellowpaw gave Lizardfang a gentle prod. "Wake up!" she mewed. "I need to ask you something."

Lizardfang twitched an ear. "Sure, ask away," he mumbled, and sank back into sleep.

Suppressing a hiss of frustration, Yellowpaw turned to Littlebird, jabbing her a bit less gently in the ribs. "Littlebird, please wake up! It's important."

Littlebird blinked up at her. "What's the matter?" She stretched her jaws in a huge yawn. "Yellowpaw . . . what do you want?"

"I have to talk to you," Yellowpaw mewed.

Roused again by the noise and movement, Lizardfang heaved himself out of his nest, scrabbling at the moss. "Is it an attack?"

"No, it's okay, Lizardfang," Yellowpaw soothed. "I just need you to answer some questions."

"Questions?" the old tom spat. "It's the middle of the night!"

Littlebird sighed. "Well, we're awake now. Ask away, Yellowpaw."

Yellowpaw took a deep breath. "What can you tell me about Raggedpelt's father?"

Lizardfang let out a disbelieving hiss. "You woke us up so

that we can gossip about Featherstorm? That's not going to happen." Turning his back on Yellowpaw, he curled up again among the moss, closed his eyes, and wrapped his tail over his nose.

Yellowpaw turned to Littlebird. "Please!" she begged. "This is really important to Raggedpelt. He has to know the truth about his father!"

The small ginger she-cat hesitated for a couple of heartbeats. "Well . . ." she began. "I'm like Lizardfang, I don't want to gossip—"

"But Raggedpelt—"

"Let me finish," Littlebird went on. "You're like all the young cats, Yellowpaw. No patience at all. What I was going to say was, I don't know very much. But in the moons before Raggedpelt and Scorchpaw were born, Featherstorm spent a lot of time near the border with the Twolegplace—not far from the big sycamore tree with the dead branch."

"I know where that is!" Yellowpaw meowed. "Do you think if I go there, I might find Raggedpelt's father?" Excitement tingled in her paws.

"Don't you do anything foolish, now," the elder warned her as she settled back in her bedding.

"I won't, I promise!"

Yellowpaw scrambled out of the elders' den. By now the dawn light was brightening, and Stonetooth was organizing the day's patrols in the middle of the clearing. Yellowpaw spotted Deerleap emerging from the warriors' den and bounded over to meet her.

There's no time to do anything about Raggedpelt's father today, she thought. *But tonight . . . I'm going to help him discover the truth!*

Yellowpaw waited impatiently for her denmates to go to sleep. Nutpaw and Scorchpaw had burrowed into their bedding immediately and the soft sound of their snoring filled the den. Rowanpaw spent some time grooming her tail, then curled up neatly with it wrapped over her nose. But Wolfpaw and Foxpaw went on chattering like a pair of starlings until Yellowpaw could have cheerfully shredded their ears.

"Settle down, you two," she meowed at last. "Can't a cat get any sleep around here?"

"You're not our mentor. You can't tell us what to do," Foxpaw muttered.

The two young cats went on telling each other about their catches at hunting practice, but to Yellowpaw's relief they soon were yawning more than they talked, and moments later both of them were quiet and breathing steadily. Yellowpaw waited a little longer to make sure they were really asleep, and then crept out.

The sky was clear and the moon filled the camp with an eerie, pale light. Nettlespot, on duty beside the entrance, looked like a cat made of ice. *We don't want her asking what we're doing outside the camp at night,* Yellowpaw thought. *We'll need to use the dirtplace tunnel to get out.*

Cautiously, slipping from shadow to shadow, she crossed the clearing to the warriors' den. She could make out Raggedpelt's tabby pelt through the gaps between the branches, but it was too far for her to reach through and prod him with a paw.

"Raggedpelt!" she whispered. "Wake up!"

She was worried that the warrior was too deeply asleep to hear her, but to her relief, Raggedpelt stirred and raised his head, looking around as if he thought the voice had come from inside the den.

"Here—outside!" Yellowpaw hissed. "It's me, Yellowpaw."

Raggedpelt peered at her through the branches. "What do you want?"

"Come here. I have to tell you something."

The tabby tom hesitated, then nodded. "Okay. Wait."

Yellowpaw flexed her claws until she saw Raggedpelt emerging from the den. He padded up to her, yawning and bleary-eyed.

"What is it?" he demanded.

"I can't tell you here," Yellowpaw replied. "We have to go outside the camp."

Raggedpelt blinked in surprise, then seemed to decide that it wasn't worth arguing.

"We can't let Nettlespot see us," Yellowpaw went on. "Follow me. We'll use the dirtplace tunnel."

She padded to the narrow gap behind the warriors' den and breathed a sigh of relief once they were well away from the camp. The air was still, and Yellowpaw sniffed deeply at the fresh scents of growing things. Not far away she could hear the gentle gurgling of a stream, and closer still the scuffling of small prey in the undergrowth, but this was no time for hunting.

"What's going on?" Raggedpelt growled, pacing alongside her. "Why have you brought me out here?"

Yellowpaw turned to him triumphantly. "We're going to find your father."

Raggedpelt halted. For a moment his eyes blazed with anger. "That's a terrible idea!"

"Why?" Yellowpaw challenged him. "You want to know who he is, and Featherstorm won't tell you, so all you can do is find out for yourself."

Raggedpelt shook his head. "We'd have to search the whole of Twolegplace," he objected. "We'd have to check out all the rogues and loners . . . and kittypets," he admitted reluctantly. "And we still wouldn't be certain of finding him."

"I know we can't be *certain*," Yellowpaw mewed. "But it's worth a try, isn't it? Or have you forgotten how much you need to know the truth?"

Raggedpelt sighed. "Okay, let's do it. I can see what you're thinking, Yellowpaw," he added. "You'll go to Twolegplace by yourself if I don't come with you, and StarClan knows what sort of trouble you'll get into."

Yellowpaw bounced on her paws with satisfaction. She set off again toward the sycamore, picking up the pace until she was pelting through the forest with the grass brushing her belly fur, the moonwashed undergrowth whirling past her. Raggedpelt raced along at her shoulder.

At last Yellowpaw halted, panting, under the bare branches of the sycamore. The walls of the Twolegplace reared up in front of her. As she gazed over the border a cloud drifted across the moon, leaving the forest around her so dark that she could barely see her own paws. The cold yellow lights of the Twolegplace seemed harsher by contrast, glaring down from thin trees made of some weird Twoleg stuff.

"What now?" Raggedpelt prompted.

"We go into Twolegplace and start asking questions, I guess," Yellowpaw meowed, with a stab of uncertainty. "Let's say one of our warriors—Amberleaf, maybe—has gone missing. We could ask the Twolegplace cats if they've seen her."

"Sounds mouse-brained to me," Raggedpelt argued. "Why would one of our Clanmates go missing in Twolegplace?"

Yellowpaw gave an exasperated sigh. "Stop being so *logical*! The Twolegplace cats won't know that, will they? And we have to start somewhere."

Raggedpelt nodded slowly; Yellowpaw thought maybe he was starting to get excited. "Let's go."

Side by side they left the pine trees behind and scrambled up a Twoleg fence. Balancing on the top, Yellowpaw looked down on a small square of grass with strong-smelling plants growing around the edges. Yellow light shone from the Twoleg den beyond. Everything was quiet.

But as soon as Yellowpaw and Raggedpelt dropped down onto the grass a flurry of barking split the silence. A door opened in the den and a small white dog shot out, still barking. A Twoleg appeared behind it, yowling at the dog as it raced toward the two cats. As if they shared the same thought, Raggedpelt and Yellowpaw split up, pelting in opposite directions. The dog skidded to a halt, not knowing which cat to chase first. By the time it plunged after Raggedpelt, the tabby tom had already reached the fence that separated this den from the next. He stood poised with his claws digging into the top of the fence, while the dog tried to jump up at him, whining in frustration.

Seeing that her Clanmate was safe, Yellowpaw bounded in a wide circle around the outside of the grass plot and scrambled up onto the fence a couple of fox-lengths farther along. Raggedpelt spotted her and gave her a nod.

"Shove off, flea-pelt," he spat at the dog, then dropped down onto the next square of grass.

Yellowpaw joined him, hearing more yowling from the Twoleg as she leaped, and the two cats stopped, panting.

"What are you doing here, strangers?"

The low growl came out of the darkness. Yellowpaw and Raggedpelt spun around, looking for the cat who had spoken. A moment later a huge ginger tom paced forward into the light from the den. He was wearing a collar, but his muscles rippled as he walked, and a torn ear showed that he had experienced at least one fight. There was a hostile gleam in his eyes.

Yellowpaw gulped. *That's a kittypet?*

Two more cats appeared from the darkness, flanking the ginger tom. One of them was what Yellowpaw had always pictured when she thought of kittypets: a fluffy white she-cat wearing a collar with a bell on it. The other was smaller and scrawny, with a badly groomed russet pelt. The softness of her features showed that she was barely out of kithood.

"You come from the forest, don't you?" the fluffy cat

mewed. Her tone was sharp. "You're not welcome here."

Yellowpaw forgot all her plans to ask clever questions. "We're looking for a tom who might have known a forest cat called Featherstorm," she blurted out.

The scrawny russet she-cat let out a hiss. "You have no right to ask us about anything!"

"Hang on a moment, Red." The big ginger tom narrowed his eyes. "Maybe we should let them ask their questions." His glittering gaze passed from Yellowpaw to Raggedpelt and back again. "That's the best way to get rid of them. Otherwise, they'll be back."

Red looked furious. "Honestly, Marmalade, you'll be making friends with dogs next! Why don't we just chase them off with a scratch or two to remember us by?"

"We might not be the only cats to get scratched," Raggedpelt growled, sliding out his claws.

"That's enough!" The white she-cat raised her tail. "If we let you ask a question, will you leave?"

Instead of answering, Raggedpelt turned to Yellowpaw. "Is it worth asking?" he mewed.

"Don't you want to know the truth?" Yellowpaw asked. *He can't give up now; we've come this far!*

"Are you going to stand there arguing?" Red asked scathingly. "Or are you coming with us?"

"We're coming," Yellowpaw decided.

The huge ginger tom leaped onto the fence at the far side of the enclosed space. Joining him, Yellowpaw saw that a narrow alley lay beyond, with a high wall of red stone at the other side.

There was a strong smell of crow-food.

As she paused at the top of the fence, the white she-cat gave her a push. "Get a move on."

Yellowpaw lost her balance and fell ungracefully into the alleyway, barely managing to twist herself in midair so that she landed paws first.

"Well done, Pixie." Red's voice was cold as she looked down from the fence. "Show them who's in charge."

Marmalade led them along the alley. The wooden fence gave way to another wall of red stone; Yellowpaw's heart raced; she felt as though she was padding along at the bottom of a crevasse. Eventually the alley led into an open space surrounded by shabby Twoleg dens. The reek of crow-food was joined by other scents: monsters and a smell that reminded Yellowpaw of a blackened stump in the forest that Deerleap told her had been struck by lightning moons ago.

Yellowpaw blinked as she spotted movement and the gleam of eyes in the shadows. *There are other cats here!*

"Just think!" she whispered, turning to Raggedpelt. "You might be about to meet your father!"

Raggedpelt didn't reply, but his eyes were troubled, and Yellowpaw could feel his pelt bristling against hers.

The three kittypets crowded around Yellowpaw and Raggedpelt, urging them into the middle of the open space. At the same time, more cats began slinking out from the shadows. Some of them were wearing collars, but others looked more like rogues, with skinny bodies and flea-bitten pelts. Yellowpaw was uncomfortably aware that they were way outnumbered if it came to a fight.

"These are cats from the forest," Marmalade announced. "They want to ask some questions."

"Hi." Yellowpaw felt hot and uncomfortable to be the focus of so many staring eyes. "I'm Yellowpaw, and this is Raggedpelt. We come from ShadowClan," she ended proudly.

"Never heard of it," a black she-cat sniffed.

"Are you really from the forest?" A gray tom padded up to Yellowpaw and her Clanmate, sniffing at them. "Yeah, you smell of trees."

"Get away from them, Boulder," Pixie snarled, giving the gray tom a shove.

"But I've always wondered what it would be like to live beyond the fence," Boulder protested.

"Sit down and be quiet." The gray tom was interrupted by a black-and-white she-cat, so old that her muzzle was grizzled and all her teeth had gone. Yellowpaw tried not to stare. *She looks even older than our elders!* "No one wants to listen to you meowing nonstop about the forest," the old cat hissed at Boulder.

Boulder sat down, looking annoyed. Yellowpaw guessed that the old cat was some kind of leader, though this collection of cats didn't look at all like a Clan. *Maybe they look up to her because she's so old.*

She spotted a black she-cat rolling her eyes, and heard her whisper to Boulder, "Don't let Jay worry you. She's just a bossy old furball."

"Questions, you said?" the old cat, Jay, rasped. "All right, you can ask *one*. Let's hear it."

Raggedpelt nudged Yellowpaw. "I told you this was a dumb idea. Let's go."

"No!" Yellowpaw gave Raggedpelt a furious glare. "One question is all it will take. We're looking for a cat who knew a forest cat called Featherstorm," she continued. "We—"

"Speak up, can't you?" Jay twitched her tail irritably. "I don't know what's the matter with you young cats. You all mumble into your fur."

"Sorry." Yellowpaw raised her voice. "A cat who knew Featherstorm?"

A small tabby-and-white she-cat flinched as Yellowpaw spoke the name, but she didn't say anything. Jay shook her head, and all the other cats did the same.

Raggedpelt looked discouraged. "I guess that's it, then," he mewed.

Marmalade stepped forward. "You got your answer. You can leave now."

Pixie and Red padded up to join them again.

"We don't need an escort," Raggedpelt snapped.

"We aren't offering one." Marmalade slid out his claws. "I said *now*."

The other Twolegplace cats were gathering behind Marmalade. Yellowpaw could see the hostility in their eyes and the anger in their bristling fur. "It's time we went," she muttered.

Raggedpelt's fur was bristling too, and he drew back his lips in a snarl. "No kittypet tells me what to do."

"Mouse-brain! There's no point in spilling their blood."

Yellowpaw shoved his shoulder hard. "What are you going to prove by fighting kittypets? Run!"

To her relief, Raggedpelt spun around and raced back down the alley, the way they had come. Yellowpaw followed; glancing back she saw Marmalade and more of the Twolegplace cats hard on their paws.

"Faster!" she gasped.

But as they came into sight of the first Twoleg fence, Marmalade and the others dropped back. "Stay away in the future!" Marmalade yowled after them.

Just as Yellowpaw bunched her muscles to leap up onto the fence, a voice from the shadows called, "Wait!"

Yellowpaw turned to see the small she-cat who had flinched at the mention of Featherstorm's name. She was beckoning with one paw, her green eyes wide and nervous.

"What do you want?" Raggedpelt growled.

"There is a cat you need to speak to," the she-cat replied. "Follow me."

Raggedpelt exchanged a glance with Yellowpaw. "It might be a trap," he murmured. "Why should she help us?"

"So that you'll stay away," the she-cat replied. "We want nothing to do with wild cats like you."

"We have to risk it," Yellowpaw insisted. "We have to know the truth!"

Raggedpelt hesitated a moment more, then shrugged. "Okay. But I still think we both have bees in our brain."

The she-cat led the way around a corner and down another alley. "There was a forest cat hanging around here a while ago," she meowed. "Her name might have been Featherstorm. I haven't seen her for ages, though."

Frustrated at coming so close to the information she needed, Yellowpaw slid out her claws. She didn't mean to be threatening, but the she-cat gave her a glance of alarm.

"That cat had nothing to do with me," she mewed defensively. She nodded toward the shadows between two Twoleg dens. "Hal knew her better than any of us. Ask him."

Yellowpaw turned to see a pair of amber eyes gleaming in the darkness. She beckoned with her tail to Raggedpelt, who padded over to her. Meanwhile the small she-cat darted away, scrambled over a wall, and was gone.

Hal blinked as Yellowpaw and Raggedpelt approached. It was so dark, it was impossible to tell what color he was. "I heard what she said," he began, before they asked him anything. "I never knew a cat called Featherstorm. I have nothing to do with forest cats."

Yellowpaw could see that Hal was a kittypet; his collar gleamed as he shifted in the shadows.

"Okay, sorry we bothered you," Raggedpelt responded, turning away.

Yellowpaw was following when instinct told her to glance back. Hal had emerged from the shadows and was slinking away along the line of Twoleg dens. Yellowpaw froze. The kittypet was a dark brown tabby, and except for the fact that his shoulders were broader and his muscles more filled out, he was the exact image of Raggedpelt.

"Wait!" Yellowpaw yowled, running after him. "You must

have known Featherstorm! Look—this is your son!"

Hal turned back, his amber eyes growing cold. For a heartbeat he looked Raggedpelt up and down. "I don't know what you're talking about," he snarled. "I have no son."

"But just look at him—" Yellowpaw began, waving her tail at Raggedpelt. Hal simply spun around and began padding away.

"We have to go," Raggedpelt interrupted. His voice was like ice. "This was a mouse-brained idea. We should never have come here."

CHAPTER 8

"Yellowpaw! Yellowpaw!"

Deerleap's voice broke into a dream where Yellowpaw was searching through the forest, though she couldn't remember what she was hunting for. It was a huge effort to open her eyes. When she tried to sit up, every muscle in her body shrieked with fatigue, and her paws were aching.

What's the matter with me? Then the events of the night before came flooding back into her mind. She and Raggedpelt had visited the Twolegplace, and dawn wasn't far off by the time they returned to their nests.

And it was a disaster!

"Yellowpaw!" Deerleap called again, sounding more impatient this time.

Yellowpaw heaved herself out of her bedding. The other apprentices were stirring around her, looking bright-eyed and energetic.

"Where did you go last night?" Rowanpaw hissed. "I woke up and you weren't in your nest."

"It doesn't matter," Yellowpaw muttered as she struggled out of the den.

Outside Stonetooth was surrounded by a larger group of cats than usual. Even though she was so tired, Yellowpaw felt a tingle of excitement.

"What's happening?" she asked Deerleap.

"We're going to raid the rats in the Carrionplace," Deerleap replied. "Prey is scarce, so Cedarstar decided to send two patrols to hunt there. With any luck, we'll catch enough to feed the whole Clan."

Mingled fear and anticipation crept through Yellowpaw. She was proud, too, that she had been chosen to go on this special raid. She could sense hopeful tension in the camp, as if every cat was looking forward to being full-fed when the raid was over.

When she and Deerleap padded up to the crowd of cats, Stonetooth was organizing the patrols. "I'll lead one, and Cedarstar the other," he meowed. "Hollyflower, Archeye, Poolcloud, Ashheart, you come with me. And Deerleap and Amberleaf, with your apprentices. Raggedpelt, you too."

As Stonetooth named the cats they stepped out of the crowd and bunched together at one side. Raggedpelt brushed past Yellowpaw as he joined the patrol, not even acknowledging that she was there.

"Did you guys have a fight?" Rowanpaw whispered to Yellowpaw. "Great StarClan, were you with him last night?"

"Can we have a bit of quiet at the back?" Finchflight hissed, before Yellowpaw could reply. "Yellowpaw, join your patrol if you're coming on this raid."

Yellowpaw shot a glare at her sister before padding off to

stand with her mentor and the others. Meanwhile, Stonetooth named the cats for Cedarstar's patrol, including Rowanpaw, Scorchpaw, and their mentors. Brightflower and Brackenfoot joined that patrol as well.

"What about us?" Foxpaw demanded, pattering up with her brother a mouse-length behind.

"You're too young," Stonetooth responded. "Rats are big enough to eat *you.*"

"So we get left behind again," Wolfpaw growled, standing beside his sister and glaring as the patrols left.

As she followed Stonetooth through the forest, Yellowpaw hung back until she could walk beside Raggedpelt, who was walking near the rear of the patrol. "Are you okay?" she meowed. "I'm sorry if I did the wrong thing last night."

Raggedpelt gave her a brief, cold glance. "I don't want to talk about it," he mewed. "As far as I'm concerned, I have no father." Not giving Yellowpaw the chance to reply, he bounded ahead until he was walking just behind Stonetooth.

Yellowpaw looked sadly after him, her pelt pricking with feelings of guilt. *I was only trying to help!* Giving her fur a shake, she padded on, trying to put the encounter with the Twolegplace cats out of her mind. *I'm a ShadowClan apprentice, and right now my job is to catch prey!*

The breeze carried the scents of rat and crow-food to the patrols long before the Carrionplace came into sight. Yellowpaw hadn't been this close since her first day as an apprentice, when Deerleap had shown her the territory. The heaps of Twoleg rubbish looked even more disgusting in daylight.

Bulging black pelts were piled up, some of them with gaping holes that let the foul stuff inside spill out onto the ground. Mixed in with them were unfamiliar things made of wood, soft pelts in strange Twoleg colors, and more sharp-edged objects made of the shiny fence-stuff, all held together by the rotting crow-food. Beyond the fence the mounds stretched into the distance, more and more of them, as far as Yellowpaw could see.

Stonetooth reached the fence and turned to pad alongside it. A few fox-lengths farther on he halted, and Yellowpaw saw that the ground had been scraped away so that there was room for a cat to wriggle underneath.

"I'll go first," Cedarstar meowed. "Once inside, we'll split up. Stonetooth, take your patrol that way"—he flicked his tail—"and we'll go this way. Let's see who can catch the most!"

Yellowpaw watched as Cedarstar squeezed his muscular body under the fence and rose to his paws on the far side. Brightflower followed with Rowanpaw close behind. Then Stonetooth began to lead his patrol through. When her turn came, Yellowpaw dived under the fence as quickly as she could, feeling it scrape along her back, then scrambled to her paws with claws extended in case a rat leaped out at her from the mounds.

When all the cats were in place, Stonetooth gathered his patrol around him; a few fox-lengths away Cedarstar was doing the same. Yellowpaw stood beside her mentor, her paws sinking into the soggy debris on the ground.

"Listen carefully," the deputy meowed. "Especially you,

apprentices—and Ashheart, this is your first rat raid, isn't it?" The gray she-cat nodded, her blue eyes gleaming with anticipation. "Never tackle a rat alone," the deputy warned. "Work in pairs and do *not* lose sight of your partner for a single heartbeat. Rats are vicious and cunning, and a rat bite can be very nasty, so do your best not to get bitten, and try to see to it that your partner doesn't get bitten, either."

Like he needs to tell us that! Yellowpaw thought.

Her heart began to beat faster, wondering if she would be partnered with Raggedpelt, but Stonetooth put the tabby tom with Nutpaw, and partnered Yellowpaw with Archeye.

"Hollyflower and I will keep watch," Stonetooth finished. "If any cat is in trouble, we'll be there to help."

"Let's show them!" Nutpaw whispered to Raggedpelt. "Let's catch the biggest rat in the Carrionplace!"

Not if I can help it! Yellowpaw thought.

She and Archeye padded cautiously alongside the nearest of the heaps. At first everything was quiet and still. A flicker of movement caught Yellowpaw's eye, but it was only Raggedpelt and Nutpaw slipping between two of the other mounds.

Archeye tapped Yellowpaw's shoulder with his tail and angled his ears to a spot deeper within the Carrionplace, where a huge yellow Twoleg monster was crouching. "I think it's asleep," he murmured.

Yellowpaw nodded. The monsters on the Thunderpath made such a racket that there would be plenty of time to get out of its way if it decided to wake up. Her whiskers twitched with impatience as she padded on. *Come on, rats! Show yourselves!*

She caught a glimpse of a wedge-shaped head poking out of one of the bulging black pelts, but as she turned to face it, it was gone.

"I think I saw one," she told Archeye softly.

Before she finished speaking, the head appeared again, lower down the mound—or perhaps it was a different rat. Yellowpaw's belly clenched as she looked at its long nose and quivering whiskers, and the hostility in its bright, bird-like eyes. She began to distinguish sounds, too: rustling and squeaking that came from deep within the mound.

This whole place is alive with rats!

Yellowpaw bounded toward the rat, but it drew its head back into the pile, and her claws sank instead into something wet and squishy inside the black pelt.

Oh, yuck!

Then she spun around at the sound of louder squeaking behind her. A rat was poking its nose out from a gap in the mound; Yellowpaw froze as it ventured farther into the open. Its whiskers twitched as it sniffed the air, and its tiny eyes glittered with malice.

"Get it!" Yellowpaw yowled to Archeye.

She landed on the rat with one huge leap, but slightly mistimed her attack, so that her claws fastened near its tail. The rat let out a high-pitched squeal and twisted around, sharp teeth snapping at Yellowpaw's neck. Yellowpaw reared back, but refused to loosen her grip.

Before the rat could bite, Archeye flung himself on its shoulders, jaws parted to sink his teeth into its neck. The rat heaved up on its hind paws; Yellowpaw lost her hold as she staggered and fell to one side. Archeye was flung backward, and for a heartbeat the rat was free, diving for the shelter of the rubbish.

"No!" Yellowpaw screeched.

Leaping in pursuit, her paws slipped on slimy debris and she almost fell, but she scrambled after the rat and sank her claws into it again. This time she got a better grip on the back of its neck, and though it struggled it couldn't shake her off. Archeye joined her, panting, and flung himself across the rat's scrabbling back legs. As the rat twisted its head, vainly trying to bite Yellowpaw, she slashed her claws across its throat. Blood gushed out and the rat went limp.

Shakily Yellowpaw rose to her paws. "Thank you, StarClan, for this prey," she mewed. "And thank you that neither of us got bitten."

"You did well there," Archeye panted. "I thought we'd lost it for sure."

Yellowpaw looked down at the dead rat. She hadn't quite realized until now how massive it was; maybe they had killed the biggest rat in Carrionplace, just like Nutpaw had hoped. "We both did it," she meowed.

Paw steps sounded behind her, and Yellowpaw spun around, expecting to see another rat. She let out a sigh of relief when she saw it was Poolcloud and Ashheart, each of them carrying a rat.

But they're not as big as ours! she thought proudly.

The rest of the patrol was gathering. Yellowpaw picked up

her rat and went to join them, with Archeye at her side.

"Great StarClan, look at that!" Nutpaw exclaimed, his voice slightly envious. "I didn't think there could be a rat as big as that." He and Raggedpelt had caught a rat too, but Yellowpaw noticed that it was quite a lot smaller than hers.

"It's an amazing catch," Deerleap agreed; her gaze was warm as it rested on her apprentice. "Are you both okay?"

"Not a scratch on either of us," Archeye meowed. "And it's Yellowpaw's rat, really. I didn't do much."

All the cats clustered around Yellowpaw, congratulating her.

"I'd have thought twice about tackling a rat that size," Stonetooth purred. "You're showing real warrior skills, Yellowpaw."

Yellowpaw felt hot with pride and embarrassment. *The Clan deputy thinks I did well!* "Archeye helped," she insisted.

Then she noticed that Raggedpelt was hanging back. She felt as though a cloud had passed over the sun. He was the only cat who hadn't said anything to her; he wasn't even looking at her.

"What's going on?" Stonetooth glanced from Yellowpaw to Raggedpelt and back again. "Raggedpelt, it's ungenerous not to praise Yellowpaw. That's not how we do things in ShadowClan."

Raggedpelt looked at his paws. "Yeah, great catch, Yellowpaw," he muttered.

Stonetooth's eyes narrowed, but he said nothing more to Raggedpelt. "It's time we went back to camp," he announced.

"We've caught as much prey as we can carry. Let's see if we can get there before Cedarstar's patrol."

Picking up her rat by its scruff, Yellowpaw set off full of pride, but before she had gone many paw steps she began to wonder if she could make it back to camp. The rat weighed more than any piece of prey she had carried before. Soon she was staggering with fatigue, her neck aching, but the sense of achievement buzzed through her like a whole colony of bees, and kept her going.

When she entered the camp she was aware of comments from the cats who had stayed behind, padding up to look as she and the rest of the patrol dropped their prey on the fresh-kill pile. For the first time she realized that Cedarstar's patrol had followed them in; the Clan leader examined her rat, then turned to her, his eyes shining with approval.

"Yellowpaw," he mewed, "you're turning into an excellent ShadowClan warrior."

"Th-thank you!" Yellowpaw stammered.

The Clan leader dipped his head to her and padded off to his den. Yellowpaw followed him with her gaze. *I can't believe the Clan leader said that to me!*

Then she noticed that Sagewhisker was standing a couple of fox-lengths away. She was looking thoughtful. Yellowpaw wondered what was on her mind, but after a moment the medicine cat turned away without speaking.

Thank StarClan! Yellowpaw thought. She had been avoiding the medicine cat ever since Silverflame died; she still felt that Sagewhisker could have done more to help the sick elder. And the depth of Sagewhisker's gaze made her feel uncomfortable.

"Yellowpaw!" Her mother's voice distracted Yellowpaw from thinking about the medicine cat. "Stonetooth says you made a great catch."

Yellowpaw ducked her head. "That's my rat," she mewed, pointing to it with her tail.

Brackenfoot dropped his own prey onto the pile. Yellowpaw noticed that her father's rat was almost as big as hers, but not quite.

"Keep going like this, and you'll be the best hunter in ShadowClan," he praised her, his eyes warm.

Brightflower gave her a lick around the ears. "You've made us so proud."

Yellowpaw gazed from one of her parents to the other, and felt as if her heart would burst with happiness.

"Are we joining a patrol today?" Yellowpaw asked Deerleap.

Two moons had passed since the raid on the Carrionplace, and the air was soft and mild, full of the scents of newleaf. Spikes of fresh green showed at the tips of the pine branches, ferns were uncoiling in the midst of clumps of dead bracken, and birdsong promised prey in the moons to come. Yellowpaw heaved a happy sigh. *The forest is so beautiful!*

"Not today," Deerleap replied.

In the last moon she hadn't been calling Yellowpaw quite so early in the morning; today the rays of the morning sun were already slanting into the camp, driving off the dawn chill. *She seems to be slowing down,* Yellowpaw thought, realizing with a pang that her mentor was growing old.

"So what are we going to do?" she asked.

"There's one more task before you can begin your final warrior assessments," Deerleap told her. "You have to travel to the Moonstone."

"Yes!" Yellowpaw was so excited that she pushed off with all four paws and gave an enormous leap into the air. Rowanpaw and Nutpaw had already made their apprentice journeys to the Moonstone, and Yellowpaw had begun to fear that her turn would never come. She landed awkwardly from her leap, feeling a hot flush of embarrassment. *Deerleap will think I'm behaving like a kit.* "When do we leave?" she mewed.

"Right away," her mentor announced. "Come with me. We need to visit Sagewhisker for traveling herbs."

"What are they?" Yellowpaw asked as they padded toward the medicine cat's den.

"Sorrel, daisy, chamomile, and burnet." Deerleap listed each herb with a twitch of her tail. "They'll give you strength and stop you from feeling hungry on the way. There won't be time to hunt."

When they slipped between the boulders into Sagewhisker's den, the medicine cat was mixing herbs together with delicate motions of one forepaw. "Here you are," she meowed, dividing the mixture into two small heaps. "Yellowpaw, the taste is bitter, but it won't last long."

Copying Deerleap, Yellowpaw licked up the herbs, chewed, and swallowed. The taste was just as bitter as Sagewhisker had warned her it would be, and she couldn't help making a face.

"Listen carefully to what StarClan tells you in your dreams," Sagewhisker prompted. "This could be the moment when you find out your destiny."

"I already know my destiny," Yellowpaw mewed. "It's to be a great ShadowClan warrior!"

Sagewhisker made no comment, just looked at Yellowpaw for a moment longer before she nodded. "Have a safe journey, both of you. May StarClan light your path."

Deerleap walked through the forest as far as the Thunderpath, then turned to follow it toward the edge of the territory. Yellowpaw wrinkled her nose as the acrid stink of monsters swamped the fresh smells of the forest. The scent of WindClan cats wafted across the Thunderpath from their territory on the far side.

I wonder what those prey-stealers are up to now? At least they haven't dared to bother us again.

Yellowpaw trotted beside Deerleap as they crossed the ShadowClan border. They soon came to a smaller Thunderpath branching off the main one.

"Do we have to cross this?" she asked her mentor, trying to hide her nervousness. There didn't seem to be a tunnel underneath like the one they used to get to Gatherings.

Deerleap nodded. "It seems scary when it's your first time, but you'll be fine as long as you remember—"

"Look, listen, and scent!" Yellowpaw interrupted, curling her tail up.

"Right." Deerleap let out a small *mrrow* of amusement. "You can look for monsters just like you look for prey."

A distant buzzing sound began as she spoke, growing quickly to a roar, and a glittering red monster swept past them and joined the main Thunderpath. Yellowpaw gagged at the stench that rolled off it in waves.

"Now," Deerleap mewed when it had gone, "these are the rules for crossing a Thunderpath. Look both ways. Can you see a monster? Listen. Can you hear one? Scent. Is the smell stronger than usual? If the answer to all those questions is no, then it's safe to cross."

"I see," Yellowpaw murmured, still feeling nervous.

"Right. So tell us when to go."

Yellowpaw stared at her. *Me? What if I get us both killed?* But Deerleap just angled her ears toward the Thunderpath, clearly waiting.

Standing near the edge of the hard black surface, Yellowpaw worked her claws into the grassy verge. She looked carefully in both directions, noting that the black strip was empty. The only sounds she could hear were the breeze in the branches and the twittering of birds. The tang of the red monster had died away.

"Okay . . . I think," she mewed.

"Then go!"

Yellowpaw bounded forward with Deerleap at her side, wincing as her paws landed on the harsh surface of the Thunderpath. Heartbeats later they had reached the safety of a clump of bushes on the other side. Another monster growled its way past as she stood there quivering and trying to get her breath.

"We made it." Deerleap gave her a nod. "One more thing to remember—once you decide it's safe, run as fast as you can and don't look back."

Yellowpaw was relieved when they left the Thunderpath behind. Beyond it, the land began to rise into moors that reminded her of WindClan territory, covered with the same short, tough grass. But the WindClan scents were fading behind them. With a tingle of excitement in her paws, Yellowpaw realized she was heading into unknown territory, where no Clan cats lived. She felt exposed in the open spaces, without the comforting shelter of pine branches.

Rabbits scampered temptingly across their path, and all Yellowpaw's instincts yowled at her to give chase. But she knew Deerleap would be annoyed if she broke off their journey to hunt, and the traveling herbs were working so she didn't feel hungry. *This is your lucky day, rabbits,* she thought.

Over to one side, beyond the big Thunderpath, she spotted a cluster of Twoleg dens.

"Do we have to go there?" she meowed, remembering what had happened when she went to the Twolegplace with Raggedpelt.

Deerleap shook her head. "We're heading for those hills," she replied, pointing with her tail. "Highstones, where the Moonstone is waiting for us."

Looking ahead, Yellowpaw saw the ground slope upward to a row of crags outlined against the sky. They looked like jagged teeth pushing out of the ground. As the cats climbed higher, the grass underpaw gave way to bare soil strewn with stones, and the slope grew steeper.

My legs have never ached like this before, Yellowpaw complained silently as she toiled upward. *What's wrong with me?*

As if her mentor had picked up her thoughts, Deerleap halted. "Let's rest for a bit."

She flopped down on a flat stone and Yellowpaw settled beside her, enjoying the sensation of sun-warmed rock on her pads and pelt. Ahead of them the sun was going down, washing the crags with an orange glow.

"I'm very proud of you, Yellowpaw," Deerleap meowed after a while.

Yellowpaw pricked her ears in surprise; Deerleap hardly ever doled out praise.

"The moons are passing," Deerleap went on, "and soon it will be my time to join the elders. You will be my last apprentice, and I know that you will become a great warrior."

Yellowpaw rested her muzzle on the she-cat's shoulder. "You've been a fantastic mentor," she murmured. "I won't let you down, I promise."

Darkness had fallen and Silverpelt was glittering across the sky before Deerleap rose to her paws. "Come," she meowed. "It's time."

The moon was still low in the sky and the rocks cast long shadows as Yellowpaw followed Deerleap up the last steep slope toward the crags. As they drew closer, she spotted a dark hole underneath a rough archway in the rock.

"Is that where we're going?"

Deerleap nodded. "That's Mothermouth. It leads to the Moonstone."

A scramble up the final slope, with stones shifting under her paws, brought Yellowpaw to the threshold of Mothermouth. A tunnel led deep into the rock; it was so dark that Yellowpaw couldn't make out anything beyond the first fox-length. She felt her heart begin to beat faster.

"Follow me," Deerleap instructed. "You won't see anything, but you'll be able to pick up my scent. There's nothing to be afraid of. I have walked this path many times." She stepped forward into the tunnel and vanished from Yellowpaw's sight.

Taking a deep breath, Yellowpaw plunged in after her. The light from the tunnel entrance died away behind her as she padded in her mentor's paw steps, and she guided herself by her whiskers brushing the rock walls, and by the thin tendril of Deerleap's scent. The rock beneath her paws was smooth and cold, and the damp air soaked into her pelt and reached deep inside her until she thought she would never be warm again. The tunnel sloped downward, and Yellowpaw tried not to think of the massive weight of rock above her head. It was too easy to imagine it collapsing on top of her, crushing her to nothing.

Then her nose twitched as she felt a fresher scent and the faint movement of air against her whiskers. Tasting the air, she picked up a faint tang of grass and rabbits. She realized that she had stepped out into a larger space.

"This is the cave of the Moonstone," Deerleap meowed.

"What do we do now?"

"We wait."

Yellowpaw shivered in the vast darkness. Above her head she could make out a single glimmering warrior of StarClan; she realized there must be a hole in the roof of the cave. But the light was too faint to reach so far into the depths of the earth.

Then, between one heartbeat and the next, a cold, white light flooded down, revealing walls of rock soaring upward for many fox-lengths. Yellowpaw couldn't hold back a squeal of surprise. In the middle of the cave was a huge rock, many tail-lengths high. The moon was shining through the gap in the roof, making the rock glitter as if all of StarClan was gathered inside it.

"That's the Moonstone?" she whispered.

Deerleap was a small, dark shape outlined against the light. She nodded. "Lie down and touch the stone with your muzzle," she mewed.

Yellowpaw settled herself and stretched out her neck to touch her nose to the rough surface of the Moonstone, closing her eyes against the dazzling light.

Instantly claws of cold gripped her. Her lids were closed, but still she saw brilliant starlight whirling around her as she was swept away. She was surrounded by cats, though she couldn't see any of their faces. Suddenly a voice echoed in her ears: "From this moment on, you will be known as Yellowfang."

My warrior name! But Yellowpaw's delight lasted no more than a single heartbeat. Pain surged through her belly, wave after wave of agony, and she realized that she was giving birth to kits. For a brief moment the whirling journey ceased; Yellowpaw curled herself around a throng of tiny bodies, and felt the joy of letting them suckle at her belly.

Then she was snatched away again. Stars fled past her, and she was overwhelmed by a feeling of loss and anger. More fury than she had ever known made her vision blur; she tried to screech out her desolation, but she couldn't make a sound.

With a bump she found herself in a green glade, with sunlight filtering through the leaves. *Home!* she thought gratefully, but there were no scents she recognized. The landscape flickered around her, showing her a stream trickling through thick moss, a stretch of flat rocks with crevices between them and a strong prey-scent all around, a narrow ravine, the gnarled roots of an oak tree, the glitter of sunlight on a wide stretch of water. The torrent of images made Yellowpaw feel sick; she tried to break free, but she felt like a drowning kit, helpless to escape from the dream that had her in its grip.

Suddenly, with a jolt that made Yellowpaw feel that she had been hurled off the top of the big ash tree, the images stopped, leaving her in darkness. Opening her eyes, Yellowpaw saw that she was still in the cave of the Moonstone, lying on the floor in the shimmering white light.

Deerleap stood at her side, her claws fastened in Yellowpaw's shoulder; Yellowpaw realized her mentor must have dragged her away from the stone.

"Wake up, Yellowpaw!" she was calling.

"I—I'm up." Yellowpaw staggered to her paws, dazed and exhausted. She tried to remember her dream, but it was all a blur of pain, anguish, and confusion. The details were slipping away from her like water through her paws.

"Come. We have to leave," Deerleap ordered.

Yellowpaw blinked at her mentor. *Did I do something wrong?* "It was . . . so weird," she began. "I felt—"

"There's no need to talk about it," Deerleap interrupted. "Follow me quickly."

She whisked into the mouth of the tunnel and Yellowpaw stumbled after her, emerging thankfully into the cold night air. She felt so exhausted that she didn't think her paws would carry her all the way back to camp.

"We'll go down the hill a little way," Deerleap meowed, sounding more like herself. "Then we'll rest and hunt before we go home." As she led the way across the stony slope, she added, "You must never tell any cat what you saw in your dreams."

I don't want to! Something struck Yellowpaw. "Did . . . did *you* see what I dreamed?"

Deerleap didn't look at her. "Only medicine cats share what StarClan tells them. Whatever you have seen of your future, use that knowledge wisely, Yellowpaw."

Disappointment clung to Yellowpaw like mist on her fur, and she felt the first stirrings of fear. *At least I know I'm going to be a warrior, right? And after that* . . . She strained her memory but the images from her dream were tumbled together in a blaze of starlight. All she knew was that something was wrong; she didn't feel excited and joyous the way she thought she would after visiting the Moonstone.

Yellowpaw looked up at the stars, but they seemed cold and remote. *Oh, StarClan, what is going to happen to me?*

CHAPTER 9

"Yellowpaw, from this time on, you shall be known as Yellowfang. StarClan honors your courage and your intelligence, and we welcome you as a warrior of ShadowClan."

Trying to keep her poise, even though she was bursting with excitement, Yellowfang bent her head and felt Cedarstar rest his muzzle on it. She licked her leader's shoulder and took a pace back.

"Yellowfang! Nutwhisker! Rowanberry!" ShadowClan yowled the names of the newly made warriors.

Beside Yellowfang, her brother and sister looked as thrilled as she felt, their eyes shining and their tails straight up in the air.

"Warriors at last!" Nutwhisker chirped. "Sometimes I thought we'd never make it!"

"We're going to be the *best* warriors ShadowClan has ever seen," Rowanberry added.

A warm, prey-laden breeze drifted across the camp, and the hot sun of greenleaf shone down, warming Yellowfang's pelt. Not a cloud could be seen in the blue sky. *What else could I wish for?* Yellowfang asked herself. *This is a perfect day.*

At the front of the cats, Brightflower and Brackenfoot were standing close together, their tails entwined as they beamed proudly at the new warriors. Deerleap gave Yellowfang a nod of warm approval.

Nearby, Foxpaw and Wolfpaw had watched the ceremony with undisguised envy. "We'll be warriors soon," Foxpaw announced as the yowls of greeting died away.

Yellowfang ignored her. "Warrior or not, she'll still be a pain in the tail," she murmured to Rowanberry, who gave a fervent nod of agreement.

Scorchwind, who had received his warrior name a moon before, shouldered his way through the crowd and gave all three new warriors a condescending nod. "Congratulations," he meowed. "If you need any tips on how warriors behave, just ask."

"We'll do that," Yellowfang responded. "I'm sure the *senior* warriors will give us loads of advice."

Scorchwind twitched his tail and padded to where his brother, Raggedpelt, was standing. Yellowfang felt a familiar stab of disappointment that Raggedpelt wasn't even looking at her. *He's ashamed because I was there when his father rejected him. I wish I could tell him that all I feel is anger toward that stupid kittypet! Hal ought to be proud to have a warrior for his son!*

But Yellowfang couldn't think of a way to start that conversation with Raggedpelt. Everything she wanted to tell him would have to remain unsaid.

"Yellowfang?"

Starting at the sound of Sagewhisker's voice behind her, Yellowfang spun around.

"Congratulations," the medicine cat meowed. "I hear your hunting assessment was especially good."

Yellowfang dipped her head. Sagewhisker still wasn't her favorite cat, but she knew that she had to get past Silverflame's death and acknowledge Sagewhisker's status within the Clan.

"Thanks," she muttered. "I guess I was lucky."

"Did you dream of serving your Clan as a warrior when you went to the Moonstone with Deerleap?" the medicine cat probed unexpectedly.

For a heartbeat, Yellowfang didn't know what to say. There was no way she was going to tell Sagewhisker what had happened. "I . . . uh . . . don't really remember what the dream was," she stammered.

"Really?" Sagewhisker's gaze was gentle but insistent. "It's a significant moment, your first Moonstone dream."

Why can't she leave it alone? "If I don't remember, it can't be that important." Turning her back on Sagewhisker, Yellowfang joined her littermates beside the fresh-kill pile, where the Clan was getting ready to celebrate the newly made warriors with a feast.

But Yellowfang couldn't resist glancing back over her shoulder. Sagewhisker was still regarding her with that persistent look, and Yellowfang would have given all her share of the fresh-kill to know what she was thinking.

Yellowfang padded silently across the thick layer of pine needles as she followed Hollyflower, Newtspeck, and Toadskip. The border patrol had left the edge of the Thunderpath and struck out toward the Twolegplace; Yellowfang could make out the walls several fox-lengths away through the trees. Her pads tingled with the unwelcome memory of the night she and Raggedpelt had visited the Twolegplace in search of Raggedpelt's father. *I don't want to go near the place ever again!*

The patrol waited while Hollyflower renewed a scent marker, then padded on with Newtspeck in the lead. A few heartbeats later the warrior halted, her head raised and her jaws parted. "What's that smell?" she muttered.

Veering away from the border, she bounded toward a sprawling clump of brambles at the foot of a pine tree. Yellowfang followed more slowly with the rest of the patrol. Before she had taken more than a couple of paw steps, she picked up the new scent, too: squirrel, but with a sweetish, rotting tang that made her neck fur bristle.

"Over here!" Newtspeck called.

Yellowfang wriggled beside Newtspeck as the black-and-ginger she-cat peered into the thicket. A half-eaten squirrel lay under the thorns, its gray fur clumped and sticky with blood. Flies crawled over its torn flesh and buzzed upward in a swarm as Newtspeck stretched out her neck and gave the crow-food a sniff.

"That's disgusting!" Toadskip exclaimed.

Newtspeck drew back, passing her tongue over her lips as if she was trying to get rid of a foul taste. "Some cat has been stealing prey!" she announced, her voice quivering with anger.

Yellowfang took a careful sniff; beneath the stink of rotting crow-food she detected other scents lingering on the cold, ripped fur. *Black stone underpaw, greasy puddles with the bitter tang of monsters, and an underlying hint of the slop that kittypets eat . . .* "The cat that killed this squirrel came from Twolegplace!" she hissed.

Toadskip gave a snort of disbelief. "Kittypets don't hunt!"

"I think Yellowfang's right," Hollyflower responded. "There's Twolegplace scent here . . . and besides, what warrior leaves prey half-eaten like this?"

"We can't let them get away with it," Toadskip snarled.

"We won't." Hollyflower gathered her patrol with a flick of her tail and led them through the trees until they crossed their own border and stood beneath the looming walls of the Twolegplace. "Split up," she ordered. "See if you can find the place where the kittypet came into the forest."

Yellowfang headed for a high fence made of interwoven strips of wood. Twoleg dens lay on the other side of it. She crept along the bottom of the barrier, jaws parted, then halted as she picked up the mingled scent of two or three kittypets. They matched up exactly with the scents on the half-eaten squirrel. "I've found it!" she called out.

Hollyflower came bounding up with the other warriors behind her, and sniffed at the place Yellowfang indicated. "Not much doubt about that," she murmured, with a look of distaste. "Toadskip, climb the fence and see what's on the other side."

The tabby tom leaped upward, digging his claws into the wood until he had scrambled to the top. For a couple of heartbeats he gazed down on the other side, then turned back with a shrug. "Nothing," he reported. "Just Twoleg grass and plants. No sign of any cats."

"That's because they only come out at night," Yellowfang meowed.

Her Clanmates gazed at her with surprise.

"How do you know that?" Newtspeck prompted.

"Oh . . . uh . . . one of the elders told me," Yellowfang mumbled. To her relief, no cat questioned her further.

"So what do we do now?" Toadskip asked, hopping down onto the grass beside the others.

Hollyflower thought for a moment. "Toadskip, you and Newtspeck had better bury that squirrel," she ordered. "And then finish the patrol. Yellowfang, you come back to camp with me. Cedarstar will want to know about this."

Moonlight shone down into the camp as the warriors of ShadowClan gathered in the clearing. Cedarstar had been as outraged as Yellowfang had expected when Hollyflower reported that kittypets had been killing prey on ShadowClan territory.

"I'll lead two patrols out there tonight," he had decided. "We'll show those kittypets that they don't mess with ShadowClan."

Yellowfang's paws tingled as she followed her Clan leader through the brambles. She felt proud that Cedarstar had chosen her for one of the patrols, but at the same time her belly was churning with nervousness.

What if one of the kittypets recognizes me?

Waiting for her turn to pass through the entrance, she tried to catch Raggedpelt's eye. She knew he must be feeling just as nervous.

What if it was Hal who killed the squirrel?

But Raggedpelt wouldn't look at her, deliberately turning his back and talking to Nutwhisker.

Yellowfang jumped as she felt a prod in her side. "Come on, move your paws," Scorchwind hissed. "Are you waiting for daylight?"

Yellowfang realized that she was blocking the gap. "Sorry," she muttered, plunging into the thorns and trying to put Raggedpelt out of her mind.

A cold breeze whispered through the pine needles as the warriors plunged into the trees. Black shadows shifted over the ground from the movement of the branches, and silver flakes of moonlight dappled the cats' fur. With Yellowfang in Cedarstar's patrol were Rowanberry, Deerleap, and Raggedpelt. Just behind them Stonetooth led the second patrol: Scorchwind, Nutwhisker, Newtspeck, and Crowtail.

When the harsh lights of the Twolegplace appeared through the trees, Cedarstar halted. All the warriors gathered around him and he spoke in a low voice. "The two patrols will split up and watch for the kittypets from opposite sides," he mewed. "All of you take cover, and don't move until I give the signal. Maybe we can finish this without a fight."

"What signal?" Stonetooth asked.

"I'll kink my tail like this," Cedarstar replied, demonstrating. He dug his claws into the ground. "You are ShadowClan warriors and I trust you. Once the fighting starts, make sure that those kittypets don't know what hit them."

Stonetooth gave a curt nod and led his patrol away. Cedarstar took his cats in the opposite direction, toward the fence where Yellowfang had scented the intruders. There wasn't much undergrowth beneath the pine trees, but they found shelter behind the brambles where Newtspeck had discovered the squirrel.

Yellowfang crouched among the thorns with Deerleap on one side of her and Raggedpelt on the other, their pelts brushing. Yellowfang was acutely aware of him, embarrassed to be so close when he refused to be her friend anymore. "Won't the kittypets scent so many of us?" she whispered. "If they know we're here, they won't come out."

Deerleap gave a disdainful sniff. "Most kittypets couldn't scent a fox if it was right in front of them."

Yellowfang gave a small *mrrow* of amusement. "I guess they never had a mentor to tell them to look, listen, and scent."

"Quiet there!" Cedarstar's low voice came from somewhere close by.

Tucking her paws underneath her, Yellowfang settled down. As she gazed along the Twoleg fence she spotted small movements among the grass that told her where Stonetooth's patrol was hiding. There was no sign of any kittypets, and the only scents Yellowfang could pick up when she tasted the air were faint and stale.

The night dragged on and nothing happened. Yellowfang grew cold and cramped; she longed to get up and stretch her legs, but she knew how angry Cedarstar would be if she so much as twitched a whisker. Cold was gripping her pelt by the time she heard Cedarstar hiss, "Look! Up there!"

Squinting through the brambles, Yellowfang spotted two cats slinking over the fence from the Twolegplace. For a moment they stood outlined against the sky. A heartbeat later they leaped down to the ground and she was able to see them more clearly. The scrawny she-cat with the untidy russet pelt was horribly familiar.

Red!

Yellowfang's belly lurched with dismay. The last thing she wanted was for her Clanmates to find out about the night she and Raggedpelt had visited the Twolegplace. *Will Red say anything?* she wondered.

As the two kittypets hesitated beside the fence, Cedarstar leaped out of the shelter of the brambles and strode toward them. "What are you doing here?" he demanded. "The forest is our place. Go back to your Twolegs."

Red faced the ShadowClan leader without a trace of fear. Yellowfang had to admire her courage as the kittypet glared at Cedarstar, who was much bigger than she was, his muscles rippling beneath his pelt.

"You can't stop us from coming here!" Red declared. "We don't live by your rules."

"We can make you stop if we want to," Cedarstar retorted.

The second cat, an older tabby tom who Yellowfang didn't recognize, took a pace forward to stand at Red's shoulder. "I'd like to see you try," he hissed. "You wild cats think you're so great! Lay one claw on us and I'll wipe that smug look off your face."

Cedarstar didn't respond in words. Instead he raised his tail and kinked it in the signal for battle. Instantly the rest of the warriors rose out of the shadows with angry yowls. They surrounded the kittypets, a barrier of furious cats with teeth bared and claws at the ready. Raggedpelt and Nutwhisker stood shoulder-to-shoulder, their lips drawn back in snarls of defiance. Rowanberry was flexing her claws as if she couldn't wait to sink them into a kittypet.

Yellowfang saw a look of sheer astonishment cross the faces of Red and the tabby. But neither of them turned to flee. The tabby tom let out a screech and three more cats jumped over the fence and landed on the ground beside the kittypets. Yellowfang winced as she recognized the skinny gray tom.

Boulder's here now! This just gets worse and worse . . .

Cedarstar launched himself at Red, and the rest of the warriors leaped into battle behind their leader. Yellowfang hung back, reluctant to tangle with a cat who might recognize her. She watched at the edge of the battle as Red shoved Cedarstar off balance, sending him stumbling against a tree stump. The Clan leader gathered himself and leaped at Red again; the russet she-cat sprang away, only to trip over a tangle of tree roots and fall on one side. Cedarstar gave her a swipe over her haunches before spinning around and hurling himself back into the thick of the fight.

Yellowfang stared at Red, who was struggling to wrench one forepaw clear of the roots. *Could I possibly talk to her?* She took a hesitant step toward Red, feeling a stab of pain shoot through her paw, then halted as Deerleap gave her a shove. "Attack!" the old cat snarled. "This is what I trained you for!"

Hot shame flooded through Yellowfang. Picking out a plump ginger tom she had never seen before, she aimed a blow at his shoulder, knocking him off balance. The tom struggled to get to his paws, but before Yellowfang could follow up her first blow, Red, free of the roots now, slipped between them, spinning around to face Yellowfang with fury in her eyes.

The she-cat aimed a blow at Yellowfang, claws unsheathed to rake across her ear. Suddenly she stopped, her eyes open wide. "It's you!" she gasped.

Newtspeck, battling the big tabby tom, heard Red's exclamation and glanced over her shoulder at Yellowfang. "What does she mean?" she demanded.

Yellowfang couldn't think of any reply. Taking advantage of Newtspeck's brief distraction, the tabby tom she'd been fighting knocked her over and landed on top of her, putting an end to any more questions.

A heartbeat later Raggedpelt charged into the tangle of cats. "Don't say a word!" he snarled into Red's ear.

Red looked startled. "About what?"

"You know very well what—"

Raggedpelt was interrupted as Scorchwind dived for Red, aiming a blow at her shoulder. Red whipped around and raced for the fence.

"There's no need to kill!" Stonetooth's voice rang out above the yowls of fighting cats. "These are kittypets! We'll soon send them wailing back to their Twolegs!"

"Pretty tough kittypets," Yellowfang muttered to herself.

She turned to see Rowanberry battling Boulder. Her sister's eyes flashed with the exhilaration of the fight as she leaped from side to side to confuse her opponent, her blows landing with precision. Slowly but inexorably she was driving the skinny gray tom back toward the fence. Blood trickled down his face from a torn ear.

Yellowfang intercepted a black-and-white tom, who was racing to help Boulder, by rearing up onto her hind legs and buffeting his ears with her forepaws. The black-and-white cat crumpled to the ground. But though Yellowfang relished the strength of her muscles and the certainty of her swiping paws, she couldn't help wincing with every blow she landed. She stung all over as if her pelt had been ripped off.

I have to toughen up, she thought. *I'm fighting for my Clan!*

She was forcing the tom back against the fence when she suddenly felt pressure on her throat, as if something was crushing her windpipe. Her attack faltered as she struggled to breathe. The tom launched himself at her again; through swirling vision Yellowfang saw that Nutwhisker had flung himself between them, giving her a moment's respite.

Her breath rasping in her throat, Yellowfang turned to see the big tabby holding Deerleap down with one paw planted on her neck. Yellowfang staggered across to them, swiping her claws down the tabby's flank. He rolled over and scrambled away.

"Thanks, Yellowfang," Deerleap gasped, struggling to her

paws. "But I was fine, really. I was just going to throw him into the brambles."

And hedgehogs might fly, Yellowfang thought, though she would never have spoken the words aloud. The pressure on her throat had vanished and she could breathe freely again, her chest heaving as she sucked air into her lungs. *What's happening to me?*

A triumphant yowl from Cedarstar distracted her. "That's right! Get out, and don't come back!"

Yellowfang saw the kittypets frantically clawing their way up the fence and vanishing over the other side. None of them looked badly injured, and glancing around at her Clanmates Yellowfang realized that they weren't seriously wounded either.

"Thank StarClan!" she breathed.

She felt so shaky that her legs would hardly hold her up, and one of her paws hurt so much that she could scarcely put it to the ground, though she couldn't remember when it had been injured. She spotted Raggedpelt a tail-length away, and this time she managed to meet his gaze. "Red nearly gave us away," she mewed. "It was so close!"

"Too close," Raggedpelt growled. Without saying more, he turned away and stalked off in the direction of the camp.

Yellowfang tried to follow, but her head spun with pain and she staggered.

"What's wrong?" Deerleap asked, stretching out her neck to give Yellowfang a concerned sniff.

"I—I'm okay," Yellowfang stammered, trying to hide her

weakness. Exhaustion wrapped around her like a heavy black cloud.

"Is something the matter?" Cedarstar padded across to Yellowfang's side, concern in his eyes. "Yellowfang, are you hurt?"

"I don't know . . ."

Deerleap sniffed Yellowfang all over and stood back with a puzzled frown. "Just a scratch or two . . . there must be something wrong that we can't see. Come on, Yellowfang, lean on my shoulder. We'll get you back to camp and let Sagewhisker take a look at you."

Yellowfang and Deerleap were the last cats to struggle back into the camp. The sky was growing pale and the stars were fading. When Yellowfang and her former mentor emerged from the tunnel, the rest of the Clan was gathered around the returned patrols in an excited huddle.

"And then I slashed him over the ear like this," Nutwhisker was meowing. "You should have heard him screech!"

Skirting the edge of the group, Yellowfang limped to Sagewhisker's den, thankful for Deerleap's shoulder supporting her. She slipped between the boulders that formed the entrance to the den, and sank down onto the moss inside.

Sagewhisker looked up from counting poppy seeds. "Yellowfang? Were you hurt in the battle?"

"I'm not sure," Deerleap meowed. "I didn't see her take any particularly bad blows, and I can't find any injuries on her, but she's exhausted and she can hardly walk. Something isn't right."

"Hmm . . ." Sagewhisker glanced from Deerleap to Yellowfang and back again. "Okay, Deerleap, you can leave her with me. I'll give her a thorough checkup."

Yellowfang looked up nervously as Sagewhisker padded over to her. The medicine cat didn't ask her any questions, just sniffed her all over, parting her fur here and there with gentle paws. Finally she sat down beside Yellowfang and wrapped her tail neatly around her forepaws.

"There's hardly a scratch on you, but you already know that, don't you?"

Yellowfang stared at her, baffled. "I must be wounded! I hurt all over."

Sagewhisker paused for a moment before replying. "Which part of you hurts the most?"

"This paw." Yellowfang stretched out a forepaw. "I can hardly put any weight on it."

"Did any other cat hurt her paw?"

Yellowfang tried to remember the chaos of the battle. "Well, Red . . . I mean, one of the kittypets got her paw stuck under a root. But that didn't have anything to do with me."

Sagewhisker didn't comment. "And what's the next worst pain?"

"My ear." Yellowfang flicked it, wincing. "It feels like some cat tore it off."

"No, it's still there, quite untouched," Sagewhisker assured her. "Did you see any cat with an injured ear?"

Yellowfang nodded, remembering Rowanberry's fight with Boulder and the blood trickling down his face.

"What about a flank injury?" the medicine cat persisted.

"How would I know?" Yellowfang retorted, irritable because Sagewhisker's questions were starting to make her feel uncomfortable. "I was *in* the battle, you know, not watching from up in a tree." When Sagewhisker didn't respond, she added uncertainly, "Maybe Cedarstar . . . he fell against a tree stump."

"I'll have to see him about that," Sagewhisker meowed.

"But what about me?" Yellowfang protested. "Aren't you going to treat my injuries?"

Sagewhisker gazed at her from calm green eyes. "I've already told you, Yellowfang, you hardly have a scratch on you. You fought well and escaped without injury. What you are feeling is the injuries of the other cats."

"What do you mean?" Yellowfang mewed shakily. "How can that happen?"

"I don't know," Sagewhisker admitted. "This isn't the first time, though, is it?"

Yellowfang thought back to the times she had been in pain. *When I fought that huge WindClan tom, I felt like I was seriously injured, but I wasn't. And there was the pain I felt when Silverflame was dying . . . and the time when my belly ached when Nutkit ate the crow-food. Great StarClan, has this been happening since I was a* kit*?*

"I guess not," Yellowfang mewed quietly. "But . . . doesn't every cat feel the same? It's not hard to see an injury and imagine how it feels!"

"This isn't your imagination," Sagewhisker told her. "StarClan must have given you these feelings for a reason, and we have to find out what it is."

"No!" Yellowfang forced herself to her paws, ignoring painful muscles that shrieked in protest. "I don't want to be different! I just want to be a warrior!"

CHAPTER 10

Yellowfang stormed out of the medicine cat's den in a whirl of fury and terror, brushing past Rowanberry, who was waiting for her.

"What's the matter?" Rowanberry called, trotting after her. "Are you okay?"

Yellowfang strode on without replying. Her paw still ached, but she did her best to ignore it. She didn't want to talk to any cat, not even her sister. She was heading for the warriors' den, but before she had covered even half the distance, Brightflower bounded up to her.

"Little one!" her mother gasped. "Are you badly hurt? I hear you fought so bravely."

"Sagewhisker fixed everything," Yellowfang muttered, not breaking stride.

Brightflower kept pace with her. "You need to rest," she fretted. "Stonetooth won't expect you to go out on patrol until you're fully healed."

"I'm fine, okay?" Yellowfang snapped, pretending not to see the shocked look in her mother's eyes.

"Hey, Yellowfang!" Archeye intercepted her as she hurried

on. "I hear you were wounded. How are you?"

"Fine."

Suddenly the clearing seemed to be full of cats, all of them bearing down on her, asking stupid questions about her injuries. *Can't they see I'm okay?*

"Leave me alone, will you?" she snarled at Foxpaw and Wolfpaw as they came scurrying up, eager to hear about the battle. She veered away from the warriors' den and ran across the clearing to the entrance.

"Stuck-up furball!" Foxpaw yowled after her.

Yellowfang plunged through the gap and headed for the shadows under the trees. Her mind was still reeling, but she was grateful for the calm and quiet of the forest. A moment later she heard the sound of paw steps and picked up a familiar scent: Rowanberry had followed her.

"What do you want?" Yellowfang growled.

"I'm worried about you," her sister responded, blinking at Yellowfang in concern. "You don't look badly hurt, but I can see something is wrong."

For a moment Yellowfang felt the urge to tell Rowanberry the crazy things that Sagewhisker had said, all the nonsense about being able to feel other cats' injuries. But as soon as she opened her jaws to speak, another sharp pain shot through her paw. With a sinking feeling in her belly she looked at Rowanberry, and saw that one of her claws was bent backward.

"What's wrong with your paw?" she asked, forcing the words out. "Did you get hurt in the battle?"

Rowanberry nodded. "It's a bit sore," she admitted.

Yellowfang knew that she could never tell her sister the truth about what she was feeling. The stab of pain had shown her that Sagewhisker was right. *If I tell Rowanberry, she'll think I'm weird. It would change everything.*

"Go see Sagewhisker," she told her sister. "Don't worry about me. I'll be fine on my own for a while."

Rowanberry hesitated for a heartbeat, then touched her nose briefly to Yellowfang's ear and scampered toward the camp.

Yellowfang watched her until she was out of sight. *I can cope with these feelings,* she told herself. *They won't stop me from being a great warrior.* With her head up, she began padding through the trees. *This changes nothing.*

Yellowfang stalked along the edge of the marshes, enjoying the warmth of sunlight on her pelt and the taste of the plump vole she carried in her jaws. Three sunrises had passed since the battle, and the pain in her body had faded away. "We've hunted well today," she mumbled to Nutwhisker around her mouthful of prey.

Nutwhisker, who was dragging a squirrel, paused for a moment and let his prey drop to the ground. "We'd do even better if we weren't stuck here in the marshes," he commented. "I can't believe that a badger would dare move into our territory."

Featherstorm, who was leading the hunting patrol, caught what Nutwhisker said and rolled her eyes. "You know very well we've always had trouble with badgers," she meowed. "Anyway, it won't be a problem for long, now that Cedarstar has ordered extra patrols to keep an eye open for it."

Blizzardwing, who padded up with Foxpaw just behind him, nodded. "We'll soon get rid of it. And then we can hunt all over the territory again."

"*I'm* not scared of badgers," Foxpaw declared, dropping the starling she was carrying. "I'd give it a good thump on the nose if it dared to chase me!"

Blizzardwing's head swiveled around and he fixed his apprentice with a freezing glare. "If you're not scared of badgers then you're a mouse-brain," he told Foxpaw. "They're the most ferocious animals in the forest—far worse than foxes. If one chases you, run away as far and as fast as you can. Now pick up your fresh-kill and let's get a move on."

Foxpaw obeyed, scowling. Yellowfang exchanged a glance with Nutwhisker before following at the rear of the patrol. *Foxpaw thinks she's so great. It will take more than a cocky little apprentice to deal with this badger!*

When the patrol returned to camp, Yellowfang was arranging the new prey on the fresh-kill pile when she heard a sudden commotion at the entrance to the camp: cats' voices raised in shock and anger, and the beat of paws on hard ground.

Is it the badger? Yellowfang wondered, her heart pounding. She spun around to see Toadskip and Nettlespot escorting two strange cats into the camp. A moment later she realized that they weren't strangers at all—not to her.

Red and Boulder! What are they doing here?

Cedarstar emerged from his den underneath the oak tree and paced across the camp. "What do they want?"

"We found them on our territory," Nettlespot explained. "They wouldn't tell us why they were there."

"Were you spying?" Cedarstar demanded, fixing a suspicious gaze on the two newcomers.

"Tear their pelts off!" Frogtail called out from the crowd.

"Yeah," Mudclaw agreed. "They've no business here."

Hostile murmurs rose from the corners of the camp. Glancing around, Yellowfang spotted Raggedpelt crouching down as if he was ready to pounce on the Twolegplace cats. A low growl came from his throat.

"Well?" Cedarstar prompted. "Why have you come here?"

Red took a pace forward with her head held high. Yellowfang couldn't help admiring her courage. She looked barely old enough to be an apprentice, yet she held Cedarstar's gaze calmly.

"My name is Red, and this is Boulder," she announced. "We want to join your Clan."

The defiant muttering changed to murmurs of disbelief.

"Right!" Nutwhisker spoke into Yellowfang's ear. "As if we'd swallow that!"

Boulder stepped forward to stand beside his friend. "We really do," he insisted. "We want to hunt and fight like you do."

"Why?" Stonetooth challenged them, padding out of the crowd to join Cedarstar. "You belong in the Twolegplace. You should go back."

"And stay there!" Amberleaf called out.

"I don't believe a single word of this," Blizzardwing put in. "It must be a trick!"

Cedarstar stared at the intruders. "Tell us why you wish to join ShadowClan," he meowed.

"It's great here in the forest!" Boulder burst out enthusiastically. "You catch your own prey, and—"

Red gave him a hard shove. "Shut up, flea-brain! That's not what's most important." Addressing Cedarstar with a polite dip of her head, she went on, "You impressed us when you fought with us. You showed us your strength and skill, but you showed us mercy, too."

"That's right," Boulder added. "You could have killed us, but you chose not to. If that's what it means to live by your warrior code—that, and the fact that you feed yourselves, and find your own shelter—then we want to be part of it."

Silence greeted the young cats' serious words, followed by a babble of comment.

"They're lying!"

"Maybe not. Maybe—"

Cedarstar raised his tail for silence. "It will be a long, hard struggle to win acceptance here in the Clan," he warned the newcomers. "Kittypets have never been welcome in the forest."

"We're not kittypets!" Red retorted, her neck fur fluffing out with indignation. "Both our mothers caught their own prey on the streets of Twolegplace. We would never live with housefolk!"

"You can't prove that!" Scorchwind scoffed.

But Cedarstar was looking thoughtful. "Very well," he began slowly. "A Clan would be foolish to turn down the prospect of new warriors, especially when times are hard. More paws to catch prey will always be a valued addition. You may stay here for one moon. If you prove your loyalty during that time, I'll consider making you part of ShadowClan."

"You won't regret it," Red mewed.

"I hope not," Cedarstar responded. Flicking his tail to beckon Brackenfoot, he continued, "Show them to the apprentices' den and teach them how to make nests for themselves."

As Brackenfoot led the rogues away, Yellowfang spotted Foxpaw watching with an expression of disgust. "Yuck!" she exclaimed to Wolfpaw. "I don't want them sleeping with us. I bet they're full of fleas."

"Don't worry," Wolfpaw replied. "We'll make sure they get all the worst jobs, like checking the elders for ticks."

Cedarstar turned to go back to his own den, but Stonetooth stood in his way. "Are you crazy?" he hissed. "These cats are our enemies. They must be spies!"

"There's no proof of that," Cedarstar responded calmly.

Stonetooth snorted. "Do you remember when we thought Featherstorm might have been visiting the Twolegplace at night?" He lowered his voice, but Yellowfang could still catch his words. "Do you want more trouble like that? We can't have our cats tangled up with—"

Cedarstar cut him off with a brusque wave of his tail. "And we can't afford to turn away strong young cats who might be telling the truth. Do you want them to go to another Clan and learn to fight against us? No, we'll give them a chance to . . ."

As the warriors moved away, Yellowfang couldn't hear any

more. She glanced around for Raggedpelt, but he had vanished. Instead, Nutwhisker turned to her, his fur bristling.

"Twolegplace cats made apprentices!" he exclaimed. "Cedarstar must be mouse-brained!"

To her surprise, Yellowfang felt defensive on behalf of Red and Boulder. "We should give them a chance," she meowed. "They're cats, the same as us. And they're not kittypets, which makes a difference, right?"

"They're still—" Nutwhisker began, but broke off as Archeye called his name from across the clearing.

"I'm leading a hunting patrol. Do you want to come?" Archeye asked.

"Sure!" Nutwhisker raced off.

Yellowfang looked at Raggedpelt, who was waiting to join Archeye's patrol. *I wish I knew what he was thinking.*

At that moment Raggedpelt noticed that she was watching him. For a heartbeat his gaze locked with hers; then he turned away with a scowl.

Annoying furball! Yellowfang thought with a flash of frustration. *When will he stop treating me like an enemy? He should know I'd never give away his secret!*

Yellowfang had been to the dirtplace and returned to camp as twilight was falling. As she emerged from the tunnel she spotted Red and Boulder sharing a vole a few tail-lengths away. She hesitated, not knowing whether to approach them or not. Before she could decide, Red looked up, then glanced at Boulder and led the way over to Yellowfang.

"You're the cat who came to see Hal, aren't you?" Boulder meowed. "With that tom over there?" He pointed with his tail toward Raggedpelt, who was sitting with his brother near the fresh-kill pile.

Yellowfang felt hot all over. "Yes," she admitted.

"I guess you weren't supposed to be hanging out with cats from Twolegplace." Red's voice was surprisingly sympathetic. "You guys have a lot of rules about where you're supposed to go."

"Yeah." Yellowfang was grateful for the young cat's understanding. "So if you don't mind . . ."

"Don't worry, your secret's safe with us," Red mewed cheerfully. "Who knows, we might want to have a few nighttime adventures of our own, once we've learned our way around!"

For a heartbeat Yellowfang felt a flash of suspicion, but she crushed it down. She guessed that most Clan cats had felt the same when they were young.

It's just as well they didn't hear us talking to Hal, Yellowfang thought. *They're too young to have been born when Featherstorm was visiting the Twolegplace, which means they have no idea that Hal could be Raggedpelt's father.*

Yellowfang trotted to the fresh-kill pile and chose a mouse for herself. She noticed that Raggedpelt was casting worried glances toward Red and Boulder, his claws flexing nervously.

I should tell him that they won't say anything about the time we went to Twolegplace. Then she let out an irritable snort. *Let him suffer! If he doesn't want to talk to me, I don't see why I should make his life easier.*

* * *

Next morning Yellowfang awoke to the sound of Cedarstar's voice ringing out across the camp. "Let all cats old enough to catch their own prey join here beneath the Clanrock for a Clan meeting!"

Yellowfang poked her head out of the warriors' den. It had rained in the night, but now sunlight glittered on shallow pools on the floor of the clearing and on droplets caught among the branches of the dens. The dawn patrol, led by Finchflight, was just returning.

Cedarstar stood on top of the rock, watching the Clan assemble below him. Sagewhisker was sitting at the entrance of her den, with Brightflower, Lizardfang, and Littlebird beside her. Foxpaw and Wolfpaw scrambled out of the apprentices' den and wriggled through the gathering crowd to find places at the front. Red and Boulder followed more slowly. They exchanged an anxious glance with each other and sat down close to the brambles that circled the clearing.

Nutwhisker and Ashheart brushed past Yellowfang on their way out of the den. "Come on!" Nutwhisker urged her. "Don't you want to know what's going on?"

Yellowfang followed them. Spotting Rowanberry sitting close to the base of the rock, she bounded over to join her. "What's all this about?" she asked.

Rowanberry licked one paw and drew it over her ear. "No idea," she mewed.

By now most of the Clan was sitting around the rock. Finchflight and the rest of the dawn patrol—including Raggedpelt, Yellowfang noticed—were the last to arrive. When they had settled down, Cedarstar spoke.

"Yesterday, two rogues from the Twolegplace came here and asked to join our Clan. Today they will begin their training as apprentices. Red, Boulder, come here."

A murmur of mingled surprise and hostility rose from the assembled cats as Red and Boulder sprang to their paws. For a moment they hesitated; Red tried to give her shoulders a quick grooming.

"What happened to waiting a moon for them to prove their loyalty?" Rowanberry muttered.

Yellowfang shrugged. "I guess they have to start training right away," she mewed. "And how can they do that without a mentor?"

"Come," Cedarstar repeated, beckoning with his tail.

Boulder and Red picked their way through the cats, who drew back to leave them an empty space at the base of the Clanrock. They halted close to Yellowfang; though they held their heads and tails high, she could see that they were both nervous.

"What happens now?" Red hissed to her out of the side of her jaws.

"You'll be fine," Yellowfang reassured her softly. "Just listen to Cedarstar."

"Red," Cedarstar began, "you have left your home in Twolegplace, and stated your wish to become a member of ShadowClan. From this time on you shall be known as Russetpaw." His gaze traveled around the cats until it rested on Featherstorm. "Featherstorm," he went on, "you are a skillful Clan cat with an excellent knowledge of the warrior code. I know that you will pass this knowledge on to your apprentice."

Yellowfang bit back an exclamation of surprise. *Cedarstar knows that Featherstorm used to hang out with Twolegplace cats! Russetpaw and Boulder might be too young to remember seeing her there, but what if they heard about her from the kittypets?*

Featherstorm, looking less than pleased, made her way to the front and stood waiting. "She's your mentor," Yellowfang whispered to Russetpaw. "Go and touch noses with her."

With a grateful look, Russetpaw obeyed, and stood beside Featherstorm while Cedarstar continued. "Boulder, you too have asked for a place in ShadowClan. From this time on you shall be known as—"

"Hang on," Boulder meowed.

Yellowfang gasped. No cat interrupted the Clan leader, especially when he spoke from the Clanrock.

"He'll be crow-food!" Rowanberry muttered.

Cedarstar's tail lashed once. "What is it?"

"I like my name," Boulder announced, obviously unaware that he had done anything unusual. "Can I keep it?"

The Clan leader paused for a couple of heartbeats. Finally, to Yellowfang's surprise, he nodded. "Very well. From this time on you will be known as Boulder. Mousewing, you will be mentor to this new apprentice. I trust that you will teach him the skills he needs and the behavior expected from a Clan cat."

The thick-furred black tom shot his apprentice a heavily

disapproving look. "You can be sure of that," he told Cedarstar.

Boulder walked over to Mousewing and touched noses with him.

"I never heard of such a thing!" Lizardfang grumbled. "Apprentices picking their own names? What's the Clan coming to?"

Littlebird replied too softly for Yellowfang to hear, though she looked more sympathetic. But Yellowfang guessed that most of the Clan would agree with Lizardfang.

"Cedarstar, have you taken leave of your senses?" Stonetooth demanded as Cedarstar leaped down from the Clanrock. "It's bad enough welcoming rogues into the Clan, but letting him keep his name . . ."

The Clan leader sighed. "You have to recognize when a battle is worth fighting," he meowed with a touch of weariness.

Stonetooth snorted.

As the Clan began to drift out of the clearing, Yellowfang spotted Raggedpelt heading in her direction. She took a pace forward, hoping that he was going to speak to her at last. But the tabby tom brushed past her as if he didn't even know that she was there.

"Suit yourself," she muttered, glaring after him. She let out a small, crushed sigh. *Is winning his trust a battle worth fighting? Is Raggedpelt worth all this worry?*

CHAPTER 11

"Look behind you, Yellowfang!" Brackenfoot's yowl rang clearly across the training area. "You're fighting two enemies, remember!"

Yellowfang whirled, ducking under the blow that Boulder was aiming at her, and in the same movement crashed into his side, trying to knock him over. But Boulder scrambled out of range, and then Yellowfang had to turn again and leap away as Russetpaw charged at her.

Turn and slash . . . leap . . . turn again . . . got you, Russetpaw! . . . duck . . . jump back . . . Great StarClan, these rogues are good!

Several sunrises had passed since Russetpaw and Boulder had come to ShadowClan. Brackenfoot had taken all the apprentices for a training session; Yellowfang and Rowanberry had gone along for the practice.

"Cedarstar's right when he says that every warrior needs to keep their battle skills sharp," Rowanberry had commented as they followed their father to the clearing. "And we'll show these rogues what it means to be a ShadowClan warrior."

But as soon as Yellowfang began the training exercise, taking on Russetpaw and Boulder at once to perfect her battle skills when she was outnumbered, she realized that practicing with them was harder than she had expected. Though the two rogues had only a scant idea of Clan battle moves, they were both strong and well muscled, and flung themselves determinedly into the fight. Yellowfang felt as though every muscle in her body was taking a beating. *I've got to get this right,* she thought, aware that her sister and the two younger apprentices were watching from the edge of the clearing.

Yellowfang was trying the move that had worked so well in the battle beside the Twoleg fence, rearing on her hind paws and battering Russetpaw around the head with her forepaws. But Russetpaw leaped backward, and before Yellowfang could follow her, Boulder crashed into her hind legs and swept her to the ground. He thumped down on top of her, his face a mouse-length from hers, his eyes gleaming.

"Do I win?" he asked smugly.

"You do," Brackenfoot replied. "Very good, Boulder—and you, Russetpaw. I'll tell your mentors you fought well."

Yellowfang scrambled to her paws, feeling bruised and indignant. It didn't help when she heard Foxpaw exclaim loudly, "Clumsy furball! She can't even keep her balance."

"That move needs work," Brackenfoot agreed more tactfully, while Yellowfang glared at the apprentice. "Try it again, Yellowfang, and this time don't forget what might be sneaking up behind you."

"Okay," Yellowfang grunted.

Facing Russetpaw again, she reared up, making sure she dug her hind paws firmly into the soft ground. She landed a couple of blows on Russetpaw's ears, her claws sheathed, then spun around at once and dropped neatly on top of Boulder as he dived at her.

"My round, I think," she meowed as he wriggled helplessly underneath her.

"Much better," Brackenfoot purred. "Now you can have a rest, Yellowfang, and we'll see how Wolfpaw and Foxpaw get on."

Panting, Yellowfang retreated to the edge of the clearing and flopped down on the moss beside Rowanberry.

"You know," Rowanberry muttered, "Russetpaw and Boulder are much better at this than I expected. Maybe they didn't lead such soft lives after all!"

Soft lives! Yellowfang opened her jaws to tell her sister just how big and scary some of the cats in Twolegplace were, then realized that she couldn't say anything without giving herself away. "They'll be good fighters when they're trained," she agreed.

Enjoying the respite, she watched as Brackenfoot took Foxpaw and Wolfpaw through the same battle moves, and then let them practice with Boulder and Russetpaw. She couldn't help a purr of satisfaction when Russetpaw landed on top of Foxpaw, squashing all the breath out of her.

"Who can't balance now?" she whispered to Rowanberry.

While Foxpaw shook moss off her pelt, Brackenfoot called Rowanberry into the center of the clearing. Then he paused and glanced up at the sun. "It's past sunhigh," he meowed. "You must be starving. Let's go back to camp for a piece of fresh-kill; then we'll come back and finish the session."

He headed through the trees toward the camp. The brambles were in sight when Yellowfang spotted Raggedpelt slinking away. He shot a glance at the returning cats, then veered off in the opposite direction.

Watching his hasty retreat, Yellowfang felt a stab of sympathy. *Maybe I should tell him that the rogues aren't going to say anything about our visit to Twolegplace.*

"Brackenfoot, I need to talk to Raggedpelt," she told her father, angling her ears toward the spot where the tabby tom had disappeared among the ferns.

Brackenfoot hesitated, as if he was going to insist that she come into the camp to eat and then return to the training session.

I've done my bit, Yellowfang thought indignantly. *And I'm a warrior now. I can make up my own mind when I train.* "It's important," she insisted.

Brackenfoot nodded. "Okay, Yellowfang. See you later."

With a nod to her Clanmates, Yellowfang bounded into the pinewoods after Raggedpelt. Everything was quiet. Yellowfang could hear her own breathing above the soft pad of her paws on the pine needles. Sunlight slanted through the trees, casting bars of light and shadow on the ground. Affection for her territory rushed over Yellowfang. *This is the best place in the forest! In the whole world!*

A terrible snarling sound from somewhere up ahead jolted Yellowfang back to reality. For a heartbeat horror froze her limbs.

That sounds like the badger!

Yellowfang raced through the trees, and found herself heading into a stretch of territory where the trunks grew more thickly, with brambles underneath to tear at her pelt and tangled undergrowth to block her path. Rounding a hazel thicket, she halted with a yelp of shock. She was standing on a small hillock, looking down into a circle of thorns where Raggedpelt was crouching. The only gap, the only way of escape, was blocked by a huge, ragged-furred badger. It had its back to Yellowfang, but she could hear its fierce snarling and its stink washed over her, making her eyes water.

Raggedpelt was lashing out bravely at the badger's head and shoulders, but the creature's thick fur softened his blows. He was backed against a tangle of brambles, unable to use his greater agility to dodge the badger's attack. A storm of pain assailed Yellowfang as the beast struck at Raggedpelt again and again with heavy, blunt claws. Its yellow teeth snapped perilously close to his neck.

Trying to ignore the stinging all over her pelt, Yellowfang bunched her muscles to leap down and join the fight. Then she noticed two tiny snouts poking out from the midst of the brambles behind Raggedpelt.

Oh, no! Raggedpelt is between the mother and her den!

Yellowfang leaped into the fray, but in the same heartbeat more terrible pain seized her, as if the badger's claws were raking across her body. She landed badly, falling onto one side, then forced herself to struggle to her paws.

You're not hurt, she told herself. *This is Raggedpelt's pain you're feeling. If you don't help him, he'll be wounded even more.*

Gritting her teeth, Yellowfang flung herself onto the badger's back. The fierce creature reared its head, snapping and snarling, but its jaws couldn't reach her. Yellowfang clung on, forcing her claws into the soft fur behind the badger's ears. She could hear the cubs squealing, and felt a momentary stab of pity. *This mother badger is only trying to protect her cubs.* Then she forced the pity down. *She's hurting my Clanmate!*

"I'll draw it away!" she gasped to Raggedpelt. "Then run!"

Yellowfang sprang off the badger's back, flinching as the animal swiveled its head and fixed its tiny, berry-bright eyes on her. Somehow, she had to entice the badger away from Raggedpelt. She limped backward, hardly needing to pretend to be injured because of the sensations that were coursing through her body.

Come on, badger! Follow me, and let Raggedpelt escape. When another wave of agony washed over her, Yellowfang had to struggle to stay on her paws. *I'm not hurt. I'm not bleeding. This is Raggedpelt's pain. I have to fight through it!*

With a roar of fury the badger lumbered toward her, one huge paw outstretched to strike. Yellowfang waited until the last moment, then sprang up, clawing at the creature's muzzle. The badger staggered sideways, leaving a narrow space between its flank and the thorns.

"Run, Raggedpelt!" Yellowfang screeched.

Raggedpelt slipped through the gap before the badger could trap him again. Once clear of the thorns he turned, crouching beside Yellowfang, ready to help her fight. Yellowfang could see that her Clanmate's pelt was clumped and spiky with blood, and more blood was welling from wounds in his shoulder and side. "Get away!" she hissed.

"You can't fight alone!" Raggedpelt gasped.

"Just go, flea-brain!"

Yellowfang darted in again, leaping to claw the badger on one side of its snout. Glancing back, she saw that Raggedpelt was limping away, leaving spatters of blood on the grass. Snarling another challenge to the badger, she slowly backed off, then spun around and fled after her Clanmate.

"Are you mouse-brained?" Raggedpelt demanded when she had caught up to him. "You didn't have to take a risk like that. You should have gone to fetch more warriors."

"There was no time," Yellowfang flashed back at him. "You would have bled to death before I got back to the camp!" Every word was an effort. Raggedpelt's hurt was flooding over her so strongly that she barely had the strength to put one paw in front of another.

"Are you okay?" Raggedpelt's anger gave way to concern. "Are you wounded?"

"I'm fine . . ." Yellowfang gasped. "You're the one who needs help. Here, lean on my shoulder." *And StarClan grant that the badger isn't chasing us!*

Whole moons seemed to pass before the entrance to the camp came into sight. Yellowfang shoved Raggedpelt into the brambles and staggered after him. The camp was quiet; Yellowfang guessed most of the cats were out on patrol, or training.

Featherstorm was sitting near the warriors' den with

Brightflower. She glanced up as her son and Yellowfang emerged into the camp. Instantly she sprang to her paws and rushed across the clearing to Raggedpelt's side.

"Raggedpelt!" she screeched. "What happened?"

As soon as he reached the clearing Raggedpelt had collapsed on his side, his chest heaving. "Badger!" he gasped.

Brightflower raced over to the medicine cat's den, calling for Sagewhisker, who ran over to examine Raggedpelt. The medicine cat gave him a few rapid sniffs, then looked up at Yellowfang. "I think we need to talk. Wait for me in my den while I look after Raggedpelt."

Words crowded into Yellowfang's mind, of protest or denial that they had anything to say to each other, but she left them all unspoken. Nodding, she paced across the clearing and slid between the rocks into Sagewhisker's den.

CHAPTER 12

Yellowfang sank down on the bare earth floor of the medicine cat's den, curling herself into a tight ball against the soreness in her pelt. She was dimly aware of Sagewhisker returning, collecting something from her herb store, and leaving again. Gradually the agony in Yellowfang's muscles began to ease, and she let herself relax.

I want to go back to my den and sleep for a moon!

She was struggling to stay awake when Sagewhisker reappeared, and she sat up, trying to look alert.

"Raggedpelt is resting," the medicine cat meowed. "I gave him some poppy seed."

Yellowfang nodded. "Good."

For a moment Sagewhisker said nothing, just padded over to her herb store and began tidying up. Then she glanced over her shoulder at Yellowfang. "What are you going to do now?" she prompted.

Yellowfang didn't understand the question. "You mean, right now? Sleep."

Sagewhisker gave a tiny shake of her head. "In the future."

"Be a warrior, of course."

"What about this pain that you feel for others?" the medicine cat asked.

"Is there some sort of herb you can give me to take it away?" Yellowfang mewed hopefully.

Sagewhisker shook her head. "There's nothing wrong with you, Yellowfang. Nothing that needs healing." She finished patting down the fern fronds that covered the herb store before she came to sit beside Yellowfang. Meeting her gaze, she continued, "You have a great ability, one that can be used to help your Clanmates."

Yellowfang shook her head. "I don't see how."

"You can tell as soon as they are injured," Sagewhisker replied. "Or where their pain is when they are sick."

"So can you—because cats tell you!" Yellowfang pointed out. Struggling to stay calm, she added, "I don't want to feel like this. It's getting in the way of being a warrior."

Sagewhisker said nothing for so long that Yellowfang grew worried. Finally she spoke. "Maybe being a warrior isn't the best use of you in ShadowClan," she mewed quietly. "Maybe you should be a medicine cat."

Yellowfang sprang to her paws. "Don't be ridiculous! I'm a warrior!" When Sagewhisker met her gaze with wide, serious eyes, she went on. "I can't help that I feel when other cats are hurt. I don't want to, and if I could get rid of it I would. You're supposed to be helping me!"

Sagewhisker sighed. "Yellowfang, that's all I ever want to do."

Suddenly Yellowfang didn't want to talk to Sagewhisker

anymore. *She doesn't understand!* Spinning around, she stormed into the clearing.

Outside, Brightflower was just emerging from the warriors' den. Spotting Yellowfang, she bounded over to her. "Raggedpelt—" Brightflower began, and broke off. "Are you okay?" she asked anxiously.

"I'm fine," Yellowfang snapped.

Brightflower blinked. "Raggedpelt is asking for you," she meowed.

Yellowfang wasn't sure she wanted to talk to any cat right now, but after a moment's hesitation she turned her paw steps in the direction of the warriors' den. Raggedpelt was curled up in his nest. It was lined with extra feathers; with a purr of amusement Yellowfang thought that the tabby warrior looked like a baby crow with a black frill around his head. As she picked her way among the other nests to his side, Raggedpelt raised his head.

"Yellowfang . . ." he murmured. "I wanted to thank you. You saved my life."

Yellowfang's pelt grew hot with embarrassment. "It was nothing," she mumbled. "Any cat would have done the same."

The secret that lay between her and Raggedpelt made her feel uncomfortable, as if ants were crawling through her fur. She took a pace back, but before she could leave, Raggedpelt reached out a paw to stop her.

"Promise me you'll never do something so mouse-brained again," he grunted. "You could have been killed."

"Well, you were nearly killed yourself," Yellowfang shot

back at him. "So I'd be in good company!"

Raggedpelt didn't reply, just let out another grunt of pain.

"Lie down," Yellowfang meowed, helping him to settle in his nest. "I'll bring you something to eat later." Glancing back before she left the den, she saw that Raggedpelt's eyes were closed. A spark of warmth woke inside her. *Maybe we can go back to being friends.*

Outside the den, Yellowfang arched her back in a long stretch. Her weariness was ebbing, and she longed to work off her energy in a run through the forest. As she relaxed from her stretch she became aware of some cat watching her, and she turned to see Foxpaw fixing her with a burning glare. *What's her problem?* But Yellowfang couldn't be bothered to confront the apprentice. She put Foxpaw out of her mind as she padded across the camp to where Stonetooth and a few of the other warriors were gathered around the fresh-kill pile. The Clan deputy was sitting with his paws tucked under him, dozing in the sunlight; he blinked awake as Yellowfang halted in front of him. As he struggled to his paws she thought he looked suddenly old, but a heartbeat later he was as crisp and efficient as ever.

"Yellowfang, I want you to lead a patrol back to where you saw the badger. We need to drive that creature out of the woods once and for all."

"Of course," Yellowfang replied, with a thrill of pride that she had been asked to take on such an important job.

"Good." Stonetooth glanced around at the other warriors near the fresh-kill pile. "Archeye, Mousewing, you can go," he mewed.

"Great!" Archeye swallowed the last of the vole he was sharing with Mousewing, and swiped his tongue around his jaws. "Now?"

Stonetooth nodded. "Right away. Scorchwind and Newtspeck, you can join them."

"And us!" Wolfpaw panted, bounding up with Foxpaw at his shoulder.

The Clan deputy shook his head. "This patrol is just for warriors."

Wolfpaw's tail dropped in disappointment, while his sister glared at Yellowfang. *Don't look at me like that,* Yellowfang thought, longing to give the annoying apprentice a cuff around the ear. *It's not my fault. And if you'd seen what that badger can do, maybe you wouldn't be so keen to go.*

"Hang on a moment," Archeye meowed. "Maybe we should let the apprentices come with us. They need the experience."

Oh, Archeye, why can't you keep your jaws shut? Yellowfang would have liked to speak the words aloud, but she had to keep quiet and not show her annoyance while the deputy considered.

Eventually Stonetooth nodded. "Very well." As Wolfpaw and Foxpaw began to bristle with excitement, he fixed them with a stern gaze. "But do exactly as Yellowfang and the senior warriors tell you," he continued. "Stay well back until they work out how to proceed."

The two apprentices nodded impatiently; Yellowfang suspected the deputy's words had gone right over their heads. Waving her tail to gather her patrol, she led the way through the brambles and into the forest. As soon as they were heading through the trees, Scorchwind put on a burst of speed to walk alongside her.

"I'll *flay* that badger," he snarled. "I'll spread her guts from here to the Twolegplace. No creature hurts my brother and gets away with it."

Yellowfang pictured the two tiny badger cubs who had peeped out from the brambles while their mother was attacking the Clan cats. *Is it fair to drive the badger and her babies out of their home? Couldn't we just stay away from that part of the forest until she has raised her cubs?*

Yellowfang knew she wasn't thinking like a warrior, but she was also certain that if it had been the other way around, she would do anything to protect her kits, including attacking any animals who strayed too close to her den.

Maybe I could say that I don't remember the way back.

Before she could decide, she heard a triumphant yowl from Mousewing, who was sniffing among the undergrowth on one side of the path. "Over here! Raggedpelt's scent, and blood on the bracken!"

Now Yellowfang had no choice but to lead the patrol straight to the clearing. She couldn't work out whether she felt relieved or disappointed. When the thorns that circled the clearing came into sight, Yellowfang raised her tail to signal her patrol to halt. "It's through there," she meowed. "Wolfpaw, Foxpaw, don't you dare move a paw until I tell you."

Remembering how Deerleap had taught her to *look, listen, and scent,* she tried to detect what the badger might be doing, and what they could expect to find when they entered the clearing. But although there was a strong stink of the creature, there was nothing to be seen, and no sound came from behind the brambles.

"Yellowfang," Archeye murmured, "we ought to have a plan before we go in there."

Yellowfang nodded. "What do you suggest?"

Beckoning the patrol closer, Archeye went on in a low voice. "When we go through the gap, we should split up. Newtspeck, Scorchwind, and Foxpaw that way"—he drew scratches on the ground with his claws—"Mousewing, you, me, and Wolfpaw this way. We'll try to surround her."

"Good," Yellowfang agreed. "I'll follow you in and help where I'm needed. Scorchwind—" She fixed the ginger tabby with a stern gaze. "You will *not* take unnecessary risks. Got that?"

Scorchwind paused, then nodded reluctantly. "Got it."

"Okay," Archeye went on. "Then, when we've pulled down the badger, we'll move on to her cubs. They shouldn't give us much trouble."

Yellowfang found herself wincing at the thought of sinking her claws into the tiny, helpless cubs. *I'm a warrior!* she told herself. *I have to do this!* "Right," she mewed. "Let's go."

Mousewing was the first of the cats to burst into the clearing. But instead of veering to the side as Archeye had planned, he halted, letting out a yowl of surprise. "The badger is gone!"

Yellowfang ran in behind him and gazed around the clearing. The thorns were trampled and the bramble tendrils torn and scattered. Fresh earth showed where the badger had frantically dragged her cubs out of the den.

Thank StarClan, thought Yellowfang. *I don't have to kill them after all!*

But then Wolfpaw called out. "Here's their trail! We can still catch them." Without waiting for any cat to respond he charged away along the badger's trail.

"Wait!" Yellowfang yowled. "You can't attack a badger by yourself!" *And* I'm *leading this patrol!* she added silently.

Wolfpaw slackened his pace enough for the rest of the cats to catch up. Yellowfang took the lead as they followed the badgers' path through trampled undergrowth that seemed soaked through with the reek of the creatures. At first the trail led toward the Twolegplace, then veered away toward the border with the unknown woods where no cat went. Soon Yellowfang began to pick up the scent of ShadowClan markers, and halted as they reached the edge of their territory.

"We should keep going until we find them and kill them," Scorchwind urged. "They might come back."

"That's mouse-brained," Yellowfang retorted. "We should be thankful that they've left without more cats getting hurt."

"You're right, Yellowfang," Archeye meowed. "And it's thanks to you that the badger took her cubs away. You showed her how fierce ShadowClan warriors can be."

"Yeah, she couldn't get out fast enough," Newtspeck agreed.

Yellowfang ducked her head, embarrassed by their praise. How could she tell them that she felt nothing but relief that they didn't need to harm the mother badger and her cubs?

CHAPTER 13

Yellowfang froze as a leaf drifted down right in front of her nose, but the lizard she was stalking through the marsh grass paid no attention. *Leaves are falling all the time now,* Yellowfang thought. Prey was becoming scarce as the foliage grew sparser, and her belly growled with hunger. The air was chilly with the promise of leaf-bare.

Setting her paws down with all the care she could muster, Yellowfang crept up on the lizard where it had halted in a clump of thicker grass. But as she was waggling her haunches in preparation to pounce, another cat flashed past her in a blur of movement. Raggedpelt's paws were outstretched, but he landed a mouse-length short. The lizard vanished, flickering away into the grass.

Yellowfang sat up. "Hey!" she yowled. "That was *my* prey."

"You were too far away for a good pounce," Raggedpelt retorted, turning to glare at her from wide amber eyes.

"Huh! And you weren't, I suppose." Yellowfang flexed her claws and felt her shoulder fur beginning to bristle. "So how come *neither* of us has any prey for the Clan?"

Raggedpelt took a breath to go on arguing, then let it out in a sigh. His tail drooped. "You're right," he admitted, ducking his head. "I'm sorry. That was mouse-brained."

Yellowfang let out a sound that was half purr, half growl. "It's okay, stupid furball," she mewed, giving his cheek a lick.

Raggedpelt stepped back, but only a little; the anger in his eyes had given way to warmth. "Since we're both after the same thing, why don't we hunt together?" he suggested.

Yellowfang blinked, holding his gaze. It felt so good to be friends with Raggedpelt again, patrolling and hunting together since he had recovered from the wounds the badger had given him. "Why not?" she agreed.

Brushing through the thorn tunnel, Yellowfang was satisfied with the result of the hunt. She was carrying a squirrel; it was thin, but it was the best piece of prey she'd spotted all day. *And I almost didn't catch it. One more heartbeat, and it would have escaped up that tree.*

Raggedpelt had caught another lizard to make up for the one he had lost. Together the two cats bounded across the clearing and dropped their prey on the fresh-kill pile.

"That went well," Raggedpelt declared. "We should hunt together more often. We make a strong team."

Yellowfang nodded. "Sounds good to me."

"Remember the other day, when you chased that rabbit right into my claws? That was—" He broke off as Foxpaw came hurtling across the clearing and skidded to a halt in front of the fresh-kill pile.

"Wow, a squirrel!" she exclaimed, her eyes stretching

wide. "Congratulations, Raggedpelt."

"It's Yellowfang's squirrel," the tabby tom responded. "It was a great catch, too."

Foxpaw's enthusiastic expression faded abruptly; Yellowfang guessed that the squirrel suddenly wasn't as impressive. With a disdainful curl of her lip the apprentice turned her back. Yellowfang rolled her eyes. *Foxpaw is always in a huff about something.*

"Yellowfang!"

At the sound of Littlebird's voice, Yellowfang turned to see the elder standing at the entrance to her den, a few taillengths away.

"Yes, what is it?"

"Oh, Yellowfang . . ." the elder began. "There's a tick at the base of my tail, and I can't reach it. I wonder if you could—"

"Aren't there any apprentices to deal with your ticks?" Yellowfang interrupted, staring pointedly at Foxpaw.

"But I'm asking *you*, Yellowfang," the elder insisted.

Yellowfang's pelt burned at the smug look on Foxpaw's face. She was conscious of the apprentice's gaze following her as she plodded over to the elders' den. Inside, the den was warm and stuffy. Lizardfang wasn't there, so there was plenty of room for Littlebird to stretch out and show Yellowfang where the tick was.

Yellowfang was still cross that Littlebird had ordered her around in front of Foxpaw. She didn't want to go to Sagewhisker for mouse bile, so she dealt with the tick by gripping it in her teeth and tugging. It came out, and she ground it into the bracken underpaw.

"That's better," Littlebird sighed, craning her neck to give her fur a lick. After a heartbeat she added casually, "I see you and Raggedpelt are getting along much better since he was attacked by the badger."

"Yeah . . . I guess," she muttered.

"I've seen the pair of you fall out before now," the elder went on, sounding concerned.

Yellowfang just gave a noncommittal grunt, not meeting Littlebird's gaze.

"You know, Yellowfang," Littlebird meowed, "I'm sure you have a long future ahead of you. There's no need to rush into pairing up with a mate."

Embarrassment prickled Yellowfang's paws. "I'm not in a rush to do anything!" she protested.

Littlebird nodded. "That's good."

"I should go," Yellowfang muttered, eager to get out of the elders' den. "Patrols . . . hunting . . ."

"Just remember what I've said," Littlebird called after her as she scrambled into the open.

More cats had gathered around the fresh-kill pile. Russetpaw and Boulder, in a patrol with their mentors, appeared laden with prey and dropped it on the pile. Poolcloud and Brightflower were sharing a pigeon, while Nutwhisker was demonstrating a battle move to Wolfpaw and Rowanberry. Foxpaw was still there, Yellowfang noticed, leaning close to Raggedpelt as he devoured a starling. Yellowfang stalked up to them in time to hear what the apprentice was saying.

"Why don't we go hunting together, Raggedpelt?"

"You can't go out on your own patrols!" Yellowfang informed her icily, before Raggedpelt could say anything. "You're an apprentice!"

"Not for much longer," Foxpaw mewed with a pert flick of her tail. "I passed my final assessment this morning!"

"Great," Yellowfang meowed, unable to summon up much enthusiasm. *She'll be twice as obnoxious once she's made a warrior!*

"Wolfpaw was a good apprentice." Brightflower dipped her head to Poolcloud. "I enjoyed training him. And Blizzardwing told me how quickly Foxpaw picks things up."

"I couldn't be more proud," Poolcloud purred, turning her head to give her shoulder a couple of quick licks. "I know that Foxpaw and Wolfpaw will impress the whole of ShadowClan when they become warriors."

"I'm sure they will," Hollyflower added, padding up in time to hear the last few words.

Yellowfang jumped as Nutwhisker's whiskers tickled her ear and he muttered, "Foxpaw is bound to be leading patrols before she even goes to her first Gathering as a warrior."

Yellowfang nodded glumly. *I don't want to patrol with her,* she thought. *But I suppose I'll have to put up with it. She'd better not try ordering me around, though!*

"Let all cats old enough to catch their own prey join here beneath the Clanrock for a meeting!"

Foxpaw gave an excited bounce. "It's our warrior ceremony!"

Cats emerged from their dens and gathered around the

Clanrock in a ragged circle. Yellowfang spotted Russetpaw and Boulder near the front, their eyes gleaming with anticipation, and realized that this was the first warrior ceremony they had seen. Featherstorm and Mousewing, their mentors, sat with them, joined after a moment by Archeye, Blizzardwing, and Deerleap. Brackenfoot bounded over to Brightflower, and the two cats sat down with Nutwhisker and Rowanberry.

Lizardfang had reappeared, and crouched outside the elders' den with Littlebird. Yellowfang could feel the old she-cat's gaze upon her as she padded over to Raggedpelt and sat beside him. To her relief, Foxpaw had gone to stand at the front with Wolfpaw. Raggedpelt acknowledged Yellowfang with a flick of his ears.

"One of the most important times in the life of a Clan is the making of new warriors," Cedarstar announced. "Today, two apprentices will take their warrior vows." His gaze searched out Brightflower, and he asked, "Is Wolfpaw ready to become a warrior?"

Brightflower dipped her head. "He is, Cedarstar."

"And Foxpaw?" The Clan leader turned toward Blizzardwing. "Is she worthy of this honor?"

"Worthy and more," Blizzardwing replied. "She will be an outstanding warrior."

Cedarstar nodded. "If that is so, it's due to your excellent training," he told the mottled white tom.

Foxpaw had puffed out her chest when she heard her mentor's praise.

"She'd better watch out," Yellowfang whispered to

Raggedpelt. "She'll explode if she gets any more pleased with herself."

Leaping down from the Clanrock, Cedarstar continued, "I, Cedarstar, call upon my warrior ancestors to look down upon these apprentices. They have trained hard to understand the ways of your noble code, and I commend them to you as warriors in their turn." He beckoned Wolfpaw and Foxpaw forward with a flick of his tail. "Foxpaw, Wolfpaw, do you promise to uphold the warrior code and to protect and defend this Clan, even at the cost of your own life?"

"I do," Wolfpaw vowed, flexing his claws.

"I do!" Foxpaw's voice rang out confidently.

"Then by the powers of StarClan," Cedarstar announced, "I give you your warrior names. Wolfpaw, from this moment you will be known as Wolfstep. StarClan honors your courage and your loyalty, and we welcome you as a full warrior of ShadowClan." He stepped forward to lay his muzzle on the top of Wolfstep's head, and Wolfstep licked his shoulder before stepping back into the ranks of his Clan.

Then Cedarstar turned to Foxpaw, repeating the same words and giving her the name of Foxheart. "StarClan honors your energy and commitment, and we welcome you as a full warrior of ShadowClan."

As Foxheart stepped back after licking her leader's shoulder, the Clan exploded into yowls of welcome and congratulation. "Foxheart! Wolfstep! Foxheart! Wolfstep!"

Yellowfang noticed that Boulder and Russetpaw were joining in enthusiastically, their eyes shining as they called out the new warriors' names. *They're not at all bitter that they haven't been made warriors too—even though Boulder must be a few moons older.*

"You know, I never thought I'd say this." The voice was Amberleaf's; Yellowfang glanced over her shoulder to see the older she-cat talking to Finchflight. "But those Twolegplace cats have really settled into the Clan. Maybe they'll make warriors after all.".

Finchflight nodded. "They work hard, and Mousewing tells me they're doing their best to understand the warrior code."

Yellowfang was pleased to hear Amberleaf—one of the strictest cats in the Clan—praising Boulder and Russetpaw. But disappointment welled up inside her when she looked back at Raggedpelt and saw that he had turned his back on the two newcomers yet again and was moving away.

"Raggedpelt, you're being mouse-brained," she hissed, bounding after him. "You have to trust those two not to say anything about the time we visited Twolegplace." When Raggedpelt just looked stubborn, she added, "They probably don't think about their old lives at all! Any cat can see that they're dedicated to ShadowClan now."

Raggedpelt gave a single lash of his tail. "They've only been in camp for three moons. We don't know them, so how can we trust them?" he growled. "They could still be spies!"

Yellowfang sighed. *Why can't Raggedpelt see what's right in front of his own nose?*

"Talk to you later," she mewed abruptly, and bounded off to join Rowanberry and Nutwhisker beside the fresh-kill pile.

* * *

"I *told* you, you have to wake up and come on patrol!"

Yellowfang woke from a deep sleep to hear Foxheart's strident tones filling the warriors' den. She was drawing breath for a stinging retort when she realized that ShadowClan's newest warrior wasn't talking to her.

Toadskip was heaving himself out of his nest a couple of tail-lengths away. "Okay, okay," he grumbled. "No need to wake the whole Clan."

"You'd better hurry," Foxheart went on. She was poking her head through the outer branches of the den. "Cedarheart and Stonetooth are waiting for you. We're going to check that the badger has really gone."

"I'm coming. Just get out of my fur, okay," Toadskip grumbled as he gave his pelt a good shake and headed out of the den.

Foxheart pulled her head back; Yellowfang heard her scolding voice receding as the two cats trotted away.

Yellowfang stretched her jaws in a massive yawn, then curled up again in the hope of going back to sleep. She still felt tired from the previous day, when she had taken part in three hunting patrols, including one after dark to look for night prey. *Hunting's so much harder in leaf-bare,* she thought drowsily. *And I'm supposed to join another patrol after sunhigh.*

But sleep wouldn't come. A sharp pain was stabbing into Yellowfang's belly, and for a moment she wondered if she'd accidentally eaten crow-food. Then she realized that the pain was different somehow. *Oh, not again! This is some other cat's pain. Get out of my fur!*

For a short while Yellowfang tried to ignore the griping in her belly, but it was growing stronger with every heartbeat. Finally she had to admit that she needed to go and see Sagewhisker. Stifling a groan, she blundered out of the den, the pangs stabbing so hard that she was almost bent double. Though she tried to avoid the sleeping bodies of the other warriors, she brushed against Nutwhisker, who raised his head and blinked sleepily at her.

"Are you okay, Yellowfang?"

"I'm fine," Yellowfang snapped. "It's just a cramp."

She shivered as she emerged into the open. An icy breeze was sweeping across the camp, and Yellowfang longed for her cozy bedding and the air inside the den, warm with her Clanmates' breath. The clearing was deserted; all the cats were either huddled in their dens or out on patrol.

Another stab of pain sent Yellowfang bounding across the clearing. Sagewhisker roused and looked up in surprise as Yellowfang slipped between the stones into her den. "Is something wrong, Yellowfang?" she asked with a yawn.

By now the pain was so bad that it was hard for Yellowfang to reply. "Is there a cat with bellyache in the Clan?" she hissed through gritted teeth.

Sagewhisker twitched her whiskers, fixing Yellowfang with a searching gaze. "What exactly do you feel?"

"Agony! It *hurts*!"

"I need a bit more detail than that," Sagewhisker responded calmly.

"It's . . . it's like I swallowed a live rat," Yellowfang gasped.

"And it's gnawing and clawing me from inside my belly."

Sagewhisker nodded. "That's hunger," she mewed. "I'd guess that you're picking up Nettlespot's pain."

That makes sense, Yellowfang thought. Nettlespot had just given birth to two kits, but one of them had died and the remaining kit was weak. "Nettlespot has always been thin," she murmured.

"I'm worried about her, and Cloudkit," Sagewhisker agreed. "This is a bad season for new arrivals."

"Why doesn't Nettlespot just ask for more food?" Yellowfang wondered aloud.

"She's too proud," Sagewhisker told her. "She's a bit old to be a mother and she's determined to prove that she can care for her kit."

Pride won't fill her belly, Yellowfang thought. "What can I do to help?" she asked. "I'll be no use to the Clan with this pain in my belly. I can hardly put one paw in front of another."

Sagewhisker gave her another close glance, then padded across her den to uncover one of her herb stores. She returned to Yellowfang with a mouthful of withered leaves. Yellowfang recognized the traveling herbs that she had eaten when she journeyed to the Moonstone.

"These will dull the edge of Nettlespot's hunger," she meowed, laying the bundle at Yellowfang's paws. "Meanwhile I'll ask one of the warriors to bring a piece of fresh-kill just for her."

Yellowfang looked at the herbs. Evidently Sagewhisker expected her to take them to the nursery for Nettlespot. *As if I was her apprentice!* But there was no point in arguing, so she picked up the leaves and staggered out of the den.

Inside the nursery, Nettlespot was hunched over her kit, using her tail to draw him closer to her belly. "Cloudkit, you must feed," she fretted.

The tiny gray scrap of fur squirmed away from her, raising his voice in a piteous mewling. "Not enough milk!"

As Yellowfang drew closer, a new spasm of pain gripped her belly, almost making her gasp and drop the herbs. Stumbling forward, she set them down in front of Nettlespot. "Eat those," she panted. "Sagewhisker will bring you some fresh-kill to eat later."

Nettlespot gazed up at her with dull, exhausted eyes. "Thanks, Yellowfang," she murmured.

But Yellowfang didn't wait for her thanks. She had already spun around and was bolting from the den, trying to shake the feelings of pain and panic from her fur. This wasn't just an inconvenience now—it was scary, and exasperating.

How can I be a warrior if I have to bear the pain of all the Clan?

CHAPTER 14

Yellowfang poked her head out of the warriors' den to see the clearing covered with a thick pelt of snow. The branches of the surrounding trees were heavy with it, and a few white flakes were still drifting down.

"It's too early in the season to be this cold," she muttered to herself.

Shivering, she waded through the powdery snow toward the fresh-kill pile, where Stonetooth was organizing the day's patrols. The older warriors gathered around him were exchanging troubled glances, and meowing to one another in low voices.

Before Yellowfang could join them, she was intercepted by Sagewhisker, who was heading toward the nursery with a few leaves of tansy in her jaws. "These are for Cloudkit," she informed Yellowfang, mumbling around the mouthful of herbs. "He's coughing a little."

Why tell me? "Okay," Yellowfang mewed. "I'm sure you'll fix him, Sagewhisker."

The medicine cat blinked at her, making Yellowfang even more uncomfortable. But all Sagewhisker said was, "Yes, the tansy should soon clear up his cough. And Nettlespot is improving since you took her the herbs the other day."

Yellowfang ducked her head. "Fine," she meowed. "Er . . . gotta go, Sagewhisker. Patrols." She headed off rapidly, aware of the medicine cat's gaze following her.

"There you are, Yellowfang," Stonetooth greeted her as she joined the group of warriors. "Crowtail's leading a border patrol. You can join him with Hollyflower and Newtspeck."

"Sure," Yellowfang responded, brightening up with the prospect of getting out of camp.

"Let's go." Crowtail waved her tail and led the way through the thorn tunnel.

Emerging into the forest, Yellowfang could hardly believe how different it looked under the covering of snow. All the humps and hollows in the ground had been smoothed out, and the surface of the snow was crisscrossed by tracks. The shadows had a bluish tinge, and every slight sound—the creak of a branch, the flutter of wings in a tree—seemed magnified in the still air.

"There's so much white stuff!" Yellowfang murmured to Hollyflower.

Her Clanmate nodded. "It's been a long time since the last snowfall. I'd almost forgotten what it's like."

I was a new apprentice then, Yellowfang thought. *So much has happened since!*

Every so often snow would shower down from one of the trees; Yellowfang suppressed a *mrrow* of laughter as Newtspeck had to skip aside to avoid being drenched. Playfully Yellowfang flicked a pawful of snow at Hollyflower; the older she-cat jumped and spun around, her jaws gaping with shock.

"I'm going to get you, Yellowfang!"

Hollyflower scooped up more snow and flung it at Yellowfang. It landed right in her face; she shook her head to get rid of it, spraying snow in all directions.

"Watch out! Snow coming!" she yowled, scuffling up more of the white stuff to throw at Hollyflower.

Crowtail, who had drawn a few paces ahead, halted and glanced back over her shoulder. "Honestly, are you kits?" she demanded. "Grow up. This is a border patrol, or had you forgotten?"

"Sorry, Crowtail," Hollyflower meowed, dipping her head and looking embarrassed.

"Sorry," Yellowfang echoed, though she tossed another pawful of snow at Hollyflower's retreating tail before following.

By the time they reached the Thunderpath, Yellowfang was becoming tired of wading through the snow and getting clots of it tangled in her belly fur. She envied her Clanmates' sleeker fur and longer legs, which kept their stomachs free.

Crowtail stopped by the two narrow tunnels that burrowed underneath the Thunderpath. "We need to make sure no cats are using these to trespass on ShadowClan's territory," she mewed. "With prey so scarce, there's no telling what the other Clans might be up to."

"Just let them try!" Yellowfang growled, sliding out her claws.

But when they examined the tunnels and the territory around them, there was no trace of enemy scent.

"Pity." Newtspeck's lip curled in the beginning of a snarl. "A good scrap with a ThunderClan patrol would warm me up!"

The patrol continued along the Thunderpath, then veered away to skirt the edge of the Twolegplace. As they drew closer to the walls and fences, Yellowfang grew more alert, watching out for kittypets who might recognize her.

Hollyflower ran lightly across the snow and leaped up onto the nearest Twoleg fence. "Look at this!" she called Yellowfang.

Yellowfang glanced back to where Crowtail and Newtspeck were investigating something at the bottom of a tree. Then she bounded up and joined Hollyflower on the fence.

"What do you suppose that is?" Hollyflower asked, pointing with her tail at a humped shape of snow in the Twoleg garden.

Yellowfang shrugged, more concerned with checking the garden for kittypets. "Who knows?"

"It looks a bit like a Twoleg," Hollyflower went on, sounding puzzled.

Yellowfang gave the shape a closer scrutiny. "It doesn't have legs," she pointed out.

"It's got a head and a body," Hollyflower countered. "And a Twoleg pelt on its head."

"It's a Noleg, then," Yellowfang mewed impatiently. *Honestly, who cares about weird Twoleg stuff?*

"I wonder what it's like, being a kittypet," Hollyflower went on after a pause. "Do you suppose they can speak Twoleg? Do you think they go up and say, 'Hey, it's time for fresh-kill! I would love to have a vole today, and make sure it's plump'?"

"I doubt it," Yellowfang returned dryly. "Do you ever see Twolegs chasing voles in the forest?"

"I guess not. Kittypets don't have to catch their own prey, though. I think that's really sad." Hollyflower let out a sigh. "Never knowing what it's like to stalk a squirrel . . ."

Remembering the kittypets she and Raggedpelt had met that night, Yellowfang was pretty sure that some of them would be able to catch their own prey. But she wasn't about to say that to Hollyflower.

"What do they *do* all day?" the gray-and-white she-cat went on. "They don't hunt, they don't train to fight, they must find it really hard to have a mate if they're shut up in a Twoleg nest all day. They hardly seem like real cats at all."

"Russetpaw and Boulder are real cats," Yellowfang pointed out.

"Yeah, but they're Clan now," Hollyflower asserted with a flick of her ears. "I'd be surprised if they even remember living over here. At any rate," she finished with satisfaction in her tone, "kittypets don't matter. As long as they stay out of our territory."

Noticing that Crowtail and Newtspeck were padding up to the fence, Yellowfang leaped down to meet them, pleased to put an end to the awkward conversation with Hollyflower. As she landed, she spotted a hole at the base of the fence, where one of the strips of wood had rotted away. There was plenty of room for a cat to slip through. Instinctively she sniffed, and froze as she picked up the scent of kittypet.

Fresh . . . she thought. *One or two cats have been through here—and not long ago, either.* There was a mess of tracks around the hole, but the traces were too confused to tell Yellowfang anything useful. She wasn't sure whether she ought to tell the others. *It will only cause trouble . . . but then, we're a border patrol. This is the sort of thing we're looking for.*

Before she could make up her mind, she noticed that Newtspeck had picked up the scent too, raising her head with a suspicious gleam in her eyes. "Kittypets!" she hissed.

Her neck fur bristling, she began searching along the base of the fence, trying to find the scent trail. Crowtail helped her, while Yellowfang stood still, flexing her claws, and Hollyflower watched intently from the top of the fence.

"It's no good," Crowtail snarled eventually. "This StarClan-cursed snow is blotting out the scent."

"But kittypets have definitely been on this side of the fence," Newtspeck meowed, her neck fur still fluffed up and her tail lashing. "Trespassing on *our* territory again. This has to stop!" She crouched, bunched her muscles, and leaped up to the top of the fence beside Hollyflower, where she let out a challenging yowl. "Stay out of our territory, kittypets!"

Yellowfang's paws tingled with frustration. *Why does Newtspeck have to go looking for a fight? Why can't we just leave one another alone?* She wasn't sure why she was so desperate not to encounter the Twolegplace cats, but she felt cold fear deep inside her, as agonizing as Nettlespot's hunger. *We mustn't fight!*

Newtspeck launched herself off the fence and vanished on the other side into the Twoleg garden. Yellowfang heard a hiss of pain from her, and in the same heartbeat felt a sharp stab in her shoulder.

"Newtspeck, what happened?" she called.

"Nothing!" the black-and-ginger she-cat called back. "I'm fine!"

Yellowfang knew that wasn't true. *My shoulder feels like it's on fire!* "We have to make them come back," she meowed to Hollyflower. "There's no point in looking for trouble."

Hollyflower looked doubtful. "We need to teach those kittypets a lesson about invading our territory," she insisted.

Reluctantly Yellowfang scrambled back onto the fence and looked down at Newtspeck. The she-cat was holding one foreleg stiffly, but she said nothing; only the waves of pain flooding over Yellowfang told her that her Clanmate was badly hurt. Crowtail leaped up beside her and dropped down to join Newtspeck in the snow. Her ears twitched and her tail lashed as she gazed around.

"Come out if you dare!" she called. "We'll teach you to trespass on our territory!"

A soft growl broke the silence that followed Crowtail's challenge. Balancing awkwardly on the fence-top, Yellowfang turned to see a huge orange tom appearing around the side of the Twoleg den.

That's Marmalade! she realized, her belly lurching. All her instincts told her to leap down from the fence before he recognized her, but she knew she couldn't abandon her Clanmates, especially when one of them was injured.

Marmalade looked up at Yellowfang with baleful yellow eyes. "What are you doing here again?" he demanded.

"What does he mean, 'again'?" Crowtail's voice was sharp. "Do you know a kittypet?"

Yellowfang didn't know how to reply. "Uh . . . sort of," she admitted. "It's not important. We're just leaving," she assured the ginger tom.

"No, we're not," Newtspeck hissed through her pain, fixing Marmalade with a fierce glare. "We're here to tell you to stay out of our territory."

Marmalade snorted. "I don't understand you wild cats and your so-called territories," he sneered. "We're far freer on this side of the fence, because we can go wherever we want."

Kittypets are free? Yellowfang had never thought of that before. To her dismay, Hollyflower dropped down from the fence to join Newtspeck and Crowtail.

Now she's joining in, Yellowfang thought helplessly. *I just want to get out of here!*

"What do kittypets know about freedom?" Hollyflower hissed. "You don't even catch your own food. Try asking Russetpaw and Boulder where they want to live, and see if they think kittypets are free!"

"Russetpaw? Who's that?" Marmalade asked.

"You knew her as Red," Hollyflower replied.

Marmalade stiffened, his gaze fixed on Hollyflower. "You know where Red and Boulder are?"

"They're part of ShadowClan now." Crowtail's voice was full of triumph. "You won't be seeing them again."

Yellowfang braced her muscles to jump down and help her Clanmates if Marmalade attacked.

But the ginger tom just narrowed his eyes. "I see," he mewed evenly. "Well, I'll let you go back to your *territory* now."

"You're not *letting* us do anything!" Hollyflower retorted, sliding out her claws.

"Stop this!" Yellowfang called desperately from the fence-top. "He's just a fat old kittypet. He's not worth fighting. Leave him alone and get out of there." She tried hard not to flinch as Marmalade turned his gaze onto her. She could almost hear his thoughts: *Fat old kittypet, huh? Come down here and say that!*

"We've shown our strength," Yellowfang persisted. "Now we need to get Newtspeck back to the camp."

"I'm fine!" Newtspeck protested.

"No, you're not," Yellowfang hissed through the stabbing sensation in her shoulder. "Hollyflower, Crowtail, help her over the fence."

"I don't need any help." Newtspeck gave a single lash of her tail and leaped up the fence. Her paws scrabbled at the top and she fell down the other side, collapsing on the ground with a screech.

"You *stupid, stupid* furball!" Yellowfang snapped. She could understand that Newtspeck didn't want to show weakness in front of Marmalade, but the flaring agony in her shoulder told her that the she-cat had made her injury worse.

Newtspeck struggled to get to her paws but she couldn't

put weight on her leg at all, and she slipped back onto her side in the snow. "Mouse dung!" she gasped.

Crowtail and Hollyflower exchanged shocked glances; clearly they hadn't known that Newtspeck was so seriously hurt.

"Come on." Yellowfang worked her shoulder underneath Newtspeck, and with her help the injured she-cat managed to stand. "Let's get you home."

Hollyflower supported her on the other side, and they began struggling back to camp, with Crowtail keeping a lookout behind in case any kittypets tried to follow them. By the time they reached the entrance, Newtspeck was barely conscious, staggering along on three paws and leaning her weight on Yellowfang and Hollyflower.

"Let's get her to Sagewhisker," Yellowfang panted; she was almost as exhausted as Newtspeck through the pain they shared.

As they approached the medicine cat's den, Hollyflower and Crowtail went to report to Stonetooth. Newtspeck collapsed on the moss, her injured leg stretched out.

"What happened?" Sagewhisker asked, bending over to examine her.

"She wrenched her shoulder jumping over a Twoleg fence," Yellowfang replied. Anger still pulsed through her along with the hurt. "And then the mouse-brain had to make it worse by jumping out again."

"I couldn't let you haul me out," Newtspeck murmured through clenched teeth. "Not with that kittypet watching."

"There was no need to go in there in the first place," Yellowfang pointed out.

"It's a bad sprain," Sagewhisker commented, giving the injured leg a sniff. "Yellowfang, fetch me some elder leaves. And give them a good chew," she added, as Yellowfang padded off to the hole where the herbs were kept.

The clean tang of the elder leaves that filled her mouth made Yellowfang feel calmer, and the hurt began to ebb as Sagewhisker plastered the poultice onto Newtspeck's leg.

"Poppy seeds, Yellowfang," Sagewhisker murmured as she applied the chewed-up leaves. "Newtspeck, you'd better sleep here for now. You can go back to your den when you've had a rest."

"Thanks, Sagewhisker," Newtspeck murmured.

Once her Clanmate was licking up the poppy seeds, Yellowfang slipped out of the den. Raggedpelt was pacing up and down outside. He whipped around to face her as she emerged.

"I heard you saw a kittypet today," he meowed. "Did it recognize you?"

Yellowfang blinked. "Yes. It was Marmalade," she admitted. "But he didn't say anything about . . . you know, Hal. There's nothing to worry about."

Raggedpelt obviously didn't agree; his neck fur was bristling and he slid his claws in and out. "I am not a kittypet! This is where I belong!" he hissed as he spun around.

"Hey, wait!" Yellowfang bounded after him. "It's okay. Calm down. Nothing happened."

Raggedpelt flicked his tail as if he were brushing away her

words. "Leave me alone, can't you?" he growled, picking up his pace until he was racing across the camp to vanish into the thorns.

Yellowfang heaved a deep sigh as she stared after him.

"Had a fight with your mate?" Rowanberry bounced up to her, a mischievous look in her eyes.

Yellowfang bit back a snarl. "He's not my mate!" she snapped. "We're just friends."

Rowanberry rolled her eyes. "There's no need to pretend," she meowed. "The whole Clan knows there's something going on between you and Raggedpelt. I think he's kind of cranky, but I guess he's handsome . . ."

Yellowfang had no time for her sister's nonsense. Without replying, she turned her back on Rowanberry and stalked away.

Twilight was gathering in the clearing as Yellowfang returned at the head of a hunting patrol. She dropped her squirrel on the fresh-kill pile and glanced around. The camp was quiet; most of her Clanmates, she guessed, were already settling down to sleep.

Archeye, Rowanberry, and Mousewing, the other members of her patrol, deposited their prey and headed for the warriors' den. Feeling thirsty, Yellowfang padded toward the stream at the edge of the camp, her paws crunching on the snow. The stream was barely a trickle in the ice, and the water was so cold that when she lapped, her tongue felt as though it were burning.

As Yellowfang raised her head and shook droplets from her whiskers, she heard the sound of a cat moving clumsily over twigs. Her ears pricked.

What's that? Apprentices slinking out? Or an elder having trouble walking?

Yellowfang glanced around the edge of the camp, peering through the trees as she tried to work out where the sound was coming from. But before she could locate it, a yowl split the silent night air. Several cats exploded out of the shadows; the thorns and brambles that surrounded the camp crackled as they burst in.

Scorchwind and Amberleaf, on guard by the tunnel entrance, leaped to their paws. "Intruders!" Scorchwind shrieked.

For a heartbeat Yellowfang stood frozen. Then she recognized the muscular ginger tom who led the intruding cats.

It's Marmalade! Great StarClan, these are the Twolegplace cats!

Chapter 15

Screeches battered Yellowfang's ears as warriors charged from their den, flinging themselves on the attackers.

Marmalade halted in the center of the clearing, his amber eyes glaring around. "Boulder! Red!" he yowled. "Where are you? We've come—" His caterwauling was cut off as Finchflight and Mudclaw leaped on top of him and he vanished in a flurry of furious teeth and claws.

Yellowfang raced across the clearing to join her Clanmates, but before she reached them she felt claws digging into her shoulders as a cat landed on her back. She staggered under the weight and almost fell. Twisting her head around, she recognized the fluffy white kittypet, Pixie.

For a moment Yellowfang was so shocked that she couldn't remember any battle moves. Then she reared up on her hind paws and let herself fall backward. Pixie released her and scrambled away to avoid being squashed underneath her. Yellowfang jumped to her paws and sidestepped as the kittypet rushed at her again. Swiping at her with sheathed claws, she knocked the white she-cat over and pinned her down with both forepaws on her chest.

"What's all this about?" she demanded as Pixie writhed beneath her paws, spitting in fury. *She's stronger than I expected,* Yellowfang thought, struggling to hold her down.

"You stole our cats!" Pixie hissed, her green eyes blazing.

"What do you mean?" Yellowfang asked, bewildered.

But there was no answer. With one desperate heave, Pixie flung her off and vanished into the crowd of battling cats. More and more of them were pouring into the clearing, attacking the ShadowClan warriors with teeth and claws. As Yellowfang stared at the heaving, screeching mass, she realized that though her Clanmates were battle-trained, the kittypets had the advantage of surprise.

Will we lose this fight? she wondered, appalled.

She spotted Nutwhisker breaking free from a clawing knot of cats and staring around him with a look of utter shock. "These are kittypets!" he exclaimed.

A rangy gray tabby aimed a blow at him. "We don't all live with housefolk!" he snarled into Nutwhisker's ear. "You aren't the only ones who can hunt down prey."

Before he had finished speaking, Yellowfang was hurtling across the clearing to stand shoulder-to-shoulder with her littermate. The gray tabby took one look at the cats facing him, claws extended, and turned tail, vanishing into the shadows.

"Get out of our camp!" Nutwhisker yowled, racing off in pursuit.

Yellowfang followed, but two more rogues lunged between her and Nutwhisker, knocking her to the ground. All the breath was driven out of her. Half-stunned, she heard the pounding paw steps of another cat and turned to face a new enemy, only to spot Raggedpelt skidding to a halt beside her. He hauled her to her paws with his claws in her scruff.

"Thanks!" she gasped.

Raggedpelt's eyes were haunted, and there was a horrified expression on his face. "What are these cats doing here?" he hissed.

"I think they're looking for Russetpaw and Boulder!" Yellowfang replied. *If Hollyflower and Newtspeck hadn't tried to boast to Marmalade, this wouldn't be happening!*

Raggedpelt opened his jaws to reply, but a loud screech cut him off.

"Help! Over here! The nursery!"

Spinning around, Yellowfang saw Rowanberry and Mousewing in the entrance to the nursery, trying to fight off a whole cluster of Twolegplace cats.

"They're attacking the queens!" Raggedpelt growled as he sprang toward them. "These cats have no honor!"

Yellowfang pelted after him, and the two warriors fell upon the intruders from behind. For several heartbeats Yellowfang struck out blindly, with three or four cats surrounding her; then she and her Clanmates forced the kittypets back into the open, away from the nursery entrance. Yellowfang glimpsed Raggedpelt chasing one of them into the bushes.

A hard blow on her shoulder made her stagger; recovering, she found herself facing Marmalade. The ginger tom aimed another blow at her; Yellowfang ducked and raked her claws across his chest fur. With a snarl of fury Marmalade threw himself on top of her and the two cats grappled together, rolling over on the ground.

"You have no right to keep Red and Boulder here!" Marmalade hissed into Yellowfang's ear.

"But they came of their own accord!" she protested. "They chose to stay!"

Marmalade wasn't paying any attention. Yellowfang knew she had to do something to stop the battle. Wriggling free from the ginger tom, knowing she left tufts of her gray pelt in his claws, she looked around frantically. "Cedarstar!" she yowled, trying to make herself heard above the storm of battle.

She spotted the Clan leader as he buffeted a rogue about the ears; the rogue turned and fled into the darkness at the edge of the camp. Yellowfang rushed across the clearing to intercept Cedarstar before he rejoined the battle.

"Cedarstar!" she panted. "I know what's going on!"

The Clan leader's claws gleamed in the starlight. "What do you mean?" he snapped. Yellowfang guessed that he hadn't heard Marmalade's yowl as he burst into the clearing.

"When we were patrolling yesterday, we told a kittypet that Russetpaw and Boulder are living in ShadowClan. The kittypets think we're keeping them imprisoned. They've come to get them back!"

"That's madness!" Cedarstar roared.

Yellowfang nodded. "I know. But the kittypets don't."

As she spoke, Marmalade staggered up, bleeding from several scratches but still on his paws. "We know Red and Boulder are here," he growled. "Give them to us!"

The Clan leader lashed his tail. "They're not here. They're out on patrol. And they're not prisoners."

Marmalade faced the Clan leader, his neck fur bristling. "So *you* say."

Yellowfang had to admire the big tom's courage. "They won't believe anything unless Russetpaw and Boulder tell them," she meowed to Cedarstar.

The Clan leader let out a snarl of anger and frustration. "Go and find them, then, and bring them back here. I know we can win this fight, but it's better for the Clan if we end it quickly."

Yellowfang dipped her head and dashed off, skirting groups of grappling cats. The patrol wasn't in sight when she emerged from the tunnel, but she knew the direction they would return and bounded off to meet them. Now that she had a moment to think, she was aware of stinging pain all over her body, and realized that she was feeling the wounds of every cat in the battle. Her head clouded with agony, and she blinked to clear it.

We must finish this quickly!

Suddenly new cat scents washed over Yellowfang. Rounding a fallen tree, she skidded to a halt as she saw Raggedpelt, Featherstorm, and Hal facing one another. All three cats were panting and wild-eyed, a terrible tension singing among them.

"Tell me this cat isn't my father," Raggedpelt growled at Featherstorm.

His mother flicked her tail. "He gave up the right to be called that long ago. It was his decision."

Raggedpelt's eyes widened as he stared at Hal. "You knew all along? But when I found you, you didn't say anything!"

Hal shrugged. "You want nothing to do with Twolegplace cats. I want nothing to do with the Clans."

"You have no idea what it was like, growing up without a father." Raggedpelt's words sounded as if he were being choked. "And now I find out that my father was a *kittypet*! Everything my Clanmates taunted me with is true!"

Yellowfang felt her heart tear with sympathy for Raggedpelt, more painful than any wound. She took a pace toward him. "That doesn't matter!" she told him. "Every cat knows that you are a ShadowClan warrior."

Raggedpelt rounded on her, his teeth bared. "Stay out of this," he snarled.

As Yellowfang gazed at him, unable to leave but not knowing what else she could say, the sounds of fighting drifted through the trees, screeches and the crackling of paws through undergrowth growing steadily nearer.

"You should never have come here," Featherstorm snapped at Hal, then bounded away toward the noise of battle.

Raggedpelt turned to his father, stiff-legged with fury, his neck fur bristling and his tail bushed out to twice its size. "Leave now," he ordered. "And never come back."

Hal gave his chest fur a slow, deliberate lick. "You can't tell me what to do, *son*," he drawled.

"I am not your son!" Raggedpelt growled, taking a threatening step forward. "I am a ShadowClan warrior!"

"A warrior with kittypet blood in your veins," Hal taunted

him. "Will your so-called Clanmates ever forget that?"

With a roar of fury Raggedpelt sprang at him; his claws slashed across Hal's throat. Yellowfang felt agony flash across her neck and through all her body, and for a heartbeat the snow-covered forest turned black in her eyes.

When she recovered, panting and blinking, she saw Hal's body lying limp on the ground with a great gush of scarlet blood flowing from his throat, staining the snow. "You killed him!" she gasped, staring in horror.

"He should have left when he had the chance," Raggedpelt snarled.

"But he was your father!" Yellowfang protested.

Raggedpelt turned to face her. Yellowfang could see her own horror reflected in his eyes, but his voice was cold. "He was nothing but a useless kittypet."

Before Yellowfang could say more, new cat scent drifted over her. Russetpaw and Boulder emerged through the trees along with Frogtail and Deerleap.

"What's going on?" Boulder demanded.

"Marmalade and the kittypets are attacking our camp," Yellowfang explained. "They think we're keeping you as prisoners."

As she spoke, Russetpaw spotted Hal's body and bounded forward to stand over him, looking down at him in dismay. "What happened?" she gasped, her voice shaking.

"He tried to attack Yellowfang," Raggedpelt replied. "I had no choice."

Russetpaw and Boulder exchanged a horrified glance.

Yellowfang opened her jaws to contradict Raggedpelt's lie, then picked up his amber glare and knew there was nothing she could say that wouldn't make everything worse.

"But the warrior code says . . ." Boulder began.

"This cat wasn't part of the warrior code," Raggedpelt interrupted. "Now come back to camp and tell the rest of these wretched cats that you don't need rescuing."

He set off toward the camp at a run. Boulder hesitated for a moment, then followed. Frogtail and Deerleap bounded after them.

Russetpaw remained standing over Hal's body, gazing down at him with grief in her eyes.

Yellowfang padded up to her and gave her a gentle nudge. "We have to go."

"He was my father," Russetpaw whispered.

Oh, StarClan. Yellowfang hoped that the young she-cat never learned that Hal was Raggedpelt's father too. *At least there are other broad-shouldered dark tabbies in the Clan who Russetpaw might assume to be Raggedpelt's father.*

Yellowfang gave Russetpaw another nudge and padded beside her until they reached the camp. Looking around, Yellowfang saw that although one or two skirmishes were still going on, most of the kittypets had surrendered. Clan cats stood over them, their flanks heaving and blood dripping from their scratches.

Cedarstar was standing in the center of the clearing. "Here are Russetpaw and Boulder." His eyes gleamed as he beckoned the two young cats with his tail. "Let them step forward."

Russetpaw and Boulder padded up to their Clan leader, a mixture of embarrassment and horror in their faces as they looked around at the battle-torn cats.

Cedarstar angled his ears toward Marmalade. "Tell this cat why you are here," he commanded.

"We wanted to see what life was like in the forest," Boulder began, raising his head confidently. "And we think it's good."

"We chose to stay," Russetpaw added, ducking her head at Marmalade. "They're not keeping us prisoners."

Marmalade's mouth fell open.

Pixie bounded up to his side, her eyes wide with astonishment. "How can you prefer to live with these wild, cruel creatures?" she demanded. "We came to rescue you!"

"Cruel?" There was an edge to Cedarstar's voice. "We aren't the cats who attacked. If you had come here peacefully and *asked*, there would have been no need for bloodshed."

"It was Hal's idea," Marmalade admitted. "He refused to give up on you, Red. Where is he, by the way?" he added, glancing around.

"He's dead," Russetpaw choked out.

Marmalade and Pixie exchanged a horrified glance. Yellowfang heard a gasp from Featherstorm, too. Glancing at her, she saw nothing that suggested grief or shock in her expression, but Yellowfang guessed that the she-cat was not as indifferent as she liked to pretend.

"He had to die," Raggedpelt growled. "He was attacking Yellowfang."

"You may take his body away," Cedarstar told Marmalade.

"Leave our territory and stay out of it. We have treated you gently this time, believe me."

Marmalade let out an angry hiss, but he turned to leave.

Pixie padded up to Russetpaw and Boulder. "If you ever change your mind, you'll always be welcome to come back."

"Thank you," Boulder replied, dipping his head. "But we're warriors now."

Pixie shook her head sadly. "Hal paid for this with his life," she mewed. "And it was all for nothing."

"He was very brave," Russetpaw murmured, her eyes still full of grief. "We won't forget him, I promise."

Yellowfang looked around for Raggedpelt, who had retreated to lurk at the edge of the clearing. *I bet there's one cat who'll try his hardest to forget him,* she thought.

Chapter 16

Yellowfang crept across the marsh, her pads sore from treading on rock-hard mud and ice-rimmed tussocks of grass. Though the snow had melted, the air was still bitterly cold, and Yellowfang's breath puffed out in a cloud. Reeds poked up at the edge of frozen pools, the rattle of their feathery tops the only thing that broke the silence. There was no sound or scent of prey.

A moon had passed since the kittypet attack, and though the Clan cats' wounds had healed, their strength hadn't returned. It seemed as if leaf-bare would go on forever. Every cat was hungry all the time. Yellowfang could feel the bones jutting through her fur, and she couldn't sleep at night because she felt the pangs of hunger in the bellies of her Clanmates.

We hunt all the time, day and night. And we still can't find enough to eat. What's going to happen to us?

She paused, watching Raggedpelt, who was padding along softly a few tail-lengths ahead of her. After a moment he stopped, his ears pricked to listen. Yellowfang slid toward him, following his gaze to a clump of grass about halfway between them. As she drew closer she heard a faint scratching among the brittle stems, and picked up the scent of a shrew.

Raggedpelt signaled to Yellowfang with his tail, then leaped at the clump of grass, swiping it with his forepaws. The shrew panicked and scuttled into the open, heading straight for Yellowfang. She dropped swiftly into the hunter's crouch, but as she pounced one of her hind paws slipped on a patch of ice and she stumbled, landing awkwardly a tail-length away from her prey. Raggedpelt bounded forward, but he was too late. The shrew darted off, taking refuge in a tangle of scrubby thorns.

"Fox dung!" the tabby tom snarled. "Yellowfang, if that's the best you can do, you'd better go back to camp."

"Don't be ridiculous," Yellowfang snapped back at him. "Have you never lost a piece of prey? You know we have to keep hunting."

Raggedpelt snorted, but said no more. As he and Yellowfang turned back toward the trees, Russetpaw and her mentor, Featherstorm, emerged from the shadow of the branches, heading toward the camp. Yellowfang bounded forward to meet them; as she drew closer she saw that Russetpaw was carrying a crow, her ears sticking up from behind a jumble of black feathers.

"You've managed to catch something!" Yellowfang meowed. "That's great! There's not so much as a mouse stirring out on the marshes."

"Russetpaw found it," Featherstorm responded, with an approving look at her apprentice.

Russetpaw's eyes shone with pride, though Yellowfang

noticed that Raggedpelt was bristling with a scowl on his face.

"The Clan will be pleased," Yellowfang mewed, walking away. "We'll see you later." When Featherstorm and her apprentice were out of earshot, she turned to Raggedpelt. "There's nothing wrong with Featherstorm praising Russetpaw. She deserved it."

Raggedpelt sniffed. "That crow was a mangy old thing," he muttered.

Impatience welled up inside Yellowfang and she let it spill over. "I've had enough of the way you always treat Russetpaw like a heap of mouse droppings," she hissed. "It's not her fault that Hal was her father, too. You have to find a way to deal with it. She's not just your Clanmate, she's your sister!"

Raggedpelt halted and stared at her. Too late, Yellowfang remembered that on the night of the battle he had headed for the camp with Boulder before Russetpaw had revealed that she was Hal's daughter.

So? It won't hurt him to face up to the truth.

"Don't ever say that again!" Raggedpelt growled with a lash of his tail. "I have no father. Russetpaw is nothing to me." He turned his back on her, then glanced over his shoulder to add, "You're lucky I was there to defend you when he started to attack. You didn't stand a chance."

Yellowfang felt her neck fur rise in shock. *That's not how it happened!* But she knew there was no point in trying to make Raggedpelt see reason. He was too desperate to distance himself from Twolegplace and the cats who lived there.

Raggedpelt began to stalk away, then stopped, angling his

ears toward a nearby clump of reeds. Easing her way around the stalks, Yellowfang spotted a blackbird pecking at the ground with its back to her. Paw step by paw step she crept up on it, while Raggedpelt edged forward on the other side.

StarClan! Don't let me miss this one. Yellowfang prayed as she dropped into a crouch. Leaping forward, she felt her claws sink into the bird as it fluttered up, then went limp between her paws.

"Great catch!" Raggedpelt exclaimed, padding up. His eyes gleamed; his bad temper had vanished. He bent to sniff the prey, then added, "I wonder when we'll get our first apprentices. We must be ready to be mentors by now."

"Sure we are," Yellowfang responded. "But it might be a while. There's only Cloudkit in the nursery."

Raggedpelt nodded. "I want us to be mentors together." He fixed his warm amber gaze on Yellowfang. "Wouldn't it be great if I was leader and you were my deputy?" He paused, and Yellowfang caught a flash of uncertainty in his eyes. "That is, if you want to be with me," he added.

Yellowfang blinked up at his handsome face and troubled eyes. She wished he could always be open to her like this, that he could curb his temper and his occasional obstinate silences. But what must it have been like, growing up without knowing who his father was? And then to discover that his father was a kittypet who wanted nothing to do with him? If Raggedpelt was angry sometimes, or reluctant to talk, wasn't that understandable? "Of course I want to be with you," she whispered.

Raggedpelt gave her ear a quick lick. "I'm glad. Now let's take your prey back to camp," he mewed.

Several cats clustered around them as Yellowfang dropped her blackbird onto the pitifully small fresh-kill pile.

"Good job, Yellowfang," Deerleap murmured, making Yellowfang feel warm with pride at the praise from her former mentor. A few more cats congratulated her, too, though she noticed that others turned away with disappointed sniffs.

"Just a scrawny blackbird," she heard Foxheart complain. "What use is that to any cat?"

Yellowfang ignored her. Since she had entered the camp a strange feeling was creeping over her: a tingling beneath her pelt, as if she was hot and cold at the same time. *What's the matter with me now?*

Leaving the cats beside the fresh-kill pile, Yellowfang tried to figure out where the feeling was coming from. Her paws carried her to the elders' den; thrusting her head inside she saw Littlebird tossing restlessly in her nest. Her eyes were glazed and she was muttering something under her breath.

Oh, no! I'm picking up Littlebird's fever!

Yellowfang raced across the camp to get Sagewhisker. "Come quickly!" she panted as she slid between the two boulders that formed the entrance to the medicine cat's den. "Littlebird has a fever."

Sagewhisker looked up from where she was counting dock leaves. "Okay, fetch the herbs she needs," she prompted.

"What?" Shock struck Yellowfang like a badger's paw. "Sagewhisker, have you got bees in your brain? I'm not a medicine cat! I'd give Littlebird the wrong thing. I might even kill her!"

Sagewhisker hesitated for a heartbeat more, then shrugged and headed for the holes where she stored her herbs. Yellowfang could see how far down she had to reach to retrieve a few shriveled borage leaves. *The store must be almost empty.* Yellowfang felt her fur bristle with fear. *There are so few herbs left, and it's too cold for fresh plants to grow. What will we do, with our cats starving and getting sick?*

Sagewhisker turned around with her mouth full of herbs. Nodding to Yellowfang, she padded out of the den. As the medicine cat bounded across the clearing, she passed Raggedpelt, who stood in the middle of the camp looking around. Yellowfang trotted over to him.

"There you are!" he exclaimed. "I've been searching everywhere for you. I thought we'd do some battle training with Foxheart and Wolfstep." He flicked his tail toward the two young warriors who were waiting eagerly behind him.

Between her hunger and the sensations of Littlebird's fever, Yellowfang knew she wouldn't be able to concentrate on practicing battle skills. "No, thanks," she replied. "I'm going out hunting again."

"Oh, come on," Raggedpelt insisted. "We hunted all morning."

Anger flared up inside Yellowfang. "Fight moves aren't going to fill our bellies," she growled. "The Clan needs to find food, not prepare for battles that might not even happen! All the other Clans are too busy trying to fill their bellies to have time to attack us."

Raggedpelt took a step back, confusion in his eyes. "I thought you wanted to be the best warrior you can be," he protested. "Let the apprentices hunt. We can't ignore battle training just because they can't find enough for us to eat."

Yellowfang opened her mouth to argue. *Since when has it been the job of the apprentices to feed the entire Clan? Especially now, when there's so little prey to be found.*

"Leave her, Raggedpelt." Foxheart pushed up close to Raggedpelt's shoulder. "I'll get Lizardstripe to come with us."

Raggedpelt nodded; then with a cold look at Yellowfang he turned his back on her and headed across the camp toward the tunnel. For a couple of heartbeats Yellowfang stared after him. *Okay, I understand why he behaves the way he does, but that doesn't mean I have to like it!* With an angry shrug, she went to look for Stonetooth. *I'll ask him to send me on another hunting patrol.*

Yellowfang found the Clan deputy talking to Cedarstar in the leader's den among the roots of the big oak tree. As she padded up, she noticed that both cats looked far older than their seasons. They were as skinny as foxes, their muzzles gray with age, their bodies curled together on the damp moss.

They don't look like the leaders of a strong and powerful Clan. They need newleaf to come, and more prey to fill their bellies.

Pausing at the entrance to the den, Yellowfang dipped her head. Cedarstar roused at the sight of her. "What is it, Yellowfang?"

"I really wanted to speak to Stonetooth," Yellowfang admitted. "Is there a hunting patrol I could join?"

It was Cedarstar who replied, his voice approving. "You're working hard, Yellowfang. Make sure you get something to eat before you go out again."

Stonetooth nodded. "Deerleap is going to lead a patrol with Toadskip and Ashheart," he meowed, angling his ears toward the fresh-kill pile, where the cats he had named were eating hurriedly. "You can go with them."

"Thanks!"

Yellowfang dashed off, reported to Deerleap, and grabbed a rather puny shrew from the fresh-kill pile. She was gulping down the last mouthful when Deerleap led the patrol out through the tunnel. The forest still seemed empty of prey. Toadskip caught a mouse that popped up from some roots almost under his nose, but that was all they saw until the walls of the Twolegplace appeared through the trees.

"I hope we don't go too close," Ashheart murmured; she and Yellowfang had dropped slightly behind the others. "I don't want to meet any kittypets. They were crazy to attack like that!"

"They won't bother us if we stay out of their way," Yellowfang responded. "Especially now that they realize we didn't steal Russetpaw and Boulder."

Ashheart looked unconvinced. "Who knows what kittypets will do? It's not like they have a warrior code." She glanced around, flexing her claws as if she expected a battle-hungry kittypet to explode out of the undergrowth. "What was it like when you had to face that big kittypet tom?" she continued. "Were you really scared? Did Raggedpelt save your life?"

Yellowfang didn't know how to reply. She didn't want to bolster Raggedpelt's lie, but she couldn't give him away to other cats. "I guess . . ." she mumbled. "It all happened so fast."

"The kittypets fought better than I'd expected," Ashheart went on; Yellowfang was relieved that she didn't probe any further into Hal's death. "But it's not like they've had warrior training. Which of our battle moves do you think worked best against them?"

At that moment Yellowfang realized that Deerleap had turned back and was padding toward them.

"We're supposed to be hunting, in case you hadn't noticed," the older she-cat rasped. "And here you are, chattering like a pair of starlings."

"Sorry, Deerleap," Yellowfang mewed.

"I should think so. Yellowfang, you see what you can find in that bramble thicket. Ashheart, try that bracken over there. Honestly, I shouldn't have to split you up like a couple of apprentices before you do any work."

Her pelt hot with shame, Yellowfang headed for the brambles. Parting her jaws to taste the air, she picked up the faint trace of something green and growing. Following the scent trail, Yellowfang came to a piece of bark lying at the edge of the thicket. Turning it over with one paw, she discovered a few stems of coltsfoot, the bright yellow petals just beginning to show in the green buds. The bark and the brambles must have sheltered them from the worst of the icy weather.

Coltsfoot—that's good for coughs, Yellowfang thought with satisfaction. Carefully she nipped off the stems with her teeth and carried them away from the brambles. Looking up, she saw that Toadskip and Deerleap were watching her with puzzled expressions.

"You're supposed to be hunting things we can eat," Toadskip pointed out.

"But Sagewhisker needs these!" Yellowfang protested around the mouthful of stems.

Deerleap nodded. "I suppose you're right. Leave them on the ground now, while you look for prey."

"Sorry, I can't," Yellowfang apologized. "If I put them on the ground they'll wither and freeze. I need to take them back to Sagewhisker right away."

Deerleap and Toadskip exchanged a glance. "For StarClan's sake!" Toadskip muttered.

"You'd better go, then," Deerleap meowed after a moment's pause. "But be as quick as you can, and come right back."

Yellowfang nodded and bounded off in the direction of the camp. Hope soared inside her. *Herbs are beginning to grow again. Newleaf can't be far off!*

As she approached the camp, she spotted Raggedpelt and Foxheart standing with jaws parted as if they were trying to pick up a scent.

Are they hunting after all? Yellowfang wondered, annoyed after Raggedpelt had made such a fuss about battle training.

"I can scent Lizardstripe," Raggedpelt mewed as Yellowfang approached. "I think she's hiding in that hazel thicket."

"You're such a great tracker, Raggedpelt," Foxheart gushed. "Let's see if we can creep up on her without her hearing us."

Side by side the two warriors crept through the grass, only to halt as Yellowfang padded up.

"Herbs?" Raggedpelt asked, staring at Yellowfang's mouthful. "Weren't you supposed to be hunting?"

Yellowfang rested her bundle carefully on one of her paws. "Sagewhisker needs these," she mewed.

Raggedpelt rolled his eyes. "Then Sagewhisker should ask the apprentices to gather them for her, not warriors!"

"It's not like it's hard," Foxheart put in.

"It's a warrior's duty to care for the Clan," Yellowfang snapped. "That means collecting herbs as well as hunting for food and fighting."

"No, it doesn't." Raggedpelt's tail-tip twitched. "You're not a medicine cat, so sick Clanmates are not your responsibility. Any cat would think you didn't want to be a warrior."

"Of course I want to be a warrior," Yellowfang retorted.

"Then let me know when you want to start battle training again," Raggedpelt meowed, brushing past her. "Hey, Lizardstripe, come on out! We know you're in there!"

Yellowfang headed into the camp, wincing at the wall of pain and hunger that hit her as soon as she emerged from the tunnel. *I wish I could tell Raggedpelt how I feel when my Clanmates are in pain. But I know he would never understand.* She sighed. *I didn't ask for this! I just want to be a warrior!*

Chapter 17

Yellowfang woke with a jerk and realized she couldn't breathe. *StarClan, help me!* She scrabbled with her paws, trying to push away the moss that she thought was suffocating her. But her feet closed on empty air. There was no moss on top of her. She opened her eyes and looked around the den. All the other warriors were sleeping, their flanks rising and falling gently as they breathed.

By now, each wheezing gasp of air took a massive effort. Yellowfang stumbled to her paws and staggered out of the den, barely managing to avoid Nutwhisker, who was curled up in his nest. Cold gripped her as she emerged into the clearing, as if claws of ice were sinking deep into her pelt. The stars glittered in a clear, black sky. Nothing stirred in the camp, but Yellowfang could hear the murmuring of voices coming from the elders' den.

Still struggling to breathe, Yellowfang limped across the clearing. As she approached the den, she could hear the same rasping breaths, and Lizardfang's voice meowing, "You can't go on like this, Littlebird. You need Sagewhisker."

Yellowfang glanced into the den and saw Littlebird lying in the moss, her chest heaving as she fought to breathe.

Lizardfang was looking on helplessly while he stroked Littlebird's shoulder with one paw.

"I'll fetch Sagewhisker," Yellowfang meowed.

When Yellowfang reached the medicine cat's den, Sagewhisker was curled up in her nest, so deeply asleep that it took several heartbeats to wake her. Yellowfang guessed that she was exhausted from caring for all the cats who had fallen ill from cold and hunger. Once she roused, she blinked up at Yellowfang in confusion. "Wha'?"

Growing impatient, Yellowfang crossed the den to the holes where the herbs were stored and pushed back the ferns that covered them. The coltsfoot she had gathered two sunrises ago had already been used, but she found a few withered juniper berries at the bottom of one hole.

Snagging a single berry on her claw, Yellowfang took it to Sagewhisker and thrust it under her nose. "Littlebird can't breathe," she told the medicine cat. "This will help, right?"

Sagewhisker nodded wearily. "Call me if there's a problem," she murmured.

Yellowfang blinked, surprised by the medicine cat's confidence in her. *Hey, I'm not your apprentice!* she thought, then shrugged and padded out with the berry.

Lizardfang looked up in alarm when Yellowfang pushed her way back into the elders' den. "Why didn't Sagewhisker come?" he meowed. "Is she okay?"

"She's fine," Yellowfang told him. "I'm just helping out. Come on, Littlebird, Sagewhisker sent you this juniper berry. It'll help you breathe."

Littlebird took the berry from Yellowfang's claw, chewed

feebly, and managed to swallow it. Then she flopped back down and closed her eyes. To Yellowfang's relief the tightness in her own chest began to relax.

"Look, Lizardfang," Yellowfang suggested, "if we build the moss up a bit on this side, Littlebird can be more upright while she rests. It should help her to breathe more easily."

Lizardfang hoisted Littlebird while Yellowfang built up a mound of moss underneath the elder's shoulders. The sick cat let out a sigh; already her breathing was starting to improve. "Thank you," she murmured.

Lizardfang curled up beside Littlebird to keep her warm, and Yellowfang headed back to Sagewhisker's den. Her own breathing had eased along with Littlebird's.

The medicine cat was still awake, and halfway sat up as Yellowfang slipped between the boulders. "How is she?"

"Better," Yellowfang replied. "I don't think you need to see her tonight."

Sagewhisker nodded. "Thanks, Yellowfang. I'll look in on her at dawn."

Thrusting her way back into the warriors' den, Yellowfang noticed that Raggedpelt was awake, his amber eyes glowing in the darkness. "Where have you been?" he whispered.

"Helping Littlebird," Yellowfang responded, weaving her way among the sleeping cats to reach her nest. "She couldn't breathe, so I fetched a juniper berry for her."

Raggedpelt's eyes narrowed. "That's Sagewhisker's responsibility, not yours."

Relieved that he hadn't asked her how she knew Littlebird

needed help, Yellowfang meowed, "I just don't want to let my Clanmates suffer, okay?"

Raggedpelt let out a snort that was half-annoyed, half-amused. "I said we'd be leader and deputy, not leader and medicine cat!"

He beckoned with his tail, and Yellowfang curled up beside him, their pelts pressed together against the cold. *This is good,* Yellowfang thought drowsily as she sank into sleep. *I wish we could always be like this.*

The full moon floated high above the ShadowClan camp. Yellowfang hadn't been chosen to go to the Gathering, but she couldn't sleep until she found out what had happened there. She sat in the warriors' den, paws tucked under her, until she heard the sound of paws racing across the packed earth floor of the camp. Raggedpelt was the first cat to appear, thrusting his broad shoulders through the outer branches of the den.

"Any news?" Yellowfang asked, springing up.

Raggedpelt's expression was grim. "All the Clans looked better fed than us," he reported, his lips drawn back in the beginning of a snarl. "And Heatherstar of WindClan told this ridiculous story about picking up ShadowClan scent on their territory."

"That's completely unfair!" Yellowfang meowed indignantly. "No cat has been over there."

"I know that, but WindClan won't believe it." Raggedpelt gave his whiskers a disgusted twitch. "And that's not all. Featherwhisker, the ThunderClan medicine cat, was asking

Foxheart and Russetpaw some very odd questions."

"What sort of questions?"

"Oh, is everything okay in ShadowClan . . . that sort of thing."

Yellowfang was puzzled. "But Featherwhisker must have seen Sagewhisker at the half-moon . . . why does he need to ask questions at a Gathering? Unless he was concerned that all our warriors look so thin."

Raggedpelt snorted. "Medicine cats should keep their noses where they belong!"

"I'm sure it's nothing to worry about," Yellowfang soothed him, resting her tail-tip on his shoulder.

By now more cats were pushing their way into the den. Foxheart scampered past, her paws scattering moss, with Lizardstripe just behind her. She halted when she saw Yellowfang. "Did you stay behind to go hunting for herbs?" she teased.

"Yeah, it must be really hard to track down leaves," Lizardstripe added.

The two she-cats exchanged a glance and let out a *mrrow* of mocking laughter.

Yellowfang rolled her eyes, but didn't bother to reply.

"You know, they have a point," Raggedpelt mewed when Foxheart and Lizardstripe had gone on to their nests. "You spend too much time helping Sagewhisker when you should be doing warrior duties."

Yellowfang bristled. "You're not Clan leader; don't tell me what to do," she muttered, turning her back on Raggedpelt.

She felt Raggedpelt's warm breath on the back of her neck. "I'm not telling you what to do," he murmured. "It's just a suggestion, okay? You're a warrior, not a medicine cat. I know that, you know that, you just need to make sure that it's clear to the rest of the Clan, too."

Yellowfang stepped forward, dipping her head to the Clan leader. "I'd like to join a hunting patrol, please, Cedarstar."

It was the morning after the Gathering. Cedarstar and Stonetooth were organizing the first patrols. The air was still icy cold but the sun gleamed in a pale blue sky, and somewhere high above, a bird was twittering. Yellowfang's heart rose at the prospect of prey.

"Fine, Yellowfang," Cedarstar meowed. "You can go with Archeye, Wolfstep, and Amberleaf."

As Yellowfang padded over to join them, she caught a look of approval from Raggedpelt. He was leading a different patrol with Blizzardwing, Brackenfoot, and Newtspeck. Though she was disappointed that she couldn't hunt with him, Yellowfang felt satisfied.

At least now he can't say I don't do warrior duties!

Archeye took the lead as the patrol headed out of the camp and across the icebound marsh. "I think we'll try the edges of the Thunderpath today," he announced. "No cat has hunted there for a few days."

Yellowfang and the others followed him until they approached the place where the tunnel led underneath the Thunderpath. The moorland of WindClan swelled on the far side, outlined sharply against the sky.

Archeye halted and stared at the hills with narrowed eyes. "I can't believe what Heatherstar said at the Gathering last night. She accused us of trespassing!"

Amberleaf flicked her tail. "Let her talk. WindClan cats are all meow and no claws."

Yellowfang wasn't so sure. She sniffed around the nearby clumps of grass for any signs of fresh herbs and prey. Suddenly she froze. She had picked up a different scent, not one she had hoped for. "Wait!" she called to the patrol, who were starting to move off again. "We may have intruders. *WindClan* intruders."

Archeye spun around. "Where?"

Yellowfang beckoned with a flick of her ears, and her Clanmates came to sniff the clump where she had detected the WindClan tang.

"That's them all right," Amberleaf confirmed with a brisk nod. "And it's fresh."

"See if you can pick up the trail," Archeye mewed softly. "And keep quiet. They may still be around."

All three cats began to cast back and forth, jaws parted to taste the air. Wolfstep was the first to pick up further traces of the invaders. He signaled with his tail, and Archeye took the lead again, following the scent trail.

How dare those mangy WindClan cats cross our border? Yellowfang thought. *They accuse* us *of trespassing, and then they set their filthy paws on* our *territory!*

The trail led toward the underground tunnels. But

before they reached the edge of the Thunderpath, the patrol rounded a spindly thicket of birches and came upon four cats, confidently surveying ShadowClan territory. Yellowfang recognized them from previous Gatherings: Dawnstripe and the young warrior Talltail, and a tom called Redclaw with his apprentice, Shrewpaw.

"What in the name of StarClan are you doing here?" Archeye demanded.

All four WindClan cats jumped at the sound of his voice, and whipped around to face the ShadowClan patrol. Yellowfang saw a flash of guilt in their faces, which vanished almost at once to be replaced with defiance.

Dawnstripe stepped forward. "ShadowClan scent has been found on WindClan territory," she asserted.

"That's not true!" Archeye's voice was furious, and his neck fur began to bristle.

Yellowfang moved forward to stand at Archeye's shoulder. Out of the corner of her eye, she could see his ribs jutting through his patchy gray coat. *Can't the WindClan cats see we're all so weak that we can barely make it to the edge of our own territory?*

"Even if we had trespassed on your territory," Amberleaf meowed, "which we didn't, that doesn't give you the right to be over here." She took a threatening step toward the intruders. "Get out now."

"Oh, can't we stay and have a look around?" Shrewpaw asked, his voice full of mock disappointment. "These skinny creatures aren't going to be able to stop us."

Without saying a word, Yellowfang and her Clanmates

stepped into a battle line. A lightning bolt of anger sliced through Yellowfang. *ShadowClan is strong! How dare WindClan cats talk to us like this?*

"Look," Archeye began, "you know you're in the wrong. Leave now, and we can avoid a fight."

The WindClan cats didn't move. Yellowfang felt tension tingling through her body from her ears to tail-tip, and she flexed her claws.

"And if we don't?" Redclaw sneered. "Are you going to eat us?"

Archeye let out a screech and leaped straight at the WindClan tom. The rest of the cats were no more than a heartbeat behind. But as the two toms clashed, Yellowfang felt a jolt of pain deep in her bones; she staggered, almost losing her balance. Talltail loomed over her, and Yellowfang struggled to get into the right position to defend herself. Beside her she caught a glimpse of Amberleaf with blood welling from a deep scratch along her flank. Then Dawnstripe leaped at her again with blood on her claws and Yellowfang shrieked with pain. She collapsed on the ground, her mind filled with visions of fur being shredded and blood gurgling in her throat, choking her. She felt Talltail's claws slicing through her pelt to the flesh below, but she could only beat her paws at him feebly as if she were a frightened kit.

"Back off, Talltail." Dawnstripe's voice reached Yellowfang through the fog of pain. "We've done enough. That will teach these mangy cats not to trespass on WindClan territory."

Yellowfang was too battered to speak. Beyond the pain,

all she could think was that the WindClan cats were going to get away with invading ShadowClan. Then the thundering of paws beat at her ears, getting louder and louder. She was conscious of cats leaping past her, and caught a whiff of Raggedpelt's scent. *The other patrol is here!* she realized, beginning to shake with relief. Blinking away the darkness that was trying to suck her away, Yellowfang raised her head to see Raggedpelt facing the WindClan cats.

"Get out!" he snarled. "If you think you can come here and attack our cats, you can think again. My claws will show you that you're wrong."

"Easy enough to say," Dawnstripe growled.

But Yellowfang saw that the WindClan cats had suffered injuries too; there was a patch of fur missing from Dawnstripe's shoulder, while both Shrewpaw and Redclaw were bleeding. Obviously they were in no mood for another fight.

"Don't you dare set paw on our territory again." Redclaw thrust out his neck so he was nose-to-nose with Raggedpelt. "Or you'll get more of the same."

Raggedpelt let out a contemptuous snort. "You terrify me."

Redclaw's only response was a glare. Then the WindClan cats were drawing back, heading for the Thunderpath and the tunnel that would lead them back to their own territory.

Yellowfang let her head rest on the ground again. She could feel blood pulsing out of her wounds, as well as the agony of every other cat's injuries. She was aware of Raggedpelt bending over her, and felt his tongue rasping warmly over her ears.

"Let's get you back to camp," he mewed.

"No!" Yellowfang muttered. "Help Amberleaf first. She's badly scratched."

She felt Raggedpelt's nose touch her ear, and his voice was unusually gentle. "Stupid furball, stop worrying about every other cat for once."

With Raggedpelt on one side and Brackenfoot on the other, Yellowfang managed to stand and stagger back to camp. As she and the other cats emerged into the clearing, their Clanmates rushed out, letting out yowls of shock and distress when they saw how badly the patrol was injured.

Brightflower rushed over to Yellowfang. "What happened?" she asked, her eyes wide with distress. "Oh, Yellowfang . . . Come straight to Sagewhisker and have those wounds looked at."

She paced beside Yellowfang as Raggedpelt and Brackenfoot supported her to the medicine cat's den. Archeye limped off with Wolfstep to report to Cedarstar.

Some cat had warned Sagewhisker, who was already gathering cobwebs to stop the bleeding. She crouched down beside Yellowfang, telling Brightflower to go with Amberleaf to the warriors' den. "Help Amberleaf clean up those scratches," she instructed. "I'll be over to see her as soon as I've dealt with Yellowfang."

The other cats left, and Sagewhisker crouched down beside Yellowfang. "It's worse this time, isn't it?" she prompted.

Yellowfang looked up at her and nodded.

Sagewhisker's eyes narrowed as if she was thinking. "This time you're not just feeling the pain of other cats," she mewed as she plastered cobweb over Yellowfang's wounds. She ran her paw lightly over the scratches on Yellowfang's shoulder. "You could easily have defended yourself from this kind of injury, but you've been badly hurt because you couldn't bring yourself to fight. You know too much about pain to inflict it on other cats. And that makes it impossible for you to be a warrior." She paused, and Yellowfang was startled by the sympathy in her eyes.

"It's time to face your destiny," Sagewhisker announced. "You have to be a medicine cat."

CHAPTER 18

The next half-moon dragged by, slow as a snail. Yellowfang remained in Sagewhisker's den, gradually recovering from the battle with WindClan. Sometimes she thought her wounds would never heal. She longed to be out in the forest, hunting for her Clan, but she felt shaky every time she rose to her paws. And she couldn't forget what Sagewhisker had said to her when she came back from the fight.

You have to be a medicine cat. . . .

She was stretching her back one morning, longing for her strength to return, when Sagewhisker slipped into the den with a worried look on her face.

"What's the matter?" Yellowfang asked.

Sagewhisker twitched her ears. "It's Nettlespot. Her milk is drying up again. Poolcloud is hunting for her, but there's so little prey in this weather, and when Poolcloud does catch something, Nettlespot doesn't seem to want it."

"That's not good," Yellowfang commented. "She'll get weaker if she won't eat."

Sagewhisker nodded. "Find me something to build up her appetite, will you?"

Yellowfang headed for the stores. "Sorrel should be good for that," she murmured, half to herself, remembering how Sagewhisker had once used it for Lizardfang when the elder refused to eat. She went to uncover the hole where the herb was kept, reached down, and brought up a few shriveled leaves, which she held out to Sagewhisker.

"Thanks," the medicine cat meowed. Giving Yellowfang's wounds a sniff, she added, "Those are almost healed. You'll be well enough to attend Russetpaw's and Boulder's warrior ceremony."

"They're being made warriors?" Yellowfang exclaimed. "Have they passed their final assessment?"

Sagewhisker nodded. "Yesterday."

"So much has happened since I've been stuck in here!" Yellowfang sighed.

Sagewhisker took the herbs from her and shot her a sharp glance. "It's only the medicine den, not the far side of the moon," she pointed out dryly. "There are worse places to be, and often it's the best place to know what's happening in every corner of the camp."

Before Yellowfang could respond, Raggedpelt ducked in between the boulders. Yellowfang let out a pleased purr at the sight of him. He had visited her every day since the battle, always asking Sagewhisker when she could return to warrior duties.

"She can try her legs outside the camp today," the medicine cat announced, forestalling the inevitable question before leaving the den with the sorrel leaves for Nettlespot.

Raggedpelt's eyes gleamed. "Great! Yellowfang, why don't we walk to the big oak tree?"

Cedarstar's voice outside interrupted them. "Let all cats old enough to catch their own prey join here beneath the Clanrock for a meeting!"

"It must be time for Russetpaw's and Boulder's warrior ceremony," Yellowfang meowed.

Raggedpelt narrowed his eyes, but he said nothing. The rest of the Clan was already gathering in the clearing. Boulder and Russetpaw stood at the front, near the base of the Clanrock. Their heads were raised, although they both looked nervous. Their mentors, Featherstorm and Mousewing, sat side by side close by.

Cedarstar signaled with his tail for silence. "These two cats," he began, "came to us from the Twolegplace. At first many of us were afraid that they would not fit into Clan life. I'm pleased to say that we were wrong. Featherstorm, has Russetpaw learned the ways of the Clan and proven herself worthy of becoming a warrior?"

Featherstorm dipped her head. "She has."

"And Mousewing, can you say the same of Boulder?"

"He is a true ShadowClan cat," Mousewing responded.

Both apprentices seemed to swell with pride. Cedarstar leaped down from the Clanrock to stand in front of them. "I, Cedarstar, call upon my warrior ancestors to look down upon these apprentices," the Clan leader began. "They have trained hard to understand the ways of your noble code, and I commend them to you as warriors in their turn. Russetpaw,

Boulder, do you promise to uphold the warrior code and to protect and defend this Clan, even at the cost of your own life?"

"I do," Boulder meowed; his voice carried strongly to the rest of the Clan.

"I do," Russetpaw vowed more quietly.

"Then by the powers of StarClan," Cedarstar continued, "I give you your warrior names. Russetpaw, from this moment you will be known as Russetfur. StarClan honors your loyalty and courage, and we welcome you as a full warrior of ShadowClan."

He laid his muzzle on the top of Russetfur's head, and Russetfur bent to lick his shoulder.

Then Cedarstar turned to Boulder. "I know that you don't wish to change your name," he mewed. "StarClan will see you are a warrior by what you do, rather than what you are called. They honor your bravery and determination, and we welcome you as a full warrior of ShadowClan."

Loud yowls of congratulation burst from the Clan. The two newcomers, regarded with such suspicion to begin with, had clearly earned their popularity among their Clanmates.

"Russetfur! Boulder! Russetfur! Boulder!"

But Raggedpelt didn't join in. He stood watching with his jaws firmly closed and a look of grim disapproval in his eyes. Yellowfang tried to yowl twice as loud to make up for his silence, knowing that there was no point in challenging him about it.

"How about that walk?" Raggedpelt meowed when the

ceremony was over and the cats split up to go about their duties. "Maybe we can pick up some prey on the way."

"Fine," Yellowfang replied, falling into step beside him. "Though I'm not sure I'll make it as far as the big oak."

Her wounds still felt sore, and her legs were weak from lack of exercise, but it was good to take in long breaths of cold, fresh air, and to see something other than the walls of the medicine cat's den.

"We must get you back into battle training," Raggedpelt decided as they padded through the forest. "Then the next time WindClan attacks, you'll be better prepared. I've been thinking about some new fighting moves . . ."

Yellowfang listened with a sinking feeling in her belly while he described his ideas to improve her skills.

"Well? What do you think?" Raggedpelt prompted when he had finished.

"I—I'm not fully healed yet." Yellowfang sought desperately for excuses. "Maybe in another quarter moon . . ."

Raggedpelt halted, his whiskers twitching. "Warriors have to be strong at all times!" he reminded. "You only feel weak because you've been sitting in a nest for too long."

Yellowfang bowed her head. "Yes, you're probably right."

By the time she and Raggedpelt returned to camp, Yellowfang was worn out. Heading for the medicine cat's den, she met Sagewhisker on her way out.

"It's the night of the half-moon," Sagewhisker meowed. "I'm going to the Moonstone to meet the other medicine cats."

"I hope all goes well," Yellowfang told her. She thought

about the way ThunderClan's medicine cat had been asking questions about ShadowClan at the last Gathering, and wondered if Featherwhisker would quiz Sagewhisker as well.

"I'm sure it will be fine," Sagewhisker replied. "Yellowfang, I want you to stay in my den for one more night. You can go back to the warriors' den tomorrow."

"Okay," Yellowfang agreed.

Raggedpelt touched his nose to her shoulder. "Let's eat first," he suggested.

After she had shared a vole with him, Yellowfang retreated to her nest in Sagewhisker's den. Her head felt fuzzy with tiredness, and as soon as she curled up in the moss she sank deeply into sleep. She woke in darkness to the sound of a startled meow and a sharp blow in her ribs as a cat tripped over her.

"Sorry, Yellowfang. I forgot you were there."

It was Poolcloud; Yellowfang made out her pale pelt in the light of the half-moon and smelled fear on her fur.

"What's the matter?" she asked.

"It's Cloudkit," Poolcloud replied anxiously. "He keeps vomiting; he must have eaten something bad when Nettlespot wasn't watching. I came to look for some herbs that will help him."

The wrong herb might kill the poor little scrap, Yellowfang thought, heaving herself out of her nest. "I'll see if I can find you something," she mewed.

Not yarrow, she decided as she padded over to the herb stores. *That will make him sicker. What we need is willow.*

When she poked a paw down the hole where the willow

leaves were kept, she found that only a tiny fragment was left. "There's not much here," she told Poolcloud. "But it's probably enough for a tiny kit like Cloudkit."

Poolcloud nodded, flustered. "Whatever you think is best, Yellowfang."

Yellowfang led the way out of the den with the scrap of leaf in her jaws. A sour smell of vomit hit her in the throat as she entered the nursery. In the dim light she made out Nettlespot crouched over Cloudkit, who was stretched out in the moss, his fur dark and clumped with sweat. As Yellowfang approached his belly heaved and he started retching, but nothing came out of his parted jaws.

"There's nothing left inside him," Poolcloud murmured. "Poor little mite!"

Nettlespot looked up as the two she-cats entered. "Please, you have to fetch Sagewhisker!" she begged. "I lost his sister, and I can't bear to lose this one as well."

"Sagewhisker has gone to the Moonstone. I've brought something to treat him with," Yellowfang meowed, setting the willow leaf down in front of Cloudkit.

"What are you doing?" Nettlespot reached out and blocked Yellowfang with one paw. "You're not a medicine cat. Leave him alone! You might make him worse!"

"It's okay, Nettlespot," Poolcloud mewed gently, resting her tail-tip on the distraught queen's shoulder. "Yellowfang knows which herb to use, and Sagewhisker isn't here, so we don't have a choice."

Nettlespot hesitated for a moment and then drew back,

letting Yellowfang get close to her kit. She watched with wide, worried eyes as Yellowfang chewed up the willow and carefully pushed the pulp into Cloudkit's mouth.

Cloudkit let out a pitiful mewling sound. "Yuck!"

"It's okay," Yellowfang comforted him, massaging his throat with one paw until she was sure he had swallowed the leaf. "It tastes nasty but it will make you feel better soon. Poolcloud, will you get me some moss soaked in water?"

The gray-and-white she-cat gave a swift nod and vanished from the den. She was back more quickly than Yellowfang could have hoped, carrying a dripping bunch of moss in her jaws. She brought it to Cloudkit, who sucked in the water eagerly. Yellowfang thought that he was already looking a little livelier. She tore off part of the wet moss and used it to clean up his face and ears. Not sure what else to do, she bent down toward the kit, pressing one of her ears against his belly; she could hear a churning sound, almost like water falling into a pool.

"That's right," she told him. "Keep drinking as much as you can."

Nettlespot had watched every movement Yellowfang made, like a hawk about to swoop on its prey. Yellowfang could feel her tension, and knew that she would lash out if anything went wrong. But Cloudkit was relaxing now, blinking up at his mother.

"Want milk," he mewed.

Nettlespot lay on her side and began drawing him closer to her with her tail.

Yellowfang thought fast. "No, don't do that," she meowed. "Keep him on water for tonight, to give his belly a rest."

Cloudkit let out a mew of protest, and Nettlespot glared at Yellowfang, then reluctantly nodded. "But only until dawn, when Sagewhisker comes back," she added.

Yellowfang clawed away the vomit-soaked bedding, and Poolcloud brought more from the far side of the nursery before going out again to fetch another bundle of wet moss. Once Nettlespot and Cloudkit were settled comfortably, Yellowfang left.

"Thank you," Poolcloud mewed, following her out of the nursery. "You were brave to step in and help. I'm sure Cloudkit will be fine until Sagewhisker comes back."

"I hope so," Yellowfang muttered, stumbling back to the medicine cat's den and collapsing into her nest.

Hardly a heartbeat seemed to pass before she was woken again by a cat prodding her in the ribs. She opened her eyes to see Poolcloud bending over her.

"Is it Cloudkit?" she asked, springing to her paws. "Is he worse?"

"No, he's fine," Poolcloud reassured her. "He slept through the night, and now he's wriggling around like a fox in a fit, wailing for milk. Nettlespot didn't give him any," she added. "She's keeping him on water, just like you said."

Yellowfang winced. *Don't listen to my advice. I'm not a medicine cat!*

She followed Poolcloud across the camp to the nursery. The dawn sky was milky pale above the camp, and a fresh breeze was blowing, ruffling Yellowfang's thick gray fur. Nettlespot was still lying in her nest, while Cloudkit jumped up and down beside her in the moss.

"I'm *hungry*!" he complained. "Why can't I have milk? I was sick *yesterday*, not today!"

"He's much better," Nettlespot meowed, with a nod to Yellowfang. Her eyes glowed as she gazed at her active kit.

Suddenly the light from the entrance to the nursery was cut off; Yellowfang glanced around to see Sagewhisker looking in.

"What's this I hear about Cloudkit?" she mewed. "He looks fine to me."

"He's better now," Nettlespot replied. "But he was so sick last night. I was scared for him."

"I gave him willow, and told Nettlespot to keep him on water overnight," Yellowfang explained a little nervously.

"And I'm *hungry*!" Cloudkit repeated.

Sagewhisker let out a soft *mrrow* of sympathy. "Let him feed for a short while," she instructed Nettlespot. "But Yellowfang was right to only allow him to have water until his belly had settled."

After Sagewhisker had examined Cloudkit and left him peacefully suckling, she led Yellowfang back to her den. "You did well," she told her. "Without you, Cloudkit might not have made it until I got back."

Yellowfang shrugged. "Well, I'm bound to have picked up something about herbs, living in here for so long."

Sagewhisker faced her with a look of gentle determination.

"Don't you think you should stop avoiding the real issue?" she pressed. "Yellowfang, your destiny is to be a medicine cat. Are you ready to accept that?"

Yellowfang felt as if the ground underneath her paws was giving way. "I'm a warrior!" she protested. "I'm too old to become an apprentice again."

"Nonsense," Sagewhisker mewed briskly. "You'll be a better medicine cat for having had extra experience. You know exactly what it's like to take part in a fight, and which wounds hurt the most. You have a good memory for herbs, too—you proved that when you took the willow to Cloudkit. And you have the courage to act on your instincts."

With every word the medicine cat spoke, Yellowfang grew more and more reluctant. *I'm* not *going to do this. She can't make me!* "You only think I should train with you because I can tell you when cats are in pain!" she blurted out.

Sagewhisker gazed seriously at Yellowfang. "You have an ability I've never come across before," she meowed. "I don't know of any other cats, even medicine cats, who can feel pain in others the way you do. It has been given to you for a reason, and I can only think it means that you should become a medicine cat yourself."

Yellowfang was startled by the somber note in Sagewhisker's voice; it made her feel uneasy. "I didn't ask for this," she whispered.

"None of us ask for our destinies," Sagewhisker pointed out. "Only StarClan knows the reason behind the paths we must walk."

"I—I need time to think about it."

"No!" Sagewhisker's voice was unexpectedly forceful. "You've had enough time! Have the courage to do this. I will help you every step of the way, but you can't keep hiding from it. We must start now, because I won't be here forever."

Yellowfang felt a sudden chill around her heart. *Sagewhisker is getting old, and she's never had an apprentice. What would ShadowClan do without a medicine cat?*

Right from being a kit, Yellowfang had wanted to be the best warrior she could, to serve her Clan. Now she had to face the fact that she might serve her Clan better by turning her paws onto another path.

"Okay." The one word took an enormous effort, and her voice shook as she went on. "If Cedarstar agrees, I will become your apprentice."

"Thank you," Sagewhisker meowed. "I'll speak to Cedarstar now." The old she-cat looked shrewdly at Yellowfang. "You should go and tell Raggedpelt, don't you think? Things are going to be very different now."

Yellowfang felt a hollow place in her belly, and a pain worse than the pangs of hunger. She hadn't thought about what effect this would have on her future with Raggedpelt. Dipping her head to Sagewhisker, Yellowfang padded out of the den. Her fur burned with awkwardness as she went looking for her mate. He wasn't in the camp, but when she headed for the training place she heard his voice raised in a savage yowl, and Crowtail's voice responding in protest. "Hey, watch it! You're not fighting WindClan cats now!"

Yellowfang reached the clearing to see Raggedpelt and Crowtail facing each other, their chests heaving and their tails lashing. "Sorry to interrupt," she called. "Crowtail, I need to talk to Raggedpelt."

The black tabby she-cat relaxed. "Okay," she puffed. "We're just about finished here anyway. That last backflip and twist worked really well, Raggedpelt." With a nod to him she headed back toward the camp.

The tabby tom bounded over to Yellowfang; she could see the excitement from the practice was still surging through him. "Are you coming back to warrior duties?" he demanded.

"No." Yellowfang gazed at him, realizing all over again how much he meant to her. The words stuck in her throat like a piece of old crow. *I have to end everything—and I've never been less sure about a decision in my life.* "I'm going to become Sagewhisker's apprentice," she whispered. "I'm so sorry."

Raggedpelt stared at her. "Not funny," he meowed.

"I'm not joking."

The next heartbeat of shocked silence seemed to stretch out for a moon. Then Raggedpelt threw back his head and sent a furious yowl into the leaf-bare trees. "Is it because you're a coward?" he snarled. "Did the fight with WindClan scare you too much?"

"Never!" Yellowfang flashed back at him. "I just cannot inflict pain on other cats, not anymore. Sagewhisker says this is my destiny."

"You'll lose me as well as your life as a warrior," Raggedpelt reminded her. "I thought you cared! I thought you wanted to spend your life with me. I—I even thought we might have kits one day."

"I thought the same," Yellowfang mewed, feeling her heart break. "I care for you so much! But I don't have a choice."

"You always have a choice," Raggedpelt growled, turning his back on her. "And I thought you had chosen me."

Chapter 19

"Are you sure about this, Yellowfang?"

Yellowfang shifted on the leaves that covered the floor of Cedarstar's den. The Clan leader had summoned her there as soon as she returned from talking to Raggedpelt.

"I want to be certain that you have thought through this decision," Cedarstar went on. "I need to know that you haven't been scared by the WindClan skirmish, or troubled by the hunger. This happens every time leaf-bare is longer and colder than usual, and even medicine cats don't have the power to feed the Clan." His tone was unexpectedly kind. "Sagewhisker believes this is your destiny," he added. "Do you believe that, too?"

Yellowfang nodded. "I've thought hard about this, Cedarstar, and I truly believe it's the path I'm meant to walk." She hoped that she wouldn't have to talk about the way she shared pain with every cat in the Clan.

To her relief, Cedarstar said nothing about that. "I'm pleased that Sagewhisker has found an apprentice," he meowed. "And you must never feel your time and training as a warrior was wasted. You'll be in a better position to understand how quickly warriors want to heal!" His warm gaze rested on her. "Good luck to you, Yellowfang. I know Sagewhisker will be an excellent mentor."

Dipping her head to the Clan leader, Yellowfang rose and left the den. Cedarstar followed her out, leaping onto the Clanrock and yowling a summons to the Clan. Yellowfang stood at the base of the rock, feeling as if the gaze of every cat was fixed on her as they emerged from their dens with murmurs of surprise at the unexpected meeting. Sagewhisker came to sit right at the front; Yellowfang thought she looked pleased but exhausted, like a cat who had just fought fiercely and won a battle.

"I have good news for the Clan," Cedarstar announced when all the cats were assembled. "Yellowfang will be Sagewhisker's apprentice, and ShadowClan's next medicine cat."

Utter silence greeted his announcement. Yellowfang's embarrassment grew; she longed to slink away from all the attention. She had spotted Raggedpelt at the back of the crowd, and she could feel the heat of his glare even from there.

I wish I could tell him that my feelings for him haven't gone away. But I must follow the code of the medicine cats now, and that means I can never have a mate. The whole Clan must mean as much to me as my own kits would.

Her gaze traveled over her Clanmates, old and young, all of them staring at her. The ground seemed to dip underneath her. Then Brightflower sprang to her paws and bounded up to her, closely followed by Brackenfoot. "This is wonderful!" Brightflower exclaimed, pressing her muzzle against Yellowfang's shoulder. "The next medicine cat—what an honor!"

"Congratulations," Brackenfoot added, dipping his head. "I know you'll do very well."

Nutwhisker and Rowanberry pushed their way through the cats to reach Yellowfang's side. Nutwhisker blinked at her with a mixture of wonder and fear in his eyes. "Wow, you'll be talking to StarClan!" he breathed.

Rowanberry looked hurt as she brushed pelts with her sister. "You were my best friend!" she mewed.

"I'll still be here," Yellowfang reminded her. "We can still be friends."

Rowanberry shook her head. "It won't be the same."

Yellowfang felt a wave of loneliness as she realized that her relationship with Raggedpelt wasn't all that she had lost. But Sagewhisker's paw tapped her on the shoulder, giving her no time to dwell on what had changed.

"Come on," the medicine cat meowed. "We have work to do."

She led the way back to her den. Yellowfang sat down in front of her, feeling rather small and apprehensive. *There's so much I don't know!*

"Your first task," Sagewhisker began, "must be to control your feelings when other cats are sick and in pain."

Yellowfang blinked in surprise. *I thought I had to do this* because *I have these feelings!*

"I can't be much help," Sagewhisker went on, "because I don't know what you actually experience, but is there any way you can block the pain coming from outside?"

Yellowfang thought hard. "It's hard to know when it's not actually happening," she explained. "But I think I might be able to shut it out if I focus on myself—that I'm healthy, I'm not in pain, and I can treat this cat's symptoms."

Sagewhisker nodded. "That sounds good. We can't test it until there is a cat in pain in the Clan, but you should practice focusing on yourself. See if you can limit your feelings to your own body."

"I'll try." *But that's like asking me to concentrate on breathing. I don't think about it; it just happens!*

"Good," Sagewhisker mewed. "Now, I want you to clear out the herb store and discard any dead leaves. You can identify what we have and when it would be used, and work out what we need to find in the forest."

That's a huge *job,* Yellowfang thought in alarm.

"But before that," Sagewhisker went on, "my nest needs more moss, and your nest needs sorting out now that you're going to sleep here permanently."

Yellowfang stared at her mentor. "Those are apprentice tasks!" she objected.

"And you're an apprentice," Sagewhisker retorted. "I'm going to see how Nettlespot and Cloudkit are, so you can get on with the bedding." Not waiting for a reply, she whisked out of the den.

Yellowfang clawed at the old nests in a mutinous daze, dragging them out into the clearing in the sharp, frosty sun that gave no warmth. As she bundled up the moss and bracken she heard a cat cough behind her, and glanced over her shoulder to see Foxheart.

"That bedding is *so* dusty!" the ginger warrior exclaimed with another exaggerated cough. "Can't you do that somewhere else where it won't bother the warriors?"

Yellowfang tried to ignore her, but Foxheart hadn't finished taunting her. "That's *such* a boring job!" she went on with false sympathy. "I wouldn't go back to being an apprentice, no way! Will you have to check the elders for ticks, too?" When Yellowfang didn't reply, she added, "After all, there are no warrior apprentices in the Clan now. Wow, you are going to be busy!" She flicked her tail at Yellowfang and ran off.

Burning with indignation, Yellowfang dragged the old bedding out into the forest, where she shoved it under a clump of brambles. As she stumbled around in the undergrowth, collecting fresh moss and dried bracken, she felt more and more resentful.

Sagewhisker just wanted someone to do all her dirty work! I never thought my destiny would include this kind of thing! I hope StarClan has a word with Sagewhisker and makes her treat me with more respect!

Puffing under her load of new bedding, Yellowfang returned to camp. Her heart sank when she spotted Lizardstripe standing near the fresh-kill pile.

"Hey, Yellowfang!" the tabby warrior called out to her. "Could you clean out my nest, too? I'd like some more feathers in it, please. And I think the elders would like some fresh-kill brought to them."

Yellowfang was too tired and cross to answer. She tried to stalk past with her head held high even though she was carrying such a huge bundle. Then she spotted Stonetooth standing outside the warriors' den.

"Lizardstripe, what are you doing?" he called, his voice annoyed. "You're supposed to be on a hunting patrol. Frogtail is waiting for you."

With a hiss of annoyance, Lizardstripe bounded off.

Stonetooth padded up to Yellowfang. "You're doing great," he meowed. "Don't worry, these mouse-brained warriors will get used to this in a couple of days, when something else catches their attention." He let out a rasping purr. "I think you'll make a fine medicine cat, Yellowfang. And remember this—when your apprenticeship is over, cats like Foxheart and Lizardstripe will be coming to you for help."

Yellowfang felt soothed by the deputy's kind tone and the twinkle in his eyes. "Thanks, Stonetooth," she mumbled, struggling on with her burden toward the medicine cat's den.

When she had arranged the bedding into two cozy nests, Yellowfang sat down to take a breath. The huge decision she had made began to sink in. This would be her life from now on. She would be separate from her Clanmates, isolated by her knowledge and her connection with StarClan, and yet she would be the cat they would come to first if they were sick or injured. She began to look around the den, really noticing it for the first time and wondering if there was anything she might want to change. Her gaze traveled over the herb stores. *I wonder if we could make a hollow somewhere to store moss for soaking. That would be much quicker than going outside the camp. And we could keep the cobwebs dry if we hung them on the thorns over there.*

"Oh, StarClan," she whispered, "if you can hear me, I think I'm okay with this. I can be a medicine cat, if that is what you want."

For a heartbeat, she felt that cats with herb-scented pelts were brushing against her, receiving her into the long line of medicine cats who had cared for her Clan for season upon season.

Paw steps sounded behind her as Sagewhisker bustled back into the den. "What are you doing?" she scolded. "Why haven't you got the herbs out yet?"

"I was just about to," Yellowfang defended herself.

"Well, you need to work faster."

Biting back a sharp retort, Yellowfang padded over to the herb stores. With Sagewhisker looking on, she began pulling out the herbs and sorting them into piles.

"No, that's borage," Sagewhisker corrected her. "It goes with the other herbs for fever, like dandelion."

"Okay." Yellowfang moved the leaves from one pile to another.

"And be a bit gentler with them," Sagewhisker warned. "Most of this stuff is so dry, it'll fall apart if you go at it with rough paws."

Yellowfang's paws tingled with a mixture of annoyance and embarrassment. She went on sorting herbs, acutely aware of Sagewhisker's alert gaze.

"How would you use those daisy leaves for back pain?" Sagewhisker asked after a while.

"Er . . . give them to the cat to eat, and—"

"No!" Sagewhisker interrupted. "Chew them up and make them into a poultice, then fasten it on with cobwebs."

Yellowfang's irritation spilled over. "Stop rushing me!" she snapped. "I'll learn, but you have to give me a chance."

Sagewhisker let out a snort, but Yellowfang was convinced she looked a little guilty. "I thought you knew more than that," Sagewhisker muttered.

"How can I?" Yellowfang meowed. "I'm a *warrior.* I can feel when cats are in pain, but I don't know how to make them better. I only knew about the willow leaf because I saw you give one to Lizardfang once when he was vomiting."

Sagewhisker nodded. "Okay, let's start again. And we'll focus on herbs that relieve pain, before we think about herbs that cure infection or give strength or stop coughing."

Yellowfang's head whirled. *There's so much to learn! Warrior training was much easier than this!*

The half-moon hung in the sky like a silver feather as Yellowfang followed Sagewhisker into the hills toward Highstones. Her belly churned with nervousness as she remembered the last time she visited the Moonstone, with Deerleap.

I had such dreadful dreams there . . . oh, StarClan, please don't make me go through that again!

She felt nervous in a different way as she and her mentor approached Mothermouth and she saw the other medicine cats waiting outside. Her pads prickled with apprehension; what would they say to her?

As she and Sagewhisker plodded up the final slope, a

graceful white she-cat with black spots on her pelt bounded forward to meet them. Her blue gaze rested on Yellowfang with friendly interest. "Greetings, Sagewhisker," she mewed. "Don't tell me you've found an apprentice at last!"

Sagewhisker shot a proud glance at Yellowfang. "I have, thank StarClan. This is Yellowfang."

The white she-cat gave Yellowfang a nod of welcome. "I'm Brambleberry, RiverClan's medicine cat," she told her. "Come and meet the others."

Yellowfang padded beside Brambleberry toward the gaping hole in the hillside, while Sagewhisker dropped back a pace. Her gaze traveled over the other three medicine cats. Two of them stood close together: an old speckled gray tom whose pale blue gaze drifted over her without interest, and a younger silver-pelted tom with a plumy tail.

I saw him once at a Gathering, talking to Sagewhisker, Yellowfang remembered.

"This is Yellowfang," Brambleberry announced as they approached the others.

"My new apprentice," Sagewhisker added. "Yellowfang, these are Goosefeather and Featherwhisker of ThunderClan, and Hawkheart of WindClan."

Yellowfang dipped her head politely. "Greetings," she meowed.

"Welcome," Featherwhisker responded. "It's always good to receive a new medicine cat."

"Th-thank you," Yellowfang stammered. "There's such a lot to learn, but I'm glad to be here."

"Yellowfang." Hawkheart, a mottled dark brown tom, stepped forward. "You have your full name already, so you must have been a warrior before you decided to follow the way of a medicine cat."

Yellowfang nodded. *Is that wrong?* she wondered.

"I was a warrior first, like you," Hawkheart continued to Yellowfang's surprise. "I've found my warrior training very useful, and I expect you will too."

"We're wasting moonlight," Goosefeather broke in tetchily. "Are we going to stand out here gossiping all night?"

I'm pleased to meet you, too, Yellowfang thought as she followed Sagewhisker into the tunnel.

The cave of the Moonstone was already drenched in brilliant silver light when the medicine cats arrived. Sagewhisker padded over to the base of the stone, and beckoned with her tail for Yellowfang to join her there. The other medicine cats sat down a few tail-lengths away.

"Yellowfang," Sagewhisker began, "is it your wish to share the deepest knowledge of StarClan as a ShadowClan medicine cat?"

Yellowfang gulped. "It is."

Sagewhisker's gaze rested warmly on Yellowfang as she continued. "Warriors of StarClan, I present to you this cat. She has shown great courage in turning aside from the path of a warrior. My pride in her could not be greater. Grant her your wisdom and insight so that she may understand your ways and heal her Clan in accordance with your will." Beckoning Yellowfang forward again, she added, "Now lie down and press your nose against the stone."

Fear flooded over Yellowfang again as she obeyed. Her eyes closed and she felt icy cold envelop her. It was as if she were floating in darkness; the stone, the cave, and her fellow medicine cats all swept away.

Then Yellowfang sensed that her paws were standing on solid ground. She opened her eyes, blinked, and looked around. She was in a lush clearing, with a stream gurgling through it and flowers of all colors scattered through the grass. Trees in full leaf surrounded the open space, their branches stirring in a warm breeze that carried scents of growth and abundant prey. Everything was bathed in sunlight.

Yellowfang rose to her paws and stretched. She had expected to find cats of StarClan waiting for her, but she was alone. *What am I supposed to do now?*

Movement caught her gaze and she realized that a cat was approaching through the trees. When it emerged into the open, Yellowfang saw it was an orange-and-gray she-cat, her fur thick and shining, with bright eyes and a frosting of starlight around her paws. Sheer astonishment struck Yellowfang as she recognized her.

"Silverflame!"

Stumbling a little, she ran forward to touch noses with the cat she had last seen as a scrawny, pain-racked elder.

"Greetings, Yellowfang," Silverflame purred. "I'm glad that I was chosen to welcome you into StarClan. It is an honor to see you here, and as a medicine cat, too!"

"It's great to see you, too," Yellowfang responded, confused.

"But I was expecting to see another medicine cat. Aren't I here to learn stuff?"

Silverflame dipped her head. "Sagewhisker will teach you all you need to know of herbs," she mewed. "But I—"

"Then you're going to send me omens!" Yellowfang interrupted, excitement tingling in her pads.

"It doesn't always work like that." There was a note of regret in Silverflame's voice. "More than anything else, a medicine cat needs to have courage in her own instincts."

Now Yellowfang was even more confused. "But you will visit me, right?" she asked anxiously. "What if I don't know the answers?"

Silverflame touched Yellowfang's ear lightly with her nose. "I will always be with you," she promised, "but you must trust yourself first."

Yellowfang blinked. "I don't understand."

"I will watch over you," the StarClan cat assured her. "Whatever choices you make, you are not alone. I have faith in you—in your decisions and your destiny."

As she spoke, she began to fade away, the outlines of her body lost in a glitter of starshine.

"Don't go!" Yellowfang called.

But Silverflame had vanished, and a heartbeat later Yellowfang opened her eyes to find herself back in the cave of the Moonstone, with the other medicine cats dreaming beside her. She stood up and backed away from the Moonstone, shaking out her fur. She had escaped the terrible dreams of her last visit, but her meeting with Silverflame had been a long way from what she expected. *Am I really expected to make my choices alone, without the guidance of StarClan?* Yet Silverflame had said she had faith in Yellowfang. If she doubted herself, she would be letting Silverflame down. *I will make you proud of me,* Yellowfang vowed to her beloved former Clanmate. *You'll see!*

Yellowfang teased out a bundle of cobwebs and began hanging them on the thorns to dry. She had been a medicine cat apprentice for five sunrises, and she felt pleased that Sagewhisker had approved her suggestion of what to do with the webs. A sudden pain stabbed into her paw. At first she thought she had picked up one of the thorns from the bush, but when she looked at her pads they were unmarked.

Another cat, then.

Yellowfang turned to see Finchflight limping between the boulders, one forepaw held in the air. She almost called out, *You've stepped on a thorn, haven't you?* before she remembered that she wasn't supposed to know about wounds until the injured cat told her.

"What can I do for you?" she asked.

Finchflight glanced around. "I was looking for Sagewhisker," he told her, then added doubtfully, "but you're a medicine cat apprentice now, so I suppose you'll do."

Thanks for your confidence, Yellowfang thought.

She winced as Finchflight hobbled forward and held out his paw for her inspection. Then she recalled talking to Sagewhisker about blocking out her feelings, and made herself aware of her own paws. *They're all fine. I have no thorns. I can feel smooth earth underneath my pads, nothing else.* The pain from Finchflight faded; Yellowfang was still aware of it, but only as a faint trace in the background of her mind. *It worked! Now I can examine Finchflight's paw without my own pain getting in the way.*

As soon as she examined the black-and-white tom's pad, Yellowfang saw the tip of the thorn just peeking out. "That looks bad," she mewed. "It must hurt a lot."

"It's a nuisance," Finchflight replied, shrugging. "I was supposed to go out on patrol. Brackenfoot is leading a raid on Carrionplace, to hunt rats."

Yellowfang shivered, remembering the time that she had taken part in the last rat raid. "It's too bad you can't go," she agreed. "Brackenfoot will need every cat."

She had seen Sagewhisker removing thorns before, so she knew what to do. She licked Finchflight's paw thoroughly around the shank of the thorn, then tried to catch it in her teeth. But it was driven in deeply, and Yellowfang accidentally closed her teeth on the soft part of Finchflight's pad.

Finchflight leaped back with a yowl, and Yellowfang felt his pain flood into her own paw again. "I'm sorry!" she gasped.

To her relief, Sagewhisker appeared in the entrance to the den. "What's all this?" the medicine cat asked.

Quickly Yellowfang explained.

"I'll take over now," Sagewhisker meowed with a nod. "But you did exactly the right thing, Yellowfang."

"Not when she bit me!" Finchflight growled.

Once Sagewhisker had extracted the thorn and sent Finchflight to catch up with his patrol, she turned to Yellowfang.

"The thing is not to rush," she advised. "Just keep licking. If you press your tongue on the outside of the pad around the thorn, it will often come out a little bit, and then you can grab it more easily."

"Thanks," Yellowfang mewed. "I'll remember that."

Sagewhisker hesitated, then asked, "How did the pain blocking go?"

"It worked really well," Yellowfang replied. "I had it under control until I bit Finchflight, and then I couldn't concentrate on keeping out that pain as well."

Sagewhisker rested her tail-tip comfortingly on Yellowfang's shoulder. "It will take time," she murmured. "Just keep trying."

The sun was rising above the trees as Yellowfang padded across to the nursery to check on Cloudkit. He was obviously in perfect health, wriggling around in the nursery and jumping on pretend mice. "I'm going to be the best hunter in ShadowClan!" he announced.

"I'm sure you will," Nettlespot purred, looking down at her kit. "He's completely better," she added to Yellowfang, who was aware of the new note of respect in her tone. "That willow cured him, just like you said. And he's grown so much in this last quarter moon!"

"I'm glad," Yellowfang began. "He should—"

She broke off at the sound of yowls from the camp entrance. At the same moment a wave of pain flooded over her: sharp stabbing wounds as well as the dull ache of scratches.

"What's that?" Nettlespot yelped, sitting up in alarm and drawing Cloudkit close to her with her tail.

Within a heartbeat Yellowfang forced herself to concentrate on the lack of injuries to her own body, until the pain eased. *I am not hurt. The pain is not mine.* Once she had it under control, she hurried out of the nursery. Sagewhisker had just appeared from her own den. Side by side she and Yellowfang bounded across the camp to meet the returning cats. Yellowfang could hear the blood rushing in her ears.

My Clanmates are wounded! But I am their medicine cat: I can help them!

Chapter 20

Brackenfoot and Deerleap hurtled out of the tunnel with Toadskip, Scorchwind, Rowanberry, and Finchflight hard on their paws. Yellowfang could see that all of them bore scratches and bitemarks.

"What happened?" Sagewhisker demanded.

"The rats happened," Scorchwind growled.

Rowanberry shuddered. "So many rats!"

The rest of the Clan was emerging from their dens, clustering around and asking the same question. Eventually the returning patrol settled down in the middle of the clearing, with their Clanmates crowding around them. Cedarstar came out of his den, followed by Stonetooth, and joined them. Yellowfang found a place to sit next to Rowanberry and pricked her ears to listen.

"No." Sagewhisker gave her a nudge. "We have to go around and check the injuries at the same time. Assess every cat, then treat the most seriously wounded first. I'll fetch the herbs we need."

Feeling embarrassed that she hadn't realized that, Yellowfang jumped up and followed her mentor.

Meanwhile, Brackenfoot explained what had happened. "As you know, we went to hunt along the edge of Carrionplace. At first everything went well. Rowanberry caught a huge rat." He gave the young warrior a nod of approval. "But then hordes of rats started pouring out of those stinking heaps and attacked us. You've never seen so many rats!"

"But rats are prey!" Newtspeck exclaimed. "Prey doesn't fight back."

"These rats do," Brackenfoot responded. He shook his head; Yellowfang could sense his shame and embarrassment, and saw that the rest of his patrol shared it. "We had to flee," he added. "There were too many for us to fight."

"You did the right thing," Cedarstar meowed, standing up to speak. "What good would it have done your Clan if you had been killed or seriously wounded? The good news is that there are plenty of rats. We just have to work out the best way to overpower them."

No warrior spoke up, but Yellowfang could see that all the Clan was thinking hard, murmuring to one another as they worked out what they might do.

Nettlespot leaned closer to Toadskip. "You can't go risking your life when you have your son, Cloudkit, to think about," she told him.

Poolcloud, who was sitting close by, swiveled her head to look at Nettlespot. "Toadskip is the father of my kits, too," she snapped. "But I wouldn't dream of telling a warrior not to fight."

Stonetooth distracted them by rising to his paws. "As I see

it," he began, "the problem is how to catch some rats without attracting the attention of the rest of them."

Amberleaf raised her tail. "Just send one or two warriors at a time?" she suggested.

"Or hunt at night, in darkness?" Mousewing put in.

"Maybe we should wait for the wind to blow in the right direction," Hollyflower added. "So it would hide our scent as we creep up?"

Sagewhisker appeared beside Yellowfang with her jaws full of herbs. "So where do we start?" she asked after setting down the dusty bundle.

"Scorchwind has a deep bite," Yellowfang reported. "That's the worst wound; it could become infected. Rowanberry has some mild scratches, and Brackenfoot has some claw marks that look sore."

"No need to fuss about me," Brackenfoot meowed, catching what his daughter said. "I've taken much worse wounds in my time."

"I'll fuss about you all I want," Yellowfang responded tartly. "You'll have some dock leaf to soothe the soreness, and like it."

Brackenfoot dipped his head; Yellowfang caught a gleam of amusement in his eyes. "Very well, medicine cat," he purred.

As Yellowfang padded around treating the wounds and keeping her pain under careful control, she noticed Raggedpelt sitting at the edge of the crowd, his amber eyes smoldering. Now he stepped forward. "Are we not warriors?" he demanded, glaring around at his Clanmates. "We are proud, afraid of no enemy, trained to fight in any battle! We will not skulk like dogs around these rats, hiding under cover of darkness, or fleeing like foxes when they bare their teeth. They are *rats*! *Prey! Fresh-kill!* We will not be scared!"

A murmur of excitement rose from the cats around him. Raggedpelt crouched down and began to score lines in the frozen earth of the camp floor. "Look! Here's Carrionplace. This is the route we should take from camp, coming out here. Patrols should attack from here, here, and here. We'll drive the rats toward a fourth patrol, and contain them in the tightest area possible. We need to find a place where we'll always be higher than the rats, to keep the advantage." His voice grew stronger and more confident with every word. "We should build barriers on either side of the spot where the rats will emerge, to keep them blocked in. We'll set a trap for them!" he ended triumphantly.

A moment of silence followed, every cat turning their gaze toward the Clan leader.

Cedarstar nodded. "It might work," he pronounced.

Several cats pushed up to Raggedpelt to congratulate him, while others started talking in quiet tones. Yellowfang knew that not every cat would feel pride in Raggedpelt's courageous plan; he was well respected in his Clan, but didn't make friends easily.

But I'm *proud of him,* she thought, catching his eye and nodding to show him that she agreed it was a great idea.

Cedarstar, Stonetooth, and the other senior warriors huddled around Raggedpelt, examining the scratch marks he had made in the earth. Yellowfang, still helping Sagewhisker deal with injuries, found herself at the back of the crowd.

"I want to be in the final patrol," Wolfstep meowed. "I'd be good at building the walls to trap the rats."

Amberleaf slid out her claws. "I'll chase the rats out of their den and into the ambush."

Yellowfang opened her jaws to make a suggestion when she was distracted by a prod from Sagewhisker. "You're not a warrior anymore," the medicine cat reminded her. "Can you go back to the den and fetch me some burdock root? That's the best cure for Scorchwind's rat bite. Or wild garlic if you can't find the burdock root."

Yellowfang padded off with a pang in her heart for what she was missing. When she got back she chewed up the burdock root while Sagewhisker put marigold on Rowanberry's scratches. When she came to treat Scorchwind's bite, he was so excited to be discussing his brother's plan that he wouldn't keep still; Yellowfang couldn't get the cobwebs to stick the poultice in place.

"Will you stop squirming around like a kit with ants in its pelt?" she meowed crossly.

Scorchwind gave her an impatient shrug. "I'm okay, Yellowfang. This is more important."

"Fine!" Yellowfang snapped. "Bleed all over the place if you want! You've got the sense of an egg if you think you can trot around the forest with a hole in your flank."

With an exaggerated sigh, Scorchwind flopped down on his side so Yellowfang could get at his rat bite. The sudden movement sent a pulse of pain shooting through him, breaking Yellowfang's careful control. More pain flooded over her: from Rowanberry and Brackenfoot; from Toadskip, who had torn a claw when fleeing from the rats; from Finchflight, whose paw was still hurting.

Yellowfang paused, taking a breath to clear her head. *I am whole and well. This is not my pain.*

"Can't you hurry up?" Scorchwind prompted her.

Yellowfang glared at him as she slapped the poultice over his bite and secured it with cobwebs. Then she turned to look at Toadskip's claw. By now Sagewhisker was finishing up with the other cats.

"That's it," she meowed to Yellowfang, who was winding cobweb around Toadskip's paw. "We're all done."

Yellowfang sank down. She felt more exhausted than if she had done a whole border patrol.

"All of you should eat now and rest." Cedarstar raised his voice to be heard by all the Clan. "After sunhigh there will be training to prepare for the rat attack tomorrow. Raggedpelt will be in charge."

Excitement welled up inside Yellowfang, banishing some of her weariness. *That's such an honor for Raggedpelt!*

She forced herself to her paws and plodded over to the tabby tom, who was in close discussion with Stonetooth and Brackenfoot. "Raggedpelt, that was a great idea," she meowed.

Raggedpelt turned to give her a nod. "Thanks, Yellowfang." He spoke lightly, but Yellowfang wanted to believe he appreciated what she said.

Sagewhisker was heading back to the den, and Yellowfang realized she should follow her, grabbing up the few leftover herbs as she went. Inside the den she sighed as she looked at the mess of overturned and rummaged herbs, all the different leaves mixed up together and scattered in the grass.

"It'll be much worse after a battle, believe me," Sagewhisker told her. "Come on, let's get it cleared up." As they began to sort through the scattered leaves, she added, "Raggedpelt has some good ideas. He'll go far, that cat. Maybe even the next deputy."

Yellowfang hid a thrilled purr. *Raggedpelt could be close to achieving his ambition.* Then a gust of regret shook her like a cold wind. *Except I won't be his deputy. I'll be his medicine cat. . . .*

The following day Yellowfang woke to see a clear, bright sky with not a breath of wind to stir the trees. *A perfect day for the attack,* she thought as she poked her head out of the den.

The Clan was gathering in the clearing, buzzing with energy like a swarm of bees as Cedarstar, Stonetooth, and Raggedpelt arranged the patrols.

"Raggedpelt, you'll lead the last group," Stonetooth announced. "You'll be responsible for killing the rats once they've been trapped."

"I'll fight beside you, blow for blow," Foxheart meowed to Raggedpelt; Yellowfang thought sourly that she looked as if she were plastered to his side with cobwebs. She felt a stab of jealousy as she remembered how proud she had felt when she and Archeye had killed a rat on their visit to Carrionplace.

Will I ever feel that kind of pride again?

Sagewhisker emerged from the den with a bundle of herbs. "Come on," she mewed, her voice muffled by the leaves. "We have to be ready to go with them."

"We're going too?" Yellowfang asked, startled.

Sagewhisker nodded. "We'll treat injuries as they occur, but stay out of the way of the fighting. That's up to the warriors, okay?" Her eyes were stern, and Yellowfang knew she was giving her an unspoken reminder that she was a medicine cat now.

Yellowfang went back into the den and loaded up with herbs and cobweb. The sticky strands made her sneeze as she tried to pick them up. *The rats will hear me coming long before we get anywhere near Carrionplace,* she thought, frustrated. Then she realized she could stick the clumps of cobweb to her thick pelt, far enough from her muzzle that they didn't make her sneeze, and went out again to join Sagewhisker, feeling pleased at her new idea.

The last of the patrols were already heading out of the camp. Yellowfang and Sagewhisker brought up the rear, following the warriors through the sparse, leaf-bare trees and across the marsh. The air was mild, and the persistent ice of leaf-bare was beginning to thaw; Yellowfang hissed in annoyance when she put her paw straight through one sheet of it into the freezing water below. After that she and Sagewhisker leaped from clump to clump of grass to keep their paws dry.

At last they drew close to the Carrionplace. Yellowfang could smell its stink before she saw the dark heaps looming up in front of her. Like before, the yellow monsters were quiet; the only sound came from big white birds that flapped and shrieked above the piles of waste.

While the patrols approached the Twoleg fence, Sagewhisker cast around among the bushes at the edge of the marsh.

"What are you doing?" Yellowfang asked.

"Finding a place under a bush," the medicine cat replied, "where we can store our herbs and stay out of sight during the fighting."

"So we'll be hiding?" Yellowfang mewed in dismay. *That feels like we're cowards!*

"No." Sagewhisker's eyes were sympathetic as she gazed at Yellowfang. "We'll be keeping ourselves safe for when our Clanmates need us."

Yellowfang still thought it was a strange way to behave, but she made no protest, and wriggled underneath a holly bush to lay out the herbs and cobweb they had brought. Her paws tingled with the urge to help as she watched Raggedpelt and his patrol pad up to the Twoleg fence. Raggedpelt found a hole in the silver mesh, and he and Featherstorm enlarged it with their teeth and claws to let cats in and rats out. Meanwhile, Foxheart and Wolfstep started dragging branches up to build the trap.

"Look what we found!" Newtspeck called from the edge of the marsh. She, Frogtail, and Lizardstripe were rolling a small tree trunk in front of them. "We managed to pull it out of the ground," she panted as they reached the fence. "Its roots are rotten, so it wasn't hard. I thought it would make a good vantage point for us to stand and jump down on the rats."

Raggedpelt nodded. "You're right; it will."

As the walls of the trap took shape he checked them carefully, leaping up on top to make sure they would bear a cat's weight. At one point the wall collapsed under him; Yellowfang gasped as he vanished in a whirl of flailing limbs and flying branches. But a moment later he crawled out, shaking debris from his pelt.

"Build it up again," he ordered, "and put a stronger branch at the bottom this time."

Raggedpelt stepped back while the rest of his patrol worked on the repairs. Yellowfang slipped out from under the holly bush and padded over to him. "Good luck," she murmured.

Raggedpelt looked at her. "I wish you were fighting alongside me," he mewed.

Yellowfang turned her head away. "I will be here," she whispered.

She expected that Raggedpelt would walk away from her in disgust; instead she felt his nose touch her ear. "I'll see you after the battle," he promised.

A screech sounded from somewhere inside the Carrionplace, telling Raggedpelt that the other patrols were in place. Raggedpelt checked that his own patrol was ready, then yowled in reply.

"Yellowfang! Over here!"

Yellowfang looked around to see Sagewhisker beckoning to her from under the bush. Reluctantly she bounded back to join her, but stayed outside the branches to watch the attack.

She realized she was holding her breath.

Silence followed the yowls, broken after a few heartbeats by faint sounds of scrabbling and hissing. *The cats are chasing the rats out of their dens in the waste!* Then Yellowfang heard squeaks growing rapidly louder, and the sound of scratching paws. She craned her neck forward, peering through the silver mesh.

Suddenly Yellowfang spotted a rat hurtling out of the heap of waste. It swerved away from the hole that Raggedpelt's patrol had made, but was driven back on course by Nutwhisker leaping down to block its way. The first rat was followed by more, and more and more—more rats than Yellowfang had ever seen before. At the same time, cats began to appear, leaping down from the waste to steer the rats toward the hole in the mesh.

Raggedpelt's patrol was waiting on top of the barriers, crouched and ready to pounce. The rats swirled at the base of the fence, beginning to panic as they realized they were trapped. Yellowfang saw Brackenfoot jump into the center of the heaving mass and shove one toward the hole.

"That way, stupid flea-pelt!" he snarled.

The other rats fled after it, thinking they had found a way of escape. But their squeaks grew louder when they realized that cats were waiting on that side of the fence, too. Raggedpelt's patrol jumped down one by one, grabbing a rat and dealing the deathblow, and scrambling back out with the fresh-kill in their jaws.

"It's working!" Foxheart yowled.

"Watch out for their teeth!" Wolfstep panted as he dragged

out a rat almost as big as he was.

It's all happening so fast! Yellowfang thought, her gaze fixed on Raggedpelt. She held her breath every time he disappeared down into the trap, and let out a gasp of relief when he reappeared with a dead rat.

Then a yelp from beyond the fence distracted her. Yellowfang let out a wail of fear when she saw that the cats on the far side of the fence were surrounded. More and more rats had poured out of the pile, too many to fit into the trap. With nowhere to escape, they had turned on the warriors, clawing and biting, and the warriors were badly outnumbered, trapped against the fence while waves of rats crashed over them.

Raggedpelt was the first in his patrol to notice what was happening. "Stop killing!" he yowled. "We have to help the others!"

But the hole in the fence was blocked by terrified rats; Raggedpelt and his cats had to scramble over the silver mesh in a desperate attempt to help their Clanmates.

Yellowfang's belly clenched as Stonetooth went down with a couple of huge rats clinging to him. More cats rushed to help him, but the swarming rats blocked their way. Cedarstar disappeared under a wave of brown bodies and lashing hairless tails.

"I can't bear this!" Yellowfang exclaimed. "We can't just stand here and do nothing!"

Sagewhisker slid out from under the bush and rested a paw on her shoulder. "We have to protect ourselves," she meowed.

Yellowfang stared at her. "There's no point if we have to

watch all our Clanmates die!"

Shaking off Sagewhisker's restraining paw, Yellowfang rushed up to the fence and flung herself over it. Just below her a huge rat was attacking Deerleap; Yellowfang leaped straight down on top of it and killed it with a single blow to its neck.

All around her, ShadowClan cats were fighting for their lives. Yellowfang spotted Foxheart battling two rats at once, killing both of them in a whirl of teeth and claws. Nutwhisker and Rowanberry dragged off a rat that had fastened its teeth in Brightflower's shoulder; then all three cats turned to help Stonetooth to his paws and fend off the rats that were attacking him. Yellowfang felt the gnawing of sharp teeth in her muscles, and concentrated on blocking it out.

She caught a glimpse of Raggedpelt diving into the snarl of rats swarming over Cedarstar. For a heartbeat he vanished, then fought his way up again, dragging Cedarstar with him, his teeth in the Clan leader's scruff.

"Clear the hole!" he yowled.

Yellowfang, Archeye, and Mudclaw fought their way through the battling rats to the hole in the fence. Yellowfang felt a savage satisfaction as she sank her claws into rat after rat and hurled them out of the way. Her warrior training flooded back and she focused on nothing but slicing and slashing, feeling warm bodies split beneath her claws.

Fighting together, the three cats managed to clear the hole so that Raggedpelt could pull Cedarstar through. Brightflower followed with a feebly staggering Stonetooth. Shoulder-to-shoulder with her Clanmates, Yellowfang fought the rats off, keeping them away from the hole so that the rest of her Clan could struggle through.

When the last cat was out, Foxheart and Mudclaw pushed the branches of the barrier up against the hole to block the rats inside, though some of them were already starting to squeeze through the mesh into ShadowClan territory.

"Back to the camp!" Raggedpelt screeched.

The cats fled, the stronger warriors helping the ones who were badly injured. Yellowfang spotted Sagewhisker fleeing with them, abandoning the herbs they had brought, and raced to catch up.

CHAPTER 21

Yellowfang paused for breath, taking a moment to control the pain she felt from her Clanmates. Around her the camp was in chaos; injured warriors lay everywhere in the clearing. Her mouth was flooded with the taste of bitter herbs. She knew she had to eke out the remaining stocks as sparingly as she could, for so little was left.

I wish we hadn't had to leave so much under that holly bush.

Two warriors in particular worried Yellowfang: Stonetooth, who had been bitten badly on his hind leg, and Hollyflower, who had a bite in her neck. She wanted to consult Sagewhisker, but the medicine cat had vanished with Cedarstar into his den, and hadn't yet reappeared.

Eventually Sagewhisker emerged from among the oak roots, looking somber, and padded over to Yellowfang. "Cedarstar has lost a life," she reported quietly. "It was hard, but he's recovering now."

Yellowfang's eyes widened in shock. She had never known the Clan leader to lose a life before. "How many lives does he have left?" she asked.

"One," Sagewhisker replied, her eyes darkening with worry.

"But keep that to yourself. Only medicine cats know how many lives the Clan leader has."

Yellowfang nodded.

"What about the other cats?" Sagewhisker prompted. "Let me see what you've done."

Yellowfang led her around the clearing, showing her the poultices she had applied, the wounds covered in cobweb, and told her which cats had been given poppy seeds for the pain.

"Very good," Sagewhisker commented. "When you've had more practice you won't need to use quite so much cobweb, and you can be a bit more generous with the poppy seed for full-grown warriors."

"We don't have much left," Yellowfang reminded her.

"True." Sagewhisker let out a sigh. "This is one of the worst defeats I can remember. The danger now is infection; rat bites can be very poisonous. We'll have to keep a close eye on Hollyflower and Stonetooth."

"I'll go out later and look for some more burdock root," Yellowfang promised. "Or if I can't find any I'll get wild garlic."

She padded over to the spot by the tiny stream at the edge of the camp, where she had piled up a heap of moss. Gripping a bundle in her jaws, she dipped it in the water and carried it over to Raggedpelt. The tabby tom was lying near the fresh-kill pile, curled up tightly on himself. He had taken a few deep scratches on his nose, which were going to leave scars. Yellowfang's belly clenched with pity, and it was a struggle for her to block out his pain.

"Here, I've brought you some wet moss," she mewed.

"I don't want it," Raggedpelt mumbled, not looking at her. "Other cats need it more."

"Other cats have had some," Yellowfang assured him, laying the moss down beside his nose. "I'm a medicine cat now. You have to listen to me, and you *will* have a drink."

Raggedpelt let out a groan, but he extended his tongue and took a couple of laps at the moss. "This is all my fault," he groaned. "I nearly killed my Clan!"

"No." Yellowfang crouched down beside him. "The plan was brilliant. It could have worked. There were just too many rats."

"I should have thought of that!" Raggedpelt snapped.

While Yellowfang was trying to figure out how she could reassure him, Crowtail limped up and halted beside Raggedpelt. "Cedarstar wants to see you," she announced.

Raggedpelt blinked despairingly up at her. "He's probably going to order me to leave the Clan," he muttered, hauling himself to his paws and heading toward the Clan leader's den.

Yellowfang fought with panic. *Cedarstar can't send Raggedpelt away!* Desperate to know what would happen, she followed Raggedpelt, and to her relief he let her come with him. Inside the dark den beneath the oak roots, Cedarstar looked weak, his eyes a little glazed as he struggled to sit up.

Raggedstar hung his head as he entered, his tail drooping. "I'm sorry," he meowed. "I have failed. Punish me as you wish."

For a moment Cedarstar was silent. "We lost the battle," he rasped. "But you did not fail. You saved me from the rats, and you did everything possible to help the rest of your Clanmates."

"But—" Raggedpelt tried to interrupt.

Cedarstar silenced him with a raised paw. "Hold your head high, Raggedpelt. There is a chance of defeat in every battle. You gave your all, and I ask for nothing more."

"I ask for more than you do, then!" Raggedpelt flashed out.

"You should be kinder to yourself," the Clan leader responded. "We can all learn lessons from today. This method of trapping can be used with other prey, one way or another. For now, the Clan must concentrate on healing and regaining our strength." He dipped his head toward Raggedpelt. "I am honored to call you a Clanmate. And this proves you are more than ready for an apprentice. Cloudkit will be yours, as soon as he's ready."

Raggedpelt stared at him. "Th-thank you, Cedarstar!" he stammered.

The Clan leader let out a purr. "Go and rest now."

Yellowfang was delighted as she followed Raggedpelt away from Cedarstar's den. But the tabby warrior's tail still dragged behind him and his shoulders were hunched. Cedarstar's praise hadn't comforted him at all.

Catching up to him, Yellowfang whispered, "You should be proud, like Cedarstar said."

Raggedpelt glared at her. "I will never be proud of defeat!" he hissed.

"Well, you stupid furball, I'm proud of you," Yellowfang snapped, letting him walk away.

* * *

Days passed, but the thaw never came. Snow lay thick on the ground, driving prey deep into their holes, and gray skies threatened more to come.

On the night of the full moon Yellowfang peered out of her den, expecting to see the sky covered with clouds. To her surprise the silver circle shone down through a gap in the dense gray covering.

"There'll be a Gathering at Fourtrees tonight," Sagewhisker mewed, coming to join her at the entrance to the den. "Are you ready?"

Yellowfang took a deep breath. "Yes."

This would be her first Gathering as a medicine cat apprentice. Though more than a moon had passed since she had made her decision, the previous Gathering hadn't taken place, as clouds had obscured the moon. She followed Sagewhisker out into the clearing where the cats who had been chosen to attend the Gathering were assembling around Cedarstar. The Clan leader had recovered well from the battle against the rats, but Stonetooth was looking frail, and Yellowfang noticed that he limped badly when he walked.

As she waited to move off, Yellowfang found that she was making a quick check of all her Clanmates, looking for signs of injury or sickness. Since she had become a medicine cat, she had gotten much better at blocking out pain; now she could do it instinctively, though sometimes it could be useful to let herself feel it, to make it easier to treat a sick or wounded cat. Now she kept the pain almost completely in check, instead looking for signs of bright eyes and healthy fur, and checking on how wounds were healing.

Cedarstar led the way out of the camp and through the forest toward the tunnel under the Thunderpath. Yellowfang would have liked to walk with Raggedpelt, but Foxheart was keeping close to his side.

"That was a great training session today," she mewed to him. "Do you think we could get together sometime and practice that new move?"

Determined not to listen, Yellowfang fell in beside Rowanberry. "I hear you caught a squirrel today," she began. "Littlebird and Lizardfang shared it, and they said it was really tasty."

"That's good," Rowanberry meowed. "I—"

"Hey, Rowanberry!"

Yellowfang's sister broke off as Wolfstep called out to her. "Sorry, I have to . . ." Rowanberry scampered off before she finished what she was saying.

Yellowfang watched her leave, trying not to feel hurt. After a few heartbeats Sagewhisker joined her. "It can be lonely," the old medicine cat murmured, as if she could read Yellowfang's thoughts. "But your Clanmates will always need you, more than you or they realize."

WindClan had already arrived at Fourtrees by the time the ShadowClan cats reached the hollow, and ThunderClan arrived at almost the same moment. Yellowfang glanced around with interest as she made her way through the clumps of fern that covered the slope. Cats were everywhere, bounding across her path, meeting together in groups from every Clan, and chattering excitedly.

"We chased a fox all the way across the moor!" a WindClan cat was boasting to a couple of ThunderClan apprentices.

"Yeah," his Clanmate added. "He won't be back anytime soon."

Cedarstar leaped up to the top of the Great Rock. "Let the Clans gather!" he yowled.

Pinestar and Heatherstar scrambled up beside him, but some cat protested that they couldn't begin the Gathering without RiverClan. While they argued, Yellowfang spotted a cat with a blue-gray pelt standing by herself under an arching fern. ThunderClan scent drifted from her. *I haven't spoken to her before,* Yellowfang thought, turning her paw steps that way.

But before she reached the blue-furred cat, the RiverClan cats began pouring into the clearing. A sturdy tabby tom padded up to the ThunderClan cat and settled down beside her, almost knocking her over. Yellowfang stared at his twisted jaw for a moment, wondering how he got his injury. She didn't want to interrupt the two of them, so she turned away and went to join Sagewhisker and the other medicine cats at the foot of the Great Rock.

As she approached, Featherwhisker rose to his paws and came to meet her. "Greetings, Yellowfang," he meowed. Yellowfang noticed that while his words were warm, his eyes were wary. "How are things going? I see that some of your Clanmates are battle-scarred. Has there been trouble recently?"

Yellowfang felt the fur on her neck and shoulders beginning

to bristle up. "Nothing we couldn't handle," she replied curtly.

"Keep your pelt on," Featherwhisker told her. "We're medicine cats. We can tell one another anything."

"And if there's anything you need to know," Sagewhisker added, appearing at Featherwhisker's side, "rest assured we'll tell you."

There was no chance for Featherwhisker to say any more, because at that moment Pinestar of ThunderClan stepped forward to the edge of the Great Rock and announced that the Gathering would begin.

Yellowfang listened as the other Clan leaders gave their news. There wasn't much of interest; she guessed that all the Clans had been hard-pressed during the cold leaf-bare, but none of the leaders would be prepared to admit it.

Finally Cedarstar paced to the front of the Great Rock and looked out across the assembled Clans. "It is with sadness that I must announce our deputy, Stonetooth, is moving to the elders' den," he announced.

A gasp of astonishment came from the ShadowClan cats. Looking around, Yellowfang realized that none of them, except for Stonetooth himself, knew anything about this.

"Stonetooth! Stonetooth!" his Clan called.

The deputy, standing at the base of the Great Rock, dipped his head solemnly.

"But it's almost moonhigh!" Yellowfang heard Rowanberry whisper to Foxheart. "Cedarstar will have to announce the new deputy *now*!"

Yellowfang could sense that tension in the clearing was

building. Cats from the other Clans were looking at one another, speculating on who the new ShadowClan deputy would be. Deputies were normally appointed within the Clan, not in public like this.

"Raggedpelt will take his place," Cedarstar went on.

"Raggedpelt! Raggedpelt!" His Clanmates yowled his name to the sky. Yellowfang tried to yowl louder than any of them, shocked and delighted.

Raggedpelt rose to his paws, his expression unreadable as he padded to the Great Rock to take his place. Still yowling his name, her heart bursting with pride, Yellowfang tried to catch Raggedpelt's eye, but he wasn't looking at her.

Cedarstar waited for the noise to die down, then continued. "There is one other piece of news to give you. Sagewhisker, this is for you to tell."

Sagewhisker rose to her paws; Yellowfang felt a pang of nervousness, knowing what the medicine cat was about to say. Gazing out across the Clans, Sagewhisker meowed, "ShadowClan has a new medicine cat. Yellowfang has agreed to become my apprentice."

A few cats from ShadowClan called Yellowfang's name, but after the excitement of Raggedpelt's promotion, the news didn't cause a big reaction. Yellowfang was relieved not to have too much attention on her. At last she managed to catch Raggedpelt's eye, and was startled at the sadness in his gaze as he looked at her. One day they would be leader and medicine cat of ShadowClan. Surely that was cause for celebration?

A stab of pain pierced Yellowfang's heart. *Is that my pain, or his? This is my destiny—isn't it?*

The thaw set in; rain fell day after day, filling every hollow and turning the floor of the camp to mud. Hissing with annoyance as she splashed through the waterlogged forest, Yellowfang paused to taste the air. A fresh, green tang led her to a fallen tree trunk, and she crouched down to wriggle her way underneath it.

"Yellowfang!"

Startled, Yellowfang jumped and banged her head on the underside of the trunk. "Mouse dung!" she spat. Scrambling to her paws, she turned to see Raggedpelt standing behind her.

"That hurt!" she complained. "Are you mouse-brained, or what?"

"Sorry." Raggedpelt blinked at her. "I had to talk to you, away from the camp." He hesitated, took a breath, and continued, "Yellowfang, are you sure you've made the right choice?"

Yellowfang gazed back at him. For once he wasn't trying to quarrel with her. His voice just sounded sad, full of such deep sorrow that there was no bottom to it.

"I miss you," he went on. "I'm going to be the leader of ShadowClan, and I wanted to have you as my deputy."

"I'll be your medicine cat," Yellowfang mewed.

"You know I want more than that," Raggedpelt told her. He took a pace toward her and his scent flooded over her. His whiskers brushed her ear. "I know you are a medicine cat hispered, "but that doesn't change the way I feel

ngs haven't changed either," Yellowfang whis-
, her voice quivering. "But this is my destiny! StarClan wants me to be a medicine cat!"

"They can have your skill with herbs." Raggedpelt's voice grew stronger. "They can even walk in your dreams. But they can't have all of you. If we do all the duties expected of us, how can this be wrong? As long as no cat knows, everything can be as it was before. This can be our secret, shared with no one else."

I wonder what Silverflame would say, Yellowfang thought. *But then, she told me to have courage in my own instincts. And my instincts are telling me that this is my destiny too.*

Yellowfang leaned closer to Raggedpelt, feeling the warmth of his fur, and crushed down a feeling of guilt. "I can keep a secret," she murmured.

CHAPTER 22

Yellowfang watched a scarlet leaf spiraling down from a branch above her head. At the last moment she sprang up and clawed it out of the air, pinning it to the ground with a triumphant yowl. More scarlet and golden leaves tumbled from the trees. Happiness bubbled up inside her. Throughout newleaf and greenleaf she and Raggedpelt had kept their promise to each other, and no cat in ShadowClan knew that they had been meeting in the remotest parts of the territory. The only cats who could possibly know were their ancestors in StarClan—and since she had received no signs warning of terrible consequences, Yellowfang had begun to believe that StarClan would allow her to be both Raggedpelt's mate and a medicine cat.

As she clambered up again Raggedpelt popped out from behind the tree and pounced on her, throwing her to the ground again and landing on top of her among the crackling leaves.

"Stop it, mouse-brain!" she gasped. "I can't breathe!"

Raggedpelt's face was close to hers, his amber eyes gleaming. "Admit defeat, then."

"Okay, okay. Just get off me!"

Raggedpelt rolled over with a purr. "You can't escape me," he meowed. "I'll always be here."

"I should be looking for herbs," Yellowfang told him, sitting up and shaking scraps of dried leaf from her pelt. "What's Sagewhisker going to say if I come back empty-pawed?"

"There's plenty of time," Raggedpelt assured her, stretching out lazily.

"But it's leaf-fall already. We have to build up our stocks of herbs before the first frosts. Remember how short of supplies we were last leaf-bare?"

"We'll go back soon. I should be preparing Cloudpaw for his final assessment." Raggedpelt let out a snort of amusement. "Do you know, that scatterbrained apprentice still hasn't learned that squirrels can climb trees faster than he can? I have to keep reminding him to stalk them in the open."

Guilt flooded over Yellowfang. "Then we have to go now."

Raggedpelt gave her a gentle nudge. "We aren't hurting any cat," he reassured her. "We meet all our responsibilities. The Clan is as safe and protected as it can be." He pressed his muzzle against her shoulder. "This is still our secret."

Yellowfang couldn't suppress a rising purr. *It's true. These times with Raggedpelt are the happiest moments I've ever known.*

"Don't forget," Raggedpelt went on, leaning close to her again, "you're only an apprentice. You can still change your mind. I would make sure that you would never have to fight in a battle. I'll be leader soon, after all, and I'll do everything to keep you safe."

Curled warmly into his fur, Yellowfang was tempted for a heartbeat. But then she thought of everything she had learned from Sagewhisker, and she knew again that this was a path she had to follow, at least for a while. She shook her head.

Raggedpelt gave her a gentle nudge. "I'll persuade you yet," he murmured.

Before Yellowfang could respond, a terrible screeching filled the forest. Together the two cats leaped to their paws.

"It's one of our patrols!" Raggedpelt exclaimed. "They're being attacked!"

Shoulder to shoulder, Yellowfang and Raggedpelt bolted through the trees, following the sound. Heartbeats later they came to a clearing. Staring across the open space, Yellowfang saw four of her Clanmates grappling with four huge rogues. The stink of Twolegplace caught her in the throat, making her gag.

Raggedpelt let out a roar of fury and leaped into the battle. He flung aside a rogue who was pinning Rowanberry down, and crashed into the flank of another who was lunging for Blizzardwing's throat. They fled screeching, and the other two, realizing they were now outnumbered, raced after them.

"Don't come back!" Raggedpelt yowled after them.

Yellowfang padded into the clearing. Rowanberry scrambled to her paws and helped Blizzardwing up. Wolfstep flung himself in pursuit of the rogues, only to come back at a sharp order from Raggedpelt. All three of them looked battered, but Yellowfang could see that their injuries weren't serious.

"It was my fault!" Rowanberry gasped. "I was leading the patrol. I should have scented them, but they jumped out on us."

"They were just looking for trouble," Raggedpelt snarled.

Yellowfang scanned the clearing. She had seen four of her

Clanmates fighting, but she could only account for three. *Where's the fourth cat?*

Then she caught a glimpse of white fur among a clump of ferns, and raced over to see Cloudpaw, lying ominously still.

"Oh, no!" she yelped.

"What's he doing here?" Raggedpelt gasped as he came to stand beside her and look down at his motionless apprentice.

"He . . . he couldn't find you," Rowanberry admitted. "So he asked if he could come on the border patrol to practice his scenting skills before his final assessment." She hesitated, then added reluctantly, "I let him take the lead. He didn't pick up the scent of the intruders until it was too late."

Trying to ignore the stricken look in Raggedpelt's eyes, Yellowfang bent over the apprentice. At first she couldn't see anything wrong with him, so she carefully let go of her control so that she could feel his pain. At once agony surged through her. She felt as if some fierce creature was inside her, trying to claw its way out through her belly. Her head reeling from it, her legs beginning to buckle, she reached out and gently turned Cloudpaw over. His belly had been slashed open; the grass underneath him was scarlet from his blood.

"Is he dead?" Rowanberry whispered.

Yellowfang shook her head; she had already spotted the faint rise and fall of Cloudpaw's chest. Forcing herself to block off the pain again, she turned to the other cats. "Wolfstep, run back to camp and warn Sagewhisker. Blizzardwing, find me some cobwebs—try under those bushes. I have to stop the bleeding before we can move him."

"I'll carry him," Raggedpelt mewed hoarsely.

Once Yellowfang had covered the wound with cobwebs, Raggedpelt insisted on taking Cloudpaw on his shoulders, even though the apprentice was nearly full-grown. Staggering under his weight, with Yellowfang and Blizzardwing on either side, he struggled back to the clearing.

Wolfstep had already alerted the Clan, who gathered around as Raggedpelt carried his apprentice through the tunnel. Nettlespot let out a piteous wail when she saw her son.

"My precious kit! Save him! You must save him!"

"We'll do our best," Yellowfang promised her.

The two newest apprentices, Nightpaw and Clawpaw, watched in alarm as Raggedpelt progressed slowly across the clearing, until their mentors, Foxheart and Crowtail, came up and swept them away.

At last Raggedpelt reached the medicine cat's den and laid Cloudpaw gently down on a bed of moss. Sagewhisker flicked him with her tail as he tried to settle down beside his apprentice.

"No, Raggedpelt," she mewed. "You've done all you can. It's time to let us take over."

Raggedpelt looked as if he was about to argue, then rose to his paws in silence. With one last look at Cloudpaw he left the den, his head and tail drooping.

Yellowfang watched as Sagewhisker bent over Cloudpaw and eased the cobwebs away from his wound. When she had laid the gash bare, the medicine cat looked up, meeting Yellowfang's gaze.

"It's very serious," she mewed. "It might be kinder to let StarClan take him now."

"No!" Yellowfang hissed. "This cat will not die! I'll care for him myself, if you're willing to give up." Furious with Sagewhisker for admitting defeat, Yellowfang went to the entrance of the den and stuck her head out. "Hey!" she called to Nutwhisker, who was padding past. "Fetch me some wet moss—as quickly as you can!"

Her brother dashed off and Yellowfang went to the herb stores and uncovered horsetail, goldenrod, and marigold, which she mixed together in a poultice. Crouching beside Cloudpaw, she licked the wound until it was as clean as she could make it, then bound the poultice in place with strands of cobweb from the thornbushes. After a moment she felt Sagewhisker beside her, holding the leaves in place while Yellowfang secured the cobweb.

"I won't stop you from trying to help him," the old medicine cat told her. "But you must be prepared for the worst."

By the time the wound was dressed, Nutwhisker was back with a jawful of dripping moss. Yellowfang squeezed some water into Cloudpaw's mouth. He was still unconscious. She watched the slight movement of his chest, the only thing that told her he was still alive. Icy fear froze Yellowfang from ears to tail-tip at the thought that those feeble breaths might stop altogether. The sun was going down behind the trees and a chilly wind rose.

"I'll stay with him," Yellowfang told Sagewhisker. She settled down beside him. "I'll keep him warm."

Sagewhisker nodded and went out to check the scratches of the other cats who had been in the fight. Darkness had fallen by the time she returned. She came over for another look at Cloudpaw, then curled into her own nest.

"Call me if there's a problem," she mewed to Yellowfang before closing her eyes.

Yellowfang sat beside the injured apprentice, gazing up at the sky as the warriors of StarClan emerged. "Was this our fault?" she whispered. "Did it happen because Raggedpelt and I were together? Please, StarClan, send me a sign, and if you're angry with us, please don't punish this apprentice. He's too young to come to you yet."

But the stars glittered coldly above her, and she didn't know if her plea had been heard.

Weariness eventually overcame Yellowfang and she fell into a doze. Then she felt a cat gently nudging her; she started up, thinking that Cloudpaw needed her, only to find herself standing in a windswept marsh. The cat beside her was holding out a leaf of comfrey. Yellowfang didn't recognize him, but he bore the scent of ShadowClan, and the scent of herbs too in his thick gray pelt. As she took the leaf, Yellowfang heard a thin wailing by her paws and looked down to see a tiny tabby kit with blood trickling from a scratched ear.

Yellowfang bent her head and chewed up the comfrey leaf so that the juice trickled onto the kit's ear. At once the wound closed up as if it had never been there, leaving no scar.

Raising her head again, Yellowfang saw the gray cat was holding out a different leaf. Beyond him was another cat and another, a line stretching out into the distance as far as Yellowfang could see. They were passing herbs to one another, sending the leaves along the line to Yellowfang in a hushed silence.

They're all medicine cats! Yellowfang realized with astonishment. *And I'm one of them. At the end of the line, treating this cat, but with all of their support and wisdom to help me.* A feeling of deep peace crept over her.

She took another leaf, catmint this time, and held it out to a little brown kit who was coughing badly. The kit swallowed it, stopped coughing, and faded away. A mist rose and blotted out the other cats and the marshland where they stood.

Yellowfang was roused by a whimpering noise close by. Cloudpaw squirmed in his nest, letting out feeble cries. His whole body was burning with fever. Yellowfang dripped more water into his mouth, and laid a paw gently on his shoulder in an effort to stop the movement. "Keep still, little one," she murmured. "You'll open your wound again."

The moment he settled, she got up to visit the herb stores again, finding what she needed more by scent than touch in the faint starlight.

Sagewhisker stirred behind her. "How is he?" she asked, her voice blurry with sleep.

"Feverish," Yellowfang responded, finally finding the herb she was looking for.

"Cloudpaw!"

The yowl startled Yellowfang, and she turned to see Nettlespot pushing her way between the boulders into the den. "I have to see my son!" she meowed.

Sagewhisker rose from her nest and blocked Nettlespot

before she could reach Cloudpaw. "It's the middle of the night," she told her. "Cloudpaw mustn't be disturbed. Come back tomorrow."

"But I need to see him!" Nettlespot insisted.

"Not now." Sagewhisker's voice was gentle. "Cloudpaw needs his rest. I promise you, if he gets worse, we *will* call you."

Nettlespot hesitated, then turned and left the den, her tail drooping. Yellowfang was glad to see her go, though she could understand her fear.

"It's hard for her," Sagewhisker commented, as she padded over to look down at Cloudpaw. Her expression grew even more worried. "Yellowfang," she whispered, "you can't save every cat."

"No, but I can save *this* one," Yellowfang growled. "I'm giving him dandelion. That should bring the fever down and help him to sleep."

Sagewhisker nodded. "Mix in a couple of borage leaves," she suggested.

Yellowfang chewed up the herbs and thrust the pulp between Cloudpaw's jaws. As the night wore on she repeated the treatment, not caring how low the stocks of the herbs were growing. *Cloudpaw must live! Nothing else matters!*

As dawn light began to seep into the sky there was movement at the entrance to the den, and Raggedpelt pushed his way between the boulders. "How is he?" he croaked.

"Holding his own," Yellowfang replied. She felt her heart ache as she watched the tabby warrior bend over the motionless form of his apprentice. As Raggedpelt drew away, she met his gaze. "I *will* save him," she vowed.

She couldn't speak of what they had been doing when Cloudpaw was hurt, and she could see that Raggedpelt would never speak of it either. Their guilt ran too deep.

"I've ordered more border patrols," Raggedpelt told her, "to make sure those rogues don't come back."

Yellowfang nodded. "Don't let the apprentices patrol there until we're sure it's safe," she advised.

Raggedpelt gave a brusque nod. "Of course not."

He left, and Yellowfang remained by Cloudpaw's side. Throughout the day, one by one, the members of ShadowClan crept into the den to visit him. Yellowfang kept guard over the apprentice, not letting any of his visitors stay for long—even Nettlespot, whose panic over her kit was no help at all.

As the sun was going down again, Sagewhisker tapped Yellowfang on the shoulder with her tail. "It's time you got out of here for a while," she meowed. "No," she went on, forestalling Yellowfang's protest. "You can't care for Cloudpaw if you fall ill yourself. Go for a walk around the camp, have some fresh-kill and a drink, and you'll feel much better. I'll keep an eye on him."

Reluctantly Yellowfang stumbled into the clearing and wandered around in a daze, aware of the glances of other cats. Every one of them knew how ill Cloudpaw was.

Brightflower bounded up to her and steered her toward the fresh-kill pile. "Here's a good juicy vole," she mewed, pushing it toward Yellowfang. "I'm going to sit with you and make sure you eat every bite!"

Yellowfang was sure she couldn't choke down a single mouthful, but as soon as she tasted the prey she realized how ravenously hungry she was. She gulped down the fresh-kill and went for a drink at the tiny stream at the edge of the camp before making her way back to her den.

Another long night's vigil with Cloudpaw stretched in front of her. The apprentice still had not recovered consciousness, but Yellowfang, watching him as if he were a piece of prey she was about to pounce on, thought that his breathing seemed a little stronger. Once again she raised her eyes to StarClan, shining in frosty splendor above her. "Take me, if you must," she prayed with all her heart. "But save him. None of this is his fault. I'm so sorry."

Eventually, worn out by grief and guilt, Yellowfang dropped into a light, troubled sleep. She woke to find Sagewhisker prodding her in the shoulder. Panicking, she sprang to her paws. "Is it Cloudpaw?" she demanded. "Is he worse?"

Sagewhisker's eyes were gleaming. "No," she purred. "He's waking up. He's still in a lot of pain, but he's asking for water."

Yellowfang gazed down at the apprentice. His blue eyes were glazed, but his breathing was normal and the fever was down.

"I'm so thirsty!" he mewed. "And my belly hurts!"

"It will hurt for a while yet," Yellowfang told him, while Sagewhisker brought him more wet moss. "But it means you're getting better. Now keep still and I'll put a fresh dressing on your wound."

Once Yellowfang had fastened a new poultice in place, she

left Sagewhisker to look after Cloudpaw while she went in search of Raggedpelt. She found him in the clearing, organizing the day's patrols. He turned away from the other cats and bounded up to her with a desperate question in his eyes.

"Cloudpaw has woken up," Yellowfang meowed before he could say anything. "He's not out of trouble yet, but the worst of the infection has cleared."

Raggedpelt closed his eyes and let out a vast sigh of relief. "Thank you," he murmured.

"A *short* walk, mind you," Sagewhisker instructed. "Just as far as the fresh-kill pile and back. You don't want to tire yourself out on your first time out of the den."

Two more days had passed. Cloudpaw was recovering fast, and was well enough to be allowed into the clearing for a little while. He scraped the earth of the den floor impatiently, though Yellowfang guessed he would be glad to get back to his nest before he had walked many paw steps.

"I'll go with him," she offered.

Outside in the camp lots of his Clanmates were waiting to greet the apprentice. "Cloudpaw! Cloudpaw!" they yowled as he appeared.

Cloudpaw gave Yellowfang a bewildered look. "Why are they calling my name?"

"Because you fought bravely," Cedarstar told him, padding up. "We'll make you a warrior as soon as you're better."

Cloudpaw stumbled as he tried to give an excited bounce. "Thank you," he mewed, dipping his head to his Clan leader.

Nettlespot dashed up, brushing past Cedarstar in her haste to get to her son. "My precious kit!" she purred. "Oh, Yellowfang, thank you, thank you!"

"I only did my duty," Yellowfang murmured.

Cloudpaw looked almost overwhelmed as Rowanberry and the other cats in the patrol clustered around him.

"Cloudpaw, it's great to see you again," Rowanberry meowed.

Before Cloudpaw could respond, Yellowfang pressed closer to his side, fixing Rowanberry and the others with a stern glance. "Give him space," she ordered. "He's barely back on his paws."

She spotted Raggedpelt on the edge of the crowd and steered Cloudpaw over to him, away from the others. Raggedpelt looked down at him, then bowed his head. "I'm sorry I let you get hurt," he meowed.

Cloudpaw looked baffled. "It wasn't your fault!" he protested. "I should have scented those rogues before they ambushed us. I let you down!"

"Not at all," Raggedpelt murmured, turning away.

Soon Yellowfang spotted pain in the apprentice's eyes and saw his head beginning to droop. She steered him back to the medicine cat's den.

"You're so good at caring for every cat," Cloudpaw mewed as she settled him in his nest. "You'd make a great mother. Do you ever regret you won't have kits of your own?"

Yellowfang blinked. "The whole Clan are my kits," she replied. "I don't have time to single any out."

Cloudpaw nodded. "I guess that's what it means to be a medicine cat. It must be tough, though," he added. "I'm really looking forward to having a mate and kits of my own."

"You're very young to be thinking about that!" Yellowfang teased him. "There's plenty of time for you to father kits with some poor queen and keep me busy!"

Cloudpaw let out a *mrrow* of laughter, then followed it with a huge yawn. He closed his eyes and immediately drifted into sleep.

Sagewhisker was tidying the herb stores. "Yellowfang, you have done a great thing by healing this cat," she meowed, her eyes glowing as she gazed at Yellowfang. "A lot of other medicine cats—and I'm one of them—would have given up on him and let StarClan decide." The medicine cat stretched out her tail and touched Yellowfang on the shoulder. "It is time you ended your apprenticeship and became a full medicine cat."

"Wow!" Yellowfang exclaimed. "Oh, Sagewhisker, thank you!"

I'm ready for this, she thought. *Saving Cloudpaw meant everything to me. I know that this is my destiny . . . so I will give up Raggedpelt and never look back.*

Chapter 23

For the first time since Cloudpaw was hurt, Yellowfang got a good night's sleep. At sunrise she enjoyed a good stretch and gave herself a thorough grooming from ears to tail.

Sagewhisker emerged from her nest and shook scraps of moss from her pelt. "I need to see Cedarstar," she meowed, "and tell him that you're ready to become a full medicine cat."

Yellowfang turned to her, a spasm of fear tingling through her paws. "Please, Sagewhisker, give me the chance to tell another cat first."

The medicine cat's eyes narrowed. "You mean Raggedpelt, don't you?"

Words failed Yellowfang; she just looked down at her paws. *How does she know?*

"You are bound by the medicine code now. This is how it is for all of us—and how it must be for you," Sagewhisker prompted, her voice firm.

"Always," Yellowfang whispered. Without waiting to hear more, she darted out. The first cat she saw was Nutwhisker, ambling over to the fresh-kill pile. "Have you seen Ragged-pelt?" she called to him.

"He took a hunting patrol out into the marshes," Nutwhisker replied. "They haven't been gone long. You'll catch up to them if you hurry."

"Thanks!" Yellowfang raced out through the tunnel and into the trees. Soon she reached the edge of the marshes and spotted Raggedpelt several fox-lengths away. Foxheart was stalking something among a clump of scrubby bushes, while Frogtail and Mudclaw were just visible farther away.

"Raggedpelt!" Yellowfang bounded from one grassy hump to the next, heading for the tabby tom. As she approached she spotted something flickering in the grass and Raggedpelt turned toward her, spitting with frustration.

"Now look what you've done! I nearly had that lizard."

"Sorry," Yellowfang panted. "But I have something to tell you."

Raggedpelt's ears flicked forward. "What? Not Cloudpaw? Is he—"

"Cloudpaw is fine." Yellowfang paused; it was harder than she had expected to deliver her news. "Sagewhisker is going to make me a full medicine cat at the half-moon Gathering tonight."

Raggedpelt stared at her. "Are you sure that's what you want? Haven't you enjoyed the last few moons with me?"

"You know I have." Yellowfang sighed. "But healing Cloudpaw has shown me where my heart lies. I must be a medicine cat."

Raggedpelt took a pace toward her, his tail lashing and his neck fur fluffing up. "You're throwing your life away!" he snarled. "I thought you'd have gotten over your fixation with herbs and cobwebs by now."

"You never take me seriously," Yellowfang retorted, her pain curdling into anger. "You have no idea what it means to be a medicine cat." Glancing across to where Foxheart had just made her catch, she added savagely, "Why don't you go and have kits with *her* instead? She's always mooning around after you."

"Foxheart means nothing to me," Raggedpelt growled. "My whole world is you, Yellowfang, and the future we could have together."

For a heartbeat Yellowfang could see that future too, and she was drawn to it in spite of herself. But she knew how impossible it was for her to turn her paws aside from the path she had chosen.

"This is my destiny," she mewed. "You cannot change it."

"No," Raggedpelt responded. "But *you* could."

Yellowfang could tell by the spring in her step that Sagewhisker was excited as they prepared to leave for the half-moon Gathering at the Moonstone. In contrast, as she checked on Cloudpaw's wound and made sure he had water and a piece of fresh-kill, Yellowfang felt hollow inside. *I've lost something so precious . . . but I can't abandon my duty to my Clan, not even for Raggedpelt.*

"This is so cool!" Cloudpaw meowed, his eyes shining. "We'll finish our apprenticeships at the same time, Yellowfang!"

Yellowfang nodded. "You'll be a good warrior, Cloudpaw."

"And you're already a *great* medicine cat!"

Sagewhisker prepared traveling herbs for both of them, and the two cats set out from the camp just after sunhigh. With every paw step Yellowfang felt as if she was leaving part of herself behind. Several of her Clanmates waited beside the tunnel to wish her good luck, but Raggedpelt was not one of them. He stood watching her from the far end of the clearing, and didn't say a word.

Yellowfang was always slightly nervous at the thought of crossing WindClan territory, even though medicine cats had the right to do so on their way to the Moonstone. To her relief, they saw only one patrol in the distance. Reedfeather, the Clan deputy, was leading it, and he simply acknowledged the two medicine cats with a wave of his tail.

Twilight was gathering by the time Yellowfang and Sagewhisker reached Highstones. The other medicine cats were already there.

"Yellowfang is here today to be made a full medicine cat," Sagewhisker mewed when greetings had been exchanged.

Hawkheart, the WindClan medicine cat, stepped forward and rested his tail-tip on Yellowfang's shoulder for a moment. "Congratulations," he murmured. "As you know, I was a warrior before I became a medicine cat, just like you. I've always found it a great help."

Goosefeather of ThunderClan ignored her, his gleaming, unfocused eyes suggesting that he was away somewhere inside his own head as usual, but Brambleberry of RiverClan pushed up beside the others, her eyes shining and her white pelt gleaming in the dusk. "I'm so excited for you!" she exclaimed.

Yellowfang thanked the two cats for their good wishes, then turned to face Featherwhisker. The second Thunder-Clan medicine cat was regarding her with the same mixture of wariness and curiosity that he always showed. "Your Clan must be pleased to have a second medicine cat," he mewed. "I trust all is well with you?"

"ShadowClan is doing fine," Sagewhisker responded brusquely.

"What about you, Yellowfang?" Featherwhisker commented. "Have you found it hard to change from being a warrior to the life of a medicine cat?"

You don't know how hard! Yellowfang thought, but she wasn't about to tell Featherwhisker that. *He needs to butt out and mind his own business!*

To her relief Sagewhisker saved her from having to reply. "Come along," she urged the others. "If we hang around gossiping we'll be late for the Moonstone."

She led the way up the last steep slope to where Mothermouth yawned in the side of the hill. As Yellowfang made her way down the twisting passage into the heart of the hill, she felt her doubts and heartaches drop away behind her.

I'm going to be a full medicine cat!

The cave of the Moonstone was still dark when they reached it. Only a faint twinkle of starlight trickled down through the ragged hole in the roof. The medicine cats took their places around the crystal and waited. Yellowfang almost let out a squeal like an excited kit when at last the moon shone through the hole and drenched the Moonstone in a cold, unearthly light.

It's the most beautiful thing in the world! Every time I see it, it still surprises me.

Sagewhisker rose to her paws, stood beside the Moonstone, and beckoned to Yellowfang with her tail. Feeling that her paws would barely support her, Yellowfang joined her at the heart of the frosty light.

Gazing up at the moon, Sagewhisker spoke. "I, Sagewhisker, medicine cat of ShadowClan, call upon my warrior ancestors to look down on this apprentice. She has trained hard to understand the way of a medicine cat, and with your help she will serve her Clan for many moons."

Yellowfang felt as if she and her mentor were standing alone in the circle of light while the rest of the world had faded away. She could hear whispers and the soft pad of paws at the edge of the cavern. Were long-dead medicine cats from StarClan here, watching? Yellowfang's paws tingled at the thought of being part of a long line of cats who had devoted their lives to caring for ShadowClan. The same line she had seen in her dream while treating Cloudpaw. All those cats, sharing their wisdom in support of her!

"Yellowfang," Sagewhisker continued, "do you promise to uphold the ways of a medicine cat, to stand apart from rivalry between Clan and Clan, and to protect all cats equally, even at the cost of your life?"

"I do," Yellowfang replied.

"Then by the powers of StarClan I declare that you are

a full medicine cat. StarClan honors your courage and your diligence. Now come, touch your nose to the Moonstone, and may all your dreams be good ones."

Yellowfang crouched down; swallowing rapidly from nerves, she stretched out her neck and touched her nose to the glimmering surface. At once everything went dark, and she felt cold creeping through her as if she were turning into a cat of ice.

StarClan, where are you?

The darkness lifted, and Yellowfang looked around. The Moonstone, the cave, and the other medicine cats had vanished. Instead she was crouching in the clearing where she had first met Silverflame, when she was made a medicine cat apprentice. But now the lush growth of greenleaf had faded; the ground felt marshy underpaw, and a chilly breeze ruffled Yellowfang's fur.

A few heartbeats later, she spotted Silverflame pushing her way through a clump of fern. "Greetings, Yellowfang," she began. "It's wonderful to see you again."

But in spite of her warm words, Yellowfang could see sadness in her eyes. "Is . . . is all well with you?" she asked.

Silverflame avoided the question. "I'm very proud of you," she mewed. "Come, walk with me."

She turned and brushed through the grass in the direction of the stream. Yellowfang padded at her shoulder, convinced there was something the old cat wasn't telling her. Silverflame followed the stream until they came to a spot where the current had carved out a wide pool. Silverflame sat on the bank and looked down into the still water.

Yellowfang sat beside her. "Why have you brought me here?"

Silverflame gestured at the surface of the pool with her tail. Yellowfang looked down and saw her own reflection staring back at her, with Silverflame's reflection beside her. Then she let out a gasp. Behind her, she saw the reflections of three kits, their tiny bodies huddled close together.

Confused, Yellowfang rose to her paws and spun around. No kits were in sight, and the grass wasn't long enough to hide them. She drew in a sharp breath, but there was no kit scent in the air.

"I saw kits!" she exclaimed to Silverflame. "Where did they go?"

There was a strange, sad knowledge in Silverflame's eyes, but she didn't reply. Instead her outline began to fade.

"No!" Yellowfang protested. "Don't go! I don't understand!"

Now Silverflame's body was no more than a shimmer by the poolside. Her voice came faintly to Yellowfang's ears. "Whatever happens, Yellowfang, know that I am always with you. Trust your instincts. Make your own choice."

The sunlight was swallowed up by darkness, and Yellowfang opened her eyes to find herself back in the cavern of the Moonstone. The silver light was gone; by the faint starshine Yellowfang could just make out the other medicine cats, all crouched as she was with their noses against the Moonstone. Yellowfang shivered, suddenly overwhelmed by the cold and the blackness. She felt an itch in her paws, an urge to run far, far away, to escape from the questions and the mystery and the responsibility of her new role.

Brambleberry was already awake, arching her back in a long stretch. "That was a lovely dream," she remarked to Featherwhisker, who was stirring beside her. "I get such great guidance from my StarClan mentor."

Featherwhisker nodded. "Mine is always quick to point out when I'm about to make a mistake!" he purred.

Yellowfang listened, puzzled. *It's not like that for me. Silverflame told me I have to trust my own instincts.*

Then Hawkheart of WindClan sat up. Blinking, he turned to Yellowfang. "How are you feeling?" he asked cheerfully.

"Er . . . fine," Yellowfang stammered. *Yes, I'm fine,* she told herself. *I'm a medicine cat of ShadowClan, just as I am destined to be.*

The warm sun of leaf-fall shone down, turning the forest to scarlet and gold. Yellowfang and Cloudpelt were collecting cobwebs in a clearing not far from the camp. Yellowfang felt warm affection as she watched the young white warrior pawing the sticky strands from the ivy growing up an oak tree. Though his wound was almost healed, he still moved stiffly, and was only allowed to perform light duties, but he was always the first to offer his help to Yellowfang. She knew his loyalty to her came from the fact that she had saved his life, and she loved him all the more for it.

The bond between us will never be broken.

Yellowfang felt a twinge in her belly and realized that

Cloudpelt was stretching too far up the tree in his efforts to reach another cobweb. Gently she nudged him out of the way. "Let me get it," she meowed. "You need to be careful not to open up that wound again."

As Cloudpelt stepped back, loud, excited squeals came from the trees at the edge of the clearing. The current apprentices, Nightpaw, Clawpaw, Blackpaw, Flintpaw, and Fernpaw, rushed past and plunged into the undergrowth on the opposite side. They were closely followed by their mentors, Foxheart, Crowtail, Rowanberry, and Scorchwind. Yellowfang suppressed a *mrrow* of amusement at how flustered all the warriors looked.

"Hey, slow down!" Scorchwind called. "This is a patrol, not a race!"

Cloudpelt rolled his eyes. "Crazy apprentices!"

Yellowfang flicked his ear with her tail. "It's only three sunrises since you were an apprentice," she pointed out.

"Ah, but I feel old in my bones," Cloudpelt responded in a quavering voice like an elder.

A sudden squeal distracted Yellowfang and she looked up to see Blackpaw reappearing from the undergrowth. The white tom was holding a single black forepaw up as he tottered across to her on three legs.

"I stepped on a thorn!"

"Let's see." Yellowfang peered at the apprentice's pads, and finally managed to spot a tiny bramble thorn at the very edge. "Great StarClan, that's *huge*!" she mewed, deftly hooking it out with her teeth. She remembered the time she'd bitten Finchflight, pleased that her skills had improved since then. "You're fine now. Give it a good lick," she told Blackpaw.

The apprentice swiped his tongue once over his pad, then charged into the undergrowth again. "Thanks, Yellowfang!" he yowled over his shoulder as he disappeared.

Yellowfang realized that Cloudpelt had watched her carefully all the time she was extracting the thorn.

"We're lucky to have you as our medicine cat," he meowed. "I'm glad StarClan chose you."

"It was my choice, too," Yellowfang responded.

The full moon shed its cold light onto the cats packed into the hollow at Fourtrees. Yellowfang felt the gaze of every single one of them fixed on her as Sagewhisker announced that she was now a full medicine cat.

"Yellowfang! Yellowfang!"

The yowls of welcome rang out around her, mainly from the other medicine cats. Yellowfang's heart swelled with a mixture of pride and comradeship at the thought that she was one of them, privileged to care for her Clan and to interpret the signs of StarClan for them.

This truly is my destiny!

Then she caught Raggedpelt's eye. He had not joined in the cheering; instead he was scowling at her. He had hardly spoken to her in the half-moon since she had taken her vows as a medicine cat.

Why can't he understand, and be glad for me? Yellowfang wondered, shooting him a look that was sharper than flint. *If he's going to be the next ShadowClan leader, I will be his medicine cat, and we will need to lead the Clan side by side. Why can't he be satisfied with that?*

Yet Yellowfang could not stifle a pang of regret for what she had lost. Instead Foxheart clung to Raggedpelt's side like a burr; she was there now, leaning close to him, whispering into his ear.

It'll change when he is leader, Yellowfang decided. *He'll just have to accept that this is the way things are.*

As Heatherstar began to speak, Yellowfang felt a strange wriggling sensation in her belly. She shifted around among the fallen leaves, trying to get comfortable.

Sagewhisker gave her a prod. "Keep still," she hissed. "I can't concentrate on what Heatherstar is saying."

"Sorry," Yellowfang muttered.

"Do you have a pain somewhere?" Sagewhisker asked. "Have you eaten crow-food by mistake?"

"That must be it," Yellowfang agreed.

But she knew what this feeling was. She'd treated enough pregnant queens now to recognize the quiver of unborn babies, even before their mother's belly had begun to swell. Yellowfang tried to block out the sensation, wondering which of the queens around her could be expecting kits. But the wriggling went on, even though Yellowfang held her breath with the effort to concentrate on her own stomach.

Which meant that these weren't the feelings belonging to another cat. These were truly inside her belly, kicking and squirming and growing. . . . A cold sensation of dread crept through Yellowfang's fur.

I'm a medicine cat now! Great StarClan, there's no way I can have kits!

Chapter 24

Yellowfang hauled herself out of her nest a few days after the Gathering. Every muscle in her body protested; she felt as exhausted as if she had run all the way around the border, three times.

"Why are you always so tired these days?" Sagewhisker asked her as Yellowfang forced herself to draw her paws over her ears in a sketchy grooming. "And you're putting on weight, too. Maybe if you didn't eat so much, you would be able to do more."

"Maybe," Yellowfang muttered. *If I weren't a medicine cat, you would know what the problem is. But you'd never even begin to guess that I'm expecting kits. What am I going to do?*

Slipping out of the den, she stood at the edge of the clearing and watched her Clanmates going about their duties. The apprentices were hauling a load of bedding out of the elders' den. As Yellowfang watched, Flintpaw rolled up a ball of moss and hurled it at Nightpaw's head.

Nightpaw batted it away. "Stop being such a mouse-brain, Flintpaw," he meowed. "We'll never get finished that way."

Flintpaw let out a yowl and hurled himself at Nightpaw. "I'm a WindClan warrior!" he screeched. The two apprentices wrestled together in the midst of the discarded bedding; Blackpaw, Clawpaw, and Fernpaw joined in with joyous mews, scattering moss everywhere.

Yellowfang wondered if she needed to intervene, but she realized that Nightpaw, who was the smallest of the apprentices, was giving as good as he got, and the squabbling was basically good-natured. A moment later Hollyflower, who was Blackpaw's, Flintpaw's, and Fernpaw's mother, strode across the clearing, grabbed Flintpaw by the scruff, and heaved him out of the fight. The other apprentices sat up with moss all over their pelts and identical disappointed expressions.

"What do you think you're doing?" Hollyflower demanded. "Clear this mess up *right now*, and get it all out of camp. If you don't finish the elders' bedding, there'll be no battle training later. I'll speak to your mentors myself."

The threat was enough to send the apprentices scurrying to gather up the scattered moss and begin hauling it toward the tunnel. Hollyflower watched until she was sure they were all working, then turned toward the fresh-kill pile.

Lizardstripe was just finishing off a blackbird; her ears twitched as the apprentices bundled past her. "You must be glad your kits are out of your paws and you can return to warrior duties," she remarked to Hollyflower.

Hollyflower sighed, gazing after the apprentices, who were heading into the tunnel with their burden of moss. "But I miss them so much! They don't seem to need me at all now."

Lizardstripe grimaced as if she had accidentally taken a mouthful of crow-food. "Didn't you feel trapped while you were in the nursery? Missing patrols, and the chance to hunt for your Clan?"

Yellowfang saw Hollyflower's puzzled expression. "Why would I feel trapped? Having kits to raise as warriors is the duty of every queen."

"Don't you think that's unfair?" Lizardstripe protested. "Toms can hunt and fight all their lives, and still have kits for the Clan."

Hollyflower reached out with her tail to give Lizardstripe a friendly flick on the shoulder. "I think that's tough on the toms! Wait until you're expecting kits, Lizardstripe, then you'll feel differently."

"Actually, I don't." Lizardstripe sniffed.

Hollyflower let out an excited squeal. "Oh, Lizardstripe, you're expecting kits! That's fabulous! Are they Mudclaw's?"

Lizardstripe nodded; Yellowfang didn't think she'd ever seen a prospective mother looking so unenthusiastic.

"You're probably just nervous," Hollyflower reassured her. "Having kits will change your life!"

"But I don't *want* my life to change," Lizardstripe meowed with a lash of her tail. "I like my life the way it is now. All I ever wanted was to be a warrior, protecting my Clan."

"Well, you'll be a warrior again, once your kits become apprentices," Hollyflower pointed out.

Her reasonable tones seemed to annoy Lizardstripe even more. "Six moons in the nursery? I'll go mad!" she exclaimed.

"You'll be fine, and so will your kits," Hollyflower promised, seeming unable to believe that Lizardstripe really meant what she said. "We have two medicine cats now, don't forget!"

With an angry shrug of her shoulders Lizardstripe got up and stalked across the camp toward the warriors' den. Staring at her, Yellowfang realized that her belly did look swollen, a little more than her own.

Two litters, neither of them wanted.

The thought made her wince. *Oh, kits, I* do *want you,* she told the tiny lives growing in her belly. *But things are going to be complicated.*

Yellowfang wished that she could talk to Lizardstripe, to confide in her about her worries, and share the experience of having kits for the first time. But Yellowfang's secret was one she would have to bear alone. Besides, she and Lizardstripe had never been friends.

And I certainly can't tell Raggedpelt. He's made it clear that my decision to become a full medicine cat means I can have nothing to do with him.

At that moment she spotted the tabby tom, hurrying from the warriors' den to Cedarstar's. She wasn't sure if he had seen her; he certainly didn't acknowledge her.

"Yellowfang, why are you standing there as if you're half-asleep?"

Yellowfang jumped as Sagewhisker bustled out of the den behind her. "We have to check Littlebird's cough," the medicine cat went on, "and bring some ointment of yarrow to Stonetooth for his cracked pads. And you promised to take Cloudpelt into the forest again. It's too soon for him to be out unless there's an experienced cat to keep an eye on him."

"Sorry, Sagewhisker," Yellowfang mewed. "I'll see to the

elders, and then find Cloudpelt." She set off for the elders' den, feeling utterly weary, her paws dragging as if they were made of stone.

Sagewhisker padded after her. "Don't forget the ointment of yarrow," she prompted. Her eyes narrowed and she studied Yellowfang more closely. "Are you all right?" she asked. "You've been very tired recently. Medicine cats do get ill themselves, you know."

Panic stabbed into Yellowfang at the thought of Sagewhisker finding out the truth. *What would she do? Strip me of being a medicine cat? Exile me from the Clan? This is my home, and my life!*

"No, I'm fine," Yellowfang replied, trying to put a spring in her step as she headed for the elders' den. *Even if they're grumpy and difficult with leaf-bare setting in, it's my duty to care for them, and I'll do that—for as long as I'm allowed.*

Yellowfang found herself standing in a dark, empty space. A few traces of starlight shone in the blackness above her head, too faint to be stars. She understood that she was dreaming, but she didn't know what the dream might mean.

"Is this StarClan?" she called. "Is there anyone there?"

A moment later a small dark-pelted cat padded out of the shadows. He gave Yellowfang a long look, and solemnly shook his head. "There is a cat coming," he meowed, "a cat who should never be born, whose life will bring fire and blood to the forest, yet StarClan is powerless to stop him!"

Yellowfang stared at him in horror. "Is there nothing we can do?"

The dark cat dipped his head. "Only one thing can stop the tide of hatred this birth-cursed cat will bring: the courage of a mother to know her destiny."

"Are you talking about one of my kits?" Yellowfang gasped. "What do you mean? Is this a prophecy?"

"It is a *warning*," the dark cat whispered. He drew back into the shadows.

Yellowfang sprang after him and woke up thrashing in her nest, with the walls of the den faintly visible as the sky paled toward dawn. Horror chilled her bones. She instinctively curled her paws around her swollen belly, desperate to protect the life within.

There's no way my kits will bring bloodshed to ShadowClan! It's not their fault that they're going to be born. For a moment, she considered describing the dream to Sagewhisker. *But Silverflame told me to trust my own instincts. And my secret would be in danger if I told her too much.*

Yellowfang raised her eyes to the few warriors of StarClan who still shone in the dawn sky. "StarClan, I speak these words before you," she whispered. "I vow to my kits that I will do everything I can to protect them. I'm sorry that I won't be the mother they might have hoped for, the mother they deserve, but I will *always* love them."

The last leaves fell from the trees. The weather was not as harsh as the previous leaf-bare, but the days were cold and endlessly wet, and none of the cats ever felt warm or dry. Life in the Clan seemed to slow down, with warriors only emerging to hunt or patrol, though no cat expected enemies to attack in such foul weather.

One morning Yellowfang lay at the mouth of her den, watching Raggedpelt sorting reluctant warriors into patrols under the perpetual drizzling rain. Cloudpelt, fully recovered now, was among them, the only cat who seemed to have any energy as he leaped and splashed through the puddles in the clearing.

"You did well to heal the young warrior." Sagewhisker came to join Yellowfang at the mouth of the den.

"He was strong enough to heal himself," Yellowfang responded, feeling uncomfortable and fat under her thick pelt.

For a moment the medicine cat was silent. Then she gave Yellowfang a nudge. "Come on, let's go for a walk. I haven't been out of the camp for days."

Unwilling, but not daring to show it, Yellowfang heaved herself to her paws and padded beside Sagewhisker out of the camp, following the departing patrols. She noticed how much the old medicine cat was showing her age, gray around the muzzle and stiff in her hind legs when the weather was damp. A pang of concern shook Yellowfang. Sagewhisker had been ShadowClan's medicine cat for as long as she could remember, a source of skill and comfort for her Clan, and it was hard to think of her getting old.

I must make sure she eats some herbs to help her pains. She needs me to take care of her, even if she doesn't want it.

Yellowfang and Sagewhisker ducked through the dripping brambles and headed out into the marshes.

"I like the open spaces when it rains," Sagewhisker meowed. "I can't stand it when rain splashes on my neck from the trees." Pausing at the edge of the marshland, she took in a deep breath. "It's bleak out here, but I love this part of the territory," she told Yellowfang. "I'm a ShadowClan cat to my bones, and I'm glad StarClan made sure I was born here."

Yellowfang murmured agreement, but her attention was mostly fixed on the wriggling in her belly. Suddenly one of her kits kicked her so hard that she let out an involuntary gasp.

Sagewhisker turned to her. "Come and sit here, on this clump of grass." As Yellowfang obeyed, she gave her a long look. "How long to go?" she asked.

Yellowfang stared at her in dismay. "You know?" she whispered.

"I'm a medicine cat," Sagewhisker replied. "I've delivered more kits for ShadowClan than you've eaten mice. Of course I know."

"Are you angry?"

"A little," Sagewhisker admitted. "You made vows, and you've broken them."

"No!" Yellowfang protested. "Raggedpelt and I haven't been together since I was made a full medicine cat at the Moonstone."

Sagewhisker flicked her tail. "You're splitting whiskers, Yellowfang. You know that you shouldn't have been with Raggedpelt when you were a medicine cat apprentice. But that's not the most important thing," she went on. "ShadowClan needs you. I will walk with StarClan soon, and you have to take my place. You have a rare gift, and you've thrown it away."

"No, I haven't!" Yellowfang insisted. "I'll deal with this, I promise. I won't stop being a medicine cat. I just need to figure out what to do . . ." Her voice trailed off.

Sagewhisker's gaze was stern. "It's time you made a decision once and for all," she mewed. "If you're to walk the path of a medicine cat, there must be no more turning aside. The Clan *must* come first."

Yellowfang nodded miserably. "I know. It will, from now on."

Sagewhisker reached out with her tail and stroked Yellowfang's shoulder, a rare gesture of affection. "You poor thing," she whispered, startling Yellowfang. "May StarClan light your path." Her tone became brisk again as she continued. "Does Raggedpelt know?"

Yellowfang shook her head.

"You should tell him," Sagewhisker meowed. "If the kits . . . are going to live, then he deserves to know."

"Of course they're going to live!" Yellowfang cried. *Does she think I would kill my own kits?*

"Then they will need their father more than ever," Sagewhisker told her. "They can't lose both their parents."

Yellowfang nodded. "I know, you're right. But it will be hard to tell him." *How will I ever find the words? And what will he do when he knows the truth?*

Later that day, Yellowfang was back in the camp, busy covering the herb stores with more fern to keep the rain out.

Sagewhisker bustled into the den and took the fern frond

she was holding. "I'll do that," she mewed. "Raggedpelt isn't on patrol. Go and tell him." More gently, she added, "You have to; you know that."

Yellowfang stared at her for a moment, then bowed her head. On reluctant paws she dragged herself out into the clearing and saw Raggedpelt gulping down a piece of prey by the fresh-kill pile.

"Can we talk?" she asked, padding up to him.

Raggedpelt eyed her coldly. "We have nothing to say to each other."

"Believe me, we do."

Yellowfang led Raggedpelt into the forest, pushing through the undergrowth until the camp was out of sight. Then she faced him under the dripping trees. "I'm going to have kits," she announced.

She braced herself for the blast of Raggedpelt's rage. Instead, the tabby tom's eyes widened in disbelief. "That's not possible!"

"Of course it's possible!"

The confusion in Raggedpelt's eyes faded, to be replaced with glowing happiness. "I'm going to be a father!" he breathed. "Yellowfang, that's great! Our kits will be the best warriors and queens the Clan has ever known. One of them might become Clan leader one day."

"But—" Yellowfang tried to interrupt. Even Raggedpelt's anger might have been better than this total refusal to see what the problem was.

"I'll be the best father," he went on enthusiastically. "I'll teach them battle moves, and show them the best places to hunt."

"But I'm a medicine cat!" Yellowfang made him listen at last. "I'm not supposed to have kits!"

Raggedpelt blinked at her. "Well, you'll have to stop being a medicine cat."

"I can't," Yellowfang choked.

Raggedpelt's voice grew dangerous. "Can't, or won't?"

"Both," Yellowfang admitted. "I will bear these kits, and love them with all my heart, but I cannot be their mother. You will have to raise them alone."

"I can't do that!" Raggedpelt yelped. "How can I stay with them in the nursery and give them milk?"

"Lizardstripe is also expecting kits," Yellowfang explained. "She can care for ours until they are old enough to feed alone. Every cat can know that they are yours, but no cats must know they are also mine." She let out a long sigh. "I'm sorry, Raggedpelt. I cannot be their mother."

Although she spoke briskly, inside Yellowfang's heart was splitting into tiny pieces. *This is the only choice I can make. I have to follow the path that StarClan has laid out for me.*

The words of the small dark cat in her dream rang in her ears, warning her about the storm of fire and blood that would be released into her Clan, but she pushed the memory away. There was no reason to believe that the black cat had been speaking of her kits. She didn't even know his name, or what Clan he had once belonged to.

Raggedpelt will be a good father. My kits will be in safe paws.

The warrior was staring at her as if he'd never seen her before. "You mean, you'd choose to be a medicine cat for Clanmates that have no kinship with you, over caring for your own kits? *Our* own kits?" His voice rose to a screech. "What kind of she-cat are you? Do you care for nothing beyond yourself?"

Yellowfang tried not to crumple to the ground in despair. "I have to do this," she muttered through gritted teeth. "Our kits will not suffer because of it."

"What do you know about growing up with only one parent?" Raggedpelt snarled.

Too late, Yellowfang realized she had forgotten about his torment over his absent father. "This will be different!" she tried to protest. "These kits will be cared for by Lizardstripe in the nursery, and they will have you as their father, to love and be proud of them! Please, you have to do this for them!"

Raggedpelt glared at her as if she were nothing more than a rat. "Very well, but on one condition," he mewed at last. "You must promise never to tell these kits the truth. It is better that they grow up without a mother than knowing that their mother chose to abandon them."

Yellowfang's heart cracked a little more as she made the promise Raggedpelt asked for. *I will never abandon you, little ones,* she whispered to her unborn babies. *I will be with you, always.*

Chapter 25

Griping pains in her belly woke Yellowfang, and she bit back a groan. She knew this time the agony was her own. *It's time. I have to go. Sagewhisker will cover for me.*

Yellowfang had already prepared the herbs she would need: chervil root and a juniper berry, folded up in a couple of nettle leaves. She had hidden the leaf wrap in her nest, so no cats who came into the den would spot it. Now Yellowfang dug the herbs out of the moss and headed for the mouth of the den. Sagewhisker was still asleep in her nest, and Yellowfang didn't wake her as she stumbled into the clearing.

Night covered the forest. A few stars showed through gaps in the clouds, but there was no moon. Yellowfang was grateful for the darkness. She could just spot Blizzardwing on guard beside the camp entrance, because of his pale pelt, but she knew that she could slink out unnoticed past the dirtplace.

Powerful ripples of pain passed through Yellowfang's belly as she skirted the dirtplace and headed through the trees. She had picked out the place where her kits would be born a few sunrises before: a dead tree across the border in the unknown forest. There the border patrols wouldn't be able to scent her, or come upon her unexpectedly.

Whatever happens after this, she thought, *I have to stay focused on my duties as a medicine cat. Nothing else matters. The Clan will always need me more than my kits.*

As Yellowfang crept into the hollow of the dead tree, she knew her kits were ready to be born. The hollow was full of dead leaves and there was a smell of toadstools and something rotting. Not even Raggedpelt would find her here.

All Yellowfang wanted was for the birth to be over. But she felt as if she was lying in that dead tree for days. Everything hurt—her whole body, down to the tips of her fur and the ends of her claws. She told herself that she was a medicine cat, able to take care of herself, but she was too weak to do anything, even eat the herbs she'd brought. Finally, after a long night of darkness and anguish, there were three small bundles next to her on the pile of leaves. Two of them were squirming; one was completely still. Yellowfang prodded it with her paw, trying to hide from herself what she knew very well. The kit had been born dead. Her eyes would never open.

Yellowfang dragged the other two, a tom and a she-cat, toward her. With all the strength she could manage she began to lick them, trying to warm them and wake them up. The tom let out an angry wail the minute she touched him; the other only whimpered slightly and jerked her paws.

I can see the tom is going to be a fighter. He had his father's dark tabby pelt, with a broad, flat face and a tiny tail bent in the middle like a broken branch. His lungs were so powerful,

Yellowfang was surprised his wails didn't bring the entire Clan running to find them. He battered his sister with his paws every time he moved, but she barely reacted.

Another dreadful certainty began to gather inside Yellowfang. She tried as long as she could, licking and licking the weak she-kit, but her breathing only got shallower and shallower, until finally it stopped altogether. Her tail twitched once and was still. Yellowfang buried her nose in the tiny scrap of fur, feeling grief crash down on her. It was a clear sign from StarClan.

These are the kits I saw in the pool, when I was in StarClan with Silverflame. But they should never have been born.

Pulling herself out of her grief, Yellowfang turned her attention to her only surviving kit, and saw the expression on his small, flat face. He was new to the world—couldn't see, could barely crawl to her belly to feed. And yet his face was already twisted with strong emotion . . .

Rage? Hatred? I've never seen such a look on any cat, let alone a newborn kit.

Fear flooded through Yellowfang, making her shiver with cold. *Maybe this kit wasn't meant to survive either,* she thought. A kit born with so much anger in him could only mean trouble for the Clan. Her fear surged higher as she remembered her dream, and the dire warning spoken by the black StarClan cat. *Is this the cat who will bring fire and blood to the forest?*

But then he squirmed over to Yellowfang and pressed his face into her fur. *He's so small, so helpless. He needs me!*

Desperately she told herself that he was only a little kit,

after all—her kit, and the son of Raggedpelt, the cat she loved. Yellowfang licked the top of his head and he let out a small purr. Her heart seemed to expand to fill her whole chest. *How can I believe that any kit should not have been born?*

Leaving the tiny tom in the hollow tree, Yellowfang buried his sisters in the unknown forest, digging deep into the soil so that no cat or fox or badger would ever sniff them out. Then she returned to her one living kit.

"Silverflame told me to trust my own instincts and make my own choices," she whispered to the tiny tom, bending to lick his head. "And I choose that you will grow up in the Clan as a warrior without knowing who your mother is." She heaved a deep sigh. "That will be best for both of us, little one."

Giving him a last lick, Yellowfang slunk back through the undergrowth, her fur matted and stinking of toadstools, the tom kit dangling from her mouth. Aware of how many questions would be asked, she stopped to clean herself in a pool near the entrance. By the time she and her kit entered the camp, no cat would have been able to guess the ordeal she had been through.

Raggedpelt spotted her the moment she pushed through the brambles. He barely even looked at her; his eyes were all for the kit, and they were full of hope and excitement. He came bounding across the clearing to follow Yellowfang into the nursery. Lizardstripe was there tending to her own two kits, born a few days earlier. Her pale brown tabby fur and white underbelly seemed to glow in the darkness of the nursery den. She looked at Yellowfang with narrow, unfriendly eyes.

Yellowfang had never really liked or trusted Lizardstripe, but she had no choice. Lizardstripe was the only nursing queen at the moment.

Yellowfang dropped the kit at Lizardstripe's paws and he let out a furious shriek.

"What," growled Lizardstripe, "is that?"

"It's a kit," Yellowfang replied.

"It's my kit," Raggedstar added proudly, shouldering his way into the den.

"Oh, yes?" Lizardstripe mewed. "What a miracle. If I'd known toms could have kits, I would have made Mudclaw have these brats of mine himself."

Raggedpelt ignored her. Yellowfang thought that the space seemed to get smaller with him in it, as if he drew all the air into himself. She wanted to press herself into his fur and tell him everything she'd been through and about the two tiny bodies in the forest. The effort of holding back left her shaking inside, but Raggedpelt still wasn't looking at her.

He crouched and sniffed at his son. The kit tried to lift his head, and then swiped his paw through the air, connecting with Raggedpelt's nose. The tabby tom jerked his head back in surprise.

"Look at that!" he cried delightedly. "He's a little warrior already!"

Lizardstripe's amber gaze was making Yellowfang uncomfortable. "His mother wishes to keep her identity secret," Yellowfang meowed. "She cannot care for this kit, and she hopes that you will take him in for her."

Lizardstripe lashed her tail. "What kind of mouse-brained nonsense is that?" she snapped. "Why should I have to put up with another mewling lump of fur? I didn't ask for these kits either, but you don't see me dumping them on some other cat. It's not my job to take care of every unwanted kit in the Clan."

Raggedpelt snarled, and Lizardstripe shrank back in her nest. "He is not unwanted," Raggedstar hissed. "He is my son, and I will always claim him as my own. You are being given a great honor, you unworthy cat. Who wouldn't want to be mother to the Clan deputy's son—and perhaps the future leader of the Clan himself?"

Lizardstripe hissed softly. But she knew better than to argue with Raggedpelt. Yellowfang thought that perhaps she saw the wisdom of his words. As the queen responsible for Raggedpelt's son—even if the Clan knew she wasn't his real mother—Lizardstripe would be a significant cat within the Clan.

"All right, fine," she spat ungraciously. "Give him to me."

As Lizardstripe nestled her son into the curve of her belly, Yellowfang felt a strong pang of unease. *What kind of life will he have, with an ambitious queen like Lizardstripe raising him? Am I making the biggest mistake of my life?*

"His name is Brokenkit," she meowed, her voice faltering. Lizardstripe nodded, stretching out a paw to touch the bend in his tail. That was where every cat would think his name came from. But Yellowfang knew the truth. She named her son for the feeling in her chest as she left him there, as if her heart were cleaving in two, as if her life had broken down the middle.

Yellowfang staggered back to the medicine cats' den and curled up in her nest. Everything within her ached, far beyond the reach of any herbs.

Sagewhisker turned from hanging cobwebs on the thorns. "Is it over?"

Yellowfang raised her head a little and nodded. "Yes. It's over." *All over.*

Sagewhisker returned to the herb store and fetched a leaf, nudging it toward her.

"Parsley?" Yellowfang asked.

The medicine cat nodded. "It will dry up your milk. You should take one leaf every day." As Yellowfang licked up the leaf, she added, "You did the right thing."

Yellowfang didn't reply. All she could think of was her tiny son, now suckling at Lizardstripe's belly. She yearned for him, yet she couldn't help feeling afraid as she remembered the rage in his face when he had first been born. She couldn't ignore her fears that he was the kit that the black cat had mentioned in his terrible prophecy. But Yellowfang hoped that by surrendering him, by giving him away to another cat, she had averted whatever doom her dream had foretold.

"The future will be different now," she hissed to StarClan as she closed her eyes. "Brokenkit is no longer my son."

CHAPTER 26

"I'll visit Lizardstripe," Sagewhisker announced the following dawn. "You can go out and collect moss. There should be plenty, with all this rain!"

Her deliberate cheerfulness didn't lift Yellowfang's spirits. She suspected that Sagewhisker was keeping her out of the nursery so that she couldn't see Brokenkit.

As Yellowfang headed across the clearing to gather moss, Brightflower fell in beside her. "Where were you yesterday morning? I looked for you and no cat knew where you were," she fretted. "Are you okay? You don't look well."

Yellowfang ached to confide in her mother, but she knew how impossible that was. "Oh, it was just medicine cat stuff," she mewed vaguely. "And I'm fine, just a bit tired."

To her relief, Brightflower looked reassured. "I'm so proud that you're a medicine cat!" she exclaimed. "I have some news for you," she added after a moment. "Nutwhisker has been spending a lot of time with Fernpaw recently, even though she's not his apprentice. I really hope he's ready to settle down with a mate. It will be so wonderful for him to father a litter of kits!"

"Great," Yellowfang meowed, trying to sound enthusiastic. "Now, if you don't mind, I have things to do."

She padded into the forest, trying to clear the scent of the camp from her head. She felt dazed, sore, and lost without the kits at her belly. *My dear daughters, I will always grieve for you. And for you, my son.* It was even more painful to think of Brokenkit, knowing that he was alive, but not with her.

Sighing, Yellowfang began collecting moss from under pieces of bark and around the roots of trees, making a pile of it beside a path ready to take back to camp later. As she worked, she drew closer to the training area. Through the trees she could see all five apprentices practicing battle moves.

"Nightpaw, don't be such a weakling." Foxheart's voice rang out shrilly. "Come on, I've shown you how to do that move before!"

"Yeah, it's no fun fighting with you," Flintpaw added.

Nightpaw's only response was a fit of coughing. Hearing it, Yellowfang dropped her moss and bounded through the trees until she reached the edge of the clearing.

"Enough!" she ordered. "Nightpaw is sick."

Foxheart turned to glare at her. "You should keep out of the training area," she snapped. "You're only a medicine cat."

"This isn't training," Yellowfang retorted. "It's illness. I'm taking Nightpaw back to the camp."

Foxheart let out a hiss of annoyance. *But there's nothing she can do to stop me,* Yellowfang thought with satisfaction.

Nightpaw recovered from his coughing fit and trotted over to her. Before he left, his brother Clawpaw touched his nose to the small apprentice's ear. "Get well soon!" he mewed.

Yellowfang gave him a nod of approval. Clawpaw was a sturdy young cat, inclined to be a bit too rough, but always kind to his weaker brother.

Nightpaw's cough eased as he and Yellowfang made their way back to camp. Passing her pile of moss, Yellowfang paused to collect a bundle.

"I can carry some of that for you," Nightpaw piped up.

Yellowfang shook her head. "No, you need to rest."

"I'll be fine, honestly," Nightpaw insisted. "Please. I'd like to help."

Yellowfang hesitated for a heartbeat and then gave in. Between them, they managed to carry about half what she had collected, and made their way companionably back to the camp. Once in the medicine den, Yellowfang checked Nightpaw from nose to tail-tip. She could hear wheezing in his chest, but his eyes were bright, his gums red, and his heartbeat steady. There was no sign of fever.

"Well, you're a puzzle," she mewed at last. "You haven't got whitecough or greencough, but I don't know—Sagewhisker?" she called as the old medicine cat came into the den. "Will you have a look at Nightpaw? He was coughing, but there doesn't seem to be anything wrong with him."

Sagewhisker examined Nightpaw, then shook her head. "Very odd," she commented. "Nightpaw, do you think you might have a furball?"

"No," the apprentice replied. "I'm sure I don't. Anyway, my pelt's so short that I don't get furballs."

"Then maybe you just swallowed a seed, or something," Sagewhisker concluded. "I don't think you need any herbs. Just be sure to drink plenty of water."

"I will, Sagewhisker. Thanks!" The apprentice turned to Yellowfang. "I feel fine now. I'll collect the rest of that moss."

When he had gone, Sagewhisker guided Yellowfang to her nest. "You need to rest for a while," she mewed. "Are you feeling okay?"

"How is Brokenkit?" Yellowfang asked, reluctantly settling down into the moss.

There was a guarded look in Sagewhisker's eyes as she replied. "He's fine. He's feeding well and already as strong as his new littermates."

Something in the old cat's voice suggested she was holding back. "There's something wrong, isn't there?" Yellowfang demanded. "What aren't you telling me?"

Sagewhisker sighed. "Lizardstripe doesn't seem entirely happy with the extra mouth to feed."

Yellowfang snorted. "Lizardstripe didn't want kits in the first place!"

Sagewhisker nodded. "I know, but it's too bad. That's the duty of a queen."

"Some queens shouldn't have kits," Yellowfang muttered. Inside, she was desperately worried about her son. *I can't bear that he might feel unwanted and unloved!*

Sagewhisker seemed to guess what she was thinking. "Yellowfang, you have to stay away from the nursery. Brokenkit needs to have a chance to bond with Lizardstripe."

Yellowfang took a short nap while Sagewhisker went out into the forest to search for herbs. She had just returned when Yellowfang awoke.

"I found more juniper berries," she meowed cheerfully. "And a whole clump of borage leaves in a sheltered spot. I'd given up hope of more of those before newleaf. They'll come in handy if Lizardstripe doesn't have enough milk."

Yellowfang rose from her nest to help Sagewhisker sort the herbs, discarding the leaves that were too shriveled to be of any use. She was still involved in the task when Foxheart burst into the den. Her fur was bristling and her eyes hot with anger.

"Why do you have the apprentices running errands for the medicine cats?" she snarled.

Yellowfang saw that Nightpaw was trailing behind his mentor with his mouth full of moss.

"Nightpaw was feeling well enough to help me," Yellowfang meowed. "Why is that a problem?"

"You should have sent him back to training!" Foxheart snapped. "Just stay out of warrior business in future!" She whipped around and stalked out of the den.

Nightpaw dropped the moss onto the pile, gave Yellowfang an apologetic shrug, and trotted after his mentor. Seething with fury, Yellowfang clawed up the moss and tossed it toward the hollow where it was kept. Her aim was poor but she didn't care. *I'd like to claw that she-cat's face, she's so full of herself!*

"Easy." Sagewhisker rested her tail-tip on Yellowfang's shoulder. "Go get a piece of fresh-kill and calm down."

Yellowfang flung a last ball of moss after the rest and

stomped out of the den. Across the clearing, Foxheart was talking to Raggedpelt, with a lot of bristling and tail-waving. *Complaining about me, I suppose,* Yellowfang thought as both cats cast glances toward her.

Trying to ignore them, she padded over to the meager fresh-kill pile and chose a shrew. As she ate, Rowanberry appeared beside her. "Have you heard about that extra kit in the nursery?" her sister asked excitedly.

"Yes, I heard," Yellowfang replied brusquely.

"Every cat thinks he's Foxheart's," Rowanberry murmured into her ear. "Look at her with Raggedpelt. They're very close."

Another stab of fury pierced Yellowfang. She wanted to yowl, *No! Brokenkit is mine!* But she made herself keep quiet and go on eating shrew.

"What sort of cat would give up her own kit?" Rowanberry went on, sounding scandalized.

"A cat who's set on becoming deputy when Raggedpelt is leader?" Ashheart suggested, padding up with Frogtail. "Foxheart has always been ambitious. She probably thinks having a kit would let another cat steal her chance." She turned to her Clanmate. "What do you think, Frogtail?"

"I don't listen to gossip," Frogtail responded. "If the kit is Foxheart's, so what? It'll be an apprentice before long, and have a mentor to take the place of its parents." He gave his tail a flick. "If I were a she-cat, I wouldn't want to be stuck in the nursery either."

Yellowfang abandoned her half-eaten shrew and withdrew to the medicine cats' den.

"What's wrong?" Sagewhisker meowed.

"The Clan is gossiping about Brokenkit," Yellowfang told her. "They all think he's Foxheart's."

Sagewhisker looked mildly surprised. "Well, it's better to have the Clan think that Brokenkit's mother is a ShadowClan cat and not a kittypet or a rogue."

Yellowfang sighed, knowing that was true. *I don't have to like it, though.* She curled up in her nest again, trying to sleep, but after two moons of having a full belly, now the emptiness kept her awake.

A few sunrises later, Yellowfang returned to the clearing with a mouthful of chervil root to see Lizardstripe emerging from the nursery. Brightflower padded over to Yellowfang as she paused, wondering why Lizardstripe was leaving her kits.

"The kits' eyes are open," Brightflower reported, her eyes gleaming. "And Lizardstripe is bringing them out for the first time."

"I hope it's not too soon," Yellowfang muttered. *It's okay to be anxious. I'm a medicine cat!*

"They'll be fine," Brightflower assured her. "It's such a beautiful day."

Several cats had gathered around the nursery to see the kits come out. Rowanberry was there with Nutwhisker and Russetfur, while Ashheart and Wolfstep stood a little farther off. All three elders watched from the entrance to their den.

Deerkit and Tanglekit bounced into the open first, only to halt and gaze around them, their eyes wide with curiosity.

Runningkit, who was the smallest of the litter, followed them more slowly, pausing in the nursery entrance while he sniffed several times. Then he suddenly decided to join his brother and sister, dashing out into the clearing and stumbling over his own paws.

Murmurs of admiration and amusement arose from the cats watching, and more of the Clan strolled up. Mudclaw joined Lizardstripe, who was licking a paw and drawing it over her ears, her eyes glinting as she heard the Clan praising her kits.

Maybe she'll be proud of them after all, Yellowfang thought, staying at the back of the crowd as she looked for Brokenkit.

He tumbled out of the nursery a heartbeat later and stood blinking in the sunlight, his dark tabby pelt bristling. Even though he was slightly younger, he was just as big as the others.

"He's a fine kit," Yellowfang heard Mousewing commenting.

Deerleap nodded. "He should make a strong warrior one day."

Yellowfang wanted to enjoy the praise of her kit, even though she couldn't acknowledge it, but there was no real warmth in the warriors' words. *They don't like the fact that no cat knows who his mother is.*

Amberleaf padded up a moment later. "Does he look like a rogue to you?" she whispered, confirming Yellowfang's suspicions. "If Foxheart is his mother, why not say so?"

Mousewing muttered agreement. "I wouldn't have said he's half kittypet, but then look at his father. Remember what they said about Raggedpelt when he was born."

Not wanting to hear any more, Yellowfang turned to leave. But Littlebird padded up and stopped her.

"You haven't come to see me for a while," she mewed.

Yellowfang fought with guilt. She had deliberately avoided the elder in case Littlebird realized she was expecting kits. "I've been busy," she replied.

"Too busy for your old friends?" Littlebird pressed. Beckoning Yellowfang with a flick of her ears, she led the way to a sunny spot away from the other cats, and settled down with her paws tucked underneath her. "Lots of kits," she commented. "Good for the Clan, but not so good in leaf-bare."

"Lizardstripe seems to be managing," Yellowfang pointed out. The elder's eyes were slitted against the sunlight, but Yellowfang still felt as if Littlebird was scrutinizing her.

"What about that extra kit?" Littlebird prompted. "Where do you think his mother is?"

Yellowfang looked away. "I have no idea. As long as Lizardstripe is willing to raise him, does it matter?"

"I think every kit deserves to know where they come from," Littlebird meowed. "I would have thought Raggedpelt would believe that more than most."

Yellowfang suddenly grew tired of the hints and comments. "Well, it's none of our business!" she snapped.

"You're a medicine cat," Littlebird commented in surprise. "Everything the Clan does is your business."

"But perhaps some secrets are best kept," Yellowfang whispered.

Chapter 27

The half-moon appeared fitfully through scattered clouds as Yellowfang toiled up the last slope toward Mothermouth. The other medicine cats were already waiting for her in the entrance to the tunnel. Yellowfang approached them nervously, worried that their experienced eyes would be able to detect signs of her recent kitting. *I wish Sagewhisker had been able to come instead of me.* But Sagewhisker was suffering from pains in her legs and deep inside her belly, so severe that Yellowfang had to struggle to block them out. The journey to Highstones would be too much for her, and Yellowfang wondered if the old medicine cat would ever travel there again.

But there was no need for Yellowfang to feel nervous. When she padded up to her fellow medicine cats their greetings were friendly, except for Goosefeather, who was muttering into his chest fur as usual, hardly aware of his surroundings.

"You look tired," Brambleberry mewed to Yellowfang. "Is there sickness in ShadowClan?"

Yellowfang shrugged, trying not to show how relieved she was that Brambleberry had given her an excuse for her weariness. "Just the usual leaf-bare stuff," she replied. "Nothing we can't cope with."

"That's good to hear," Featherwhisker murmured, with that oddly curious look that Yellowfang knew well. "And everything else is going well for ShadowClan?"

"Everything's fine," Yellowfang told him. "Isn't it time we were heading for the Moonstone?"

"We know that!" Goosefeather snapped at her. "Young cats, think they have to teach their elders to eat mice . . ." He lapsed into his mumbling again.

"Come on, Goosefeather," Brambleberry meowed kindly, laying her tail on the old cat's shoulders. "Let's you and I lead the way." She padded into the tunnel with Goosefeather by her side.

Wanting to avoid any more of Featherwhisker's probing questions, Yellowfang fell into step beside Hawkheart, leaving the second ThunderClan medicine cat to bring up the rear.

"How are you finding life as a medicine cat?" Hawkheart asked her. "It took me a while to forget that I wasn't a warrior anymore."

"Me too," Yellowfang agreed, remembering the battle with the rats.

"It helps if I remember that I'm more use to my Clan where I am now," Hawkheart went on, his voice warm and friendly in the darkness. "Every cat has the potential to be a warrior, but only a few of us can be medicine cats."

"That's true," Yellowfang acknowledged.

"When I look at a wounded cat," Hawkheart went on, "I try to imagine how the wound was caused. That's often a help in knowing the best treatment."

"Oh, I get that!" Yellowfang meowed, beginning to relax and enjoy the talk. "Like, whether it was teeth or claws or a sharp bit of a branch."

"Right," Hawkheart agreed. "Sometimes—" He broke off.

Ahead of them, Goosefeather had halted suddenly, and Yellowfang had to take a pace back to avoid bumping into him. *I'd never hear the end of it if I did!*

Hawkheart stumbled into her, thrown off balance by the sudden change in direction. "Sorry," he muttered, then added, "Is that parsley I can smell on you?"

Yellowfang's belly clenched. She had forgotten that she might be carrying the scent of the herb she used to dry up her milk. *Mouse dung! I should have rolled in some ferns or something on the way here to hide the scent.*

"I'm surprised you still have stocks of that in leaf-bare," Hawkheart continued as they set off again down the passage.

Yellowfang couldn't think what to say. "I guess we're lucky," she mewed after a moment. "I found a sheltered clump just the other day."

She sent a silent prayer of thanks to StarClan that they reached the cave of the Moonstone at that moment. The moon was already shining through the hole in the roof, waking a frosty light in the heart of the stone. There was no more time for talking. Yellowfang closed her eyes and leaned her muzzle against the cool surface of the crystal. Every muscle in her body ached with fatigue. *Sagewhisker and I would never let a queen leave the camp so soon after kitting!* Gratefully she sank into sleep.

A warm breeze ruffled Yellowfang's pelt. She jolted awake to find herself on a sunlit stretch of marshland. The sound of trickling water filled the air, and unseen birds sang overhead. A feeling of being watched crept over Yellowfang as she lay enjoying the sunlight on her fur. Sitting up, she noticed Silverflame beside her, gazing at her with eyes that were soft with sympathy.

"Oh, Yellowfang," she murmured.

"You knew, didn't you?" Yellowfang demanded with a snarl. "The night Sagewhisker made me a full medicine cat, I saw the reflection of three kits behind me. Why didn't you tell me what was going to happen?"

Silverflame sighed. "What good would that have done? I couldn't change your future. Better that you didn't grieve before it happened."

"I should have stopped seeing Raggedpelt!" Yellowfang protested.

Silverflame regarded her gravely. "It was already too late. And not even the medicine cat code was strong enough to make you do that."

Yellowfang sprang up and started to pace, sending lizards and frogs skittering from her paws. *Is it my imagination*, she wondered, *or is the breeze turning colder?* "Silverflame, what else do you know about the kits?" she asked, turning back toward the StarClan cat. "Do you know a small cat with black fur? Has he said anything to you? Is he from ShadowClan?"

"A small black cat? Oh, you must mean Molepelt." Silverflame hesitated, and Yellowfang wondered if she was hiding something. "Molepelt was the ShadowClan medicine cat many, many seasons ago. He makes little sense at the best of times," Silverflame mewed. "He is treated with kindness, but it doesn't always pay to listen too closely."

"He told me that a kit will be born that will bring fire and blood to the forest!" Yellowfang hissed, her voice shaking. "Why would he tell me if it wasn't one of my kits? There's something about Brokenkit . . ."

Yellowfang choked on the rest of her words as Silverflame swept her tail across her mouth.

"A mother says nothing bad about her kits," the StarClan warrior warned. "If you do not love them, who will?"

"But I can't be a proper mother to Brokenkit," Yellowfang meowed wretchedly.

"No, because you are a medicine cat, and your Clan must always come first." Silverflame took a pace toward Yellowfang, and there was warmth in her gaze. "But that doesn't mean you cannot be his friend, and a force for good in his life. Don't give up on him, Yellowfang. You could be his only hope."

As Silverflame finished speaking the marshland around her started to fade, and Yellowfang knew she was waking up. "Wait!" she cried. "Where are my daughters? Are they here?"

Silverflame was already no more than a glimmering outline, but as Yellowfang stared around, she caught a glimpse of two tiny, pale shapes watching her from a clump of grass. *My precious kits!*

Yellowfang's heart began pounding in her chest. She tried to run to the kits but instead of moving toward them she felt her legs paddling against cold, hard stone. She opened her eyes to find herself back in the cavern, fresh waves of grief surging over her until she could barely stop herself from screeching aloud.

As she and the other cats rose to their paws, preparing to leave, Brambleberry padded up to Yellowfang. "Bad news?" she murmured into Yellowfang's ear.

Yellowfang shook her head. "Sad dreams, that's all," she replied.

Yellowfang slipped out of camp before the dawn patrols had left. Pale light was trickling through the trees, but shadows still lay deep among the undergrowth. Dew clung to every blade of grass and cobweb. Fluffing up her fur against the chill, Yellowfang suppressed a yawn. The weather would warm up later in the day, and here and there she could spot a hint of green on the branches. With newleaf not far off, she was out early every morning, searching the forest for the herbs the Clan needed so badly after the cold of leaf-bare. She would dig carefully through the leaf mold to find the tiniest shoots, clearing away debris so that they could reach the sunlight, and bringing back what she could.

The sun dazzled her eyes by the time Yellowfang returned to camp. She had found a few precious comfrey leaves and tansy to soothe Nightpaw's persistent cough, as well as a few blackbird feathers for Sagewhisker's nest. As Yellowfang approached the camp, the first hunting patrol emerged from the tunnel. Raggedpelt was in the lead, with Foxheart beside him, followed by Mudclaw, Deerleap, and Russetfur, who gave Yellowfang a friendly wave of her tail as she passed.

Raggedpelt and Foxheart were talking together; Foxheart broke off to give Yellowfang a scornful glance as they passed by. Raggedpelt didn't even look at her.

Yellowfang sighed as she plodded on toward the camp entrance. *If they go on like that, they'll only fuel the rumors that Brokenkit is Foxheart's. I'd have chosen any other queen in the Clan to be his mother!*

Emerging into the clearing, Yellowfang spotted Lizardstripe in a warm patch of sunlight near the fresh-kill pile, sharing tongues with Nettlespot and Ashheart. There was no sign of her kits. Yellowfang assumed they were in the nursery, but as she approached her den she heard shrill squeaking coming from behind it.

Peering around the boulders, she found Deerkit, Tanglekit, and Runningkit all surrounding Brokenkit, who faced them with his dark tabby fur fluffed up.

"We don't want to play with you," Deerkit squeaked, screwing up his nose. "You smell funny."

"Yeah," Tanglekit added. "Every cat says you're a kittypet, like your father."

"My father is not a kittypet!" Brokenkit yowled, lashing out with one paw.

Tanglekit leaped back to avoid the blow. Brokenkit was bigger and stronger than the others now. Runningkit and Deerkit shrank away from him too.

"My father is the Clan deputy; he's the best warrior in

ShadowClan!" Brokenkit spat.

"But who's your mother?" Runningkit asked with a sniff. "Even you don't know!"

"Yeah, she could be anyone," Deerkit mewed. "A rogue, a kittypet, a *badger*! Badger-stinky! Badger-stinky!"

The other two kits joined in. "Badger-stinky!"

Yellowfang dropped her herbs and feathers and strode into the middle of the group. "Enough!" she exclaimed, glaring around at Lizardstripe's kits. "Deerkit, Tanglekit, Runningkit, you ought to be ashamed of yourselves! How dare you treat your Clanmate like this?"

Runningkit had the grace to look ashamed, staring down at his paws and sniffling wretchedly. Deerkit and Tanglekit just looked defiant, though they didn't dare say anything to a medicine cat.

"Brokenkit, come with me," Yellowfang meowed. She curled her thick tail around him and swept him away.

Brokenkit stomped crossly beside her. "Now they'll think I'm scared of them! I could have beaten them if you hadn't turned up! They're so weak, I don't care if there's three of them and only one of me!"

Yellowfang felt confused. She'd expected her kit to be grateful that she'd rescued him from the bullies. "Well, fighting isn't the answer to everything," she told him. "Your littermates need to learn how to behave. I'll tell Lizardstripe and she'll punish them."

Brokenkit ran in front of her and turned to face her, his eyes wide and pleading. "Please don't do that!" he begged.

"Lizardstripe will only blame me! She doesn't like me; she thinks I'm stealing milk from her kits."

"Of course she doesn't think that!" Yellowfang exclaimed, shocked.

"Yes, she does!" Brokenkit insisted. "I heard her saying it to Amberleaf. Nobody likes me."

Yellowfang's heart twisted with love and regret. "I like you," she mewed. "And so will all your Clanmates, once they get to know you. Now, why don't you help me collect all these herbs and feathers and carry them into my den? You're so strong, you probably don't need me to help you!"

Brokenkit's chest puffed out proudly as he collected as much as he could manage, scattering a few leaves and feathers as he marched into Sagewhisker's den.

Sagewhisker was curled in her nest. She raised her head in surprise as the kit appeared, followed by Yellowfang. "Shouldn't he be playing with his littermates?" she asked Yellowfang.

Yellowfang knew that the old cat was giving her a warning. She didn't reply, just showed Brokenkit where to put down his burden.

"My littermates are stupid," Brokenkit snorted. "Yellowfang's my friend now."

Yellowfang could feel the heat of Sagewhisker's gaze on her fur but refused to share the old cat's concern or even acknowledge it. *What harm am I doing?* "Brokenkit, would you like to help me fetch some clean moss?"

Brokenkit nodded, bouncing on his paws. "I can carry more

moss than any cat!" he boasted.

Yellowfang knew that she couldn't take him out of the camp, but there were some pieces of bark behind the elders' den where moss grew. She led him across the clearing, aware of some startled glances from her Clanmates.

"Now, you hold up the bark," she instructed Brokenkit, "so I can peel the moss from underneath."

"Like this?" Brokenkit burrowed under a piece of bark and sat up with it balanced on his head like an extra bit of pelt.

Yellowfang *mrrowed* with amusement. "Not quite," she meowed. "A squirrel might think that you're a tree and try to climb up you."

Brokenkit let out a squeal. "I'm a tree! I'm a tree!" He jumped up and down until the bark fell off his head.

Yellowfang showed him how to hold up the bark with one paw while she gathered the moss. When they had collected a good pile they bundled it together and Brokenkit helped her carry it back to her den.

Admiring her son's sturdy body and gleaming fur, Yellowfang glowed with pride. *Why did I ever doubt his right to be born? He might grow up to be* my *apprentice,* she thought, *and work by my side for the rest of my life. That would be an even greater gift than being acknowledged as his mother!*

Chapter 28

The bright newleaf sun shone down as Yellowfang laid out a bundle of borage leaves and some coltsfoot to dry on the flat ground outside her den. Brokenkit was playing close by, sometimes pouncing on the end of her tail, or batting a piece of moss into the air.

"Take that, ThunderClan flea-pelt!" he growled, swiping at it with his paw. "That'll teach you to stay out of the ShadowClan camp!"

"Look, Brokenkit," Yellowfang meowed. "These leaves are called borage. They're good for treating cats who have a fever. And this is—"

"Why are you telling me this stuff?" Brokenkit interrupted. "I'm not going to be a medicine cat! I'm going to be a warrior! Grrr! Watch me pounce!" He fell on the moss ball and shredded it to tiny scraps with his claws.

Yellowfang watched him fondly. She knew that Sagewhisker didn't approve of the time Brokenkit spent with her rather than with his littermates. *But I don't see why Brokenkit should be treated like an outcast when I can look after him and make him feel special.*

She twitched an ear at the sound of sniffling, and looked up to see Runningkit crouched a few tail-lengths away, gazing at her intently as she sorted the herbs. "Hi," she mewed. "Come and look if you want to."

Runningkit started, his fur fluffing up in alarm. For a heartbeat he hesitated, blinking anxiously, then with another huge sniff scampered off toward the nursery.

Yellowfang shrugged, turning back to Brokenkit. In two more moons her son would be apprenticed, and then she would hardly see him because he would be so busy training with his mentor. For a heartbeat she felt a pang that he wouldn't be training with her as a medicine cat, but she consoled herself with the thought that he was clearly going to be a great warrior.

Brokenkit bounced off to find another moss ball and Yellowfang continued laying out her herbs until she saw Nightpelt padding up. He had been made a warrior two sunrises before, and Yellowfang could see his pride by the way he walked and held his head high. But he was still coughing.

I've tried everything: herbs, honey, planning his choice of fresh-kill so he never eats anything with feathers. But nothing works.

Every time the young warrior exerted himself, he would start coughing and gasping for breath. Yellowfang could see his frustration as he came up to her, coughing again as he tried to speak. *He looks tired and thin, when he should be young and strong like his littermates.*

"Sit down," Yellowfang meowed. "Just breathe gently. I'll get you some wet moss."

"There must be some way of fixing this!" Nightpelt rasped when she returned.

Yellowfang shook her head. "No herbs will help," she told him as she set the moss down beside him. "You just need to calm down and relax."

"I know. But it's not easy," Nightpelt retorted. For all his troubles, there was no anger in his voice; he was still friendly and good-humored.

"I mentioned you to Hawkheart at a recent half-moon Gathering," Yellowfang went on, as Nightpelt gratefully lapped the water from the moss. "He said that a WindClan cat had the same symptoms—coughing after running around—but without any signs of a fever or sickness. Hawkheart didn't have a name for it; it was just something the cat had to live with."

Nightpelt looked up apprehensively. "And what happened to the cat?"

Yellowfang half wished she hadn't brought the subject up because there wasn't any good news to give the young warrior. "He was unable to do all his warrior duties, and had to retire to the elders' den early," she admitted.

"I'll never do that!" Nightpelt exclaimed. "I want to be a warrior! ShadowClan deserves that!"

Yellowfang stretched out her tail to rest it comfortingly on Nightpelt's shoulder. "ShadowClan doesn't expect its cats to work themselves to the bone when they're not fit enough. Now, sit down and be quiet until you can breathe normally."

Sagewhisker bustled out of the medicine cats' den, thrusting

Brokenkit in front of her. Her blue eyes were snapping with annoyance.

Yellowfang rose and went to meet them. "Is there a problem?"

"I caught this kit taking moss from the store inside the den!" Sagewhisker meowed crossly. "As if we didn't have to work to collect it!"

Brokenkit gazed up at the old cat with defiance in his eyes. "I wanted some to play with! You can always get more!"

Sagewhisker fixed Yellowfang with a stern gaze, clearly expecting her to deal with him.

"Brokenkit, if you want moss you know where to get some," Yellowfang mewed. "There's plenty behind the elders' den. But please don't take the moss from our store." *Does Sagewhisker expect me to punish him?* she wondered. *He's only a kit!*

She was trying to figure what to do when Deerkit and Tanglekit tumbled out of the nursery and bounded across to Brokenkit.

"Still hanging out with the medicine cats?" Deerkit sneered. "Old she-cats and a sick warrior are the only friends you've got!"

Tanglekit padded forward until she was almost nose-to-nose with Brokenkit. "What skills are you learning?" she asked in a mock-interested voice. "How to dry herbs? Ooh, our enemies will be scared!"

"Yeah, I can just hear him in a battle!" Deerkit added. "'Come one step closer and I'll slap you with this leaf!'"

Brokenkit's neck fur bristled up and he swiped at Deerkit,

catching him a blow on the nose.

Deerkit let out an outraged yowl. "That hurt!"

"And it serves you right," Yellowfang snapped. "Go back to the nursery until you learn how to be nice."

The two kits trailed off, casting resentful glances behind them as they went.

"Don't listen to them, Brokenkit," Yellowfang went on when they had gone. "There's nothing wrong with—"

Brokenkit turned on her, anger flaring in his eyes. "They're right. I'm not learning anything useful here! You're just a dumb old medicine cat, not a warrior. Why do you make me come here all the time?"

"I don't *make* you." Shocked, Yellowfang reached out her tail to him, but Brokenkit batted it away.

"Quit bugging me, and leave me alone!" With a furious hiss, he ran off.

Yellowfang stared after him miserably. *What have I done?*

"Perhaps it's for the best," Sagewhisker murmured in her ear. "He needs to grow up as normal as possible so that he's not singled out any more than he already has been."

Yellowfang rounded on her. "What would you know?" she demanded. "He's *my son*! I'd do *anything* to stop him from being hurt!"

In the days that followed, Brokenkit avoided the medicine cats' den. Yellowfang never gave up hope that he would come back. Every time she heard him outside she would rush to the entrance, but he always turned away from her. Yet he was constantly alone; his littermates went on ignoring him, even Runningkit, who had never joined in the bullying since Yellowfang had interrupted them.

Watching Brokenkit wrestle with a stick in the middle of the clearing, Yellowfang's heart ached for him. He was so strong and confident and handsome; even his crooked tail didn't show so much now that his fur had thickened. *But he doesn't have any friends.*

"Brokenkit never plays with the others."

Yellowfang was startled to hear her own thoughts spoken aloud. The voice was Amberleaf's; the dark orange she-cat was strolling past with Blizzardwing, on their way to join Raggedpelt, who was sorting out the patrols near the camp entrance.

"Well, he's not like the others, is he?" Blizzardwing commented. "But he's a strong young cat. He'll be fine once he's an apprentice."

The two cats padded on, out of earshot. Yellowfang gazed after them, trying to comfort herself with the thought that Blizzardwing was right.

When the patrols had left, Raggedpelt bounded over to where Brokenkit was playing and stood watching him. After a moment, Brokenkit realized that he was there and looked up.

"Try attacking with both paws at once," Raggedpelt advised. "If it was a real enemy, you'd need to leap on him with the full power of your claws."

Brokenkit nodded and leaped on the stick again, smashing both paws down on it so that it splintered. Raggedpelt gave him a nod of approval.

Cedarstar had emerged from his den to watch the exchange between Raggedpelt and his son. "He looks very strong," he remarked to Raggedpelt.

"Yes, he's ready to be an apprentice," Raggedpelt responded proudly.

Yellowfang glimpsed a flash of trouble in Cedarstar's eyes as he studied Brokenkit battering the stick. "Being an apprentice isn't just about being able to fight our enemies," he meowed. "Brokenkit needs to learn the importance of patience, honor, and loyalty as well, just like any young cat."

"He'll have all of those!" Raggedpelt assured him. "Just you wait!"

As Yellowfang watched Brokenkit glowering over the pieces of stick, she tried to suppress the memory of Molepelt's dire warning. *Brokenkit is going to be fine!*

A heart-wrenching cry from her den drove these thoughts from Yellowfang's mind. She spun around and raced inside to find Sagewhisker sprawled on her side next to the herb stores, gasping in pain. In the same heartbeat Yellowfang felt a searing agony in her chest. For a moment her heart seemed to stop, and she couldn't breathe.

No! Sagewhisker!

Using all the control she had taught herself, Yellowfang fought through the pain and staggered to Sagewhisker's side. "Hold on!" she begged. "Please hold on! I'll help you. . . ."

"I can't . . . it's too much," Sagewhisker hissed through clenched teeth. "StarClan needs me now. . . ."

"What's happening?" Brightflower appeared at the

entrance to the den and rushed across to Sagewhisker.

At the same moment Sagewhisker's whole body convulsed and then was still. Her clear blue eyes clouded over, gazing at nothing.

"Sagewhisker . . ." Yellowfang whispered.

"She hunts with StarClan now," Brightflower murmured, laying her tail across Yellowfang's shoulder and drawing her away. "She served her Clan well," she meowed. "No Shadow-Clan cat will ever forget her."

Yellowfang nodded, but she was too stunned to say anything. She was aware of Brightflower leaving the den, and a short while later Cedarstar appeared. Yellowfang watched in a blur as he stood beside Sagewhisker's body and dipped his head in a gesture of respect.

"Farewell, Clanmate," he meowed. "You were a good medicine cat and a good friend. May you continue to guide ShadowClan as you walk in the stars."

The elders followed the Clan leader into the den and carried Sagewhisker's body into the clearing for the vigil. Yellowfang stumbled after them, numb with grief. The rest of the Clan padded up, touching their noses to Sagewhisker's cold fur, quietly sharing memories of her as they gathered around.

Yellowfang crouched beside her mentor all the rest of that day and all night, while the stars whirled overhead. "I'm sorry, Sagewhisker," she murmured. "I'm so sorry for letting you down. I promise to uphold the code of the medicine cats until my very last breath." Her voice cracked. "I owe you so much. . . ."

The sky was milky pale when the elders arrived to take Sagewhisker's body away for burial. Yellowfang rose to her paws, feeling stiff and dazed after the long vigil.

"May StarClan light your path, Sagewhisker," she mewed, her voice ringing out over the camp as she spoke the ancient farewell for all lost Clanmates. "May you find good hunting, swift running, and shelter when you sleep." Then she stood back to let Littlebird, Stonetooth, and Lizardfang pick up the body.

Littlebird paused beside her. "You'll be a good medicine cat," she murmured kindly. "Just as Sagewhisker was. ShadowClan is lucky to have you."

Yellowfang watched as the three elders bore Sagewhisker's body out of the camp.

Oh, Littlebird, I wish I could believe you!

Chapter 29

"Nightpelt, you are an intelligent and dedicated warrior," Cedarstar meowed. "I know that you will do your best to pass on these qualities to Brokenpaw."

Nightpelt dipped his head to the Clan leader. "I'll do my best, Cedarstar," he promised, his eyes shining with pride. He had hardly coughed at all through the apprentice ceremony.

"Brokenpaw! Brokenpaw!"

Yellowfang's heart swelled with pride as the Clan greeted her son by his new name. She felt a rush of relief, too, that Cedarstar had chosen Nightpelt as his mentor. Nightpelt was sensible and wise, and would teach Brokenpaw that there was more to the warrior code than fighting.

But she was disconcerted to see the shock in Brokenpaw's face when Cedarstar named his mentor. He hesitated for a moment before padding over to Nightpelt to touch noses with him. She was even more worried when she heard him mutter to Deerpaw, "How come I got the sick cat? That's so not fair!" Yellowfang was sure that Nightpelt must have heard him too, although he gave no sign of it.

Deerpaw had been apprenticed to Cloudpelt, and

Tanglepaw to Wolfstep. Both of them looked ready to burst with pride and excitement, and even Lizardstripe looked pleased. In contrast Brokenpaw just stood glowering at his paws.

It will be all right, Yellowfang tried to tell herself. *Once Brokenpaw starts training, he'll realize how much Nightpelt has to teach him.*

She tried to put Brokenpaw out of her mind as Cedarstar raised his tail for silence once again. *I've got something important to do, too,* she thought, with a tingle of excitement in her paws. Runningkit looked excited as well, his eyes shining as he gazed at his Clan leader.

"Come forward," Cedarstar called to Yellowfang, beckoning her with his tail. As she stepped toward him, he went on, "The last two moons have been hard without Sagewhisker, and I know that within ShadowClan our former medicine cat will be mourned forever."

A murmur of agreement rose from the Clan, and Yellowfang felt a fresh pang of grief for the old cat who had taught her so much.

"But the line of ShadowClan medicine cats will continue," Cedarstar announced, "with a new apprentice, Runningkit. Yellowfang, you have already proven yourself to be a skilled and loyal medicine cat. I know that you will pass on all your knowledge to Runningkit."

"I will, Cedarstar," Yellowfang promised.

"Runningkit," the Clan leader meowed, "do you accept the post of apprentice to Yellowfang?"

"Yes, Cedarstar." Runningkit's voice went up in an excited

squeak, and he scuffled his front paws in embarrassment.

"Then from this moment you shall be known as Runningpaw. And the good wishes of ShadowClan go with you," the Clan leader finished.

"Runningpaw! Runningpaw!"

As his Clan greeted him, Runningpaw scampered over to Yellowfang, gave a huge sniff, then reached up to touch noses with her.

Yellowfang winced. *The first thing I'll teach him will be to cure his own sniffles.*

"I'll take you to the half-moon Gathering soon to meet the other medicine cats," she whispered to Runningpaw, who danced on the spot.

As the cats separated—Lizardstripe rejoining the warriors with a huge sigh of relief—Yellowfang followed the other mentors and their apprentices out of the camp for their first tour of the territory. Runningpaw bounced by her side.

"Will we see cats from other Clans?" he panted. "What happens if we do?"

"We might spot a patrol on the other side of the Thunderpath," Yellowfang admitted. "If we do, we greet them and go on our way." She hesitated, then added, "Later I'll teach you some fighting moves. You need to be able to defend yourself. But never forget that you're a medicine cat, not a warrior. You don't go looking for trouble, and you never—*never*—attack first."

Runningpaw nodded seriously. "I'll remember, Yellowfang."

As they toured the territory, Yellowfang enjoyed seeing her apprentice's astonishment when he realized how big the forest was, which made her recall her own first exploration with Deerleap. The sight of the Carrionplace shocked him and he shivered when Yellowfang told him about the battle with the rats.

"But never forget," Yellowfang warned as they padded past at a safe distance, "rats are dangerous, but warriors are more dangerous! And medicine cats know just what to do for rat bites."

"Cobwebs for bleeding, right?" Runningpaw mewed.

"Right, but some wounds get infected. Marigold and horsetail are good for that, but best of all for rat bites is wild garlic or burdock root."

"Marigold . . . horsetail . . . wild garlic . . . burdock root . . ." Runningpaw muttered under his breath. "Great StarClan, there's a lot to learn!"

He halted, shocked, when they reached the Thunderpath with monsters roaring past. "Mudclaw told us about it," he gasped, "but I never thought it would be like this! Are those monsters dangerous?"

"Only if you try to cross the Thunderpath," Yellowfang told him. "I don't know why, but they never leave it."

"But we have to cross it to get to Fourtrees, don't we?"

Yellowfang shook her head. "There's a tunnel that goes underneath it, leading to a little bit of ShadowClan territory that borders ThunderClan and WindClan."

Runningpaw's eyes sparkled. "So we could visit

ThunderClan territory? Great!"

"We could," Yellowfang replied severely, "but we're not going to because we're too courteous and honorable to go wandering over another Clan's borders without good reason. There's another tunnel, too, that leads directly onto WindClan territory, over there." She waved her tail at the swell of moorland beyond the Thunderpath. "And before you ask, no, WindClan warriors aren't just rabbit-eating nuisances, even if that's what you've heard. But you don't need to be afraid of them, either." She felt a warm glow of pride as she added, "ShadowClan is a match for any Clan."

Yellowfang started to look for herbs as they continued, to teach her apprentice what they looked like and what they were used for. But she hurried more quickly past the border with the Twolegplace, even though Runningpaw wanted to linger.

"Do we ever go there?" he asked, staring curiously at the sharp red Twoleg dens. "I think it'd be cool to meet a kittypet!"

Yellowfang felt her fur bristle as she thought of Hal and the other kittypets who had attacked the camp. "No, it wouldn't be cool," she snapped. "We don't go there and they don't come here. We don't bother one another, and that's best for all of us."

"Okay." Runningpaw blinked, looking slightly disappointed. Then he brightened up and pattered along beside Yellowfang as she headed back to the camp.

As they approached the camp entrance, Yellowfang heard a voice raised angrily, and flinched as she recognized that it was Brokenpaw's.

"But I *want* to! *Why* can't I?"

Rounding a bramble thicket, Yellowfang came upon Brokenpaw and Nightpelt glaring at each other. Brokenpaw's fur was bushed out to twice his size, and his yellow eyes shone.

"Because we've done enough for one day, touring the whole territory," Nightpelt explained. "We—" He had to break off to cough, the only sign that he was under stress, for his tone was calm and patient.

"But I want to learn battle moves!" his apprentice insisted.

"Training will begin tomorrow. We'll start with hunting practice. Don't you want to catch your own prey?"

"I want to fight," Brokenpaw growled, tearing at a clump of ferns with unsheathed claws. "Look how strong I am! I'm bigger than the other apprentices. They can do the hunting and the boring stuff around the camp. Let me do battle with the other warriors!"

Nightpelt's tail-tip twitched. "There are no battles to fight at the moment, Brokenpaw. You'll have a chance to learn everything, but you need to go at the right pace. Don't be impatient!"

Brokenpaw glared at his mentor for a heartbeat longer, then spun around and stalked away. "Coughing old fool!" he muttered under his breath.

"Off you go back to camp," Yellowfang told Runningpaw. "You can choose a piece of prey from the fresh-kill pile."

"Thanks, Yellowfang!" her apprentice exclaimed. "And thanks for today. It was awesome!"

When he had scampered off, Yellowfang padded over to Nightpelt. "Couldn't you have shown Brokenpaw a couple of moves?" she meowed. "He's right about being bigger than the other apprentices, and he seems to be getting bored. There's no reason he can't learn more quickly, is there?"

Nightpelt's eyes narrowed, and Yellowfang realized she might have gone too far. "I'm his mentor, and I'll decide when he learns to fight!" the warrior retorted. Another coughing fit seized him; when it was over he dipped his head to Yellowfang. "I'm sorry I snapped at you," he rasped. "The tour of the territory wore me out. I'm going to rest."

As he limped off, Yellowfang stared after him with concern. *He's looking old before his time—and if his cough interferes with training, that won't be fair to Brokenpaw.*

Emerging from the tunnel, Yellowfang spotted Cedarstar lying with his back against the warm Clanrock, watching his Clanmates feed. Yellowfang marched over to him. But as she approached, she passed a group of elders, stretched out in a sunny spot as they shared tongues and fresh-kill.

"You don't get squirrels like you did when I was a warrior," Deerleap meowed; she had recently moved to the elders' den with Crowtail and Archeye. "I could climb the highest tree in the forest after a squirrel, no trouble."

"Ah, but could you climb down again?" Archeye asked with a *mrrow* of amusement.

"I'm not still up there, am I?" Deerleap snapped, slapping at him with her tail.

Yellowfang noticed that Littlebird was listening with a look of fond indulgence, while Lizardfang shifted restlessly, pushing away his share of the squirrel.

"I'm too old to need feeding," he sighed. "I'll be heading for StarClan soon."

"Nonsense!" Littlebird meowed. "You've seasons in you yet, Lizardfang." She clawed at a piece of squirrel and set it in front of him. "Here, try this. It's lovely and fresh. Rowanberry caught it just for us."

Affection for Littlebird surged over Yellowfang, seeing the elder choosing the softest parts of the squirrel for her denmate to eat. She realized that Cedarstar was watching too.

"The Clan is growing older," the leader commented softly to her. "Myself included. It's time to prepare new cats to take over the responsibilities of running the Clan." Looking Yellowfang up and down, he added, "Sagewhisker chose well in you, Yellowfang. I admit that I had some doubts at first . . ."

Oh, no! Yellowfang thought. *Does he know about Raggedpelt?*

"But you have more than proven your loyalty and skill," Cedarstar went on. "Runningpaw is lucky to have you as a mentor."

"It was mentoring that I wanted to talk to you about," Yellowfang meowed, taking the chance Cedarstar offered her. "It's Nightpelt. His cough is still really bad, and I think it will hinder him being a mentor. Brokenpaw is so strong and fit; he needs a mentor who can keep up with him, and I don't think Nightpelt can do that."

Cedarstar gazed keenly at Yellowfang from narrowed eyes.

"I chose Nightpelt deliberately," he explained, "because I think Brokenpaw has lessons to learn in patience and selflessness. He is a cat who needs to choose between two paths: one that will serve his Clan loyally and one that . . . will be less helpful."

His words chilled Yellowfang. *Does he know about Molepelt's prophecy?*

Cedarstar rose to his paws, dipping his head slightly to show that the conversation was at an end. "I will watch all of the apprentices to make sure they are progressing well," he meowed. There was a hint of warning in his voice as he added, "Brokenpaw is not to be singled out, at any cost."

Reluctantly, Yellowfang nodded.

"Tell me about the other medicine cats!" Runningpaw begged, bouncing around the medicine cats' den and getting under Yellowfang's paws.

"What for? You'll meet them soon," Yellowfang responded.

Runningpaw had been her apprentice for a quarter moon, and tonight he would go with her to his first full-moon Gathering.

"But I'm nervous! I won't know what to say. *Please*, Yellowfang!"

"Okay, but let me sort these herbs at the same time." Yellowfang uncovered the first store and plunged her paw into the hole. "Let's see . . . Goosefeather is the ThunderClan medicine cat. He's a bit . . . strange. If he snaps at you, pay no attention; he doesn't mean anything. ThunderClan has a second medicine cat, Featherwhisker. He tends to ask too many questions about ShadowClan." Yellowfang turned to her apprentice and gave him a hard stare. "Whatever you do, *don't* tell him anything."

"I won't, Yellowfang," Runningpaw promised, eyes wide.

"Then there's Hawkheart of WindClan," Yellowfang went on. "He can sound gruff, but he's a good cat. And Brambleberry of RiverClan—you'll like her, she's so kind and friendly."

Yellowfang covered up the first hole, took more herbs out of another one, then laid everything out in front of Runningpaw. "These are for Lizardfang," she announced. "He says he's always thirsty, and he's losing a lot of weight. Now, tell me what these herbs are and why I'm giving them to him."

Runningpaw studied the herbs. "That's sorrel," he mewed, pointing with one paw. "That's to build up Lizardfang's appetite. That one is burnet, to make him feel generally better and stronger, and the juniper berry . . . oh, StarClan, I've forgotten!" He hesitated a moment, gave a sniff, then added, "Is the juniper to strengthen his stomach?"

"Very good," Yellowfang purred.

"I'll take them to Lizardfang, if you like," Runningpaw offered. "And I'll make sure he has wet moss."

"Thanks, Runningpaw," Yellowfang responded. "Be as quick as you can, and meet me in the clearing. It's almost time to go."

Her apprentice tucked the herbs into a neat leaf wrap and hurried off. Yellowfang made sure the den was tidy, then followed him out. The cats who were going to the Gathering had assembled around Cedarstar and Raggedpelt in the middle of the clearing. Darkness had fallen, though the moon still hadn't risen above the trees. The sky was clear except for a few thin puffs of cloud.

Yellowfang strained to see Brokenpaw. It took her a few moments to spot him; he wasn't with his mentor, like the other apprentices. She finally saw him standing beside Raggedpelt, who was letting him stay there instead of sending him back to his proper place. Nightpelt just looked resigned. A flash of indignation seared through Yellowfang. *Why can't Nightpelt keep his apprentice under better control?*

Cedarstar waved his tail as the signal to move off. Yellowfang looked around for Runningpaw, who dashed to her side as she was waiting to go through the thorn tunnel.

"Lizardfang's okay," he panted. "He ate the herbs. Littlebird says she'll fetch him more water if he needs it."

"Great." Yellowfang gave him a nod of approval.

The Clan trekked through the forest and along the tunnel that led to the patch of ShadowClan territory on the far side of the Thunderpath. As they headed toward Fourtrees, Brokenpaw suddenly shot away from the rest of his Clanmates, racing for the ThunderClan border.

Cedarstar halted, his tail lashing, and Raggedpelt yowled, "Brokenpaw! Get back here!"

Brokenpaw paused on the border for a couple of heartbeats before padding back to the group. "I was just making sure that the ThunderClan scent marks were on the right side of the border," he explained. "This is a vulnerable piece of territory. We can't neglect it, when getting to Fourtrees is so important."

Raggedpelt nodded. "True. But next time ask before you go dashing off."

Yellowfang noticed two or three of the older warriors echoing Raggedpelt's approval, and her heart swelled with pride.

"Good call," Blackfoot purred.

"Yes," Russetfur added. "I can see you're going to make your Clan strong, Brokenpaw."

"You'll be a great warrior," Boulder agreed.

The ShadowClan cats were the first to arrive at Fourtrees. By now the moon was floating high above, shedding its silvery light over the meeting place. Runningpaw halted at the top of the hollow, his eyes wide with awe as he gazed down. "It's *huge*!" he gasped. "Yellowfang, is that the Great Rock where the leaders stand?"

"That's right," Yellowfang told him. "They—"

She broke off at a triumphant yowl from Brokenpaw. He hurtled down the slope into the hollow, outstripping all the other cats, and dashed straight for the Great Rock. He was bunching his muscles to leap when Nightpelt called him back.

"You can't go up there," he scolded. "That's only for the leaders."

For a heartbeat Brokenpaw looked angry; then he flicked his tail. "One day," he promised. He raced off to explore the rest of the hollow.

Before Yellowfang and Runningpaw were halfway down the slope, Brokenpaw was back. "More cats are coming!" he announced.

Pinestar appeared at the top of the hollow with the cats of ThunderClan behind him. Yellowfang spotted Featherwhisker, and led Runningpaw down to meet him.

"Greetings," mewed the ThunderClan medicine cat. "So you have a new apprentice. Welcome," he greeted Runningpaw. "I hope to see you at the Moonstone soon."

Runningpaw ducked his head. "Thank you."

"Where's Goosefeather?" Yellowfang asked.

Featherwhisker shook his head. "Ill, I'm afraid," he replied. "He can't be here tonight."

"I'm sorry," Yellowfang began, then broke off as more cats poured into the clearing. WindClan and RiverClan had arrived together, and Runningpaw was looking a bit daunted.

"Stay by my side," Yellowfang told him. "We'll head for the Great Rock. The medicine cats always sit together at the bottom."

Together she and Runningpaw squirmed through the crowd, followed by Featherwhisker. Brambleberry and Hawkheart welcomed Runningpaw warmly, and Yellowfang saw that another young cat was sitting with Hawkheart.

"This is my new apprentice," Hawkheart meowed. "His name is Barkpaw."

"Oh, great!" Runningpaw exclaimed, sitting beside the brown tom. "We can learn together."

Barkpaw gave him a shy nod. "I don't know much yet," he mewed. "There are so many different herbs, I get confused."

"So do I," Runningpaw admitted. "I'm really good at clearing out old bedding, though!"

Glancing up at the Great Rock, Yellowfang saw the four leaders looking down at their Clans, ready to start the Gathering. She silenced the apprentices with a wave of her tail.

Cedarstar was the first of the leaders to step forward to the front of the Great Rock. "ShadowClan has good news to report," he meowed. "We have made four new apprentices. Tanglepaw, Brokenpaw, and Deerpaw will train as warriors, while Runningpaw is apprenticed to Yellowfang and will become a medicine cat."

The cats in the clearing—especially the ShadowClan cats—began to yowl the names of the new apprentices. Runningpaw sat upright, eyes shining with pride and his whiskers quivering. Yellowfang couldn't spot Brokenpaw in the throng.

"The Clan has been strengthening its borders," Cedarstar went on as the noise died down. "We look forward to good hunting throughout newleaf and greenleaf." He gave a meaningful glance around at the other Clans, then stepped back to give his place to Pinestar, who was followed by Hailstar of RiverClan and Heatherstar of WindClan.

All the other leaders had good news to report, and Yellowfang was impressed by how well they looked. *Except Pinestar,* she thought, wondering if anything was wrong with the ThunderClan leader. *He looks a bit listless and distracted.*

The WindClan leader announced Barkpaw's apprenticeship, and the cats yowled his name too. Barkpaw sat beside Runningpaw looking very proud and embarrassed. As Heatherstar continued to talk about plentiful rabbits and some fleet-footed young cats, Yellowfang heard a commotion break out at the edge of the clearing. Yowls and screeches drowned what the WindClan leader was trying to say.

Craning her neck, Yellowfang spotted a familiar dark brown shape. *Brokenpaw!* He was wrestling with two young cats. From their skinny frames Yellowfang guessed they were from WindClan.

From his place on top of the great Rock, Cedarstar leaped to his paws. His voice rang out above the turmoil. "Brokenpaw! Stop fighting at once! This is a Gathering!" Turning to Heatherstar, he dipped his head and added, "I am sorry, Heatherstar. He is a young apprentice and it's his first time at a Gathering. I will deal with him afterward."

Heatherstar dipped her head. "No cat blames you, Cedarstar," she meowed with dignity. "But be sure to remind your apprentices of the importance of keeping the truce at full-moon. I shall speak to my own apprentices, too."

Yellowfang's heart sank. Brokenpaw had violated one of the most important rules of the warrior code, and in full view of the four Clan leaders. The young cats had broken apart, but Yellowfang couldn't see what was happening now. Beside her, Runningpaw was standing on the tips of his paws, craning to see over the heads of the crowd. "What happened?" he mewed. "What was Brokenpaw *thinking*?"

"I'd guess he wasn't thinking at all," Featherwhisker muttered.

Cats were shifting around, whispering. Eventually Yellowfang heard Russetfur speaking to Raggedpelt. "Apparently Brokenpaw accused the WindClan apprentices of coming through the tunnel under the Thunderpath to steal prey. He jumped on them when they denied it."

Runningpaw had overheard Russetfur's words too. "What will happen to the Gathering?" he gasped, his eyes wide with shock.

It was Featherwhisker who replied. "We'll carry on, because the moon is still clear. If StarClan wanted us to stop, they'd send clouds to cover the moon."

Yellowfang glanced up—not at the moon, but at the glittering stars that surrounded it, scattered thickly across the sky. *Are the warriors of StarClan watching Brokenpaw now?*

When Heatherstar had finished her interrupted speech, the four leaders sprang down from the Great Rock. The cats below relaxed and started to share news with friends in other Clans. But Cedarstar gathered the ShadowClan cats around him with a flick of his tail. "We're leaving," he growled.

"What?" Blizzardwing protested. "Already?"

Yellowfang saw Nightpelt padding up with Brokenpaw beside him; the black warrior was clearly furious, but Brokenpaw only looked sullen and defiant.

"One of our apprentices doesn't deserve to stay and meet others." Cedarstar glared at Brokenpaw, then turned and led the way out of the hollow.

Yellowfang was walking just behind Cedarstar, with Runningpaw at her side. Before they reached the top of the hollow she was shoved roughly aside, almost losing her balance. Runningpaw steadied her. When Yellowfang turned to glare at the cat who had pushed her, she saw it was Raggedpelt.

The tabby tom had fallen in beside Cedarstar. "You didn't have to single out Brokenpaw in front of all the Clans like that!" he challenged his leader angrily. "Or scold him like that. There were two other apprentices involved! Brokenpaw was only defending ShadowClan honor!"

"Your son broke the rules of the truce." Cedarstar's anger was colder and more controlled. "I cannot let that happen."

Raggedpelt snorted. "Loyalty and courage mean more than rules," he growled.

But that kind of loyalty and courage starts battles, Yellowfang thought, with a flutter of alarm in her belly. *Oh, StarClan, please let Brokenpaw learn to curb his temper.*

CHAPTER 30

The mellow sunlight of late greenleaf shone over the camp. Sunhigh was just past, and hunting patrols were returning, their jaws laden with prey. Yellowfang and Runningpaw pushed through the brambles after an herb-gathering expedition in the marshes.

"I'll put these away," Yellowfang meowed as they dropped the bunches of herbs in their den. "You go check on Littlebird. Take her some wet moss."

"Sure, Yellowfang." Runningpaw hurried away.

Yellowfang sighed. Lizardfang joined StarClan two moons ago, and now Littlebird was growing very frail. Yellowfang was worried that soon she would have to say farewell to her old friend.

She had begun to sort the herbs when she heard a paw step outside the den and Tanglepaw hopped in on three legs.

"What happened to you?" Yellowfang asked.

"I got scratched." Tanglepaw turned to show Yellowfang a nasty claw mark scored across one of her haunches.

"How did you get this?" Yellowfang gasped, wondering if there was a fox in the territory.

"I was practicing a battle move with Brokenpaw," Tanglepaw explained, not sounding particularly bothered.

Yellowfang gazed at the young she-cat in horror. "You're supposed to fight with claws sheathed! You know that!"

"Yes, but Brokenpaw said we'd get even better if there was a real threat of getting hurt!" Tanglepaw's eyes were shining with admiration for her denmate.

"And are you a better fighter?" Yellowfang asked dryly.

"I will be next time!" Tanglepaw promised.

Yellowfang got her to lick the wound clean while she took some marigold out of the store. Rubbing the leaves on her wound, she told Tanglepaw, "Keep it dry and rested for at least one day. And don't fight with claws out again. I don't care what Brokenpaw says. I don't collect herbs just to treat mouse-brained apprentices!"

She could tell her warning had gone straight over Tanglepaw's head. "I'm going back to the training area," she announced as she hopped away. "I want to watch Brokenpaw beat Deerpaw!"

When she had finished tidying the herbs, Yellowfang padded into the clearing and spotted Nightpelt by the fresh-kill pile. "Do you know the apprentices were fighting with claws out?" she asked as she joined him.

Nightpelt nodded, looking exhausted as usual.

"You should stop them," Yellowfang warned. "Tanglepaw will be okay, but one day there could be a real accident."

"Oh, you should know better than to think that Brokenpaw would listen to me." Nightpelt's tone was full of unexpected bitterness. Then he flicked his ears as if he were chasing away a fly. "I'm sorry for being so tired and crabby," he added, ending with a cough.

"I'll send Runningpaw out to find more honey for your throat. It must hurt from all the coughing," Yellowfang mewed sympathetically.

"Only two more moons and I won't have to worry about being a mentor anymore," Nightpelt murmured. "I can't wait."

"No cat could do his duty better," Yellowfang assured him, though privately she thought Nightpelt needed to have fewer duties to conserve his strength. *And I was right that he's the wrong mentor for Brokenpaw. If only Cedarstar had listened to me!*

A stabbing feeling in her belly woke Yellowfang. Careful not to disturb Runningpaw, asleep in his nest, she stumbled out into the clearing. Drawn-out groans were coming from Cedarstar's den. Peering underneath the oak roots Yellowfang saw Cedarstar thrashing around in his bedding, his limbs contorted in agony.

"Cedarstar, what's wrong?" she whispered.

There was no reply, just another groan. Yellowfang could tell that Cedarstar was not fully conscious. She slipped into the den and let herself feel his pain to guide her. She was running her paws over his belly when she became aware of another cat standing in the entrance to the den. She glanced over her shoulder to see Raggedpelt, his eyes gleaming in the starlight.

"What's going on? I heard groaning."

"Cedarstar is very sick," Yellowfang mewed. "I'm not sure I can help him."

Raggedstar nodded. "I know you'll do your best," he told her, for once not sounding hostile.

Cedarstar arched his back in a fresh spasm of agony. His eyes blinked, then focused on Raggedpelt. "My last life!" he gasped. "StarClan is calling me. Raggedpelt, lead my Clan well." His body contorted again and he struggled for breath.

Yellowfang watched his heaving chest, knowing that there was nothing she or any other medicine cat could do now. Cedarstar fought on for a few heartbeats that felt like many seasons; then he went limp, falling back into the moss. Life faded from his eyes.

Yellowfang crouched beside him, reeling with sadness. She had loved the calm, wise leader, and trusted him to care for her Clan. She'd had no idea he was so close to losing his ninth life; there had been no lingering sickness, no injury that became infected, not even a frailty that she would associate with elders. Whatever had killed him had taken him swiftly, with little suffering. Perhaps that was what they should be most grateful for.

Raggedpelt bent his head to pay homage to his dead leader, then straightened up. "I must summon the Clan," he told her. "Will we go to the Moonstone tonight so I can claim my nine lives?"

Yellowfang stared at him in surprise. *Cedarstar's body is still warm!* "If . . . if you wish," she stammered.

"I do wish," Raggedpelt declared. "But first let me tell the Clan."

Yellowfang followed him out of the den. Raggedpelt jumped onto the Clanrock and raised his voice in a yowl. "Let all cats old enough to catch their own prey join here beneath the Clanrock for a meeting!"

The ShadowClan cats stumbled sleepily from their dens, gathering around the Clanrock in bewildered silence. Raggedpelt waited until they had all appeared.

"Cedarstar has lost his ninth life," he announced. "Now he walks in StarClan, a great warrior among the lights of our ancestors."

There was a stunned pause.

Brokenpaw broke the silence. "Raggedstar! Raggedstar!"

No other cats joined in. Raggedpelt looked very proud for a moment, then lowered his head to gaze at his son. "Don't call me by that name yet," he warned. "I cannot claim it until I've been to the Moonstone to receive my nine lives from StarClan." Glancing at Yellowfang, he added, "I'll go there at once, while the rest of you sit vigil over Cedarstar."

Deerleap and Crowtail entered the Clan leader's den and dragged his body into the clearing. Yellowfang watched as the cats lined up to pay their respects.

Russetfur's gaze was deeply sad as she bent her head over Cedarstar's body. "Thank you, Cedarstar," she whispered, "for giving me a chance to become a warrior."

Boulder padded up beside her and gave her ear a comforting lick. "And me also, Cedarstar," he added. "Your generosity transformed our lives, and we will never forget you."

Raggedpelt was already waiting at the entrance to the camp. As soon as Yellowfang joined him, he bounded out, his powerful muscles pumping until he was racing over the ground. Yellowfang struggled to keep up. Her belly was churning with nervousness at being alone with Raggedpelt again after so long. But he said nothing about what had happened in the past.

Instead, as she ran alongside him, he meowed, "I have waited a long time for this. I will make ShadowClan stronger than it has ever been!"

Yellowfang didn't have enough breath to reply.

They crossed WindClan territory without meeting any WindClan warriors, and reached Highstones as a milky line of dawn appeared on the horizon. *There'll be just enough moonlight left to hit the Moonstone.*

Without pausing to catch their breath, she and Raggedpelt plunged into the darkness of Mothermouth. The tabby warrior was so eager that Yellowfang was left behind. By the time she reached the cavern, Raggedpelt was sitting on the ground, gazing in awe at the glimmering crystal. "Now it's my turn," he whispered.

"Lie down with your nose touching the stone," Yellowfang instructed him, gesturing with her tail. "Close your eyes, and StarClan will call you to them. And remember," she added, "you may not speak to any cat of what happens to you now. Except to me, if there's something you need to discuss."

Raggedpelt gave her a brief nod and stretched out his nose to touch the Moonstone. Yellowfang settled down beside him. The cold of the stone seeped into her bones. Heartbeats later she opened her eyes and found herself in the marshy space where she had met Silverflame. Now it was shrouded in mist, through which she could hear the piping of birds and the soft lapping of water.

Raggedpelt was standing beside her. The mist began to clear, and cats appeared all around Raggedpelt, nine of them, with Cedarstar at their head. Yellowfang recognized Lizardfang and Sagewhisker, but the others were unknown to her, although she had spotted them in the distance in StarClan on previous visits.

As the cats of StarClan gathered around Raggedpelt, Yellowfang heard her name being called. "Yellowfang! Yellowfang, over here!"

She scrambled up to a clump of pine trees on a rocky bluff overlooking the marsh. To her horror, Molepelt was waiting for her there.

"The time has nearly come!" he hissed. "Darkness lies ahead! Beware the cat with blood on his paws!"

Yellowfang let anger surge through her, driving away her fear. "Go away!" she snapped. "If you can't give me more detail, what use is this prophecy?"

Molepelt leaned closer. "The truth lies in your heart," he hissed. "You cannot be blind to it for much longer."

Yellowfang bunched her muscles and sprang at the black cat as if he were a piece of prey. But her paws thumped to the ground, her claws digging into earth instead of into Molepelt's body. A swirl of mist blinded her eyes, and when it cleared again he was gone.

Turning back, Yellowfang saw the circle of StarClan

warriors still surrounding Raggedpelt. As she padded across the marsh to join them, she saw the last of the nine cats step forward to speak to the new ShadowClan leader. This was a graceful she-cat with creamy brown fur who carried herself with the authority of a leader.

"My name is Dawnstar," she meowed, her brilliant green gaze resting on Raggedpelt. "I was leader of ShadowClan many seasons ago. I give you a life for putting ShadowClan above all others. There are four Clans in the forest, but ShadowClan will always be the greatest."

She touched her nose to Raggedpelt's; he flinched and staggered a little, as if the pain of receiving his nine lives was becoming too much to bear.

As Dawnstar stepped back into the circle of cats, all the StarClan warriors threw back their heads and let out a howl of triumph that echoed across the marshes and rose to the glittering stars.

"Raggedstar! Raggedstar!"

Yellowfang jerked awake, shaking with cold. Raggedstar was awake too, pacing across the cavern with powerful strides. "I have nine lives!" he declared in the pale light of dawn that seeped down from the hole in the roof. "I am Raggedstar, leader of ShadowClan!"

When Raggedstar and Yellowfang returned to the camp, Yellowfang's first duty was to go with the elders as they carried the body of their former leader out for burial. She looked up at the stars as she spoke the ritual words, wondering which of them was Cedarstar, and whether he was looking down on them now.

"May StarClan light your path," she meowed, and added in a whisper, "Burn bright, dear friend, and watch over your Clan."

By the time she and the elders returned, dusk was falling. Raggedstar was standing on the Clanrock, with the rest of the Clan gathered around.

Runningpaw rushed over to Yellowfang. "Raggedstar is going to appoint the new deputy!" he mewed.

Raggedstar's gaze traveled over his Clan. "I say these words before StarClan," he announced, "that the spirits of our ancestors may hear and approve my choice." Once again his gaze swept around the clearing, and Yellowfang wondered if he was deliberately trying to draw out the tension. "Foxheart," Raggedstar meowed at last, "will you do me the honor of being my deputy?"

Foxheart dipped her head, her eyes shining. "I will, Raggedstar."

Murmurs rose up from the crowd of cats, not all of them approving. "I *knew* there was something going on between those two!" Brightflower exclaimed.

"Great StarClan, she'll be insufferable now!" Amberleaf muttered.

"Foxheart! Foxheart!" The murmuring was drowned out as the Clan obediently called out Foxheart's name, and Raggedstar bowed his head.

I'd have picked any other cat, Yellowfang thought as she joined in the yowling. *But it wasn't up to me. I will just have to put up with it.*

As the noise died down, Yellowfang heard Deerpaw meow to Brokenpaw, "Wow, your father is the leader of the Clan!"

"Yeah," Brokenpaw chirped. "I bet he wishes I was a warrior already so I could be his deputy!"

"I don't think so," Tanglepaw retorted crushingly.

As Brokenpaw bristled, Fernshade brushed his shoulder with the tip of her tail. "It won't be long," she meowed, "if you keep practicing the way you are."

Yellowfang was distracted by Runningpaw giving her a nudge. "Littlebird says she has a pain in her head," he reported, angling his ears to where the elder stood. "Should I give her something to help her sleep?"

"I'll do it," Yellowfang replied. "Come to my den, Littlebird."

Once there, she got the poppy seeds out of the store and carefully divided one in half. "That should be enough," she warned as Littlebird licked it up. "These seeds can be very strong."

Littlebird sighed. "My dreams are so troubled lately, I don't want to close my eyes."

Yellowfang pressed her muzzle into the old cat's shoulder. "Then I will ask StarClan to send you peaceful dreams." *Is Littlebird dreaming of blood and fire? Oh, StarClan, if you have any omens to share, send them to me! Don't make my Clanmates frightened to sleep!*

Yellowfang was clearing a pile of dead leaves from the entrance to her den when she heard Raggedstar yowling a summons to the Clan, and looked up to see him standing on the Clanrock, his fur ruffled by the cold wind. Almost two moons had passed since Cedarstar's death, and Raggedstar had won approval from his Clanmates by allowing them to continue as they had always done, patrolling and training and guarding their borders with the protectiveness of a mother over her kits.

Calling to Runningpaw, who was busy counting juniper berries inside the den, Yellowfang headed into the clearing. Brightflower and Brackenfoot emerged from the warriors' den, closely followed by Amberleaf, Blizzardwing, and Frogtail. Russetfur and Boulder hurried in together through the brambles, giving Yellowfang a friendly nod as they sat down close to her. The other apprentices and their mentors bounded across from the fresh-kill pile. The elders appeared at the entrance to their den.

Raggedstar gazed down at them. "I am proud of my Clan," he began. "You are all I could have hoped for as a leader. With warriors like these, I could fight any battle! And there will be a new warrior today. Brokenpaw, step forward."

A gasp rose from the Clan as Brokenpaw bounded forward to stand at the base of the Clanrock. Yellowfang shared her Clanmates' astonishment. *He's only been an apprentice for five moons!*

"Raggedstar," Nightpelt meowed, stepping forward, "Brokenpaw hasn't completed his final assessments yet."

Brokenpaw shot a furious look at his mentor, while Raggedstar flicked his tail dismissively. "I know a cat who is ready to be a warrior when I see one," he declared. Leaping down from the Clanrock, he faced Brokenpaw. "I, Raggedstar," he continued, "call upon my warrior ancestors to look down on this apprentice. He has trained hard to understand the ways of your noble code, and I commend him to you as a warrior in his turn. Brokenpaw, do you promise to uphold the warrior code, and to protect and defend this Clan, even at the cost of your own life?"

Brokenpaw puffed out his chest importantly as he replied, "I do."

"Then by the powers of StarClan," his father went on, "I give you your warrior name. Brokenpaw, from this moment you will be known as Brokentail—but let no cat see this as a sign of weakness. You are one of the strongest cats I have ever known, and I look forward to fighting alongside you! StarClan honors your courage and your fighting skills, and we welcome you as a full warrior of ShadowClan." He rested his muzzle on Brokentail's head, and Brokentail licked his shoulder.

"Brokentail! Brokentail!" ShadowClan acclaimed the new warrior, but Yellowfang could see that some of the cats were less than happy. Though the warriors yowled his name with approval, his fellow apprentices were staring at one another with a mixture of dismay and anger. Yellowfang was close enough to hear Deerpaw mutter, "This is so unfair! Just because his father is Clan leader!"

"This would never have happened in my day," Archeye commented from where he sat in front of the elders' den. "What's next? Kit warriors?"

Brokentail stood in the center of the clearing, lapping up

his Clan's yowls of welcome. As Yellowfang looked at him more closely, a thrill of horror passed through her. His legs were stained with blood, the brown fur dark and wet. The air stirred beside her and a voice whispered, "Beware the cat with blood on his paws. . . ."

Yellowfang whirled around, looking for Molepelt, but she saw only her Clanmates, still watching the new warrior. Pushing her way through the crowd, she reached Brokentail's side. "Are you okay?" she whispered. "Is that blood on your fur?"

Brokentail looked surprised. "No, it's water. I got wet when I was chasing a lizard in the marshes, that's all."

Relief surged through Yellowfang. Now that she was close enough to smell his fur, she realized that it was just peaty water turning his legs dark.

Everything's fine. And stay away from me, Molepelt, with your stupid prophecies!

She stepped back as other cats padded up to congratulate her son.

"You're welcome on my patrols anytime," Blackfoot meowed.

"And mine," Nutwhisker added. "And can you show me that tricky claw-and-leap battle move? I saw you can do it, but I haven't got it quite right."

"Sure." Brokentail dipped his head, his eyes gleaming with pleasure.

Boulder loped up and gave him a friendly cuff on the shoulder. "I'm looking forward to chasing foxes with you," he told Brokentail.

The new warrior gave Boulder a return cuff that sent him

staggering. "We'll shred them," he agreed.

Then Foxheart shouldered her way through the crowd. "Congratulations, Brokentail," she meowed graciously. "ShadowClan needs keen young warriors like you."

Does she think she's Clan leader already? Yellowfang wondered, bristling at the deputy's superior tones.

She realized that Raggedstar was standing beside her. "My son will go far," he murmured in her ear. "He is everything I ever hoped for." He looked at Yellowfang with a challenge in his eyes, as if he was daring her to say that Brokentail was her son too.

I won't play that game. I know I have given up any claim to him that I once had.

Politely Yellowfang dipped her head to the cat who had once meant everything to her. "I'm sure he has a bright future in the Clan," she meowed.

CHAPTER 31

Yellowfang shivered beneath her thick pelt. Leaf-bare had descended on the forest and the clearing was covered in snow. Her paws sank deeply into it; her pads felt as if they were about to fall off, they were so cold. Flicking a bit of leaf from behind her ear, Yellowfang knew that she needed to give herself a good grooming. *But there never seems to be time. . . .*

Now she headed for Raggedstar's den, ducking beneath the oak roots out of the worst of the snow. To her dismay she saw that Foxheart was there, her head bent close to the leader's as they talked together.

It was Foxheart who noticed Yellowfang first. "What do you want?"

Yellowfang refused to let the Clan deputy's rudeness get to her. "I need to speak to Raggedstar."

"Can't you see he's busy?" Foxheart snapped. "Come back later."

Yellowfang merely waited, her gaze fixed on Raggedstar.

"No, you can speak now." The Clan leader's voice had an impatient edge. "What is it?"

"I don't think Nightpelt can continue with his warrior

duties," Yellowfang told him. "His cough is getting much worse, and he's too tired and weak for patrols."

Foxheart's eyes widened. "Are you saying you can't cure him? Aren't you supposed to be the medicine cat?"

"I've tried everything," Yellowfang hissed through gritted teeth. "Some cats have coughs that don't go away. I think it has something to do with his breathing. If he doesn't give up his duties, he'll just get sicker and sicker."

"We need all our warriors!" Foxheart protested.

Raggedstar stretched out his tail and laid it on Foxheart's shoulder. "Send Nightpelt to me," he ordered Yellowfang. "If it's what he wants, then I won't force him to continue with warrior duties. But it's his decision, Yellowfang!"

Returning to her den, Yellowfang found Boulder waiting for her. "What can I do for you?" she asked.

Boulder stretched out one forepaw. "I've got a thorn in it," he announced cheerfully. "I tried to get it out myself, but I can't shift it."

"Well, that's what your medicine cat is for," Yellowfang responded. "Let's have a look."

The thorn had been pushed a long way into Boulder's pad, and it took a lot of licking before Yellowfang could catch it in her teeth.

"I was on patrol with Brokentail," Boulder meowed as she worked. "Great StarClan, he's a good warrior! We should all try to be like him."

Yellowfang, vigorously licking, tried not to react to this praise of her son.

"I was just a bit too keen on chasing a blackbird," Boulder went on. "To tell you the truth, I think I was trying to impress Brokentail. The bird went into a thornbush, and I was fool enough to go after it."

"Did you catch it?" Yellowfang meowed.

"Yes—ow!" Boulder let out a yelp as the thorn came free.

"Then you weren't a fool. Give your paw a good lick," Yellowfang instructed him, "and come back if the paw swells or if it continues to hurt."

"Thanks, Yellowfang." Boulder ran his tongue over his pad a few times, then rose to his paws. "I'd better get back on patrol." He dashed off.

Runningpaw, who had been tidying the herb stores at the back of the den, turned to look at his mentor. "I wouldn't want to live in a Clan full of Brokentails," he remarked. "He's too . . . fierce!" He went back to his herbs, then stopped, looking thoughtful, with a borage leaf in one paw. "I wonder who Brokentail's mother is. Do you have any ideas, Yellowfang? Was she a kittypet, like some cats say? Or was it Foxheart all along?"

"I don't have time for idle gossip," Yellowfang snorted. "Why are you standing there like an uneaten bit of fresh-kill, instead of sorting the comfrey from the foxgloves?"

Runningpaw sniffed as he gave her an injured look, but yowls from the clearing outside interrupted any reply he was about to make. Looking out between the boulders, Yellowfang saw cats bursting through the thorns, and recognized Lizardstripe's border patrol. A single glance told her that some of the cats had been badly scratched.

"Bring cobweb and marigold," she ordered Runningpaw, then bounded to meet the wounded cats in the center of the clearing.

Raggedstar and Foxheart emerged from the leader's den and raced to join the others. "What happened?" Raggedstar demanded.

"Rats attacked us near the Carrionplace," Lizardstripe panted. Her fur was bristling and blood dripped from a scratch on her belly.

"And we weren't even hunting them!" Wolfstep added indignantly.

While Lizardstripe described in more detail what had happened, Yellowfang and Runningpaw started to treat the wounds. Wolfstep had a torn ear, but it had already stopped bleeding; Yellowfang licked it clean, then gave him a marigold leaf to rub on it.

"Look at this bite," Runningpaw mewed, beckoning Yellowfang over to Tangleburr. "I think it might get infected."

Yellowfang nodded as she examined the bite on Tangleburr's shoulder. "That's always a risk with rat bites. Tangleburr, wait for me in my den, and I'll find you some burdock root."

"Thanks, Yellowfang." The young she-cat limped off.

Yellowfang padded over to Lizardstripe. "I need to see that scratch on your belly," she told her.

Lizardstripe flicked her tail. "Not now. Can't you see I'm talking to Raggedstar?"

Suit yourself, Yellowfang thought. *Bleed all over the camp. See if I care.*

While she was checking Brackenfoot and Fernshade, more cats appeared at the entrance to the camp. Yellowfang looked up to see Brokentail and his hunting patrol, laden with prey.

Brokentail, carrying a huge pigeon, padded up to the group in the middle of the clearing. "What's going on?" he asked, dropping the dead bird.

"Rats attacked us near the Carrionplace," Fernshade told him, while Wolfstep exclaimed, "Great catch, Brokentail!"

"Yeah, I climbed a tree to get it," Brokentail mewed casually, then turned to Raggedstar. "How long are we going to put up with these rats?" he demanded with a lash of his tail. "We need to teach them a lesson!"

"What do you suggest?" Raggedstar prompted.

Yellowfang remembered the doomed attack on Carrionplace seasons before, when Cedarstar had lost a life. *Please, StarClan, not that again!*

"We can't fight all the rats," Brokentail told Raggedstar. "We don't know how many there are. Instead, we should single out a few of them and kill them in view of the others, as a warning."

Yellowfang heard a few doubtful murmurs from the cats surrounding Brokentail, but others were nodding in agreement.

"It might be worth a try," Fernshade murmured.

"Right," Foxheart meowed. "We tried ambushing them with a mass attack, and it didn't work. Perhaps this is the only way."

Raggedstar looked thoughtful, then straightened up. "Brokentail, come with me to my den. We'll discuss this in more detail." He led the way across the camp with Brokentail padding at his shoulder. Foxheart followed them.

Yellowfang sent Runningpaw back to the den to prepare a burdock root poultice for Tangleburr. Meanwhile she managed to persuade Lizardstripe to let her look at the scratch. By now it had stopped bleeding. Relieved that she didn't have to do more, Yellowfang gave Lizardstripe some marigold and sent her to rest in the warriors' den.

Tangleburr was just leaving when Yellowfang got back to her den, the burdock root poultice securely in place. "Let me have another look at that tomorrow," Yellowfang told her.

Tangleburr thanked her and went off with a wave of her tail.

"That poultice was a neat bit of work," Yellowfang told Runningpaw. "Now we need to sort out some herbs for this battle with the rats."

Runningpaw gulped. "You mean *we'll* be in the battle?"

"No, but we'll be nearby. If there are injuries, we can treat them on the spot. Get out more marigold, and some chervil, and we'd better have burdock root too."

"I heard about the last battle with the rats," Runningpaw mewed as he began uncovering the herb stores. He gave Yellowfang a look in which excitement mingled with nervousness. "What do you think will happen this time?"

"I don't know," Yellowfang responded grimly, "but I'm not happy about our chances. There are just too many rats." Padding over to the thornbush to unhook some cobwebs, she realized that their stocks were low. "I'm going out to get some more of this," she told Runningpaw. "Make leaf wraps of those herbs so we can carry them easily."

Once out of the camp, Yellowfang headed for a nearby oak tree that was covered with ivy, a perfect place for gathering cobwebs. As she stretched up to reach them, a voice spoke behind her.

"Do you need any help with that?"

Yellowfang turned to see Nightpelt. He began clawing cobwebs down and collecting them in a ball at the foot of the tree. "This is for the rat battle, right?" he mewed.

Yellowfang nodded.

"You know I won't be taking part?" Nightpelt went on quietly. "I've decided to join the elders."

Yellowfang stopped gathering cobwebs to gaze at him, sadness welling up inside her. "I'm so sorry that I was never able to cure you," she mewed.

Nightpelt started to speak, broke off to cough, then continued, "It's not your fault. I know you tried. I just wish StarClan would tell me why they made this my destiny!" He let out a long sigh. "I wanted to be a great warrior!"

"And you are," Yellowfang assured him. "But your Clan needs you to be safe and well more than they need your hunting skills. You can still be part of the life of the Clan. Try telling Littlebird she's less important than she used to be!"

Nightpelt nodded, but Yellowfang could see that she hadn't managed to chase the depression from his eyes.

Dawn was breaking as the ShadowClan cats gathered around Raggedstar in the center of the clearing. Gray clouds covered the sky and a thin sleet was falling. Yellowfang shivered as she and Runningpaw joined the back of the crowd.

"This is the plan," Raggedstar meowed, raising his voice so that all the Clan could hear. "Two cats—that's Foxheart and me—will draw the rats out by pretending to hunt at the edge of Carrionplace. Brokentail, Cloudpelt, Blackfoot, and Finchflight will lie in wait to jump out and circle the first few rats to appear. Brokentail will give the signal. Brackenfoot, Newtspeck, Clawface, Fernshade, and Scorchwind, you will hold back any other rats so they can watch while we kill their denmates." His gaze swept around the warriors. "Any questions?"

No cat responded. Brokentail's eyes were gleaming.

"Then let's go!" Raggedstar yowled.

Yellowfang and Runningpaw picked up their supplies and followed the patrol as the Clan leader led the way out of camp. Yellowfang spotted Nightpelt watching them with the other elders outside their den. *You're better off out of this,* she thought, though she understood how disappointed the young cat must feel, seeing his Clanmates go off to battle without him.

As the Carrionplace loomed into sight, Yellowfang flinched at the familiar stink and the shrieks of the white birds that flapped over the heaps of Twoleg garbage. She began to brace herself to block out the pain of the wounds that would inevitably come. *I am whole and well, I have no injuries, I feel no pain.*

She led Runningpaw to the same holly bush where she and Sagewhisker had sheltered during the previous battle, though her belly felt cold at the memories it conjured up. As she set her herbs down beneath the branches, Yellowfang noticed that part of the silver mesh had fallen down, so it was easy for the cats to get into the Carrionplace. *And the rats can get out to where Brokentail is waiting.*

Brackenfoot led his part of the patrol in among the rotting piles, where they swiftly disappeared. Meanwhile Brokentail directed the cats under his command into hiding places among the trees and bushes. Raggedstar and Foxheart were left alone in front of the gap in the silver mesh, at the edge of the closest pile of waste.

"They're really brave!" Runningpaw commented.

Yellowfang murmured agreement as she watched the two cats go through the motions of hunting: tasting the air, sniffing around the roots of trees, crouching to creep up on tangles of bramble or clumps of fern. She kept watching, her heart pounding, as a rat poked its head out, then edged its way into the open. It was soon joined by another, then a third, then more. They crept forward, almost as far as the silver mesh. Their glittering gaze was fixed on the cats who were apparently too stupid to notice them.

But Raggedstar and Foxheart clearly knew they were there. Skillfully they moved farther away, tempting the rats away from the safety of the heaps. Once they were well clear of the silver mesh, Brokentail, Cloudpelt, Blizzardwing, and Finchflight leaped out of their hiding places. Raggedstar and Foxheart sprang forward, until the rats were surrounded.

"Prepare to die!" Brokentail snarled.

CHAPTER 32

A rustle of rat noise came from the heaps of waste, but Brackenfoot and his patrol sprang out of hiding and guarded the holes. Yellowfang could see twitching noses and the gleam of malignant eyes, but for the moment at least none of the rats dared emerge.

"Don't let them out!" Brackenfoot yowled. "But keep far enough back so they can watch what happens!"

"Flea-pelts!" Brokentail taunted the captured rats, springing forward to score his claws down the flank of the nearest, then darting out again. "Crow-food eaters!"

The rest of the patrol copied him, driving the rats together into a tight knot and wounding them while staying out of reach of their claws. Yellowfang dug her claws into the ground. "Get on with it, before something goes wrong!" she muttered.

A heartbeat later, two rats, terrified and desperate, sprang out of the huddle and leaped upon Foxheart. Yellowfang stared in disbelief at how precise their movements were, like trained hunters. Foxheart let out a screech and crumpled to the ground, blood gushing from her neck.

"No!" Raggedstar yowled.

In the same instant, Brokentail and Cloudpelt leaped on the two rats who had attacked Foxheart, breaking their necks and tossing them into the air. Raggedstar hurled himself into the center of the knot of rats, his Clanmates only a heartbeat behind, their claws slashing and tearing. The orderly plan broke up into a chaos of shrieks and blood.

"Great StarClan!" Runningpaw whispered.

Even Yellowfang was awed as she watched the slaughter, the rats struggling to escape only to be clawed back. They hurled themselves on the warriors, who met their onslaught with teeth that ripped into them and left the rats twitching as their blood soaked into the snow.

Within moments it was over. The last of the rats that had been tempted out were dead and the ShadowClan warriors stood over them, panting. Apart from Foxheart, who lay ominously still, none of them seemed to have serious injuries. Raggedstar called Brackenfoot and the others out of the Carrionplace, while Brokentail worked himself underneath Foxheart's body and draped her over his shoulders. He was covered in blood but as far as Yellowfang could see, it all belonged to the rats.

"We won," Runningpaw mewed, sounding stunned.

"Yes," Yellowfang agreed grimly, gazing at Foxheart's body. *But we paid a high price. I didn't like her. I didn't want to serve under her as leader. But she was too young to die.*

The elders and the few cats who had remained in the camp gathered around as the warriors returned. Yellowfang spotted

Rowanberry looking in horror from the entrance to the nursery as Brokentail laid Foxheart's body in the middle of the clearing. A flash of joy warmed Yellowfang at the sight of her sister's kits, Cinderkit and Stumpykit, peering out curiously beside their mother.

Warriors die, but the Clan survives.

Foxheart's mother, Poolcloud, dashed out of the warriors' den and flung herself to the ground beside her daughter. "StarClan, no!" she wailed. "Why did you have to take her?"

Wolfstep followed his mother out and crouched beside her, pushing his nose into his sister's blood-soaked fur. "Goodbye," he rasped. "We were so proud of you. You would have made a great leader."

Cloudpelt, who shared a father with Wolfstep and Foxheart, padded over to her and bowed his head. "She died like a warrior," he meowed.

Yellowfang took her place beside Foxheart's head. "We will keep vigil for her," she announced.

Raggedstar stayed for a short time beside the body of his deputy, then vanished into his den, reappearing as the moon rose above the trees. Leaping onto the Clanrock he summoned the Clan, though most of them were already in the clearing, clustered around Foxheart.

"I grieve for Foxheart," the Clan leader began. "She served us well, and should have continued to do so for many seasons to come. But she died bravely, protecting her Clan from rats. She will have a place of honor in StarClan." He paused, looking down at his Clan, and Yellowfang could feel the tension mounting, for every cat knew that this was the moment when Raggedstar must announce the name of his new deputy. Several of the cats glanced at Brokentail, who was looking particularly alert, his eyes gleaming.

"However much we miss Foxheart," Raggedstar went on, "the Clan needs a new deputy. I say these words in the presence of her body, that her spirit may hear and approve my choice. Cloudpelt will be the new deputy of ShadowClan."

Both Cloudpelt and Brokentail looked equally astonished. Yellowfang could see bitter disappointment in Brokentail's eyes, and he bared his teeth in a snarl.

"Wow!" Runningpaw whispered. "I guess we all know who was hoping to be deputy!"

Cloudpelt rose to his paws and stammered, "Th-thank you, Raggedstar. I promise I will serve my Clan well."

Raggedstar jumped down from the Clanrock while the rest of the Clan raised their voices in yowls of welcome to Cloudpelt. Yellowfang could see that he was a popular choice. She was pleased with the decision, too; she knew that Cloudpelt would make a far better leader than Foxheart, if she had lived.

Then Yellowfang spotted Brokentail cornering Raggedstar as the Clan leader tried to return to his den. *I need to hear what they're saying!* Unobtrusively she eased her way over to them, halting in the shadow of the Clanrock.

"I should have been made deputy!" Brokentail growled. "The rat attack was my idea, and it worked!"

Raggedstar gazed at him with slitted eyes. "Use your brain," he snapped. "I'm your father, and I have to be careful not to show favoritism in front of the other warriors. Besides, you need an apprentice before you can be deputy. But don't worry. I've many seasons left in me, and if anything should happen to Cloudpelt, it will be your turn next."

The thaw came and gradually newleaf crept through the forest. Pushing her way through a fresh growth of fern, Yellowfang reveled in the feeling of the sun on her thick pelt, and the sight of green shoots springing up everywhere in the frost-burned forest. Nightpelt, who had accompanied her, jumped up to swipe at a butterfly that was fluttering above the grass. Yellowfang watched him fondly as he chased it, reflecting that his cough was much better now that he wasn't trying to keep up with all the warrior duties.

"Are you a kit?" she teased him as he came panting back to her.

"Not anymore," Nightpelt replied with a *mrrow* of amusement. "I guess I'm just enjoying the sunshine." He took a deep breath with jaws parted. "And all the prey-scent. I'm sure there's a mouse around here somewhere." He began to follow the scent trail and disappeared into a thick stretch of ferns. Moments later Yellowfang heard a gasp, and then his voice was raised in a startled yelp.

"Yellowfang, come here!"

Yellowfang pushed her way through the ferns. When she emerged on the other side, she found herself gazing at a small hawthorn tree. One of the newest apprentices, Stumpypaw, Rowanberry's kit, was hanging from the lowest branch by his teeth.

"Stumpypaw!" Yellowfang exclaimed. "What in the name of StarClan are you doing?"

When Stumpypaw opened his mouth to reply, he crashed to the ground in a tangle of legs and tail. "Now I'm going to be in big trouble!" he wailed as he picked himself up. "Brokentail told me I had to stay there until he came back!"

"What?" Yellowfang exchanged an incredulous look with Nightpelt. "No mentor would do that! You must have misunderstood."

Stumpypaw hung his head. "I was chattering during battle training, so Brokentail said I needed to learn how to keep my jaws shut."

"There must be a better way than this!" Yellowfang meowed to Nightpelt. *Stumpypaw could have permanently injured his jaw!*

"Not if I say so." Yellowfang spun around at the growled words behind her and found herself facing Brokentail. "Don't interfere with my business, medicine cat," he warned her.

Yellowfang blinked at the savagery in his yellow eyes. "It is my business," she insisted, trying to stay calm. "Harsh treatment like that could injure an apprentice."

"Nonsense!" Brokentail snarled. Jerking his head at Stumpypaw, he added, "Get back to the training area."

Stumpypaw dashed off, and Brokentail followed with a last glare at Yellowfang. "Keep out of it!" he ordered.

"I never punished him like that when he was my apprentice," Nightpelt commented when Brokentail had disappeared.

A pang of fear shook Yellowfang. "Maybe you should have," she muttered.

When she returned to the camp, Yellowfang spotted the

other apprentice, Cinderpaw, tucking into the fresh-kill pile with his mentor, Nutwhisker. When Stumpypaw started making his way over to join them, Brokentail stood in front of him, blocking him.

"You can eat when you've caught enough prey to feed the elders," he snapped.

Stumpypaw just nodded unhappily and trailed off toward the camp entrance. Yellowfang thought he looked tired out. *That's not fair!* Anger smoldering inside her, she went looking for Cloudpelt.

The Clan deputy was sitting in a patch of sunlight near the warriors' den with Amberleaf and Finchflight, discussing the best places to hunt.

"Cloudpelt, may I talk to you in private?" Yellowfang asked as she padded up.

"Sure." Cloudpelt rose to his paws and drew her away a couple of fox-lengths so no cat could overhear them. "What is it?"

Yellowfang mustered her courage, knowing that not even a medicine cat should question the way a mentor chose to deal with his apprentice. "It's Brokentail," she began. "I'm not happy about his mentoring. Have you seen how he is with Stumpypaw?"

She could see from the flicker in Cloudpelt's eyes that he knew what she was talking about. "All mentors train in different ways," he meowed. "It's not my place to interfere."

"But some cat has to do something," Yellowfang insisted. "You can't imagine what I saw earlier today. . . ." She told

Cloudpelt the story of Stumpypaw hanging from the tree branch.

"Was Stumpypaw injured at all?" Cloudpelt asked.

"No," Yellowfang admitted. "But he could have been!"

"In that case, I can't get involved—and I wouldn't want to," Cloudpelt told her. "Look, Yellowfang, I understand your concern for every member of the Clan, but it's been a long time since you were a warrior. Perhaps you've forgotten how tough it can be for apprentices!"

There was nothing more that Yellowfang could say. Dipping her head coldly to the deputy, she turned and stalked back to her own den.

"Look, I brought you a vole," Runningpaw announced as she slipped between the boulders. "It's really fresh."

"Thanks, Runningpaw." Yellowfang flopped down beside the fresh-kill and took a bite.

"Nightpelt said you had an argument with Brokentail," Runningpaw chirped. He sniffed and then continued, "If you don't mind me saying so, you ought to be careful what you say to that cat. He's bad news."

Yellowfang blinked at him, grateful for his concern. "You know," she mewed, "it's time you stopped being my apprentice."

For a heartbeat Runningpaw looked horrified, until he understood what she was really saying. "You mean I can become a full medicine cat? Wow!"

"You more than deserve it," Yellowfang told him. "I am lucky to have had you as my apprentice."

"And I'm lucky to have had you as a mentor."

Yellowfang snorted with amusement. "Even if I haven't taught you how to cure your sniff yet!"

Yellowfang and Runningpaw, with the other medicine cats, sat in the dark cave of the Moonstone as they waited for the moon to shine through the hole in the roof.

"I have sad news," Featherwhisker reported. "Goosefeather has gone to join StarClan."

"I'm sorry," Brambleberry meowed, with her ready sympathy. "How do you feel, being ThunderClan's only medicine cat?"

Relieved he doesn't have to cope with Goosefeather muttering on, Yellowfang thought, though she would never have dreamed of saying that out loud.

"I'm coping," Featherwhisker replied. "There's a very promising new arrival called Spottedkit. She's already taking an interest in my herbs, so if StarClan approves I'll make her my apprentice."

"I have some good news, too," Yellowfang put in. "Tonight I'm going to make Runningpaw a full medicine cat."

All the other medicine cats chimed in with their congratulations. In the faint starshine, Yellowfang could see that Runningpaw looked happily embarrassed.

"You're so lucky!" Barkpaw purred.

"It will be your turn soon," Runningpaw told him.

As he spoke the moon floated into sight, and the Moonstone woke into life, its icy radiance filling the cavern.

Yellowfang rose to her paws and beckoned to Runningpaw to join her beside the shining stone. He was shivering with excitement as he padded up to her.

Yellowfang took a breath, remembering the words from her own ceremony. "I, Yellowfang, medicine cat of Shadow-Clan, call upon my warrior ancestors to look down on this apprentice. He has trained hard to understand the way of a medicine cat, and with your help he will serve his Clan for many moons. Runningpaw," she meowed, "do you promise to uphold the ways of a medicine cat, to stand apart from rivalry between Clan and Clan, and to protect all cats equally, even at the cost of your life?"

"I do," Runningpaw replied in an awed whisper.

"Then by the powers of StarClan I give you your true name as a medicine cat. Runningpaw, from this moment you will be known as Runningnose. Your name will be a reminder that medicine cats cannot cure everything—but we always need to have faith enough to try. StarClan honors your intelligence and your dedication. Now come, touch your muzzle to the Moonstone, and may all your dreams be good ones."

Runningnose crept forward and rested his nose against the shining surface. Yellowfang crouched down beside him and the rest of the medicine cats took their places.

When Yellowfang closed her eyes she was immediately swept out into a place of darkness and cold. She could feel her paws standing on rock, but she couldn't see anything. Then jagged flashes of scarlet broke up the darkness, and high-pitched shrieking battered at her ears. The shapes of kits appeared before Yellowfang's eyes, but these were not the warm, furry bundles of her Clan's nursery. Instead, their tiny bodies were ripped from their mothers' bellies in fountains of blood, while the mother cats clutched at them helplessly.

Yellowfang rushed to and fro trying to save the kits from the unseen claws that were tearing them away. But her pads slipped on the blood, the stench of it filling her nose and throat. However hard she struggled, the dying kits were always just out of reach of her stretching paws.

"No! No!" she yowled.

Something hard pressed into her side. Yellowfang opened her eyes to see Runningnose poking her with one paw. His eyes were wide and scared.

"I—I'm sorry," he stammered. "But you were crying out. I hope I didn't do the wrong thing by waking you?"

"No . . . no, I'm fine," Yellowfang rasped, tottering to her paws. The light from the moon had gone, and the cave was illuminated by the faint sheen of stars. In the faint glimmer she could see the other medicine cats watching her anxiously. "I'm fine," she repeated. "It was just a bad dream."

"It was more than that," Runningnose insisted. "Yellowfang—"

"Enough!" Yellowfang snapped. "We only share our dreams with our leader. They are not for idle gossip!"

Whirling around, she stomped up the passage ahead of the others.

CHAPTER 33

Yellowfang crossed the clearing toward the nursery. A chilly breeze ruffled her fur, warning her that greenleaf was almost at an end. Soon the leaves would fall from the trees and another leaf-bare would set in.

At least these kits will be big and strong before then, she thought.

She was on her way to check on Featherstorm's new litter, Molekit, Dawnkit, and Volekit. They had been born two sunrises before, so they hadn't yet opened their eyes. As she entered the nursery she gazed with satisfaction at the three little wriggling bodies snuggling up to their mother's belly. *At least these kits aren't the ones I saw in that terrible dream at the Moonstone.*

Featherstorm raised her head to greet Yellowfang. "I'm glad you've come," she meowed, looking proudly down at her kits. "I want you to listen to their chests and check their ears for mites."

"Of course."

Yellowfang was pretty sure that there was nothing to worry about, but she knew that an older queen like Featherstorm was bound to be concerned. Besides, she enjoyed spending time with the little squirming creatures, who approached her boldly and sniffed with eager curiosity at her, even though they couldn't see.

While she was examining the kits, their father, Blizzardwing, popped his head through the entrance. "Everything okay?" he called. "Can I do anything?"

"We're all fine," Featherstorm responded with a flick of her tail. "You can fetch me a piece of fresh-kill—something nice and tasty, please. Toms!" she added to Yellowfang when Blizzardwing had disappeared. "I've never found them to be much use around kits."

Hal wouldn't have been, that's for sure, Yellowfang thought, picturing Featherstorm's long-ago mate from the Twolegplace. *He wanted nothing to do with his kits.*

She was heading back across the clearing when the sound of crashing branches broke out in the entrance tunnel. Yellowfang spun around to see Brokentail rushing in with half a rabbit in his jaws.

"Raggedstar! Raggedstar!" he yowled, dropping the rabbit in the middle of the clearing.

The Clan leader appeared from his den, while several other cats rushed up and gathered around Brokentail and the fresh-kill. The elders peered out of their den, and Runningnose came bounding out of the medicine cats' den to join Yellowfang.

"What's going on?" he panted.

"I don't know," Yellowfang replied, padding closer with Runningnose at her side. "Brokentail just came back with that fresh-kill."

"I found this dead rabbit near the tunnel that leads to

WindClan territory," Brokentail announced, his eyes flashing with anger. "It proves that WindClan warriors have been killing prey inside ShadowClan's borders!"

Scorchwind stepped forward with Stumpytail and Cinderfur just behind him. "We patrolled that border earlier," he meowed, "and we didn't find any trace of WindClan scent."

"The rabbit is still warm," Brokentail pointed out. "They must have just caught it! We need to attack at once!"

"Wait a moment," Raggedstar ordered. "We need to make sure the rabbit didn't stagger over the border wounded before dying."

Brokentail let out a hiss of annoyance and thrust the tattered body in front of his leader. "Look! There are bitemarks in it! This was clearly an invasion!" He paused briefly and added, "If you're too scared to challenge those prey-stealers, I'll lead the patrol myself!"

Some of the other warriors nodded agreement, as if they were willing to go with him. Yellowfang noticed that Stumpytail and Flintfang were among them.

"Hang on!" Raggedstar exclaimed as Brokentail turned as if he was about to head off. "Of course I am not afraid. But these things need planning. Brokentail, come with me and Cloudpelt."

When the three cats had gone, Yellowfang padded over and gave the rabbit a thorough sniff. She picked up some WindClan scent on its fur, but the bitemarks had a stronger scent of Brokentail. Yellowfang felt her neck fur begin to rise. *Okay, so he carried it back to the camp, but could this be the shape of* his *teeth in the rabbit's flesh? What if he caught the rabbit himself, after it strayed of its own accord under the Thunderpath?* She began to shake. *Should I tell Raggedstar?*

Just then, Brokentail and Cloudpelt bustled out of the leader's den and started calling to warriors to join them beside the thorn tunnel. Seizing her chance, Yellowfang took a deep breath and slipped underneath the oak roots to see Raggedstar.

"Are you sure that Brokentail is telling the truth?" she demanded boldly. "What if he caught the rabbit himself?"

Raggedstar bristled. "No son of mine would lie! How dare you question him?" He bared his teeth in a snarl. "Now get out of my way."

Bruised by his fury, Yellowfang stepped aside, then followed him out of the den. She watched him race across the camp toward Brokentail, Cloudpelt, and the warriors they had gathered: Stumpytail, Flintfang, and Scorchwind. With a wave of his tail, Raggedstar hurtled through the tunnel with the patrol hard on his paws.

Runningnose padded over to her with dismay in his eyes. "Are we going to follow with herbs?"

Yellowfang shook her head. "This will just be a border skirmish. There won't be any serious injuries." But as she spoke her paws were itching to carry her after the patrol. The camp suddenly felt too small, as if the circle of brambles was closing in on her.

I have to get out!

"I'm going to look for comfrey," she told Runningnose, heading for the tunnel.

"But we have plenty!" he called after her, sounding bewildered.

Yellowfang ignored him. Once out of the camp she raced toward the Thunderpath. Everything was silent. *Perhaps the patrol will just set new border markers and leave,* she thought hopefully.

Panting, Yellowfang emerged from the trees close to the place where the tunnel led into WindClan territory. She couldn't see Brokentail or his patrol, but her heart sank when she sniffed around the entrance to the tunnel and scented ShadowClan warriors heading through it. Yellowfang padded forward, her pelt brushing the tunnel walls. For a few paw steps, light from the opening lit her path, but soon that faded, leaving her in the dark. She jumped, her belly lurching, as a roar sounded from overhead, echoing around the tunnel until she thought her ears would burst.

It's only a monster, she told herself. *Why are you so jumpy? One of those huge things would never get down here.*

Gradually the end of the tunnel appeared, a bright circle in the dimness. Yellowfang's ears rang from the noise of monsters as she clambered out. Dreadful shrieks rose into the air from somewhere up ahead. *Oh, no! Cats are fighting!*

She broke into a run, scrambling up a short, steep slope covered with tough moorland grass, and clawed her way across a sandy overhang. Reaching the top, she looked down into a narrow valley with a stream running along the bottom. The ShadowClan patrol was grappling with WindClan cats. Yellowfang recognized Talltail and a small, russet-furred tom called Redclaw. The others were strangers to her.

"Trespassers!" Talltail growled as he launched himself at Brokentail. "Get off our territory!"

"Prey-stealers!" Brokentail retorted, raking his claws down Talltail's side.

"Stop!" Yellowfang screeched, but no cat heard her.

For a heartbeat she wanted to hurl herself into the battle and help her Clanmates, but she stopped herself. *I am a medicine cat. I must keep apart from Clan rivalries.*

She watched, horrified, as Raggedstar and Redclaw tussled together in a shrieking ball of fur, battering at each other with their strong hind paws as both cats strove to break free. Cloudpelt jumped on top of another WindClan warrior, lashing at his ears until the blood ran freely. Then he sprang off and flung himself at Talltail, who had pinned Brokentail down and was clawing at his face. Scorchwind had fallen beneath the paws of a tabby tom, who was trying to sink his teeth into the ShadowClan warrior's throat.

Yellowfang's heart began to pound harder as she realized that her Clanmates were being beaten back toward the tunnel. Even though the patrol was made up of ShadowClan's best fighters, they were no match for WindClan's fury.

Raggedstar broke away from his battle with Redclaw and staggered to his paws. "Retreat!" he yowled.

Brokentail snarled with rage, in spite of the blood running down his face, but Raggedstar gathered the patrol together and they gradually fought their way back toward the tunnel, still harried by the WindClan cats. Yellowfang gasped as a stabbing pain shot through her throat. She scanned her

Clanmates and saw Cloudpelt stumble to the ground. His thick white fur was turning red.

As she rushed forward to support Cloudpelt, she heard Raggedstar hiss, "What are you doing here?"

Yellowfang ignored the question. "We have to get Cloudpelt back to camp!" she gasped.

To her relief, they were only a few fox-lengths away from the tunnel mouth, and the WindClan cats, satisfied with their victory, drew back at last.

"Don't set paw on our territory again!" Talltail yowled after them.

Yellowfang helped Cloudpelt through the tunnel, stumbling through the darkness with the roar of monsters all around them. The Clan deputy scarcely seemed conscious, and she had to take all his weight. At the other end of the tunnel Scorchwind came to Cloudpelt's other side to prop him up, and the patrol struggled back to the camp.

"Cobwebs! Quickly!" Yellowfang snapped at Runningnose as she dragged Cloudpelt into her den. She remembered how she had battled to save his life before, when the rogues leaped out at him. *I succeeded then. I will succeed now.* "StarClan, wait your turn!" she hissed aloud.

The other members of the patrol crowded in after them, but Yellowfang only had eyes for the white warrior, who had collapsed onto the ground.

"Get a juniper berry," she ordered as Runningnose brought her a thick pad of cobweb. "Crush it and see if you can get the juice into him." She pressed the cobweb to the gash in

Cloudpelt's throat, but his blood soaked through almost at once. Runningnose dropped another pad beside her before fetching the juniper berry.

"I need marigold and thyme!" Yellowfang ordered, pressing the fresh cobweb to Cloudpelt's wound.

As she worked she was vaguely aware of dismayed wails coming from the clearing, as the rest of the Clan heard about the patrol's defeat. Meanwhile Runningnose dealt with the injuries of the rest of the patrol; none of them were serious.

"Get off me!" Brokentail snapped when Runningnose tried to help him clean up the scratches on his face. "I don't need a stupid medicine cat pawing over me."

Runningnose shrugged. "Suit yourself," he muttered. He watched Brokentail stride out of the den, then turned to examine the claw marks on Scorchwind's flank.

This is all my fault, Yellowfang thought as she listened to Cloudpelt's wavering breath. *I should have forced Raggedstar to listen to me about that rabbit.* WindClan had fought this fiercely because they had been falsely accused.

The rest of the patrol left the den after Runningnose had finished treating them. Yellowfang looked up to see that daylight was already fading; she had lost all track of time. "You'd better get some sleep," she told Runningnose. "I'll call you if I need anything."

Runningnose nodded, glancing anxiously down at Cloudpelt, then curled up in his nest and closed his eyes.

The night dragged on. Yellowfang never moved from Cloudpelt's side, listening to his shallow breathing and watching the ooze of blood that still trickled from his neck. She wasn't sure how long she had been sitting there when the young warrior's eyelids fluttered and he opened his eyes.

"Yellowfang?" he murmured feebly.

"I'm here." Yellowfang rested a paw reassuringly on Cloudpelt's shoulder. "I won't leave you." She reached for a ball of wet moss and held it so that Cloudpelt could lap at it.

"That's good . . ." Cloudpelt sighed out the words. "Am I going to StarClan?"

"Not if I can help it," Yellowfang muttered grimly.

Cloudpelt twitched his whiskers. "Maybe I'll see you there . . ." His voice faded and his eyes closed again.

Her heart clenched with grief, Yellowfang stayed by his side. Gradually she became aware that another cat was standing beside her. She looked up to see Brokentail.

"Have you come to have your wounds treated?" she asked.

"No," Brokentail sneered. "I've come to tell you not to waste your efforts with Cloudpelt. His time is over. He would never have been able to lead ShadowClan." He drew himself up, his eyes gleaming in the darkness. "There is only one cat who can do that after Raggedstar. I will be the next leader of ShadowClan."

"How can you say that?" Yellowfang gasped. "I am a medicine cat, and I will always do everything I can to save my Clanmates!"

Brokentail did not respond, just looked down at Cloudpelt with eyes that glittered with hostility. Then without another word, he stalked out of the den.

Brokentail lied about the rabbit, I'm sure of it. And now Cloudpelt is terribly injured. Yellowfang remembered what Raggedstar had said to his son when he made Cloudpelt deputy. *Don't worry. I've many seasons left in me, and if anything should happen to Cloudpelt, it will be your turn next.* She forced her darkest fears away. Even if Brokentail had deliberately caught the rabbit to start a battle with WindClan, he couldn't have known how badly Cloudpelt would be hurt. *Brokentail is ambitious, but that's a good thing for a warrior. I can still be proud of him.*

Throughout the night Yellowfang tried every herb, every trace of knowledge she possessed, to help Cloudpelt, but as the sun slid into the den through the branches overhead, the white warrior's faint breathing grew more ragged, then sank into silence. His tail-tip twitched once, and then was still.

He has gone to hunt with StarClan. Yellowfang bent over the deputy's body, grief-stricken and scared deep inside. *Things are going terribly wrong.*

As she crouched over Cloudpelt's body, she heard a rustling from Runningnose's nest. His voice came from behind her, blurred with sleep. "How is Cloudpelt?"

"He's dead," Yellowfang choked out.

"No!" Runningnose got up and came to stand beside her, scraps of moss still clinging to his pelt. "Do you want me to break the news to Raggedstar?"

Yellowfang shook her head. "No. Thank you, but I have to do that myself." She stumbled into the clearing and padded over to Raggedstar's den. Creeping under the oak roots, she saw the Clan leader curled in his nest. "Wake up!" she meowed.

Raggedstar lifted his head, then scrambled up when he saw Yellowfang. "What news?"

"The worst," Yellowfang admitted. "Cloudpelt walks with StarClan now."

Raggedstar bowed his head. "He died the death of the noblest warrior."

"But it was a battle that should never have been fought!" Yellowfang flashed back at him.

"Do not say that!" Raggedstar roared. "You dishonor Cloudpelt's memory if that's what you truly believe!"

"I would never do that," Yellowfang assured him, forcing herself to meet her leader's gaze steadily. "But I think Brokentail looked for this battle. Cloudpelt died unnecessarily."

Raggedstar narrowed his eyes. "What exactly are you saying?"

Yellowfang flinched. "I don't think you should make Brokentail deputy in his place."

"I will not listen to this!" Raggedstar snarled. His amber gaze, alight with anger, rested on her like a flame. "You are my medicine cat, Yellowfang, and your loyalty should only be to me and my warriors. Never question me again!"

The moon was rising above the trees. In the clearing, the ShadowClan cats kept vigil for Cloudpelt. Yellowfang sat near his head. She remembered the eager apprentice he had been, looking forward to having a mate and kits.

I'm so sorry that will never happen. But you were a fine deputy for your Clan, and you died with a warrior's courage.

Movement alerted Yellowfang, and she looked up to see

Raggedstar leaping up onto the Clanrock.

"Cats of ShadowClan!" he began. "We have lost Cloudpelt, and we grieve for him. But the life of the Clan must continue. It is time to appoint a new deputy." He paused, but this time there was no sense of anticipation among the Clan. Every cat knew who the Cloudpelt's successor would be.

"I say these words before the body of Cloudpelt, and in the presence of the spirits of my ancestors, that they may hear and approve my choice," Raggedstar announced. "Brokentail will be the new deputy of ShadowClan." He raised his tail for silence before the Clan could break into the usual cheers. "True, Brokentail is still younger than most of you, but ShadowClan has never had a braver or more skillful warrior. He is an example to us all, and it will be a great honor to lead the Clan with him."

Yowls rose up to welcome Brokentail. The warrior stood in the center of the clearing with his head held high and his eyes gleaming like two yellow moons. Yellowfang thought back to the time when he had been a friendless kit because no cat knew who his mother was. She had felt sorry for him then, and terribly guilty for abandoning her only son. But so much had happened since then, all of it overshadowed by Molepelt's strange warning of blood and fire. However hard she tried, Yellowfang couldn't feel pride in the warrior that stood before her now. Only fear and a deep sense of dread for the future.

He has come so far since he was a motherless kit. How much further will he go?

Chapter 34

The sound of cats crashing through the brambles woke Yellowfang. She sat up in her nest. The night was starless, pitch-black, and a brisk leaf-fall wind scoured across the camp. *Are we being attacked?*

Then the sound of familiar voices drifted into the medicine cats' den. Yellowfang let the fur on her neck lie down. *It's only a night patrol returning.*

A moon before, shortly after he became deputy, Brokentail had decided that the Clan should start patrolling the borders at night. "Other Clans might attack us under cover of darkness," he had stated. "But they'll discover that ShadowClan is ready for them."

Runningnose stirred in his nest beside Yellowfang. "These night patrols are a waste of time," he complained. "We're no more at risk of attack than the other Clans, because they're all *sleeping* like we are."

"Fox dung! StarClan-cursed thorns!" A voice sounded a couple of tail-lengths away.

"At least we should be sleeping," Runningnose added dryly.

There was a rustle of movement as a cat slipped between

the boulders into the den; Yellowfang recognized Frogtail by his scent. "What is it?" she called.

"I wrenched my shoulder jumping down from a tree trunk while I was on patrol," Frogtail explained. "You can't see your paw in front of your face on a night like this."

Yellowfang sighed. "Come over here."

She did her best to examine Frogtail's shoulder in the dark. She could feel heat in his muscles and she let down her defenses, allowing herself to feel his pain briefly so that she could judge how bad it was. "You'll live," she grunted.

"Do I need herbs?" Frogtail meowed. "Poppy seeds to sleep?"

"No, your pain isn't that bad," Yellowfang told him. Brokentail's new schedule of extra patrols and training had meant more injuries than usual and stocks of herbs were low. "You'll be fine if you just rest."

"Are you sure?" Frogtail sounded disappointed. "I can't afford to miss any training, or Brokentail will put me back on apprentice duties."

ShadowClan had no apprentices at the moment: Featherstorm's litter, Mosskit, Volekit, and Dawnkit, were still too young, and Newtspeck had only recently given birth to Wetkit, Littlekit, and Brownkit. Until more kits could be apprenticed, the warriors were taking turns performing the duties.

"That's not necessarily a bad thing," Yellowfang suggested. "Apprentice duties will be easier on your shoulder than training and patrolling."

"I guess," Frogtail muttered. "Thanks anyway, Yellowfang," he added as he padded out of the den.

Runningnose had already curled up again, but when Yellowfang returned to her nest, sleep eluded her. As soon as the sky began to grow pale with dawn, she made her way into the clearing. The ground was cold beneath her paws and in the dim light she could see a white rim of frost on every leaf and twig. *Leaf-bare is almost upon us.*

From the nursery she could hear the joyful squeaking of kits, and she pictured six warm, furry bodies squirming among the moss and pine needles. Yellowfang glowed with warmth as she imagined them growing big and strong over the next moons. But her hope was tinged with worry. *Our ranks are swelling; it might become hard to feed us all.* She wondered if she should pay the nursery a visit, then decided there was no need. *Featherstorm is an experienced queen, and Newtspeck has really good mothering instincts.*

A cough sounded behind Yellowfang. Startled, she turned to see that Nightpelt had emerged from the elders' den. He was looking strained; his cough always troubled him more when the cold weather started to set in.

"I thought I'd go for a walk," Yellowfang meowed. "Do you want to come?"

The black tom nodded and fell in beside her. The two cats slipped through the brambles, past Mousewing on guard, and padded into the trees. Yellowfang heaved a contented sigh as she gazed around at the territory, caught like crystal in the silver dawn. The trees and bushes were white with frost and every puddle was rimmed with ice that glittered in the growing light.

I'm so glad this is my home.

"I trained here once with Flintpaw and Clawpaw," Nightpelt mewed as they reached a thicket of dense bushes. "Flintpaw ran into a bees' nest in that tree over there—I've never heard a cat yowl so loud!"

"I remember," Yellowfang responded; she had used up most of her stocks of dock leaves treating the young cat's stings. "He was very brave about the pain."

Nightpelt nodded. "He'd only just healed when he convinced us to go fishing in the stream near the big ash tree. We all came back soaking wet, and we didn't catch a thing."

"And Stonetooth told you to leave fishing to RiverClan," Yellowfang recalled. "You and your denmates were always causing trouble!" She padded on a few paw steps, then asked, "Do you mind not being a warrior anymore?"

Nightpelt paused before replying. "I am still a warrior inside," he mewed at last. "I have the same spirit, the same loyalty to my Clan. I hope that one day I will find new ways to prove this, besides warrior duties."

"I'm sure you'll never stop finding ways to prove your love for ShadowClan," Yellowfang told him, touching him lightly on the shoulder with her tail-tip.

As they headed back toward the camp, they met a patrol on their way out. Stumpytail and Tangleburr were bounding in the lead, closely followed by Rowanberry, Blackfoot, and Deerfoot. Brokentail brought up the rear.

"Are you going hunting?" Yellowfang called.

"No, this is battle training," Stumpytail announced, his whiskers quivering with excitement. "Brokentail has asked us to be dogs, and chase our Clanmates through the forest."

Yellowfang blinked. "Doesn't the Clan need feeding first?"

Deerfoot flicked his tail. "They can wait. It's not like we'll be long."

Yellowfang and Nightpelt watched the patrol as it charged off through the trees.

"I'm going to climb a tree!" Stumpytail meowed. "Then I'll jump down on the dogs and *shred* them!"

"But we'll be too fast for you," Tangleburr countered. "So you can stay up your tree until you freeze!"

"Brokentail has really inspired them," Nightpelt commented as he and Yellowfang went on toward the camp. "The next cats to trespass on our territory won't spend long on the wrong side of the border."

Yellowfang nodded. "The Clan is certainly strong at the moment." She sensed they were both being careful about what they said. *Brokentail's methods can sometimes be harsh; I'm sure Nightpelt would agree with me on that.* The silence hung heavily between them as they pushed through the brambles into the camp.

As soon as they emerged into the clearing, Featherstorm came dashing toward them from the nursery. "Oh, Yellowfang, thank StarClan you're back!" she exclaimed. "Volekit has started coughing."

"I'll come and look at him right away," Yellowfang mewed.

She could hear the kit's persistent cough as she slid through the entrance to the nursery. Volekit was squatting in his bedding, a miserable bundle of fur, his tiny body shaken by coughs. His two littermates looked on with wide, anxious eyes.

Yellowfang placed a paw on his chest and felt feverish heat striking through her pads. "How long has he been like this?" she asked Featherstorm.

"It came on in the night," the she-cat replied. "How bad is it, Yellowfang? Is it whitecough?"

"I don't think so," Yellowfang meowed. "I'll bring him a tansy leaf. That should do the trick." Stroking the tiny tom's brown pelt, she added, "You'll feel better soon, little kit."

On her way out of the nursery she paused beside Newtspeck, whose young litter—their eyes not open yet—was huddled into the curve of her belly. "If I were you, I'd keep the little ones away from Volekit until his cough clears up," she advised.

Newtspeck nodded and curled her tail protectively around her kits.

On her way back from delivering the tansy leaf, Yellowfang was hailed by Hollyflower from the entrance to the elders' den. "Poolcloud's joints are aching," she announced when the medicine cat padded up. "Do you have anything for her?"

Yellowfang nodded. "I'll bring her a poultice of daisy leaves," she replied. "And a poppy seed to help her sleep."

But before she fetched the herbs, Yellowfang poked her head into the warriors' den to make sure Frogtail was resting, and beckoned to Amberleaf, who was gathering up soiled bedding. "Come with me," Yellowfang ordered. "It's time I renewed that dressing on your ear." Amberleaf had torn her ear in a training exercise and the wound had been reluctant to heal.

Amberleaf sighed as she rose to her paws. "Okay, Yellowfang. When can I return to warrior duties?"

"When I'm satisfied that ear isn't infected," Yellowfang retorted.

When she peeled off the wrapping of cobweb and goldenrod leaves, she was pleased to see that Amberleaf's wound looked clean and healthy. "You don't need another poultice," she commented as she rubbed the scratch with marigold. "You can go back to your duties tomorrow provided it's no worse."

"Great!" Amberleaf meowed. "I think if I have to take one more tick off the elders I'll go mad as a fox in a fit."

Yellowfang sent her away and collected the daisy leaves and the poppy seed for Poolcloud. At the entrance to the elders' den she met Runningnose, staggering under the weight of a huge bundle of dripping moss.

"I don't want the elders to get their paws wet by the stream," he explained, mumbling around his burden. "Their bedding needs changing, too."

"Hasn't Brokentail put any cat on apprentice duties?" Yellowfang asked.

Runningnose shook his head. "No, they're all out battle training. Except for Amberleaf, and she's stuck doing the warriors' bedding all on her own."

Yellowfang sighed. *Runningnose shouldn't have to work so hard when he's no younger or less experienced than the other warriors.* "Never mind," she meowed. "I'll help you with the elders' nests as soon as I've taken care of Littlebird."

Once Littlebird was dosed and comfortable, Yellowfang went into the forest again, her pleasure in the bright day dimmed by her anxiety about using so many herbs. She was carrying a bundle of moss and feathers across the clearing when Raggedstar padded up to her.

"Have you seen any hunting patrols?" he asked her.

Yellowfang shook her head. "As far as I know, they're battle training first."

The Clan leader's amber eyes grew troubled. "There are hungry bellies in the Clan," he mewed. "Elders, kits, and warriors all need feeding."

You should talk to your deputy about that, not your medicine cat, Yellowfang thought. "Well, I have some traveling herbs that could take the edge off the worst hunger," she suggested, "but I'm not sure I should use them up so soon before leaf-bare."

"I don't want my Clanmates eating your herbs!" Raggedstar's eyes widened in shock and anger. "They should have fresh-kill!"

As he was speaking, movement by the entrance caught Yellowfang's eye, and Brokentail plunged into the clearing. Blood spattered his muzzle and his eyes shone with triumph.

"Excellent training session," he announced, bounding up to Raggedstar and Yellowfang. "Rowanberry and Stumpytail cornered the dogs before they were halfway to the border!"

The two dog-hunters had followed him into the camp, panting and exhausted but clearly very pleased with themselves. The other three warriors staggered into the camp; Yellowfang was shocked to see how bedraggled and battered they looked. Deerfoot was limping, Blackfoot's shoulder was bleeding, and Tangleburr had a lump of fur missing from her side.

They must have been the dogs, Yellowfang thought. *They've certainly had the worst of it.*

"Next time, you'll run faster!" Brokentail told them. "Now, clean yourselves up and get back to the training area. I need you to practice your defense moves."

"They can rest first, I think," Raggedstar meowed.

"And I ought to check those wounds," Yellowfang added.

Brokentail stared at Raggedstar. "Rest?" He sounded surprised. "We can't stop a battle just because we get tired! I said they can clean themselves up; then we'll continue."

"What about the hunting patrols?" Raggedstar prompted.

"Don't worry," Brokentail assured him cheerfully. "I've sent some cats off to find fresh-kill. That's if they haven't scared all the prey into hiding!"

Yellowfang gazed at Brokentail. *You have so much ambition, so much drive to make your Clanmates as strong and fearless as you,* she thought. *I wonder where your spirit comes from. Is it partly from me?*

Yellowfang was putting away a fresh supply of dock leaves when Runningnose padded up behind her and touched her shoulder with his tail.

"Have you forgotten it's the half-moon? We should be on our way to the Moonstone."

Yellowfang blinked at him in confusion. "There's so much to do here, it slipped my mind," she confessed.

Runningnose gave her shoulder a brief stroke. "I'll stay behind and get on with the work, if you like," he offered. "I don't mind missing the meeting for once."

Yellowfang pushed her nose into his shoulder fur, grateful for his sensitivity. "I'm sure it will be routine," she mewed. "I haven't heard anything from the other medicine cats lately."

With a quick farewell, Yellowfang headed out of the camp and across the forest to the tunnel that led into WindClan territory. Emerging from the other end, she bounded over the tough moorland grass, suddenly anxious that she would be late and miss the moment when light poured down onto the Moonstone. She was relieved to spot Featherwhisker of ThunderClan and Brambleberry of RiverClan padding ahead of her, and picked up her pace to catch up to them. Brambleberry had a younger cat with her who was a stranger to Yellowfang.

"This is Mudpaw, my new apprentice," she announced proudly when she had greeted Yellowfang.

Yellowfang dipped her head to the young tom. "Welcome to the company of medicine cats."

"Thank you." Mudpaw's eyes shone. "I can't believe I'm going to meet our ancestors!"

"I should have an apprentice of my own next time," Featherwhisker announced. "Spottedkit will be Spottedpaw by then. She's always poking about my stores; I think she's going to be a great medicine cat!"

"I'm looking forward to meeting her," Brambleberry mewed.

At the far side of the territory Hawkheart and his

apprentice, Barkpaw, were waiting, and all the medicine cats traveled on together. They trekked through the farm, where a young black-and-white tom watched them from his perch on top of a wall. Yellowfang recognized him from her last visit to Highstones. He'd recently arrived there and was friendly enough to the passing Clan cats.

"Hi, Barley," Hawkheart meowed. "Settling in okay?"

Barley dipped his head. "Everything's fine, thanks, Hawkheart. The old barn is crawling with mice! You can all stop and eat if you like."

"Thanks, but we don't have time," Featherwhisker told him. "Maybe on the way back."

The two apprentices were walking side by side. There was a bounce in Mudpaw's step, as if his paws were itching to run flat out to the hills.

"What's it like, meeting a StarClan cat?" he asked Barkpaw. "What do you say to them?"

"It's different for every cat," Barkpaw told him. "But don't worry. You'll be fine."

"And do you only meet with cats from your own Clan?" Mudpaw went on. "Yellowfang, do you only see ShadowClan cats?"

Yellowfang shook her head, suppressing a shudder at the thought of some of the cats she had walked with in her dreams. "You might see more of your own Clan than others," she replied to the eager young cat. "But not always. There's no telling who you'll meet in StarClan."

Mudpaw's eyes sparkled. "I can't wait!"

In the cavern of the Moonstone Yellowfang found it was a bit of a squeeze for all six cats to get into position. As she settled herself she was a bit disconcerted to see Featherwhisker deliberately wriggle between her and Hawkheart.

Why does he want to be next to me? For once he hasn't been asking his annoying questions, so what's on his mind now? Does he think he'll get to walk in my dreams?

The long walk had tired Yellowfang, and she relaxed as she closed her eyes. But her relief was short-lived. Darkness swirled around her like black fog, torn apart by slashing claws and tumbling, shrieking bodies. Yellowfang was in the middle of a terrible battle, choking on air that was thick with blood and fury. But there was something different about these warriors. . . . Yellowfang loomed over them, taller by more than a mouse-length. And their shrieks were high-pitched, as piercing as rat squeals.

These were not warriors fighting, but *kits*!

Yellowfang stared down at the tiny mewling things, some with their eyes still closed, but when their little paws struck they left gouges that spilled with blood, and their puny teeth sank deep into one another's fur.

Oh, StarClan, no! Yellowfang wailed silently. *Why are you showing me this?*

She plunged into the battle, trying to stop the kits from tearing one another apart, but they ignored her and kept on ripping and biting. Blood flowed over the ground and rose up around Yellowfang's legs and belly like a river, clinging to her pelt.

A screech sounded behind her and she whipped around to see Molepelt, standing on a mound of earth above the battle and blood.

"Fire and blood will destroy the Clans!" he yowled.

Yellowfang tried to fight her way toward him but the tide of battling kits swept her away. Blood gurgled in her throat and thick, choking darkness covered her.

Yellowfang crouched, trembling in darkness and silence. She forced her eyes open, expecting to find herself back in the cavern of the Moonstone. Instead she was curled up in a star-lit glade. A soft breeze whispered in the grass, and the air was filled with the scent of fresh green growth. Silverflame was licking her fur, as if Yellowfang were a kit once more, with her pelt ruffled from playing with her littermates.

For a couple of heartbeats Yellowfang surrendered herself to Silverflame's gentle care. Then she whispered, "The kits! They were fighting! Why?"

Silverflame looked at her with eyes full of grief. "Terrible times are coming," she mewed. "I'm so sorry."

"Why are you sorry?" Yellowfang asked, springing to her paws. "Just tell me how I can change things!"

Silverflame shook her head. "You can't. The tide has turned already."

"But there must be something I can do!" Yellowfang protested.

"Knowing something is going to happen does not give us the power to change it," Silverflame mewed, so softly that Yellowfang could only just hear her. "Now, lie down and rest while you can. Your Clan needs you more than ever."

In spite of her desperate anxiety, Yellowfang let the she-cat's steady lapping soothe her, and closed her eyes. After a little while, two tiny tongues joined in with Silverflame's, and Yellowfang smelled the heartbreaking scent of her daughters.

I must be strong for my Clan, she told herself. *But StarClan, why do you make it so hard?*

A moment later Yellowfang felt a cat nudging her in the side. She opened her eyes to meet the curious gaze of Featherwhisker. The moonlight was gone, and dawn light trickled in through the gap in the roof of the cave.

"Are you okay?" the ThunderClan medicine cat inquired. "What did you see?"

The ghastly vision of battling kits flooded back into Yellowfang's memory. Ignoring Featherwhisker's question, she yelped, "I have to get back to the camp!"

Leaving the other medicine cats behind, Yellowfang raced up the tunnel and hurled herself down the steep slope outside, her paws skidding and sliding on the pebbles. She ran all the way back to the ShadowClan camp and arrived, panting, at cold, crisp sunhigh.

Bursting through the brambles, she headed toward Raggedstar's den. *He has to know what I saw!*

But before Yellowfang could reach the Clan leader's den, he rushed out to meet her. "I must talk to you," he meowed urgently.

Raggedstar spun her around and thrust her back through the tunnel and into the trees, away from the camp. When they were beyond the hearing of their Clanmates, he halted and faced her.

"I had a dream," he told her, his voice shaking. "Kits fighting! Killing one another, way beyond their strength! The ground ran with blood, and I could do nothing to stop them. Yellowfang, what does it mean?"

CHAPTER 35

Sheer horror choked Yellowfang's words before she could speak. "I had the same dream," she managed to whisper at last.

Raggedstar stared at her in dismay. "Great StarClan, why would we both have this vision? I would never send kits into battle! It's against the warrior code!"

"I know you wouldn't," Yellowfang assured him.

Just then, the sounds of battling cats drifted through the trees. A screech split the cold, bright air, followed by Brokentail's voice, loud and hectoring.

"No, Deerfoot, not like that! I've seen *rabbits* that could fight harder than you! And don't snigger, Tangleburr. You're just as feeble. Let me see that move again, and put some strength into it this time!"

Yellowfang met Raggedstar's gaze. The Clan leader opened his jaws to speak, only to break off when they heard another vicious growl from Brokentail.

"You're soft, all of you! Will you stop in the middle of a battle to lick your wounds? If you get hurt, you'll learn more quickly how to avoid getting hit."

"I've made a terrible mistake, haven't I?" Raggedstar

murmured. "Our son wants to do nothing but lead Shadow-Clan into battle. I should never have made him deputy! What can we do to stop him?"

A flash of rage pulsed through Yellowfang. "He's *our* son now, is he?" she snarled. "I have never been allowed to be his mother! You said you would only keep my secret if I never called him my son. What can I possibly do to change him? Brokentail is your problem, Raggedstar."

"But—" The Clan leader tried to interrupt.

Yellowfang ignored him. "You have told me too many times that I am nothing more than a medicine cat. I heal my Clan, that's all. You are responsible for what your warriors do."

Raggedstar blinked, shocked to silence.

Yellowfang glared at him for a heartbeat, then spun around and stormed off. *How dare he expect me to have any influence over Brokentail now? There was never anything I could do.*

As she returned to the camp, she tried to calm herself. She took deep breaths and forced her paws into a dignified walk.

"Yellowfang!" Fernshade came rushing across to her from the warriors' den. "You'll never guess—I'm going to have Wolfstep's kits!"

Yellowfang just looked at her.

"I know I'm a bit old to be having my first litter," Fernshade chattered on happily, "and with leaf-bare approaching, it isn't the best time, but after all, the Clan needs young blood!"

At the mention of young blood, Yellowfang froze, seeing again the scarlet tide that had risen around her from the battling kits. *No!* she wanted to screech aloud. *Don't have these kits!*

They can't be born! Terrible things lie ahead!

Instead she forced herself to mew, "That's great. Come with me and I'll give you some herbs to help with your strength."

Yellowfang was relieved to see Runningnose in their den, and she passed Fernshade's care over to him.

"Kits!" Runningnose exclaimed, his eyes gleaming with delight. "Fernshade, that's wonderful. Lie down here and let me check how they're doing."

Yellowfang watched as Runningnose ran his paws over Fernshade's barely swollen belly, then leaned close to press his ear against the smooth curve. "Hi, little kits," he purred. "Can you hear me in there? Make sure you grow big and strong so you'll be good warriors for your Clan."

Fernshade let out a little *mrrow* of happiness. "I'm sure they'll be fine, with both of you to look after them."

Yellowfang fetched burnet leaves, which were good for all expectant queens, and Fernshade swallowed them obediently.

"Come back every day for more," Runningnose instructed, "and make sure you get enough to eat. Don't be afraid of taking as much fresh-kill as you need. It's important for your kits that you feed well."

Yellowfang was distracted by voices chattering outside the den.

"I couldn't believe what Raggedstar did!" That was Deerfoot, sounding shocked, though Yellowfang had a feeling that he was enjoying passing on gossip.

"What happened?" Tangleburr prompted.

"He interrupted our battle training and tried to tell Brokentail how to run the session! He thought Brokentail was being too hard on us."

"Well, Raggedstar is Clan leader," Tangleburr pointed out. "He has the right to tell any cat what to do, even his deputy."

"He's got no right to mess up Brokentail's battle training!" Deerleap retorted hotly. "Brokentail is tough, sure, but he's made me a better warrior already!"

"So what did Brokentail say?"

"He did what Raggedstar told him. He's a loyal deputy. But I could tell he wasn't happy . . ."

The young cats began to move off, and Yellowfang couldn't hear any more of their conversation, but she felt a stir of concern in her belly. *Will Brokentail start to defy his Clan leader when he knows that he has the support of the warriors?*

After Fernshade had left the den, Yellowfang tracked down Raggedstar near the fresh-kill pile. "Is everything okay?" she asked, bounding over to join him.

"Fine," Raggedstar replied. "I spoke to Brokentail and asked him to be a bit less fierce in training."

And you trust him to do that? Yellowfang didn't voice her doubts out loud.

"In three moons, Featherstorm's and then Newtspeck's kits will be ready to be apprenticed," Raggedstar went on, "but until then Brokentail needs to focus on keeping the Clan fed and fit through the cold season."

Yellowfang murmured agreement. "Fernshade is expecting kits," she informed the Clan leader.

Raggedstar's eyes widened in delight. "That's excellent news!"

"But what about the dream we had?" Yellowfang whispered.

"It must mean something terrible for the Clan."

"Kits are always a good thing," Raggedstar meowed; there was a hint of warning in his voice, as if he didn't want to be contradicted.

Yellowfang knew there was no point in persisting. Instead she dipped her head and slipped past him to the fresh-kill pile.

What a miserable little heap!

With hunting so badly neglected, there was hardly any prey worth eating. The best pieces were a vole and a starling, but Yellowfang spotted Archeye and Poolcloud padding up with gloomy expressions as they surveyed the scanty pile. *The elders need to be fed,* Yellowfang thought. *I'll choose something else.*

She took a scrawny shrew, while Archeye and Poolcloud settled down with the vole and the starling. But before they could start to eat, Frogtail bounded up to the fresh-kill pile and shouldered the elders away.

"I need this prey!" he announced. "I'm a warrior. I have to keep my strength up."

"What?" Poolcloud bristled. "Kits and elders eat first! That's the warrior code."

"Let him have them," Archeye mewed wearily, patting the vole and starling across to Frogtail. "It's not worth arguing."

Poolcloud still looked indignant.

Frogtail was crouching down to take his first bite of vole when Brokentail strode across the clearing and fixed him with a stern look. "Frogtail, what are you doing?" he demanded.

"Taking our food, the prey-stealer," Poolcloud grumbled.

"What?" Brokentail's eyes narrowed and his voice dropped

to a soft snarl. "Frogtail, give the prey back right now. The warrior code tells us that kits and elders feed first."

"Told you!" Poolcloud mewed smugly.

"I'm shocked and disappointed in you, Frogtail," Brokentail went on. "This isn't the way a ShadowClan warrior behaves."

"But you said—" Frogtail protested.

"I'm sure I never told you to steal food from those who need it more," Brokentail interrupted, not giving Frogtail the chance to speak.

"Brokentail is right." Raggedstar, who had been listening, padded up to join the group. "Archeye, Poolcloud, eat your fill. Frogtail, you can take out a hunting patrol and see if you can restock the fresh-kill pile."

Frogtail sullenly rose to his paws with a glare at the elders, who crouched down and began to eat in swift bites, in case their leader changed his mind.

Meanwhile, Brokentail glanced around the camp, signaling to nearby warriors with a sweep of his tail. "Brackenfoot, Stumpytail, Blackfoot, you need to join Frogtail on a hunting patrol."

The Clan leader and his deputy stood side by side as the patrol left the camp. Yellowfang saw that Raggedstar's eyes gleamed with approval and satisfaction.

He and Brokentail seem to be in agreement for now, she thought uneasily. *But how long will it last?*

Yellowfang shifted in her nest, blinking up at the warriors of StarClan above her head. She felt exhausted, but her growling belly wouldn't let her sleep. Frogtail's patrol had brought back only a meager collection of prey, and she had ended up sharing a skinny blackbird with Runningnose.

"Honestly, Yellowfang!" Runningnose's voice came from his own nest. "They can probably hear your belly rumbling in ThunderClan! Why don't you go and catch yourself something? The night patrol went out a while ago, so make sure they don't think you're an intruder and flay your fur."

"I might just do that." Yellowfang heaved herself stiffly out of her nest and headed into the clearing. Instead of leaving the camp, she padded over to the fresh-kill pile and began nosing around the area for scraps.

She was gulping down a morsel of mouse when she heard a noise from the entrance tunnel: a cat's voice raised in a wail of unbearable anguish. Every hair on Yellowfang's pelt rose. Whipping around, she saw Brokentail burst into the camp. His fur was bushed out and his eyes were wild and distraught.

"WindClan ambushed us by the tunnel!" he yowled. "Raggedstar is dead!"

Yellowfang froze. The solid floor of the camp seemed to give way under her paws, and she was falling, falling into darkness. Then her head cleared and she forced her paws to move, racing over to Brokentail.

"What happened?" she demanded.

"They were waiting for us . . ." The deputy's voice shook; he seemed dazed with grief and anger. "We fought. Raggedstar led us . . . then a WindClan cat tore out his throat." He shook his head helplessly. "I couldn't save him . . ."

"And the rest of your patrol?" Yellowfang asked, fear surging up inside her. *Not more cats dead . . .*

"Chasing the WindClan cats across the moor," Brokentail replied.

Not waiting to hear any more, Yellowfang raced out of the camp and across the marshes toward the tunnel that led to WindClan. The reek of blood caught in her throat before she came within sight of it. At the mouth of the tunnel, Raggedstar lay stretched out. A circle of torn-up grass and fern surrounded him, and the ground was soaked with his blood. His eyes were glazed, staring sightlessly up into the sky.

Yellowfang lay down beside him and pushed her muzzle into his fur. Until then she had hoped that he hadn't lost all his lives, or that her medicine cat skills might be enough to revive him, or even that Brokentail had mistaken the Clan leader's losing a life for true death. But now her hope had gone. Raggedstar's wounds were so severe they had drained all his lives at once. He hunted with StarClan now.

"I loved you so much," she murmured. "You were all I ever wanted. We fought and hunted together, and played in the sunlight . . . What went wrong? How did we ever come to this?"

A memory of giving birth to Brokentail flashed into Yellowfang's mind, and she saw once again the rage that fueled the tiny body. Another pang of grief shook her, but she pushed the memory away.

"Hunt well in StarClan," she told Raggedstar, drawing her

tongue over his fur in a long, caressing lick. "I will see you again."

Running paw steps alerted her and she looked up to see Blackfoot, Scorchwind, and Boulder racing out of the tunnel. Spotting her with Raggedstar, they halted and stared with growing horror in their eyes.

"We fought with some WindClan cats," Boulder mewed hoarsely. "But we didn't know that Raggedstar was hurt."

"How can he be dead?" Scorchwind whispered, taking a pace forward to look down at the body of his brother. "He still had nine lives!"

"A leader can lose all his lives at once if the wounds are severe enough," Yellowfang told him quietly. "Now you must carry his body back to camp."

As the patrol gathered around, Brokentail rushed up, the wild look still in his eyes. "Stay away from my father!" he ordered. "I will carry him, no one else!"

A rush of pity engulfed Yellowfang. *My poor son . . .*

As Boulder and Scorchwind heaved Raggedstar's body onto Brokentail's back, she rested her tail across his shoulders, and in a rare moment of gentleness Brokentail let it stay there while they walked slowly back to camp.

CHAPTER 36

Yellowfang stood beside Raggedstar's body in the center of the camp while the cats of ShadowClan filed out of their dens to sit vigil for their dead leader. Every cat's eyes held the same stunned expression, as if they couldn't believe that their leader was dead.

The older warriors and elders in particular were struggling with grief. "Raggedstar was leader for such a short time," Archeye mewed. "He should have cared for his Clan for many seasons yet."

"How terrible, to lose nine lives at once!" Hollyflower murmured.

Brokentail was crouching beside his father's head with one paw resting on Raggedstar's cold fur. "Those WindClan maggots must have been determined to send him to StarClan," he rasped.

Struggling to focus through her aching sadness, Yellowfang padded to stand at Brokentail's shoulder. "You must go to Moonstone to receive your lives," she reminded him. "You are leader of ShadowClan now!"

Brokentail looked up at her with fury in his eyes. "I will

not leave my father's body in the cold!" he hissed. "We will go tomorrow."

Startled—*I thought becoming leader was all he ever wanted*—Yellowfang didn't try to argue. She bowed her head. "Of course. StarClan will understand," she murmured.

As dawn crept into the sky, the elders gathered around to carry Raggedstar's body outside the camp for burial.

"May StarClan light your path, Raggedstar," Yellowfang announced. "May you find good hunting, swift running, and shelter when you sleep."

She watched the elders bear their former leader's body away, and felt a tremor of fear in her belly. *If WindClan did this to us, we must prepare for war.* Hearing angry voices, she noticed Scorchwind and Blackfoot huddled beside Tangleburr and Cinderfur.

"WindClan might attack us at any moment," Cinderfur meowed. "They'll think we're weak without a leader. What are we going to do?"

"That's for Brokentail to decide," Tangleburr reminded him. Her tail-tip was twitching, but she was clearly trying to control her fury. "But he can't do anything until he gets his nine lives."

"Then he needs to get a move on," Blackfoot hissed.

"We have to attack!" Scorchwind declared. "We can't let WindClan get away with this."

Brokentail, who had been watching his father's body vanish into the brambles, looked over his shoulder. "Vengeance can wait until we have grieved, Scorchwind," he murmured wretchedly.

He seems further from launching an attack on WindClan than ever before, Yellowfang thought, not sure whether that was a good thing or not. *Surely he wants to avenge Raggedstar's death?*

Returning to her den, she found Runningnose halfheartedly rolling more balls of moss for the store. "Do you think Brokentail even wants to be leader?" he asked, echoing Yellowfang's own thoughts. "He's only just become deputy." He sighed. "It's a big responsibility for him."

"It will be difficult," Yellowfang admitted, "but he is strong enough." She added, "And he is not alone. We will be with him. He needs us to get him through this dark time." *Most of all, he needs his mother.*

She left her den and went to find Brokentail. He wasn't in the camp; guessing where he might be, Yellowfang padded through the brambles and discovered him beside the mound of earth where Raggedstar was buried. He was staring at the soil, one huge paw resting on the disturbed leaves.

"Brokentail, it's time for you to come to the Moonstone with me," Yellowfang mewed.

Brokentail started and looked up. "It's too soon. . . ." he protested.

Yellowfang shook her head. "You cannot leave your Clan without a leader."

Brokentail hesitated, then took a deep breath. "Very well. I will do this for the Clan. For *my* Clan."

He seemed sad and quiet as he padded at Yellowfang's shoulder across the marshes. But when the WindClan tunnel came into sight he halted with a flash of fury in his eyes. "I will not set paw on the territory of that evil Clan," he declared.

Yellowfang sighed. The journey would be even longer if they couldn't go through WindClan. But she made no protest, just led the way farther up the Thunderpath until the moorland fell away behind them. They crossed beside a small cluster of Twoleg dens; Yellowfang worked her claws impatiently into the grass as she waited for a chance to race over the hard black surface between the snarling monsters. Their route took them across frostbitten fields where the grass was hard and cold under their paws. A bitter, icy wind blew into their faces. Brokentail plodded with his head down, the freezing gusts plastering his fur to his sides.

Darkness had fallen by the time they reached Mothermouth. Yellowfang led Brokentail down the long tunnel and into the cave, where dazzling light was already pouring from the Moonstone. As she waved her tail to beckon Brokentail closer, and showed him where to lie with his nose against the stone, she winced at the memory of her previous dream.

Please, StarClan, spare me from that.

But no shrieking, bloodstained kits met Yellowfang's gaze as she woke within her dream. Instead she was standing on a bleak and windy stretch of marsh that might have been somewhere within ShadowClan territory. Looking around for Brokentail, Yellowfang saw that the quiet, grief-stricken cat of their journey had vanished. Now the tabby tom stood strong and erect, his kinked tail held high like a signal. His eyes shone and he quivered with excitement.

"Where are they?" he demanded. "My StarClan ancestors?"

Yellowfang glimpsed movement in the distance, and

pointed with her tail to where a line of cats was advancing steadily over the marshes. A frosty glimmer came from their pelts, and the light of stars was in their eyes. Cedarstar was in the lead, with his deputy, Stonetooth, padding at his shoulder. Sagewhisker and Lizardfang were there too, and other cats Yellowfang didn't know, though she recognized some of them as cats who had given lives to Raggedstar when he became Clan leader.

At first Yellowfang could only count eight cats, until she noticed that one of them was a tiny kit, skipping through the long grass in Cedarstar's paw steps.

"My daughter . . . oh, my daughter," she whispered.

She felt a moment's surprise to see that Raggedstar was not among the nine. *Surely he would want to give a life to his son?* Then she told herself that Raggedstar's spirit must still be traveling to StarClan. *He will watch over Brokentail as he leads his Clan.*

Cedarstar was the first of the nine cats to step forward. He bowed his head to Brokentail and meowed, "I give you a life to live by the warrior code. Remember it well, Brokentail, and let it be your guide. Wiser cats than you or I have lost their way without it."

Yellowfang detected a veiled warning in his words, though Brokentail showed no loss of confidence as he touched noses with Cedarstar to receive the life. Yellowfang knew what agony the leader had to endure with each new life, but Brokentail gave little hint of the pain beyond a flaring of his nostrils and a twitch of his eyes.

Cedarstar stepped back into the circle of nine cats that had formed around Brokentail, and Stonetooth took his place. "I give you a life for duty," he meowed. "Remember what you owe to your Clan as well as what your Clan owes to you." He touched noses with Brokentail, who flexed his claws briefly and then was still.

The next StarClan warrior to step forward was Dawnstar, the former ShadowClan leader who had given a life to Raggedstar. "I give you a life for honor," she told Brokentail. "Honor is expected from all cats, but most of all, from a Clan leader. Use the honor of leadership carefully."

For the first time Brokentail showed emotion as he received his third life. His eyes closed as if he was in pain, and his claws dug hard into the earth. As the StarClan she-cat withdrew, Brokentail opened his eyes again and fixed her with a challenging gaze as if he blamed her for the torture of receiving her life, but Dawnstar did not react as she took her place once more in the circle.

The fourth cat stepped forward; Yellowfang didn't know his name. He was a skinny gray tom, and he studied Brokentail carefully before he spoke. "I give you a life for truth. Without it, kin is set against kin, Clan against Clan. Hold fast to truth in all your dealings and let it guide your words." The skinny tom hesitated before darting his head forward like a striking snake and touching Brokentail's nose to give him his life.

As Yellowfang looked on from outside the circle of cats, she began to feel uneasy. All the lives Brokentail had received so far seemed to come with a warning, almost a threat, and she sensed a reluctance among the StarClan cats that was unlike anything she had experienced when she had accompanied Raggedstar to his ceremony.

Then she dismissed these thoughts with a lash of her tail. *Brokentail was the Clan deputy, so he has to be the new leader. Even StarClan can't change that, and why would they want to? Brokentail is a strong and loyal cat. When he has more experience he will be a great leader.*

Lizardfang was the next warrior to come forward. Yellowfang rejoiced to see his frail limbs strong again, and his tabby pelt thick and healthy. "I give you a life for judgment," he meowed. "ShadowClan stands at a place where the path ahead divides. Choose to follow the right path, for the good of your Clan."

As Brokentail received his fifth life, instead of appearing unmoved, his limbs and his tail twitched as if they were briefly out of his control. He staggered at the touch of Lizardfang's nose, recovering himself with an effort. Something huge, something overwhelming, seemed to hover around him, as if an unseen battle were going on in the very air he breathed.

Can he stand to receive four more lives? Yellowfang wondered. Then she saw the next cat in line and bit back a cry of pain. *Oh, my precious love. I miss you with every beat of my heart.*

Tail held high, Brokentail's tiny sister pattered forward into the circle to stand beside him. "I give you a life for love of kin," she mewed, the wisdom in her voice startling Yellowfang as it came from so small a body. "And as Clan leader, remember that every Clan cat is your kin."

Brokentail had to bend his head to receive the life from the young kit. As their noses touched a spasm of agony shook him, and he closed his eyes, jerking his head aside as if for a heartbeat he had seen something he could not bear.

The seventh cat was a stranger to Yellowfang, a small brown tabby with a depth of gentleness in her eyes. "I give you a life for clear sight," she meowed. "Brokentail, know yourself and your destiny, but know too that destiny can be changed if you choose the right path."

Again Brokentail staggered as he received the new life. Yellowfang thought he looked exhausted. Yet throughout he hadn't uttered the slightest sound of pain, not even a whimper.

The eighth cat, a plump black-and-white tom, had also given a life to Raggedstar. He padded up to Brokentail and spoke swiftly. "I give you a life for strength. This is the time you and your Clan will stand or fall. You need to be stronger than ever."

What do they mean? Yellowfang wondered. So many of the cats had spoken of a divided path for ShadowClan, a time when decisions must be made about the destiny of all the cats. *What are Brokentail's choices, and will he make the right ones?*

This time, when Brokentail received the life, he seemed to revive, as if the strength the tom had promised was already flowing into his limbs and his heart. With the end of the ceremony in sight, Yellowfang began to breathe more easily.

All this while, Sagewhisker had stood silently in the circle of cats, her gaze fixed on Brokentail. Now she stepped forward to give him his last life. "Brokentail, I give you a life for compassion. Use it to shelter the weakest in your Clan, the kits and elders and the sick. Use it to show mercy to your enemies and to choose the path your paw steps will follow."

Yellowfang watched the spasm of pain rippling through Brokentail as Sagewhisker gave him his ninth life. For a moment she was afraid that he wouldn't be able to stay on his paws.

But the discomfort passed. As the nine cats acclaimed him by his new name, Brokenstar stood strong and proud again, his eyes gleaming as he heard the yowls rise up to the stars.

"Brokenstar! Brokenstar!"

As the yowling died away, he dipped his head. "My ancestors, I thank you," he meowed solemnly. "I promise that I will make ShadowClan the strongest and most feared that it has ever been."

The StarClan warriors began to fade, their outlines shimmering faintly with starlight until they vanished, leaving Yellowfang and Brokenstar alone in the bleak marshes.

Brokenstar turned to Yellowfang. "It is time to return," he announced. His voice dropped to a savage snarl, and he lashed his tail. "It is time for *vengeance*!"

Dusk was falling by the time Yellowfang and Brokenstar returned to camp. Brokenstar raced across to the Clanrock and summoned the Clan together. "Let all cats join here beneath the Clanrock for a meeting!"

Yellowfang was surprised that he had left out the words "old enough to catch their own prey," but guessed that he had forgotten. *He's new to this. He'll get the words right when he's had more practice.*

Newtspeck emerged from the nursery with Littlekit, Wetkit, and Brownkit scampering around her feet. Featherstorm followed, but there was no sign of Mosskit, Volekit, or Dawnkit.

Brokenstar gazed down at Featherstorm with a disapproving expression. "Where are your kits? Fetch them at once!"

"But they've just gone to sleep!" Featherstorm protested. "And it's very cold out here. Besides, they're not old enough to catch their own prey and usually—"

Brokenstar cut her off. "Are they part of ShadowClan?" he growled. "Then get them!"

So he does want the kits here, Yellowfang thought. *Why?*

Featherstorm hesitated, anger clear in her eyes, but she could not hold Brokenstar's gaze. She retreated into the nursery and reappeared a few heartbeats later, guiding her kits in front of her. All three stumbled sleepily into the open and collapsed into a bundle of fur close to their mother. Brokenstar gave Featherstorm a curt nod.

"I will not rest until WindClan has been punished, and until ShadowClan is feared by every cat in the forest," he announced to his Clan. His voice rose to a roar. "They will bow down before us! From now on warriors will only fight and train for battle. Hunting is of little importance, and cats will have to find food where they can."

He paused, but the Clan was silent; Yellowfang thought that shock—and perhaps a little fear—had closed their jaws as they exchanged uncertain glances.

"Meanwhile," Brokenstar went on, "it is time for me to

choose a deputy. I say these words before the spirits of my ancestors, that they may hear and approve my choice. Blackfoot will be the next deputy of ShadowClan."

The big white warrior rose from his pace and walked to the Clanrock. His black paw looked like a shadow in the moonlight and his eyes shone with pride. "Brokenstar, your choice honors me," he meowed. "I'll do my best to serve you and our Clan well."

Yellowfang felt the Clan relax around her. Blackfoot was popular. *He hasn't had an apprentice, but then, we haven't had any kits ready to give him.*

"Now," Brokenstar went on, "I need an apprentice. Mosskit, step forward."

"Wait!" Yellowfang, broke in. "He's not old enough."

"Quiet!" Brokenstar's voice cut across mutters of agreement from other cats. "I am the leader and this is my decision."

Featherstorm, clearly reluctant, prodded Mosskit awake. He was a big, healthy kit, but even so, Yellowfang knew he wasn't ready to be an apprentice. He stepped forward, glancing around him uncertainly.

"From this time on," Brokenstar announced, "you will be known as Mosspaw. I will be your mentor." He jumped down from the Clanrock to touch noses with the little cat, who looked startled.

"That's not fair!" Volekit complained, gazing at his brother with undisguised envy.

"That's right!" Dawnkit agreed. "We're just as old as he is!"

"I promise you will be made apprentices as soon as you're

as tall as your brother," Brokenstar mewed. "Blackfoot will be your mentor, Dawnkit, and Clawface can have Volekit."

At once Volekit arched his back and stood on his toes, as if he was trying to grow taller right away.

"Stop that!" Featherstorm snapped. "Your brother is too young to be an apprentice, and so are you."

"But it's a great honor," Blackfoot assured her. "You should be proud."

Newtspeck said nothing, just drew her kits closer to her with her tail.

Though some of the cats were still looking worried, Yellowfang could see that most of them thought it was a good idea.

"We don't have any apprentices just now," Wolfstep commented. "And we need to start training young cats."

Flintfang nodded. "Mosspaw is big and strong. He'll be fine."

Runningnose padded up to Yellowfang and spoke into her ear. "I guess we'd better stock up on marigold for scratches." His voice sounded concerned but resigned. "You're looking troubled, but don't be," he went on. "Everything will be fine, you'll see!" He paused, then added, "WindClan is going to regret killing Raggedstar, that's for sure."

CHAPTER 37

Fernshade lay stretched out on the floor of the nursery. A powerful ripple passed along her swollen belly, and she bit down hard on the stick Runningnose had brought to stifle her shriek of agony. Yellowfang blocked the she-cat's pain so that she could concentrate and ran her paw over Fernshade's belly. She could only feel one kit inside, but it was a big one, and it was stubbornly refusing to be born.

A lively ball of fur bounced against Yellowfang's shoulder. "Is the kit here yet?" Volekit squeaked. "I want to see!"

Yellowfang bit back a sharp retort. It was difficult enough delivering this stubborn kit without the other five and their mothers watching her every move. *The nursery is so full I can hardly move a whisker!*

"All of you kits, out of here!" she hissed. "Go over to the apprentices' den and play with Mosspaw."

"Aw, we want to say hi to the new kit," Dawnkit protested, disappointed.

"And you can," Runningnose promised from his place beside Fernshade's head. "Just not yet. I'll call you when it's time."

There was a brief moment of squealing as the five kits bundled out of the den.

"I'll go keep an eye on them," Featherstorm muttered.

When she and the kits had gone, Yellowfang had room to breathe. She watched another spasm of pain pass through Fernshade. "You're doing very well," she praised her. "It won't be long now."

Her gaze met Runningnose's and she saw her own worry reflected in his eyes. Fernshade was exhausted, and there was no sign that the kit inside her was making any progress.

"Feel here," Yellowfang murmured to Runningnose, placing her paw on Fernshade's belly. "I think her kit is the wrong way around."

Runningnose reached out his front paw, then nodded. "You're right. What do we do now?"

"Massage her belly just there," Yellowfang instructed, "and I'll give the kit a push like this . . ."

For a moment nothing happened, except that Fernshade bit down on her stick again, her eyes dull and glazed with pain. Then the kit gave a great heave inside her. The stick splintered in Fernshade's jaws, and a small black-and-white shape slid out of her onto the soft moss.

"Yes!" Yellowfang gave an exultant yowl. "Well done, Fernshade!"

"It's a fine, handsome tom," Runningnose announced.

The exhausted queen curled around her son, her eyes full of love as she began to lick his fur and guide him toward her belly so he could suckle.

"His face is striped just like a badger," Yellowfang observed.

"Then that's his name," Fernshade murmured. "Badgerkit."

Worn out, but full of joy at the successful birth, Yellowfang rose to her paws and climbed out of the nursery.

Outside, Wolfstep was pacing back and forth; he whipped around as soon as Yellowfang emerged. "Well?" he demanded.

"You have a son," Yellowfang told him, seeing delight spring up in Wolfstep's eyes. "You can go in, but be careful. Fernshade is very weak."

She followed Wolfstep back in, noting with approval how gentle he was as he settled down beside his mate and licked her ear.

"Isn't he beautiful?" Fernshade whispered, pressing her muzzle against Wolfstep's shoulder. "His name is Badgerkit."

"He's the most beautiful kit in the forest," Wolfstep responded, looking down at his son with love and pride in his eyes. "And that's a really good name."

Watching them, Yellowfang felt a warm thrill of satisfaction. "This is the best part of being a medicine cat," she told Runningnose. "Breathing new life into the Clan." *And we haven't seen enough of it lately.*

Since Brokenstar had become leader, the Clan had seemed to be a dark place. Yellowfang felt as though she spent all her time now treating wounds and overseeing burials. Stonetooth had died peacefully in his sleep; Yellowfang was glad that he hadn't had to witness the battles Brokenstar had led his warriors into. Vengeance had been taken on WindClan more times than Yellowfang could count, with stolen rabbits regularly appearing on the ShadowClan fresh-kill pile. A hint of ThunderClan scent on the wrong side of the border near Fourtrees had led Brokenstar to extend patrols beyond the Thunderpath until warriors returned with tufts of ThunderClan fur caught in their claws and the scent of their rivals' blood on their pelts. It seemed as if ShadowClan was at war with every cat, and amid all this turmoil the birth of new kits felt even more precious.

Leaving the new family together, Yellowfang slipped out of the nursery to see light growing in the sky, the trees outlined against a bright morning. Yellowfang took in a deep breath and arched her back in a long stretch.

"You're exhausted," Runningnose commented, emerging from the nursery behind her. "Why don't you go back to the den and sleep? I'll fetch some wet moss for Fernshade."

Yellowfang opened her jaws to protest, then realized that she was so tired she could scarcely hold her head up. "Okay, thanks," she mumbled, and headed for her nest.

She hardly seemed to have slept for a heartbeat when she was awoken by a small nose prodding her in her side. "Excuse me, Yellowfang," a voice squeaked. "I'm hurting."

Yellowfang opened her eyes to see Brownkit standing in front of her, holding up one paw. "Is it a thorn?" She yawned as she scrambled out of her nest. "Let me look."

But however carefully Yellowfang searched, she couldn't find a thorn in the tiny paw. Letting down her defenses, she tracked Brownkit's pain and realized that it came from his shoulder. Somehow he had wrenched it.

"How did this happen?" she asked him. "What have you been up to?"

"Brokenstar let all the kits go with Mosspaw to the training area, to give Fernshade some peace and quiet," Brownkit explained. His eyes glowed at the memory. "It was great! We learned some battle moves; watch this—ouch!" He broke off with a gasp of pain as he tried to swipe with his injured leg.

"You're too young to leave the camp, let alone start training," Yellowfang growled as she went to look for some daisy leaves to treat the sprain.

"Am not!" Brownkit squeaked. "I'm nearly three moons old, like Mosspaw when he became Brokenstar's apprentice. You should see him fighting now! He's awesome!"

"I'm sure he is, but no more training for you!" Yellowfang warned him.

"You're not the leader of the Clan!" Brownkit retorted. "Brokenstar is! And if he says I can train, then I will!"

Yellowfang didn't speak, just prepared the poultice for Brownkit, plastering it on securely with cobweb. "Now go rest in the nursery," she told him, "and see me again tomorrow."

As the kit left he passed Runningnose in the entrance to the den. "Fernshade and Badgerkit are doing well," he told Yellowfang. "She seems to have plenty of milk, thank StarClan!"

Yellowfang acknowledged his news with a nod. "I'm going to speak to Brokenstar," she meowed. "Apparently he took the kits training this morning."

Runningnose blinked. "That's not necessarily a bad thing," he pointed out. "It's good for them to get some exercise away from the nursery, especially when Fernshade needs to rest."

"Not if they get injured!" Yellowfang retorted. She headed into the clearing, aiming for the leader's den among the oak roots, but before she reached it Brokenstar appeared and leaped up onto the Clanrock, yowling a summons.

ShadowClan warriors began pushing their way out of their den to gather around the rock. Blackfoot sat at the base, his ears pricked. Flintfang and Tangleburr came to join him. Glancing around at her Clanmates, Yellowfang thought how hungry and skinny they all looked, and nearly every warrior bore a new scar from one border skirmish or another.

Rowanberry and Nutwhisker bounded over to Yellowfang. "What's this all about?" Nutwhisker mewed.

Yellowfang shrugged. "I have no idea."

The elders emerged at the entrance to their den, and all the kits—even Brownkit, hobbling bravely on three paws—scrambled out of the nursery and clustered together at the front of the crowd. Their whiskers quivered with anticipation; Yellowfang guessed that they were all hoping to be made apprentices.

"Where is Fernshade?" Brokenstar demanded.

Runningnose, who was sitting beside Yellowfang, rose to his paws and dipped his head politely to his Clan leader. "She's asleep, Brokenstar," he meowed. "We shouldn't wake her."

Brokenstar hesitated, then gave a reluctant nod. "Cats of ShadowClan," he began. "You have fought well in our recent battles. Our Clan has scored victories in ThunderClan and WindClan, and even defeated some kittypets foolish enough to stray into the forest from Twolegplace. But I think the Clan can still be stronger," he went on, his eyes gleaming.

Blackfoot sprang up from his place at the foot of the Clanrock. "What about battle training every day?" he suggested. "That would really sharpen our skills."

And how do you suppose we're going to fill our bellies, mouse-brain? Yellowfang thought.

"We could patrol at sunhigh as well as dawn and evening," Russetfur suggested. "Let ThunderClan and WindClan know that we're *always* watching."

"We could even put a permanent patrol across the Thunderpath," Deerfoot added.

Yellowfang exchanged a glance with Runningnose, and saw her own doubts reflected in his eyes. *We don't have enough time or cats to do all this!*

Brokenstar looked at all the cats gathered around the Clanrock, and his gaze rested longest on the elders. "Even our elders have a role to play," Brokenstar announced, his gaze still firmly fixed on the old cats, who were beginning to look uneasy.

Great StarClan! Yellowfang thought. *He's not going to ask them to train young cats, is he? Or hunt? That's not fair!*

Brokenstar drew one paw over the rock. "I know they would do anything to make us stronger and more powerful. And with that in mind, I have decided that they can best help their Clan by leaving the camp."

A stunned silence followed. Then yowls of protest rose up from all over the clearing. "You can't do that!" Rowanberry called out. "It's against the warrior code!"

"Yes, they've earned their place with us," Wolfstep declared.

For a moment, Yellowfang refused to believe what she was hearing. The elders were just as shocked, turning to one another with looks of indignation and growing fear.

"The elders are no use for fighting or hunting or having kits," Brokenstar explained, dismissing the cats' protests with a wave of his tail. "So they can't take up precious room or prey. They must go."

To Yellowfang's horror, she saw that some of the warriors were beginning to convince themselves that Brokenstar was right.

"They might be more comfortable away from the camp," Deerfoot commented.

Cinderfur nodded. "True. Especially with so many kits scampering around. You know how the little ones are always bothering the elders."

Yellowfang didn't want to hear any more. She padded over to where the elders were clustered together in front of their den.

Poolcloud's shoulder fur was bristling, and she lashed her tail. "Brokenstar can't do this to us!" she snarled. "Has he forgotten how well we've served our Clan?"

Archeye nodded; he was working his claws into the ground, rage flaring in his eyes. "If he remembers, he obviously doesn't care," he spat. "What would he do if we refused to go?"

"I don't think we want to find out," Nightpelt warned, resting his tail on the older cat's shoulder. "He could make us fight, prove that we can still be warriors by invading the other Clans. Do you want to be a part of that?" In a lower voice he added, "We all know that these battles aren't necessary."

Hollyflower sighed. "Let's just go," she growled. "This isn't the ShadowClan I knew, not anymore." She brushed her tail along Crowtail's side. "Come on, let's collect our bedding."

Nightpelt gazed up to where Brokenstar still stood on the Clanrock. "We will go, Brokenstar."

"Good," the Clan leader meowed. "Move out at once, and good luck with your hunting."

As the elders filed back into their den more murmurs of protest followed them, but no cat dared to speak out loud.

Yellowfang halted Nightpelt with a paw on his shoulder. "This is wrong, and you know it," she hissed.

Nightpelt looked at her with troubled eyes. "I know," he murmured, "but Brokenstar is our leader. StarClan gave him nine lives. They have done nothing to stop him so far. This must be their will as well as his."

Yellowfang couldn't think of an argument against that. *No! This* can't *be the will of StarClan!*

Inwardly seething, she slipped into the elders' den and helped them to gather up their favorite soft bits of bedding. Runningnose followed her and rolled up the moss and fern into bundles for carrying. When everything was ready, Yellowfang led the way back into the clearing. Refusing to look at Brokenstar, she headed for the entrance, hotly aware that the gaze of all the rest of the Clan was fixed on her and the elders.

The group of cats trekked out of the camp in silence and

padded across the marsh. Yellowfang took them to a spindly copse of trees that offered some shelter; it was still within ShadowClan territory, and not too far from the camp. There she found a spot where rock had fallen away to make a hollow in a bank, shaded by overarching clumps of fern. Yellowfang and Runningnose cleared away the debris inside and dug out more soil to enlarge the space until it was big enough for all the elders. Nightpelt tried to help, but the vigorous exercise brought on a fit of coughing.

"Let us finish this," Yellowfang told him. "You scout around to see if you can find any prey."

When the den was ready, the elders brought in their bedding and began arranging it into nests.

"This is okay," Crowtail mewed, sounding determined. "We'll be fine here, Yellowfang."

Yellowfang wondered if the black tabby she-cat was trying to convince herself as well as her denmates. "I'll visit every day with herbs and whatever prey I can catch," she promised.

"Don't neglect your duties," Poolcloud sneered, "or Brokenstar might banish you as well."

"You haven't been banished!" Yellowfang protested. "You're still part of ShadowClan. You still live in our territory."

Nightpelt trotted up with a mouse dangling from his jaws, in time to hear her last words. "It feels like banishment," he commented quietly.

Yellowfang left Runningnose to finish settling in the elders, and marched off to find Brokenstar. Shrill squealing from the training area alerted her as she approached the camp, and she turned her paw steps toward the sound. When she reached the edge of the clearing she saw all five kits and Mosspaw stalking one another, leaping and swiping as they practiced battle moves. Brokenstar sat on an ivy-covered tree stump, watching them with a gleam of satisfaction in his eyes.

Yellowfang strode over to Brokenstar. "I have to speak with you," she meowed.

Brokenstar stared down at her. "Go on, then. Speak."

Yellowfang took a deep breath. "What are you doing?" she demanded. "Training kits who are too young to fight? Sending the elders away from their den? This isn't part of the warrior code!"

Brokenstar narrowed his eyes. "Nor is questioning your Clan leader," he hissed. "You are *my* medicine cat, so you do as I say. Are the elders safe? Sheltered?"

"Yes," Yellowfang answered reluctantly. "But—"

"Then they are fine," Brokenstar interrupted. "And if the kits want to learn how to fight, why should I stop them? We have many enemies, Yellowfang."

You have made us many enemies, you mean, Yellowfang thought.

Brokenstar had turned away from her and was shouting instructions to the cats in the clearing. "No, Littlekit! Use your hind paws! Brownkit, Wetkit, try the double attack again on Mosspaw. Remember to strike him at exactly the same time."

Yellowfang knew that there was no point in trying to argue with Brokenstar any further. Turning to leave, she halted at the sound of a squeal from the far side of the clearing. She spun around to see Brownkit and Wetkit backing away from

Mosspaw. The tiny apprentice was lying ominously still.

"We were trying that double-attack trick, like you said," Brownkit squeaked. "Did we do it right?"

A horrible suspicion rose to choke Yellowfang as she bounded over to Mosspaw. His head was wrenched at an awkward angle and his eyes were open but glazed.

Great StarClan, he's dead!

Striving to keep calm, Yellowfang stepped between the kits and Mosspaw's body. "Go straight back to the camp," she ordered them. "Go on, all of you!"

The five kits gave one another bewildered looks, then scampered obediently away. "I guess Mosspaw must be hurt real bad!" Volekit exclaimed as they left.

Brokenstar strode across and confronted Yellowfang. "What's going on? Why have you stopped the training?"

Yellowfang was so horrified it was hard for her to keep all her paws on the ground and not leap at her Clan leader, clawing at his eyes. "Look what happened!" she yowled.

Brokenstar gazed down at the tiny limp body. "I should have taught them better," he mewed. "They must have got the angle wrong."

"That's not the point!" Yellowfang snarled. "An apprentice is dead!"

Brokenstar bowed his head. "You're right, it's terrible." There was genuine regret in his voice. "The Clan needs apprentices more than ever."

Her heart wailing with grief, Yellowfang picked up Mosspaw's body by his scruff and carried him back to the camp. *He wasn't even four moons old!*

In their den, Runningnose looked startled and shocked as Yellowfang laid Mosspaw's body down and began to smooth his ruffled fur. "What in the name of Starclan—" he began.

Yellowfang cut off his question. "Get Featherstorm," she ordered.

Runningnose hurried off at once and returned a few heartbeats later with Mosspaw's mother. For a moment Featherstorm stood rigid, staring at the lifeless body of her son.

"I'm so sorry," Yellowfang mewed.

Featherstorm seemed not to have heard her. She flung her head back and let out an anguished shriek. "No! No!"

"I'll get her some thyme leaves for the shock," Runningnose murmured, slipping past Yellowfang.

Featherstorm turned to Yellowfang, her eyes full of grief and confusion. "He was only training," she meowed, her voice shaking. "How could this have happened?"

Yellowfang was determined that the kits shouldn't be blamed for killing a Clanmate. "It was a terrible accident," she replied.

As Featherstorm crouched beside her son, pushing her nose into his fur, Yellowfang heard Brokenstar's voice raised in a summons to the Clan. "What now?" she growled as she headed out into the clearing.

Brokenstar stood once more upon the Clanrock. The rest of the Clan was gathering, and Yellowfang couldn't help glancing toward the elders' den, waiting for them to emerge. *It feels so strange, that they aren't here!*

"I have some very sad news," Brokenstar announced. "Mosspaw is dead."

Brownkit and Wetkit let out a shriek, while murmurs of shock and disbelief rose from the rest of the Clan.

"It was just an accident," Brokenstar went on. "You kits were all very brave. To reward you, I'm going to make you all apprentices."

The kits' shock changed to squeals of excitement. Yellowfang closed her eyes. *Has Brokenstar learned nothing?*

"Volepaw, you will be my apprentice," Brokenstar mewed briskly, not bothering to speak the usual words of the apprentice ceremony. "Clawface, I know I promised him to you, but you can have Littlepaw instead. I owe it to Mosspaw to train his brother in his place. Blackfoot, you take Dawnpaw. Boulder, you will have Wetpaw, and Stumpytail will have Brownpaw."

The crowd of cats shifted as four of the kits scampered up to their new mentors to touch noses with them. Only Volepaw remained at the foot of the Clanrock, gazing up at Brokenstar with shining eyes.

"I am proud of my Clan," Brokenstar declared. "We have five new apprentices! Victory will be ours in every battle!" Glancing around, he asked, "Where is Featherstorm?"

"In my den," Yellowfang replied.

"Fetch her."

Before Yellowfang could move, Featherstorm emerged from the medicine cats' den. Her head was bowed and her tail trailed in the dust.

"ShadowClan owes you a great debt for mothering so many warriors," Brokenstar told her. "I think it would be best if you join the elders now, where you can rest and be proud."

For a heartbeat Featherstorm did not move, her eyes puzzled as she gazed at Brokenstar. Yellowfang wondered if she expected the Clan leader to acknowledge that they were kin, that she was his father's mother. Then she nodded without saying a word. Yellowfang stared after her in dismay as she stumbled across the clearing and vanished into the brambles.

"There's another cat gone," Rowanberry murmured worriedly to Clawface. "What is Brokenstar thinking?"

"StarClan knows," her mate responded with a twitch of his whiskers. "If he's not careful, there'll be more of us out there than in camp."

"Just watch what you say!" Tangleburr hissed beside him. "Don't go asking for trouble. Brokenstar hears everything!"

The crowd of cats began to break up, and the new mentors led their apprentices out for the tour of the borders. The little cats weren't as excited as new apprentices usually were because they had already left the camp to practice their battle moves, but they might be more impressed when they realized how far ShadowClan stretched.

As Yellowfang watched them go, she realized that Brightflower had padded up to her side. The she-cat looked excited but apprehensive, her whiskers quivering. "Brackenfoot and I are expecting kits!" she announced.

Yellowfang wished she could be as thrilled as usual at the prospect of new kits for the Clan, but this time all she could do was stare at her mother as a wave of despair washed over her.

"May StarClan help you all," she whispered.

Chapter 38

Brokenstar stood on top of the Great Rock with the bare branches of the oaks at Fourtrees creaking over his head. A cold wind drove shreds of cloud across the sky where the full moon shone fitfully. Blackfoot sat at the foot of the rock, with Russetfur, Stumpytail, Brownpaw, and Brackenfoot huddled together close by. Brightflower hadn't come to the Gathering this time because her kits were almost ready to be born.

Yellowfang sat with the other medicine cats, though she no longer felt at ease among them. Had StarClan told them in their dreams what was going on in ShadowClan? Her own dreams of StarClan were limited to visions of blood and death, of battles between cats too young to open their eyes. If these were omens, ShadowClan was doomed—and it seemed that she could do nothing to help. Yellowfang listened apprehensively as her Clan leader began his report.

"ShadowClan is stronger than ever," Brokenstar announced with triumph in his eyes. "We have been challenged on each border, but have won in every battle!" His gaze raked across the cats in the clearing below. "Let all Clans know that we will tolerate no trespassing, no prey-stealing, no dishonor."

He narrowed his eyes, as if he was defying any of the cats to comment. "And we have a new apprentice: Badgerpaw," he finished.

Yellowfang watched Badgerpaw rise to his paws beside his mentor, Flintfang. The black-and-white tom held his head high, but he still looked tiny.

He's barely three moons old!

"Badgerpaw! Badgerpaw!"

The other ShadowClan apprentices cheered loudly beside their Clanmate, though Yellowfang couldn't help thinking about how small they looked beside the apprentices from the other Clans. Her belly clenched with the memory of grief. One ShadowClan apprentice was missing since the last Gathering: Volepaw had died of an infected wound from a fight with rats.

Brokenstar makes a rat fight part of every apprentice's training now. Is he mad?

As the cheers for Badgerpaw died away, Barkface leaned over and whispered into Yellowfang's ear. "Tell me that apprentice is old enough to start training!" His voice was taut, and there was disapproval in his gaze.

Spottedleaf, the new ThunderClan medicine cat, opened her eyes wide with anxiety. "No cat would train kits younger than six moons, would they?"

"StarClan wouldn't allow that, surely?" Barkface added.

"It would be completely against the warrior code," Mudfur declared.

There was weight in the tone of all the medicine cats,

suggesting that Yellowfang should do something to stop the training of kits.

How can I admit that I'm powerless when it comes to influencing Brokenstar? she thought with an irritable flick of her ears. "Brokenstar knows what he's doing," she mewed aloud, turning her back on the other medicine cats. "It's none of your business."

She could hear them muttering about what a dreadful temper she had, but she ignored them. *There's no way I can defend Brokenstar, so it's better that I don't speak to them at all.*

Yellowfang had given up hoping that her Clanmates would stand up to their leader. Brokenstar had convinced them that every living creature was their enemy, and his cats would do anything, even surrender their own kits, to keep their Clan safe. And the elders, whose wisdom had once been so important in guiding the Clan, were still exiled in the marshes.

He has complete power now! Great StarClan, is there nothing any cat can do?

At the end of the Gathering, Brokenstar swept away from Fourtrees at the head of his Clan. Badgerpaw was pattering along beside him, his eyes still full of excitement at seeing the other Clans for the first time. Walking behind them, Yellowfang was able to overhear their conversation.

"You'll be able to fight in your first real battle soon," Brokenstar promised the apprentice. "You've been training for half a moon, so you're ready."

"Really?" Badgerpaw gasped.

Brokenstar nodded. "I've scented traces of WindClan on our territory, so we will attack at dawn! Those rabbit-eaters will soon discover they can't set paw in ShadowClan territory and get away with it."

Ready to burst with excitement and pride, Badgerpaw darted off to his mentor, Flintfang. "I'm going to fight!" he announced, dancing along beside the powerful gray tom. "Brokenstar said! I'll use that two-pawed move you taught me, and the leap-and-scratch . . ."

Flintfang gazed down at him. "Just remember everything I've taught you, and that there's no shame in losing your first battle," he meowed. His tone was heavy, and Yellowfang wondered just how keen he was to lead his tiny apprentice into a hostile Clan.

Fernshade, who was walking beside Yellowfang, looked fondly across at Badgerpaw. "I'm so proud of him!" she exclaimed. "I thought I'd never manage to give birth to him, and he's everything to me. And now he's going to be a true ShadowClan warrior!"

Yellowfang drew a breath to speak, but bit back the words. *He shouldn't even be an apprentice yet!*

Yellowfang crouched in the prickly grass, listening to the sounds of the skirmish with WindClan that came from the far side of the Thunderpath. The sun shone brightly over her head and branches in the fresh green of newleaf rustled at the edge of the forest.

This is not a day when cats should die.

Paw steps sounded behind Yellowfang and she turned her head to see Nightpelt approaching with the limp body of a vole in his jaws. In spite of the elders' exile, the young black cat looked settled and confident. Yellowfang knew he had found a purpose in life, doing most of the hunting for his companions, keeping up their spirits when they were far from the camp where they had expected to live out their days.

Nightpelt set down his prey and sat beside Yellowfang, his ears pricked as he listened to the screeches and thuds from the battle. "How long will this continue, do you think?" he murmured.

"Until every cat is dead," Yellowfang replied bitterly, "either here or in WindClan."

"Why does StarClan let Brokenstar do it?" Nightpelt asked.

"Perhaps they are proud of him," Yellowfang responded. *I have begged StarClan for reasons, but they ignore me. They have abandoned us to wherever Brokenstar leads.* "After all," she went on out loud, "ShadowClan is the strongest and most feared of all the Clans now."

Nightpelt shook his head. "I cannot believe our ancestors would find any glory in this constant bloodshed." With a deep sigh, he picked up his prey and headed for the elders' den in the copse.

Yellowfang felt a pang of guilt. Every night her dreams were full of blood and darkness, demonstrating over and over that what Brokenstar was doing was absolutely wrong. But there was no guidance from StarClan, not even an appearance from Silverflame to promise that all would be well in the end. Whatever Yellowfang did, it was up to her alone. *I have to stop him!* she thought. *I am his medicine cat; he* must *listen to me!*

Just then, Russetfur came panting up. "Yellowfang!" she gasped. "Runningnose sent me to find you! Brightflower's kits are coming!"

Yellowfang sprang to her paws and raced back to the camp. But when she reached the nursery, she found Brightflower already curled around two furry little scraps, while Runningnose looked on with satisfaction.

"Oh, they're beautiful!" Yellowfang exclaimed, with a nod of approval for Runningnose. "Have you named them yet?"

Brightflower looked up from licking a tiny tortoiseshell she-cat. "This is Marigoldkit," she purred, "and the little gray tom is Mintkit. Kits, this is Yellowfang. She's your big sister."

Both kits looked strong and healthy, suckling at Brightflower's belly with their eyes tightly shut and their soft paws kneading rhythmically. A stab of pain struck Yellowfang as she pictured her own daughters, who had gone to StarClan before they had a chance at life. She bent her head and touched each tiny head gently with her nose. "Hello, kits," she murmured. "Welcome to ShadowClan."

"You would have been a great mother," Brightflower whispered.

Yellowfang tensed. "Never!" she hissed. "This is my life now."

Then she saw Marigoldkit pummeling at her mother with tiny paws, and love and longing swept over her again. "They're perfect!" she breathed.

The noise of cats returning to the camp intruded on the blissful silence inside the nursery. Yellowfang raised her head. "Is that news of the battle?"

She scrambled out of the nursery to see Flintfang emerging from the entrance with a crooked black-and-white shape dangling from his jaws.

"Oh, no!" Yellowfang yowled. "Badgerpaw!"

She raced across to Flintfang, meeting him in the center of the clearing. The gray tom laid his burden down and smoothed the fur on his apprentice's head with one paw. The warrior's eyes were glazed as if he still saw the blood and terror of the battle.

"He fought like a lion," Flintfang meowed hoarsely, turning his shocked gaze on Yellowfang. "He should not have died because he should not have been fighting! I will never train kits again. It's wrong, and it brings shame to our Clan."

Yellowfang crouched down beside Badgerpaw's puny body, licking him to clean away the blood and filth of battle. "You will go to StarClan, Badgerpaw," she murmured between the strong strokes of her tongue. "You will shine so brightly, I promise you."

"He's not Badgerpaw anymore," Flintfang gently corrected her. "I gave him his warrior name before he died. I hope that's okay. He's called Badgerfang now."

A surge of compassion swelled up in Yellowfang for this bewildered, grieving warrior. "It's a great name," she told him, "and he earned it. You're right. This has to stop." She finished her licking and stood up. "I must tell Fernshade what happened."

"I'll tell her," Flintfang mewed bravely. "I owe her that

much, and I can assure her that her son died like a true warrior."

As Flintfang walked toward the warriors' den, there was more noise from the entrance. Brokenstar bounded through the thorns with the rest of his patrol. Every cat was buoyant with pride, tails fluffed up and their eyes shining.

"We will feast tonight!" Brokenstar announced, calling to the apprentices. "Off you go," he ordered when they stood in front of him. "Bring back fresh-kill. We must celebrate. ShadowClan is victorious again!"

As the apprentices dashed off, Yellowfang marched up to Brokenstar. "I have news for you," she snarled.

Brokenstar stared at her for a moment, then nodded and led the way to his den. He seemed to fill the space between the oak roots with fur and muscle and gleaming eyes.

"Badgerfang is dead. Or did you know that already?" Yellowfang challenged him.

For a second she thought Brokenstar looked shocked, but his confidence returned so quickly that she couldn't be sure. "That's a shame," he meowed. "He would have made a great warrior."

Yellowfang felt the biting fangs of anger, sharper than a fox's jaws. "Maybe one day, but he was too young!" she snapped. "You must stop training kits before they are six moons old. You will destroy our Clan before they can become warriors!"

"That is my decision, not yours," Brokenstar growled.

"Then I will walk with StarClan in my dreams," Yellowfang threatened him, grief and fury making her paws throb.

"I will let them know exactly what you're doing, and they will take away your nine lives."

Brokenstar burst into an incredulous *mrrow* of laughter. "StarClan will do nothing to stop me, old cat," he retorted. "I have made their Clan glorious! Let them try! *You* certainly won't stop me." He flicked his tail at her. "Now, do your duty and heal my warriors before we celebrate."

Seething with anger, Yellowfang left. Across the clearing she spotted a line of injured cats already waiting outside her den. *There are so many battles now, every cat knows to come straight to my den as soon as they return,* she thought. *Being wounded is just routine.*

She bounded across the clearing and slipped between the boulders into her den. Runningnose was binding a poultice of marigold onto Scorchwind's shoulder. Warmth flickered into Yellowfang's heart at the sight of her companion. *I couldn't hope for a more patient and loyal medicine cat to have beside me.*

Scorchwind kept turning his head to talk to Boulder, who was waiting with blood dripping from a torn ear. "Did you see me scratch that WindClan tom?" he prompted. "I showed that furball who's the strongest!"

"You should have seen me fighting with their deputy," Boulder responded. "I think he must be still running!"

Do they even know that Badgerfang died today?

Yellowfang sighed and went to fetch marigold, goldenrod, and cobweb. "Let me look at that ear," she snapped at Boulder. "And for StarClan's sake, keep still!"

While she was cleaning up the savaged ear, Littlepaw crept into the den, holding out one paw that was bleeding where a claw had been torn away. "Is it true?" he mewed. "Is Badgerfang really dead?"

"Yes," Yellowfang replied curtly.

To her astonishment, Littlepaw's eyes shone. "Wow, he's a true warrior now! I hope he's watching me from StarClan!"

Grief struck Yellowfang like a blow. *These tiny cats are far too accepting of death in battle. The warrior code has been trampled in the dust if they have no hope of living long enough to become elders.*

When the last injured warrior had been treated, Runningnose helped Yellowfang clean up the leftover herbs. "Are you coming to the feast?" he asked.

Yellowfang shook her head. "I'm not hungry. You go."

When Runningnose had left the den, Yellowfang did her best to ignore the sounds of celebration outside, and curled up in her nest. As sleep claimed her, she turned her thoughts toward StarClan. *They cannot hide from me forever! I have to speak with them!*

Opening her eyes within her dream, Yellowfang found herself in the windswept marsh where Brokenstar had received his nine lives. She paced among the reeds and scrubby bushes until she found Cedarstar, his head lowered as he lapped from a pool.

All the pent-up anger of the last moons burst from Yellowfang at once. "Why did you let Brokenstar become leader?" she shrieked. "What were you thinking, you mouse-brained foxes?"

Cedarstar raised his head and shook droplets of water from his whiskers. His gaze was solemn. "What choice did we have?" he asked. "Brokenstar was Raggedstar's deputy. When Raggedstar died, we had to make him leader. That is the way of the warrior code."

"Well, you made a mistake!" Yellowfang retorted. "There are kits here who shouldn't even have been apprentices, let alone fighting in battle! You have to stop him."

Cedarstar turned away. "There's nothing we can do. Brokenstar promised to make ShadowClan the most feared Clan in the forest, and he has kept his promise."

"What, even feared by *StarClan*?" Yellowfang sneered. Frustration and fury and compassion for the innocent dead spilled over inside her. "A curse upon you for letting us suffer like this!"

As she screeched out the words she awoke with a jolt in her own nest. StarClan, Cedarstar, the scent of her ancestors had all vanished. Her questions remained unanswered. StarClan could do nothing to help. Yellowfang's anger ebbed, leaving behind nothing but emptiness and a strange sense of loss. She had never felt more alone, more abandoned by the ancestors who should have protected her. *From now on, I cannot even trust StarClan.*

"It's the meeting tonight," Runningnose remarked. "We should go to the Moonstone."

Half a moon had passed since Yellowfang had dreamed of Cedarstar. Since then she had had no contact with StarClan, not even in dreams of violence and blood. She knew that she could not go meet the other medicine cats, press her nose against the Moonstone, and pretend that nothing had changed. "Go without me," she meowed. "I have nothing to say to them or to our ancestors."

Runningnose's voice was urgent. "You cannot give up hope."

"As long as Brokenstar rules this Clan, there is no hope!" Yellowfang snarled.

"Then don't give up on your Clanmates," Runningnose pleaded. "They need you. I need you. Please, Yellowfang, you have to keep going."

"What, keep on burying kits who should still be at their mother's bellies?" Yellowfang let her fury spill out in a low-voiced snarl. "Keep on treating wounds from battles that should not have been fought? Keep on sending the elders to the farthest corner of the territory because their wisdom is valued less than dirt?"

Runningnose shook his head. "I made a vow to serve ShadowClan," he mewed quietly, "and that will outlast any leader."

Yellowfang touched Runningnose on the shoulder with her tail. "Your loyalty is admirable," she murmured. "I chose well when I made you my apprentice."

Following her friend into the clearing, Yellowfang watched him leave for the meeting. Her hatred of StarClan was a cold, hard knot inside her. Around her the life of the Clan went on; Blackfoot was leading a patrol out, while the apprentices dragged bedding out of the warriors' den. Yet there were no elders sunning themselves at the entrance to their den, and no hunters returning laden with fresh-kill.

ShadowClan is victorious and feared by all the Clans, just as Brokenstar promised. But darkness lies at its heart.

Excited squeaks from the other side of the clearing jerked Yellowfang out of her black mood. Her heart lifted as she watched Brightflower's kits playing outside the nursery. Then she realized that Marigoldkit was pouncing on a ball of moss, shredding it to bits with tiny claws, while Mintkit was dragging a feather along the ground, worrying at it as if it were a defeated enemy.

So young, and already playing at battle?

Yellowfang bounded across the clearing. "I know a better game," she announced. "See if you can catch my tail." She twitched the tip invitingly in front of Mintkit.

Both kits stopped what they were doing. They looked at Yellowfang's tail, then at each other, but neither of them moved.

If a cat had offered that to me or my littermates, Yellowfang thought, *their tail would have been shredded by now.*

"Okay," she mewed. "What about this?" She held her tail out level with the ground. "Let's see how high you can jump."

"Is that part of warrior training?" Mintkit squeaked.

"Well, not exactly," Yellowfang admitted.

"In that case," Marigoldkit mewed with a polite dip of her head, "we'll keep practicing our battle moves, thanks. Brokenstar said it's important to be as strong as we can before he gives us our mentors."

Yellowfang recalled her own early days in the nursery, playing with Nutwhisker and Rowanberry. *Attacking the elders' tails was the closest we got to fighting. Yes, we pretended they were WindClan invaders, but we knew real battles were moons away. These kits could be fighting to their deaths by the end of greenleaf.*

She watched, sick at heart, as Marigoldkit went back to her moss and Mintkit to his feather.

A few moments later Brightflower emerged from the nursery and came to stand by Yellowfang's side. "They're so strong already," she meowed, though Yellowfang could see a flicker of fear in her eyes.

"They're certainly lively," Yellowfang commented. "They must keep you busy!"

Her mother nodded. "I'll be joining the elders as soon as they leave the nursery," she revealed. "It seems so strange, not to have them around," she added, "though I'd never say so in front of Brokenstar."

"They should be here," Yellowfang meowed.

Brightflower gave a swift glance around. "Don't let our leader hear you say that!"

Yellowfang twitched her ears. "Well, the elders seem happy enough in their new home." It was hard to force out the words when she thought of that tiny hollow in the marshes. "Nightpelt hunts for them."

"And I'll help him when I go to join them," Brightflower declared. "I'm looking forward to the quiet. I'm feeling my age with these kits around!"

A pulse of shock ran through Yellowfang. "Brightflower, you're not old!"

"Yes, I am," her mother purred gently. "And so are you,

Yellowfang. None of us survives forever."

Yellowfang looked around at her Clanmates, from the traces of gray on her mother's muzzle to the kits wrestling with moss and feathers beside her. Suddenly everything seemed as fragile as a moth's wing, as fleeting as a drop of dew.

Nothing survives forever—not even ShadowClan, with Brokenstar as our leader.

CHAPTER 39

"Yellowfang, wake up!"

Something was prodding Yellowfang in her flank. She opened her eyes to see Brightflower standing beside her nest. Her fur was fluffed up and her eyes wide with anxiety.

"What's the matter?" Yellowfang leaped to her paws. "Is it the kits?"

Brightflower nodded. "They're not in the nursery. They were with me when I went to sleep, but now they're gone!"

"We'll find them," Yellowfang mewed reassuringly.

She looked for Runningnose to ask him for help in the search, but he was deeply asleep after the long journey from the Moonstone, and she decided not to disturb him unless she had to. Stifling a trickle of fear, Yellowfang led the way out into the clearing. The night was dark, the moon showing fitfully in a sky ribbed with cloud. "Let's try the apprentices' den first," she suggested.

But when she and Brightflower peered into the den they saw only the four remaining cats in training, curled up and snuffling gently in their sleep.

"The warriors' den?" Brightflower guessed.

When she poked her head through the branches, Yellowfang saw nothing but dark lumps of slumbering fur. Thrusting herself completely inside, she roused Clawface, who was nearest, with a sharp tug on his tail.

"Ow! Get off!" Clawface looked up sleepily. "Oh, it's you, Yellowfang. What do you want?"

"Have you seen Brightflower's kits?" Yellowfang asked. "They've gone missing."

Clawface shook his head. "They're not here. But maybe they snuck out with the night patrol. They talked about wanting to join it tonight, but I told them they had to wait until they were apprenticed."

Like they'd listen! Yellowfang thought. "Thanks, Clawface," she mewed.

The gray tom curled up again as Yellowfang left the den and joined Brightflower, who was pacing back and forth across the clearing. Her expression cleared as Yellowfang told her what Clawface had said.

"That must be where they are!" Brightflower exclaimed. "They should be fine if they're with their Clanmates."

As she spoke, the night patrol pushed its way back into the camp: Blackfoot leading Russetfur and Wolfstep. Mintkit and Marigoldkit weren't with them. Yellowfang and Brightflower bounded over.

"Have you seen my kits?" Brightflower demanded as she halted in front of Blackfoot.

Blackfoot shook his head. "No. Should we have?"

Brightflower let out a wail of terror, and Yellowfang

rested her tail-tip on her shoulder. "They're missing. Clawface thought they might have gone with you," she explained to Blackfoot.

"We'll go out at once to look for them," Russetfur meowed, her voice full of concern.

Wolfstep nodded. "Do you think they tried to follow us, but couldn't keep up?"

"It's possible," Yellowfang admitted.

"We went through the trees as far as the border with the unknown forest," Russetfur told her, "and then along by the Twolegplace and back here."

"Great StarClan!" Brightflower exclaimed, flattening her ears in distress. "They could have been stolen by Twolegs!"

"They're probably just lost," Yellowfang calmed her. "They're only half a moon old; they couldn't have gotten far. I'll follow the patrol's route and look for them. And meanwhile," she added, knowing how important it was to keep Brightflower occupied, "you should give the rest of the camp a really thorough search. Russetfur, perhaps you could help?" She looked meaningfully at the warrior, trying to indicate that Brightflower needed some company.

"Of course," Russetfur meowed. "Let me know if you want me to search the forest later on."

Yellowfang hurried out of the camp and picked up the trail of the night patrol. The cloud cover had thickened and the moon was scarcely visible. It was hard going through the trees and undergrowth, and Yellowfang concentrated so as not to lose the scent. Then she heard the bark of a fox from somewhere up ahead, and quickened her pace. *I hope it hasn't found the kits. . . .*

Another harsh tang mixed with the traces of the night patrol. Yellowfang's heart started to pound and she broke into a run, her nostrils flared with the scent of blood. The night patrol had reported no skirmishes on any of the boundaries, yet somewhere a cat was badly hurt. Yellowfang's fur stood on end as all her instincts pricked with alarm. *Something is terribly wrong!*

She burst through a line of trees and stumbled to a halt in a small clearing. Panting hard, she gazed around and saw a thin shaft of starlight breaking through the branches. It rested on two tiny heaps of fur, as still as rocks in the cold air. One tortoiseshell, one gray, both ripped apart by the jaws of some cruel creature who couldn't even be bothered to stay and eat his prey.

Oh, no! StarClan, not even you could be this cruel.

Yellowfang bounded across the clearing to where the little bodies lay, their blood spattering the ferns. She bent over them, desperately checking for signs of life, and opened herself to their pain in the hope that it would prove they were still alive. But she was too distraught to be sure if she could feel the flicker that would tell her there was still hope.

Desperately summoning her medicine cat skills, Yellowfang looked around for anything nearby that she could treat them with or pad their wounds. But the clearing was barren: no sign of a scrap of cobweb or marigold leaf. Clinging to the last traces of hope, Yellowfang curled her body around the kits, licking their still-warm fur.

Come on, little ones! Live!

Crashing paw steps disturbed her, followed by a ghastly wail. Yellowfang looked up to see Brightflower standing on the other side of the clearing, staring in horror. Brokenstar was just behind her.

"What happened?" Brokenstar demanded.

"I found them like this," Yellowfang replied, her voice shaking. "It must have been a fox!"

Brokenstar sniffed the air. "I don't smell any fox."

"It was here!" Yellowfang insisted. "I heard it just before I found them."

Brightflower padded forward and gazed down at the two tiny shapes. "My babies, my babies!"

Yellowfang stared at Brokenstar. "You need to look for the fox! It could be close by!"

"Yellowfang, I can only pick up your scent," Brokenstar mewed quietly. "Come back to the camp with me."

"What about the fox?"

"There is no fox here," Brokenstar growled. "Come."

Dazed, Yellowfang rose to her paws. Her fur was sticky with blood and her mouth was full of the taste of death. "I'll carry one of the kits," she mewed.

"No," Brokenstar ordered. "I'll send warriors to bring them. Brightflower, you wait here."

Brightflower took Yellowfang's place and folded her body around her kits. She didn't look up at Yellowfang or Brokenstar as they left the clearing.

Brokenstar padded beside Yellowfang as they returned to

camp. The moon was setting by the time they reached the clearing. The sky was gray with cloud and there was a tang of rain in the air. All the cats were out of their dens, busily searching for the kits. Boulder was the first to notice Yellowfang, and halted, staring at her. Gradually the other cats realized that she had returned and stopped what they were doing, until Yellowfang felt as if the gaze of every cat in the Clan was fixed on her. She could read shock in their eyes, and a flicker of unease joined the grief she felt for Mintkit and Marigoldkit.

"Russetfur. Frogtail." Brokenstar's voice cut into the silence, and he beckoned with his tail. "Follow our scent trail, and bring Brightflower and the kits back to the camp."

He waited until the two warriors had left, then crossed to the foot of the Clanrock, jerking his head for Yellowfang to follow him. "Come closer," he ordered the Clan, as if he was too distressed to leap onto the rock and summon them formally.

As the Clan gathered, silent and apprehensive, Runningnose bounded across to Yellowfang from the medicine cats' den. "Are you hurt?" he gasped. "All this blood . . ."

"It's not my blood," Yellowfang choked out, as if telling him would make the terrible truth more real. "It's . . . the kits'."

A stunned murmur rose from the Clan, and Brackenfoot stepped forward, his eyes huge with fear. "Tell me what happened."

"I found them in a clearing—" Yellowfang began.

Brokenstar cut her off with a lash of his tail. "Yellowfang

went to look for the kits after Brightflower told her they were missing," he announced. "When I found her, she was with the kits, but they were both dead. Yellowfang claimed they had been attacked by a fox."

"A fox!" Newtspeck exclaimed, her eyes wide with fear. "On our territory? It could kill us all!"

"We have to send out a patrol to track it," Blackfoot meowed.

More fearful cries came from the Clan, but Brokenstar silenced them with a flick of his tail. "I found no trace of fox anywhere near the kits."

"Then how did they die?" Stumpytail asked.

"Yes, how?" Deerfoot echoed. "We have to know!"

Brokenstar took a step away from Yellowfang. "Only one cat knows the truth," he meowed softly.

Brackenfoot stared at Yellowfang in horror. "Did *you* kill them?" he whispered.

"Of course not!" Yellowfang shrieked. In her worst nightmares she had never imagined that her own father could accuse her of something so terrible. "They were dead when I found them!"

"We have no reason to believe that Yellowfang killed them," Brokenstar put in. "Why would she?"

"She's been under a lot of strain recently, with all the battles," Wolfstep pointed out.

"She said she didn't want to treat my scratch because it was a waste of herbs!" Dawnpaw added with an indignant flourish of her tail.

"Yes, she hasn't been herself lately," Tangleburr meowed. "I asked her about a pain in my belly, and she practically bit my ear off."

"But then gave you a juniper berry to take the pain away," Runningnose reminded her, but no cat seemed to be listening.

"She acts like the whole Clan is a nuisance," Cinderfur sniffed.

Newtspeck stepped forward with a furious hiss. "Are you seriously suggesting that Yellowfang would kill our own kits so she wouldn't have to treat their injuries later on?"

There was a deafening silence as Yellowfang waited for her Clanmates to realize that Newtspeck was speaking sense. It was broken by a wail from Brightflower, who had just entered the camp. Russetfur and Frogtail followed, each carrying a pitiful broken scrap of fur.

Brightflower plunged at Yellowfang with a snarl. "Did you kill my kits?"

Yellowfang was frozen to the spot with horror. Before she could react, Runningnose leaped in front of her. "Don't be ridiculous, Brightflower!" he yowled.

Brokenstar held up his tail for silence. "We will never know what happened tonight," he meowed, his voice cracking with sorrow. "All we know is that two young kits, two promising warriors, are dead, and that Yellowfang was with them. Yellowfang, as our medicine cat, there must have been something you could have done."

"I tried, but—" Yellowfang began to protest.

Brokenstar ignored her. "Russetfur," he continued, "is

there any evidence that she treated their wounds?"

Reluctantly Russetfur shook her head. "No, Brokenstar."

"They were dead when I found them!" Yellowfang exclaimed. Her head was whirling. She couldn't believe that this was happening to her, that any cat would take these crazy accusations seriously.

"Frogtail, were their bodies cold?" Brokenstar went on.

Frogtail ducked his head. "Well . . . no."

Yowls of shock and hatred rose from the Clan. Rowanberry and Nutwhisker both pushed through the crowd to stand beside Yellowfang, along with Runningnose and Newtspeck, but their protests went unheard. Yellowfang knew that there was too much suspicion, too much grief over these latest deaths to expect a rational response from her Clanmates.

Brokenstar turned to face her. "Yellowfang, you cannot stay here. For your own safety, you must leave."

"You mean, j-join the elders?" Yellowfang stammered. *I could be at peace there, and still help my Clanmates if they came to me.*

"No." Brokenstar curled his lip, showing a hint of sharp yellow teeth. "I cannot protect you within this territory after what has happened. Your Clanmates are too angry over these deaths. You have to understand that I don't want to do this, but I have no choice. I must banish you from ShadowClan."

At his words everything became clear to Yellowfang, clear as spring water gurgling from a rock. She had threatened to speak with StarClan about what Brokenstar was doing, get him stripped of his leadership and his nine lives. And this was his way of making sure that never happened. She had made herself a problem—and he was solving it.

Yellowfang took a deep breath. Brokenstar had scared this Clan into silence for too long. Fury overwhelmed her fear. If she held her tongue any longer she betrayed all her Clanmates, including the memory of the dead kits. "This is exactly what you wanted!" she hissed. "You couldn't have known that those kits would die, but this is your perfect opportunity to get rid of me! I am the ShadowClan medicine cat! This is where I belong!"

Blackfoot stepped forward, his voice weighty and regretful. "Not anymore, Yellowfang. Come, I'll escort you to the border."

He reached out his tail to rest it on her shoulder, but Yellowfang batted it away. "Get off me!" she snapped. "I'll find my own way!"

Still dazed, she stumbled toward the entrance; her Clanmates parted to let her go.

"I'm so sorry!" Runningnose gasped, bounding alongside her. "I'll prove it was a fox! You'll be back soon! Come to the next half-moon Gathering!"

Yellowfang stopped at the entrance and looked at him. "Runningnose," she meowed, "you have been a dear and loyal friend, but I cannot stay here. Not as long as Brokenstar rules. This is not the ShadowClan I pledged to serve." Glancing at the cats clustered around the Clanrock, she added, "They are lucky to have you. May StarClan light your path, always."

"But, Yellowfang—" Runningnose wailed.

Yellowfang couldn't listen to him anymore. Turning, she plunged through the brambles and staggered out of the camp.

CHAPTER 40

Half-mad with grief and fury, Yellowfang stumbled across the territory, howling her rage to the stars. Finding herself at the edge of the marshes, she turned her paw steps away from the elders' den.

I can't unleash this disaster on them. They'll find out soon enough.

At last the entrance to the tunnel that led to Fourtrees loomed up in front of Yellowfang. Forcing her paws to carry her forward, she padded into the echoing darkness. Water dripped around her, sounding unnaturally loud, and her paws slipped on the slimy tunnel floor.

After what seemed like seasons, Yellowfang spotted a pale gap in front of her and clambered out of the tunnel to see that dawn light was seeping into the sky. Her limbs heavy with exhaustion, she staggered across the last few fox-lengths of ShadowClan territory, and half scrambled, half fell into the hollow where she came to rest in the shelter of the spiky branches of a holly bush.

Yellowfang lay in the undergrowth while the morning light strengthened into a chilly, gray day. Soon a thin rain began to fall, but Yellowfang had no energy to find better shelter. She tried to sleep, but the heavy branches of the four great oaks loomed over her, rustling in a threatening way that sounded more like thunder. Yellowfang stayed where she was, too stunned to think about moving or eating, the harsh words of her Clanmates echoing over and over again in her mind. *StarClan, can you see me? Do you know what Brokenstar has done now?* There was no reply, no sign that her ancestors had even heard. If Yellowfang had felt alone before, that was nothing compared to her solitude now.

Eventually the dead holly leaves underneath her began to prickle through her ungroomed pelt, and she hauled herself to her paws. Night had fallen again, with barely a hint of starlight to pick out the four giant oaks. Not that it mattered to Yellowfang. If StarClan had given up on her, Fourtrees meant nothing except a place where too many cats came to crow about hollow victories every full moon. She started walking, not because she had anywhere to go, but because she was tired of staying still. Her belly growled but she felt no hunger. Maybe she would eat again one day; maybe not. She couldn't be bothered to care.

She thought of Marigoldkit and Mintkit, cold and still in the shadows. She hoped they were in StarClan now, playing with her daughters, being cared for by Silverflame. They were better off there than in ShadowClan, where Brokenstar seemed to delight in sending cats to die before they were old enough to catch their own prey. But that didn't stop Yellowfang's dreadful feelings of guilt that she hadn't been able to help them.

Oh Marigoldkit, Mintkit, I'm so sorry you had to die alone and scared. I would have saved you if I could, I promise.

Yellowfang stumbled up the side of the hollow and through a line of ferns that caught in her tangled pelt. She was dimly aware of scent markers—ThunderClan's, she thought—but she couldn't bring herself to care. She was a medicine cat; she could go wherever she wanted. Or if she wasn't a medicine cat, she would be chased off like a rogue, and be hungry and lost somewhere else. It didn't matter.

Her legs started to tremble with tiredness, even though she had barely traveled out of sight of Fourtrees. She pushed her way into a clump of ferns and lay down beneath the arching green fronds. The horror of being exiled, her grief for the kits, and her exhaustion sapped her strength so that she couldn't block her senses anymore. Her body convulsed as she felt the pain of her Clanmates' wounds far away, the agony of a vixen giving birth somewhere nearby, the flash of fear and anguish as a mouse fell prey to a ThunderClan warrior's paws. The suffering of every creature in the forest flooded through her limbs and assailed her heart.

At last, worn out, she slept.

Yellowfang was never sure how many sunrises she saw from under the ferns, drifting in and out of consciousness. She knew that she ought to hunt, to groom herself, and to find shelter as far as possible from these StarClan-cursed Clans, but for a long time she couldn't rouse herself to do anything.

Eventually she became aware of sunlight filtering through the ferns, warming her pelt, reminding her of times when she had been happy in her home among the pine trees. A slow-burning anger began to replace her grief. *My Clan banished me, and I have done nothing wrong! I will not give in!*

A trickle of strength returned to her limbs. She could scent water, and hear the gurgling of a nearby stream. *I need to drink, hunt, and get off ThunderClan territory.*

But as she forced herself to her paws, she heard a faint growl from the direction of the stream. Peering out from among the ferns, she spotted a young cat with a flame-colored coat heading straight for her in the hunter's crouch, as if he was stalking prey. Yellowfang realized that the wind must have carried her scent straight toward him.

Fox dung! A ThunderClan cat would have to turn up just now. He's bound to stop me if I try to escape. Yellowfang unsheathed her claws, sinking them into the soft forest floor. *I'll have to fight my way out.*

Yellowfang eased herself from the ferns and crept into the shelter of a clump of bushes. Now the breeze worked to her advantage, and she caught the reek of ThunderClan. The young cat paused, glancing around him with a puzzled expression. He sniffed the air again, as if he couldn't work out what had happened to the scent.

Prey doesn't keep still, mouse-brain!

Letting out a snarl, Yellowfang burst out of the bushes and slammed into the orange tom, knocking him sideways. He let out a screech of shock. Yellowfang felt a savage delight as her paws clamped down on his shoulders and her jaws closed on the back of his neck.

"Murr-oww!" the young cat grunted. For a heartbeat he

struggled to free himself, then suddenly relaxed his muscles with a howl of alarm and went limp.

Still pinning him down with her paws, Yellowfang opened her jaws and let out a yowl of triumph. "Ah, a puny apprentice!" she hissed. "Easy prey for Yellowfang."

She bit down once more on the ThunderClan cat's neck, but at the same moment he surged upward, exploding with all the strength of a powerful young body. Yellowfang let out a snarl of surprise as she was thrown clear, tumbling back into a gorse bush.

The tom steadied himself on his paws and gave his pelt a shake. "Not such easy prey, huh?" he meowed.

Yellowfang ripped herself free from the prickly branches, hissing curses at the thorns. "Not bad, young apprentice!" she spat back. "But you'll need to do a lot better!"

The young cat puffed out his chest. "You're in ThunderClan's hunting ground. Move on!"

"Who's going to make me?" Yellowfang curled her lip. "I will hunt. *Then* I will leave. Or maybe I'll just stay a while. . . ."

"Enough talk," the young cat flashed back at her.

Yellowfang sensed a change in him. She could tell that he was eager to fight, to defend his territory and protect his Clan. *For an apprentice, he has courage,* she thought with the first flicker of respect. *I'll need to use a little cunning here. . . .*

Dipping her head, breaking eye contact with the young tom, she began to back off. "No need to be hasty now," she purred in a silky tone.

The apprentice wasn't deceived. He let out a furious

growl and leaped forward. Yellowfang sprang forward to meet him, digging her claws into his shoulders, and they rolled over together in a whirl of claws and teeth. Breaking free, Yellowfang reared up on her hind legs and lunged at the young tom's head. To her frustration, he jerked away just in time and her teeth closed on empty air a mouse-length from his ear.

Before Yellowfang could lash out again, the apprentice swiped at her with one paw, dealing her a hard blow over her ear. Stunned, she dropped to all fours, shaking her head to clear it. As she tried to recover, her opponent flung himself forward and clamped his jaws tight on her back leg.

Yellowfang screeched, whipping around to snap at the young tom's tail. Satisfaction flooded through her as her teeth connected.

The apprentice ripped his tail from her grip and lashed it in rage. His green eyes gleamed with fury. Yellowfang crouched for a fresh attack, but she could feel her strength ebbing. Her breath wheezed, and hunger gnawed at her like a live rat in her belly.

For a heartbeat the flame-colored cat hesitated. Yellowfang lunged, trying to reach up onto his shoulders and get a killing grip, but now she was hampered by her wounded leg.

"Get off!" the apprentice snapped, arching his back in an effort to throw her off.

But Yellowfang managed to dig her claws in and held on tight, using her greater weight to force the young cat to the ground. He twisted as he tried to avoid her thrashing hind legs; once more they rolled over together, biting and snapping.

Yellowfang knew that she had lost her chance to win. Her hind legs would hardly support her and she loosened her grip on the young tom.

"Had enough yet?" he growled.

"Never!" Yellowfang spat. But her injured leg gave way and she slumped to the ground. Glaring at the apprentice, she hissed, "If I wasn't so hungry and tired, I'd have shredded you into mouse-dust." Her mouth twisted in pain. "Finish me off. I won't stop you."

And then it will be over. No more pain, no more struggle . . .

The young tom hesitated, something in his eyes that Yellowfang couldn't read.

"What are you waiting for?" Yellowfang taunted him. "You're dithering like a kittypet!"

Rage flared in his green eyes. "I'm an apprentice warrior of ThunderClan!" he snarled.

Yellowfang narrowed her eyes. She had seen the cat flinch at her words, and she knew she had hit a nerve. "Ha," she snorted. "Don't tell me ThunderClan are so desperate they have to recruit kittypets now?"

"ThunderClan are not desperate!" the tom hissed.

"Prove it, then!" Yellowfang challenged him. "Act like a warrior and finish me off. You'll be doing me a favor."

The apprentice stared at her. She saw his muscles relax as a spark of curiosity woke in his eyes. "You seem in an awful hurry to die," he meowed.

"Yeah? Well, that's my business, mouse-fodder," Yellowfang

snapped. "What's your problem, kitty? Are you trying to *talk* me to death?"

But her hunger and exhaustion were sapping her strength with every heartbeat. She knew she could do no more; she was at this cat's mercy. *Has it really come to this, StarClan? Is this the end I deserve?*

"Wait here," the young cat ordered at last.

"Are you kidding, kitty? I'm going nowhere," Yellowfang grunted, limping toward a patch of soft heather. She flopped down and began licking her leg wound.

The flame-colored tom turned, then glanced back at her over his shoulder with a hiss of exasperation before heading for the trees. Yellowfang watched him go. She still felt numb with shock, well past caring what would happen to her. *Will ThunderClan keep me a prisoner, or send me back to ShadowClan?* she wondered. She knew she didn't have the strength to get off ThunderClan territory before she was found by the ginger tom or some other patrol. Did this mean that she was giving up without a fight?

And yet there was something about that bold little apprentice, some spark that reminded her of herself when she was young. "Not that I'd let him know it, arrogant mouse-brain," she muttered.

She would wait for him to come back. *I have no Clan now, no destiny, no place to be, and no duties to tend to. Let the future bring what it will.*

Yellowfang sighed, but a quiet determination began to grow inside her. Somehow, she felt less bleak, less hopeless.

This wasn't her home, but the heavy-branched trees and whispering ferns promised more peace than she had known for a while. She didn't know any ThunderClan cats well—she didn't know *any* cats well, apart from Runningnose, perhaps—but Brokenstar had denounced them for being too full of pity and soft on their enemies. So perhaps they would view her with kindness, a refugee from the troubled Clan across the border. Besides, whatever they did to her could not be worse than what her own son had done.

My son! Yellowfang drew a long, quivering breath. She could not leave the forest. Even if she had to seek shelter in a hostile Clan, there was still work for her to do, questions that only she could answer. Vengeance that she had to seek on behalf of Marigoldkit and Mintkit, Cloudpelt and the banished elders, all the cats whom Brokenstar had destroyed with his ambition. Alone, hungry, crushed by betrayal, Yellowfang made the most solemn vow of her life.

I know my path will cross with Brokenstar's again. And one day I will do something to stop this tide of fire and blood that he has unleashed on the forest.

Keep reading for an

exclusive manga adventure . . .

Created by

ERIN HUNTER

Written by

DAN JOLLEY

Art by

JAMES L. BARRY

MY NAME IS YELLOWFANG.
I'M THE THUNDERCLAN MEDICINE CAT NOW.
I KNOW HOW TO HEAL MORE AILMENTS THAN I CAN COUNT.
CUTS, SCRAPES, BITES, WHITECOUGH. JUST TRY ME.
ONE THING I'VE NEVER BEEN ABLE TO CURE, THOUGH, IS BAD DREAMS.
AS OFTEN AS I HAVE THEM THESE DAYS, STARCLAN KNOWS I WISH I COULD.
TIGERCLAW'S GONE!
HE WAS A TRAITOR!
TIGERCLAW TRIED TO KILL BLUESTAR!
HE WON'T COME BACK, WILL HE?

THE WOUNDED CAT IS BROKENTAIL. HE'S PROVEN HIMSELF TO BE THE WORST KIND OF TRAITOR. BETRAYED HIS CLAN. CAUSED MANY DEATHS.
AND NOW HE'S HORRIBLY WOUNDED.
EAT THESE BERRIES, AND THE PAIN WILL GO AWAY FOR GOOD.
I KNOW YOU CARE FOR NOTHING, BROKENTAIL.
NOT YOUR CLAN, NOR YOUR HONOR, NOR YOUR OWN KIN.
I HAVE NO KIN.
WRONG. YOUR KIN HAS BEEN CLOSER TO YOU THAN YOU EVER DREAMED.
I'M YOUR MOTHER, BROKENTAIL.
AND YOU MURDERED RAGGEDSTAR. YOUR OWN FATHER.
NOW IT IS TIME TO PUT AN END TO ALL THIS TREACHERY.
THE PAIN HE'S FEELING... THE HORROR. IT'S NOT FROM THE DEATHBERRIES. NOT YET.
MY WORDS HAVE CAUSED THIS.
WHAT MEDICINE CAT WOULD DO SUCH A THING?
YELLOWFANG! YELLOWFANG!

YELLOWFANG, WAKE UP! YOU WERE HAVING A BAD DREAM.
MRRRH. I SUPPOSE I WAS.
WHAT DO YOU NEED?
I HAVE AN IDEA, ABOUT HOW TO TREAT SMALLEAR'S PAW. I WANT TO USE MARIGOLD.
...IS THAT ALL RIGHT WITH YOU? MAY I GO AHEAD WITH IT?
OF COURSE I LET CINDERPAW GO AHEAD WITH SMALLEAR'S TREATMENT. IT MIGHT WORK...
...PLUS IT GIVES ME MORE TIME TO MYSELF, TO COME FULLY BACK FROM THE DREAM.
GOOD MORNING, BRIGHTPAW. SWIFTPAW.
DON'T FORGET YOU NEED TO CHECK THE ELDERS FOR TICKS TODAY.
AWWWW!
GOOD MORNING, YELLOWFANG!
I SHOULD HAVE SAID THIS TO YOU BEFORE NOW. BLUESTAR TRULY MADE THE RIGHT DECISION, INVITING YOU TO BE OUR CLAN'S MEDICINE CAT.
NO THUNDERCLAN CAT WOULD EVER DOUBT YOUR LOYALTY TO US.
WELL, THAT'S...AN ODD THING FOR FIREHEART TO SAY. I CAN'T HELP BUT WONDER IF HE KNOWS WHAT HAPPENED TO BROKENTAIL...
...BUT HE DOESN'T SAY ANYTHING ELSE ABOUT IT. SO NEITHER DO I.
CINDERPAW SEEMS TO BE DOING WELL AS APPRENTICE MEDICINE CAT.
EH...SHE'S FINE AS LONG AS SHE KEEPS HER HEAD STRAIGHT.
WHEN DO YOU THINK SHE'LL GET HER FULL MEDICINE CAT NAME?
THERE'S PLENTY OF TIME.
THAT MAY BE TRUE... BUT THE CLAN WILL ONLY BE STRONGER WITH TWO MEDICINE CATS. YOU KNOW THAT.
I'D SAY CINDERPAW'S WAITED LONG ENOUGH.

FIREHEART'S RIGHT. I KNOW THAT. BUT IF I TAKE CINDERPAW TO THE MOONSTONE... LET HER RECEIVE HER NAME...
I'M ASHAMED TO ADMIT IT TO MYSELF, BUT I'M FRIGHTENED. IF I TALK TO STARCLAN...WHAT WILL MY ANCESTORS SAY TO ME?
BROKENTAIL DIED AT MY PAW. WHAT IF THEY WON'T LET ME BE A MEDICINE CAT ANYMORE?
I TAKE A WALK TO CLEAR MY HEAD, BUT THE FOREST DISTRACTS ME ON ITS OWN.
I MISS THE MARSHES AND PINE TREES OF SHADOWCLAN.
ONE THING I WILL SAY ABOUT IT, THOUGH. SOUND CARRIES WELL HERE.
I KNOW CINDERPAW'S COMING LONG BEFORE I SEE HER.
YELLOWFANG! SMALLEAR'S PAW IS MUCH BETTER! I ASKED HIM TO STAND IN THE STREAM...
...AND I THINK IT WASHED THE INFECTION OUT. NOW I'VE GOT THE NEW MARIGOLD POULTICE ON IT.
HMPH. NOT BAD, I SUPPOSE.
SO...I WAS WONDERING... DO YOU THINK I'M READY TO GET MY FULL NAME?
WHAT CAN I SAY TO THAT? SOMETHING? ANYTHING? ...I SETTLE ON NOTHING.
DON'T YOU THINK I'M READY? ...WHAT ELSE DO I NEED TO LEARN?
IT'S NOT THAT, CINDERPAW. YOU'VE EARNED YOUR NAME. IT'S...IT'S ME. I DID SOMETHING TERRIBLE...
...AND IF OUR ANCESTORS ARE ANGRY WITH ME...THEY MIGHT NOT LET YOU HAVE YOUR MEDICINE CAT NAME.

YELLOWFANG, I... I WON'T ASK WHAT YOU DID. NOT IF YOU DON'T WANT TO TELL ME.
BUT I REFUSE TO BELIEVE YOU DID ANYTHING TO HARM THUNDERCLAN!
I TRUST YOU. THE ANCESTORS WILL TRUST YOU.
YOU JUST NEED TO TRUST YOURSELF.
I CAN ONLY TELL HER I'LL TRY.
TWO DAYS LATER, WE SET OUT ON OUR JOURNEY.
THE JOURNEY GOES SMOOTHLY, FOR WHICH I THANK STARCLAN.
WE CROSS WINDCLAN'S MOOR...
AND CLIMB UP TO THE HIGHSTONES WITHOUT ANY TROUBLE.
THE OTHER CLANS' MEDICINE CATS ARRIVE AT THE APPOINTED TIME.
MUDFUR FROM RIVERCLAN... BARKFACE FROM WINDCLAN... MY OLD APPRENTICE, RUNNINGNOSE, FROM SHADOWCLAN.

THE TUNNEL DOWN TO THE MOONSTONE FEELS LONGER SOMEHOW.
I'M EVEN BEGINNING TO WONDER IF WE'VE GOTTEN LOST...
...WHEN WE COME OUT INTO THE CHAMBER.
THE MOONSTONE IS MORE BEAUTIFUL THAN EVER.
WARRIORS OF STARCLAN.
I BRING TO YOU A NEW MEDICINE CAT, WHO IS LOYAL AND COMMITTED IN HER SERVICE TO THUNDERCLAN.
I NAME HER CINDERPELT.
THE NAME ECHOES AROUND THE CHAMBER AS THE OTHER MEDICINE CATS REPEAT IT IN TURN. CINDERPELT.
NOW, CINDERPELT.
IT'S TIME TO WALK WITH YOUR ANCESTORS.
STARCLAN, PLEASE BE KIND.

YELLOWFANG...
...I'M SCARED.
IT'S ALL RIGHT. TRUST OUR ANCESTORS TO KNOW THE TRUTH IN YOUR HEART.
IN MY MIND, WORDS RING OUT:
WHATEVER YOU THINK OF ME, STARCLAN...PLEASE BE GENTLE WITH HER. SHE'S A GOOD MEDICINE CAT.
AND I CROSS INTO THE DREAMING...
I'VE BEEN HERE MANY TIMES...
BUT NEVER BEFORE HAVE I BEEN SO TWISTED WITH FEAR.
WHO WILL I SEE? WHAT WILL THEY TELL ME?
I KNOW THIS CAT. HIS NAME IS MOLEPELT. I'VE SEEN HIM OFTEN IN DREAMS...DREAMS ABOUT SHADOWCLAN. DARK DREAMS.
IF I'M LOOKING FOR A MESSAGE OF HOPE FROM MY ANCESTORS, THIS IS NOT THE CAT I WOULD EXPECT TO DELIVER IT.

THE WORDS SLIP OUT OF MY MOUTH BEFORE I CAN THINK TWICE.
WHAT DO YOU WANT NOW, MOLEPELT? RIVERS OF BLOOD CAME TO SHADOWCLAN, JUST AS YOU PROMISED.
HAVE YOU COME TO GLOAT?
I WOULD NEVER GLOAT, YELLOWFANG. SHADOWCLAN WAS MY CLAN ONCE, JUST AS IT WAS ONCE YOURS.
I HAVE COME TO TELL YOU THAT I AM TRULY SORRY ABOUT BROKENTAIL.
WHAT DO YOU MEAN... WHY WOULD YOU... YOU'RE SORRY?
WHY ARE YOU SORRY? HOW CAN ANYTHING TO DO WITH BROKENTAIL BE YOUR FAULT?
I WAS HIS MOTHER! I CHOSE HIS PATH!
NO, YELLOWFANG.
YOU SUFFERED MOST BECAUSE YOU GAVE BIRTH TO HIM, BUT THERE WAS NOTHING YOU COULD HAVE DONE TO CHANGE HIS DESTINY.
HE HAD A CHOICE OF WHICH PATH TO FOLLOW. AND HE CHOSE THE ONE THAT LED TO BLOODSHED AND MISERY.
I CAN'T...CAN'T BELIEVE WHAT I'VE JUST HEARD...
I'VE ONLY JUST BEGUN TO UNDERSTAND HIS WORDS FULLY WHEN HE STARTS TO LEAVE.
WAIT! NO!
COME BACK!

IF MOLEPELT BROUGHT DREAD AND ANGER WITH HIS ARRIVAL, THE NEXT CAT TO SPEAK FILLS ME WITH WARMTH.
YELLOWFANG?
IT'S MY OLD SHADOWCLAN MENTOR. THANK YOU, STARCLAN!
SAGEWHISKER! IT'S SO GOOD TO SEE YOU!
OH, YELLOWFANG...
IF I HAD KNOWN WHAT LAY AHEAD FOR YOU,
I WOULD NEVER HAVE FORCED YOU TO TAKE THE PATH OF A MEDICINE CAT.
WHAT? YOU DIDN'T FORCE ME.
IT WAS MY OWN CHOICE. AND I'VE NEVER REGRETTED A SINGLE DAY OF IT.
ALWAYS SO STRONG. YELLOWFANG...I KNOW HOW MUCH PAIN YOU'RE IN. WE ALL DO.
I CAN LIVE WITH MY PAIN. WHAT MATTERS NOW IS CINDERPELT. WILL YOU LET HER HAVE HER MEDICINE CAT NAME?
WE WILL, YELLOWFANG. YOU CHOSE YOUR APPRENTICE WELL.
YOU WILL LEAVE A STRONG LEGACY IN THUNDERCLAN. ALL THEIR MEDICINE CATS WILL BE EXCEPTIONAL.

AND BROKENTAIL? WHAT ABOUT HIM? I...
SAGEWHISKER, I KILLED HIM.
BROKENTAIL BROUGHT HIS DEATH UPON HIMSELF.
THE WARRIOR CODE PLACES LOYALTY ABOVE ALL THINGS. AND YOU HAVE PROVEN YOURSELF MORE THAN LOYAL TO THUNDERCLAN.
"GO WELL, YELLOWFANG. I WILL WALK WITH YOU, ALWAYS."
YELLOWFANG! YELLOWFANG!
I SAW STARCLAN!
IT WAS WONDERFUL!
I TURN THE WORD OVER IN MY HEAD. WONDERFUL. AND I THINK SHE'S RIGHT. THE ANCESTORS UNDERSTAND.
IT WAS WONDERFUL.
NOT THAT I'LL LET ANYONE KNOW IT.
REMEMBER, THIS IS ONLY THE START OF YOUR HARD WORK!
NOW, MY OLD BONES ARE ACHING FROM THIS COLD STONE.
LET'S GO HOME.
THE END

DON'T MISS
SUPER EDITION
WARRIORS
TALLSTAR'S
REVENGE
THE #1 NATIONAL BESTSELLING SERIES
WARRIORS
SUPER EDITION
TALLSTAR'S
REVENGE
EXCLUSIVE
MANGA
ADVENTURE
INSIDE!
ERIN HUNTER

Chapter 1

"Be careful, Tallkit!"

Tallkit paused when he heard Palebird's anxious call. "I'll be okay!" he mewed. He glanced back at the nursery. The warm, milky scent of his mother drifted from the entrance.

Inside the thick gorse den, Brackenwing soothed her. "Barkkit and Shrewkit will watch out for him, I promise."

Tallkit shivered. This was only his second sunrise outside the nursery, and his paws pricked with excitement. A light dusting of snow had turned the camp white, frosting the tussocky grass and thick heather walls. The freezing air stung his nose. He fluffed up his fur.

Barkkit pawed at the white tip of Tallkit's black tail. "You look like you're turning to ice as well."

Tallkit flicked his tail away, purring with amusement. His white muzzle and white paws would just make it easier for him to hide in the snow!

Shrewkit bounced past him. "Let's show him the Hunting Stones, Barkkit!"

Tallkit stared at his denmates. They were three moons older and twice his size, but he was determined to keep up with them. "I thought we were going to climb Tallrock again," he protested. "I *know* I'll make it this time." His eyes stung in the bright, cold air. He'd only opened them for the first time a few sunrises ago and they were still slowly adjusting to sunlight after the cozy gloom of the nursery.

He blinked up at the high slab of granite where Barkkit had told him Heatherstar stood to address the Clan. It loomed, jagged and dark, from a wide, sandy crater, which encircled it like an empty pool.

The Meeting Hollow.

Tallkit gazed into it wide-eyed. At the bottom, Heatherstar, Hawkheart, and Reedfeather huddled beside the stone, their breath billowing as they spoke.

Hawkheart looked up and caught Tallkit's eye over the rim. "Our youngest kit is exploring again," he murmured.

Tallkit shifted his paws. The dark glint in the medicine cat's gaze made him nervous. Palebird had warned him to stay away from the gray-brown tom; he had little patience for kits.

"Stay under cover, Tallkit." Hawkheart narrowed his eyes. "We don't want you attracting buzzards to the camp."

"Buzzards?" Tallkit's heart lurched.

"Kits are their favorite prey," Hawkheart warned. "And they can spot you from Highstones."

Reedfeather's whiskers twitched. "Don't scare the poor kit." There was a purr in his throat as he nodded to Shrewkit, who had popped up beside Tallkit. "What are you showing him today?"

Shrewkit flicked his tail. "The Hunting Stones."

Heatherstar shook frost from her thick gray pelt. "Be careful," she cautioned. "The stones will be icy."

"Don't come mewling to me if you sprain a paw," Hawkheart called.

"Come," the WindClan leader urged her deputy and medicine cat. "It's too cold to sit here. Let's go to my den."

As Heatherstar hopped out of the Meeting Hollow, Hawkheart and Reedfeather followed, their tails twitching as they ducked into the shelter of the leader's den beneath a gorse bush at the far end of the clearing.

"Can we play sliding in the hollow?" Barkkit mewed.

"I want to go to the Hunting Stones," Shrewkit insisted. He scraped up a pawful of snow and flung it at Barkkit. The wind snatched the flakes and tossed them back into his whiskers.

As he sneezed, Barkkit purred with amusement. "Wow! You're scary!"

"I'll show you!" Shrewkit hurled himself at his brother and sent him rolling over the grass.

Tallkit backed away as their dark brown pelts scuffed the snow. *It must be fun to have a littermate to playfight with. If only Finchkit hadn't died.*

Shrewkit leaped free of his brother's grip. "Look at Tallkit!" he teased. "He's blinking like he's just opened his eyes!"

Tallkit bristled. "I'm nearly half a moon old and Sandgorse says I opened my eyes quicker than *any* kit in the nursery." He glared at his denmates. "I'm just not used to snow." The ground sparkled, and the heather that formed the camp boundary—so dark against the sky yesterday—now glittered brightly with frost. What would the moor look like when the heavy snows came and the world turned completely white? Palebird had warned Tallkit that leaf-bare hit WindClan hardest of all the Clans, because the moor touched the sky. But this also made them more special, and safer.

"We're closer to Silverpelt than any Clan," she'd told him as she snuggled him in their mossy nest. "Which means that StarClan watches us more closely."

Tallkit heard worry in her mew. "Is that why we tunnel under the moor?" he asked. "To hide from the dead warriors in other Clans?"

"Don't be silly." Palebird had licked his ear. "We tunnel because we're stronger and cleverer than all the other Clans together." Her washing became brisker, silencing him.

"I'm going to the Hunting Stones!" Shrewkit charged across the grass.

Barkkit raced after him. "What about sliding in the hollow?"

"There's not enough snow for real sliding." Shrewkit veered away from Tallrock.

"You're just scared." Barkkit swerved after his brother, sending a shower of frozen flakes up from his paws.

"Am not!" Shrewkit called back.

Tallkit followed, not caring where they chose to play. It felt great to be outside, the grass cold on his pads as he raced across it.

"Watch out!"

Tallkit skidded to a halt as Cloudrunner yowled at him. The pale gray tom was crossing his path with Aspenfall. The warriors were heading to the prey heap, carrying fresh-kill. Wind-ruffled from the moor, they'd brought food for the Clan. Tallkit gazed at them, impressed by their long legs and wiry tails. They were moor runners, which meant they served WindClan by hunting and patroling the borders, and Tallkit could smell heather on their pelts.

In the brittle patch of bracken where the tunnelers made their nests, Woollytail looked up from washing his mud-streaked belly. Like all the cats who served the Clan by carving out new tunnels and shoring up old ones far beneath the moor, his pelt was permanently stained with sand and dust. He nodded at the rabbit swinging from Cloudrunner's jaws. "Did you catch that on the high-moor?"

"Yes." At the prey heap, Cloudrunner kicked away a stale mouse left from the previous day's hunt and dropped his catch. "You're right, as usual, Woollytail."

Tallkit blinked at Woollytail. "How did you know?"

"I can smell the sand in its fur." Woollytail flicked his tail and returned to washing.

Hickorynose, his tunnelmate, shifted on the bracken beside him. "You only find sand tunnels on the high-moor." The brown tom lifted a forepaw and rubbed dirt from his ear. "Not like the gorge tunnel. *That's* all soil and grit. But it'll open the way to fresh prey beside the river."

Cloudrunner snorted. "If you ever find a way to stop the cave-ins."

Aspenfall laid a vole beside the rabbit. "The grit makes it

unstable. It's not safe to tunnel there."

Woollytail narrowed his eyes. "It is if you know what you're doing."

Tallkit glanced from tunneler to moor runner as an awkward silence fell between them.

Heatherstar cut through it. She padded from her den and followed the rim of the Meeting Hollow. Passing the grass nests of the moor runners, she brushed by Cloudrunner and stopped beside the bracken patch. "Will the new tunnels be ready before newleaf, Woollytail?"

Woollytail sniffed. "It takes time to shore up the roofs."

Heatherstar flicked her tail. "I'm sure you'll find a way." She turned back to the prey heap and sniffed Cloudrunner's rabbit.

Does Heatherstar ever patrol underground? Tallkit watched the WindClan leader curiously. She'd trained as a moor runner, but surely as leader, she needed to understand what it was like to be a tunneler too.

"Hurry up, Tallkit!" Barkkit called.

Tallkit jerked his attention away and scurried after his denmates. Barkkit and Shrewkit were already at the Hunting Stones. The smooth, low rocks huddled like rabbits in the grass near the elders' den. Sprigs of heather poked between them and moss clumped at their base. Shrewkit leaped onto the highest stone and crowed down at Barkkit. "I am leader of the Hunting Stones!"

Barkkit scrambled onto the boulder beside him. "I'm deputy!"

Tallkit reached the rocks and waded through the thick

moss at the bottom. Reaching up with his forepaws, he kicked out with his hind legs and tried to jump up beside Barkkit. His claws slithered on the frosty stone and he slid back into the chilly moss.

"Hey, Wormkit!" Shrewkit called down. "Why don't you tunnel underneath? You're not supposed to be a moor runner like us!"

Tallkit's pelt pricked with confusion. "I'm not Wormkit. I'm *Tall*kit!"

"You're going to spend your life wriggling underground like a worm, aren't you?" Shrewkit taunted. "That's where you should be now—*under* the rocks, not on them."

Tallkit frowned. He knew that his mother and father were tunnelers, but did that really mean he couldn't play on the Hunting Stones?

Barkkit reached down with his forepaw. "Ignore him and try again, Tallkit!" he mewed.

Tallkit leaped for his denmate's paw and felt it curl beneath his own. He churned his hind legs while Barkkit heaved. Scrabbling against the stone, he flung himself onto the rock. "Thanks!" He sat up beside Barkkit, his pads stinging on the frozen rock.

He gazed across the camp. Sun shone from a crisp, blue sky, thawing the grassy hummocks, which bulged like clumped fur across the frosty clearing. The tunnelers' bracken patch glowed orange while the long grass enclosing the moor runners' nests drooped lower as the frost slowly loosened its grip.

A white face appeared at the entrance of the elders' den.

"You young'uns are up early." Whiteberry slid out and sat gingerly on the cold grass a tail-length from the Hunting Stones.

Lilywhisker limped after him and stood tasting the air. She was the youngest in the elders' den, far younger than Whiteberry, Flamepelt, and Flailfoot. She'd retired to the den after a tunnel collapse had smashed her hind leg and left it useless. "Do you want to come onto the moor?" she asked Whiteberry.

The white elder looked at her. "So long as you don't try to get me down any rabbit holes."

"Not after last time," Lilywhisker purred. "I've never seen a cat chased out of a tunnel by a rabbit."

Whiteberry shifted his paws. "I *thought* it was a fox."

"Your sense of smell must be worn out." Flicking her tail teasingly, Lilywhisker hopped toward the camp entrance. Her lifeless hind leg left a trail through the shallow snow.

Whiteberry heaved himself to his paws and followed. "Yours will wear out too after a few more moons sharing a den with Flailfoot. He's got fox-breath."

"It's not that bad," Lilywhisker called over her shoulder.

"Do you want to swap nests?" Whiteberry caught up to her. "Last night he snored right in my muzzle. I dreamed I'd fallen into a badger den."

As they disappeared into the heather tunnel, a pale ginger tom nosed his way past them, heading into camp. *Sandgorse!* Tallkit lifted his tail as his father trotted into the clearing.

The ginger warrior's pelt was speckled with earth. "I've left a stack of sticks at the tunnel entrance," he called to Woollytail.

The gray-and-white tunneler lifted his nose. "Great!" he meowed. "We can start shoring up the roof this afternoon."

"You'll have to manage without me." Sandgorse headed toward the Hunting Stones. "Tallkit! I want to show you something."

Tallkit blinked excitedly at his father. "What is it?" Was Sandgorse going to show him the moor? Tallkit slid off the rock and scrambled over the tussocky grass. He skidded to a halt at Sandgorse's paws.

Sandgorse licked a sprig of moss from Tallkit's ear and spat it onto the grass. "It's time you learned to dig."

Disappointment dropped like a stone in Tallkit's belly. He didn't want to dig. He wanted to see the moor and feel the wind in his pelt.

"Tallkit's going to go worming!" Shrewkit jeered from the Hunting Stones.

Tallkit spun around crossly. "Worms don't *dig*!"

"Ignore Shrewkit!" Barkkit stepped in front of his littermate. "He's just teasing."

Sandgorse snorted. "Typical moor-kit, scared of getting sand in his eyes." He headed for the tunnelers' bracken patch. Tallkit scrambled after him and ducked under Sandgorse's belly as he stopped beside Woollytail's nest. Tallkit peeped out, relishing the warmth of his father's fur on his spine.

"Do you think sticks will be strong enough to hold up the roof?" Sandgorse wondered.

Woollytail frowned. "They'll do until we can roll stones into place."

"Perhaps we should take a different route to the gorge." Above Tallkit's head, Sandgorse's belly twitched.

Woollytail shook his head. "We can't be far from clay now. It'll be harder digging, but there'll be fewer cave-ins."

Sandgorse glanced toward the elders' den. Tallkit guessed he was thinking about Lilywhisker's crushed leg. "Perhaps we should explore the rabbit warrens higher up. There may be a clay seam there we can dig into."

"But we've made so much progress over leaf-bare," Woollytail argued. "It'd be a shame to start again." The tom's muscular shoulders twitched. They were as wide and toned as Sandgorse's.

Will I have shoulders like that when I'm a tunneler? Tallkit's gaze strayed across the camp to Cloudrunner and Aspenfall. They were much sleeker: built for speed, not strength. Tallkit wondered what it felt like to run across the moor with the wind rushing through his fur. Surely that would be better than being squashed underground? He imagined his ears and nose filling up with mud, and shuddered.

"Come on, Tallkit." Sandgorse's mew broke into his thoughts. His father was heading for the moor runners' nests. Tallkit scampered after him and followed him past the swishing stalks to a patch of bare earth behind Tallrock.

"There's good digging here," Sandgorse explained, running his paw over the ground. "This is where I first learned to tunnel."

Tallkit gazed down at the churned earth and wondered how many times this patch had been dug and refilled, ready for new tunnelers to practice. "Don't you ever get bored of digging?" he mewed.

"Being a tunneler doesn't just mean digging," Sandgorse retorted. "Hollowing out new earthroutes is part of being a tunneler. But we patrol them, too, and it's a great place to hunt, especially during leaf-bare. Don't forget, that's why Shattered Ice first tunneled through the rabbit warrens."

Tallkit already knew the legend of Shattered Ice. It was one of the first nursery stories Palebird ever told him. Long ago, the moor was gripped by the worst leaf-bare the Clan had ever known. There was no prey to be found in the snow-drowned stretches of heather and gorse. So one of WindClan's bravest warriors had gone into the rabbit warrens and dug deep beyond them in search of food for their Clan.

"He cared more for his Clan than his own safety," Sandgorse meowed solemnly. "And he didn't have any of the training or experience we have now."

He had only his courage and strength. Tallkit stifled a yawn.

"He had only his courage and strength," Sandgorse went on. "WindClan has tunneled ever since, learning more with each generation." He lifted his chin. "Without its tunnelers, WindClan would have suffered many hungry, preyless moons."

Tallkit's pelt pricked guiltily. How could he dream of running across the moors like Cloudrunner and Aspenfall? One day his Clan would depend on him. He should be proud to follow in his father's paw steps.

ENTER THE WORLD OF WARRIORS

Warriors: Dawn of the Clans

Discover how the warrior Clans came to be.

Warriors

Sinister perils threaten the four warrior Clans. Into the midst of this turmoil comes Rusty, an ordinary housecat, who may just be the bravest of them all.

Download the free Warriors app at www.warriorcats.com

HARPER

An Imprint of HarperCollins*Publishers*

Visit www.warriorcats.com for the free Warriors app, games, Clan lore, and much more!

Warriors: The New Prophecy

Follow the next generation of heroic cats as they set off on a quest to save the Clans from destruction.

Warriors: Power of Three

Firestar's grandchildren begin their training as warrior cats. Prophecy foretells that they will hold more power than any cats before them.

Warriors: Omen of the Stars

Includes Warriors Adventure Game

Which ThunderClan apprentice will complete the prophecy that foretells that three Clanmates hold the future of the Clans in their paws?

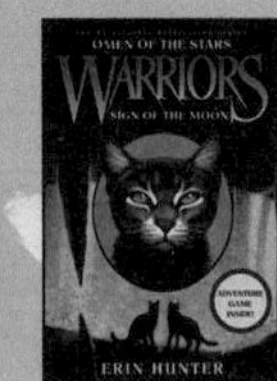

HARPER
An Imprint of HarperCollinsPublishers

All Warriors, Seekers, and Survivors books are available as ebooks from HarperCollins.

Visit www.warriorcats.com for the free Warriors app, games, Clan lore, and much more!

Warriors Stories
Download the separate ebook novellas or read them all together in the paperback bind-up!
WARRIORS
Hollyleaf's Story
SHORT STORY EBOOK EXCLUSIVE!
ERIN HUNTER
WARRIORS
Mistystar's Omen
SHORT STORY EBOOK EXCLUSIVE!
ERIN HUNTER
WARRIORS
Cloudstar's Journey
SHORT STORY EBOOK EXCLUSIVE!
ERIN HUNTER
WARRIORS
The Untold Stories
Paperback
ERIN HUNTER
WARRIORS
Tigerclaw's Fury
SHORT STORY EBOOK EXCLUSIVE!
ERIN HUNTER
Read the new ebook novella!
Don't Miss the Stand-Alone Adventures
WARRIORS
Firestar's Quest
ERIN HUNTER
WARRIORS
Bluestar's Prophecy
ERIN HUNTER
WARRIORS
Skyclan's Destiny
ERIN HUNTER
WARRIORS
Crookedstar's Promise
ERIN HUNTER
WARRIORS
Yellowfang's Secret
ERIN HUNTER
WARRIORS
Tallstar's Revenge
ERIN HUNTER
Delve Deeper into the Clans
WARRIORS
Field Guide
Secrets of the Clans
ERIN HUNTER
WARRIORS
Cats of the Clans
ERIN HUNTER
WARRIORS
Code of the Clans
ERIN HUNTER
WARRIORS
Battles of the Clans
ERIN HUNTER
WARRIORS
Enter the Clans
ERIN HUNTER
WARRIORS
The Ultimate Guide
ERIN HUNTER
BONUS POSTER INSIDE
HARPER
An Imprint of HarperCollinsPublishers
Visit www.warriorcats.com for the free Warriors app, games, Clan lore, and much more!

Warrior Cats Come to Life in Manga!
HARPER
An Imprint of HarperCollinsPublishers
Visit www.warriorcats.com for the free Warriors app, games, Clan lore, and much more!